D0802768

WILLOWTREE PRESS, L.L.C.

The Law Of Three

A Rowan Gant Investigation

A Novel of Suspense and Magick

By

M. R. Sellars

E.M.A. Mysteries

THE LAW OF THREE: A Rowan Gant Investigation
A WillowTree Press Book

PRINTING HISTORY
WillowTree Press First Trade Paper Edition / July 2003
Second Printing / May 2006

ISBN: 0-9678221-8-1
EAN : 978-0-9678221-8-1

10 9 8 7 6 5 4 3 2

PRINTED IN THE U.S.A.
by
TCS Printing
North Kansas City, Missouri

Books By M. R. Sellars

Praise for M. R. Sellars and the Rowan Gant Investigations:

"Fans of *Hamilton* and *Lackey* will want to religiously follow the exploits of Mr. Rowan Gant."
> — Harriet Klausner
> Literary Reviewer

"Fans of *Mercedes Lackey's* defunct *Diana Tregarde Mysteries* rejoice— a new witch is in town!"
> — Melanie C. Duncan,
> The BookDragon Review

"These books should be marketed as controlled substances..."
> — Kathleen Hill,
> Founder/Moderator,
> Pagan Page Turners Book Club

"Hooray for M.R. Sellars, the master of Pagan fiction!"
> — Dorothy Morrison
> Author of *Everyday Magic* and *The Craft*

"Rowan Gant is a detective in the tradition of *Diana Tregarde* and *Anita Blake*."
> — Rosemary Edghill
> Author, The Bast Mysteries

"I am impressed with M. R. Sellars' latest book. *The Law of Three* is a fascinating study in religious fanaticism and mental illness. The characters are refreshing and feel authentic. Sellars captures the politics of major police investigations... an entertaining read."
> — Kerr Cuhulain
> Author of *Wiccan Warrior* and
> *The Law Enforcement Guide to Wicca*

ACKNOWLEDGEMENTS

There are so many people who have come into and gone out of my life over the years that I've lost count, and each of them is in some part responsible for what happens between the pages of my novels. It is literally impossible for me to thank each and every one of them here individually, but there are some who stand out in the crowd, and I feel it a moral imperative that they be mentioned—

Dorothy Morrison: Friend, mentor, and supreme conjuress of the "Bobble Head."

Officer Scott Ruddle, SLPD: Best-Bud, confidant, and real life "copper"— Ben Storm without the ancestry.

Roy Osbourn: Teller of wonderful stories, purveyor of invaluable information, and barbecued rib chef extraordinaire.

Tammi Nesser: Thanks for letting me borrow your neuroses and phobias.

Trish Telesco and A.J Drew: Friends, cohorts in crime, and charter members of the "Bobble Head Coalition."

My long distance family: Mystic Moon Coven.

Duane, Chell, Angel, and Randal: I love you guys.

Lexi Kavanaugh: Über Publicist

All of my good friends from the various acronyms: C.A.S.T., F.O.C.A.S.M.I., H.S.A., M.E.C., S.I.P.A., and S.P.I.R.A.L.

Patrick Owen: What can I say, brother? A Romeo and Julietta Churchill, VSOP, and an easy chair—I'll be there.

My parents: I will never be able to thank you enough for introducing me to the written word.

Chell, Cindy, Dorothy and Kathy: The team who tirelessly reads, re-reads, and then reads some more.

"Chunkee": Who not only reads and re-reads but also has the guts to argue with me. My friend, you ARE the Rowan Gant scholar, and I cannot write these without you.

Johnathan Minton: A sorcerer of graphic art, who can take my innocuous ramblings about a cover idea and create a masterpiece worth well more than a thousand words.

My daughter: For being my daughter.

My wife, Kat: For story editing; running the household; putting up with my dual career; making sure I get where I am supposed to be, when I am supposed to be, while still making me look presentable to the public—and she looks gorgeous doing it. Then, after all that, she claims that she still loves me.

Of course, Chris, Evelyn, and all the wonderful folks at WestCan PG up in the Great White North.

And, as always, everyone who takes the time to pick up one of my novels, read it, and then recommends it to a friend.

For Dorothy.
Thank you for reminding me
that this is supposed to be fun…

Ribbit!

AUTHOR'S NOTE:

While the city of St. Louis and its various notable landmarks are certainly real, many names have been changed and liberties taken with some of the details in this book. They are fabrications. They are pieces of fiction within fiction to create an illusion of reality to be experienced and enjoyed.

In short, I made them up because it helped me make the story more entertaining—or in some cases, just because I wanted to do so.

Note also that this book is a first-person narrative. You are seeing this story through the eyes of Rowan Gant. The words you are reading are his thoughts. In first person writing, the narrative should match the dialogue of the character telling the story. Since Rowan (and anyone else that I know of for that matter) does not speak in perfect, unblemished English throughout his dialogue, he will not do so throughout his narrative. Therefore, you will notice that some grammatical anomalies have been retained (under protest from editors) in order to support this illusion of reality.

Let me repeat something—I DID IT ON PURPOSE. Do NOT send me an email complaining about my grammar. It is a rude thing to do, and it does nothing more than waste your valuable time. If you find a typo, that is a different story. Even editors miss a few now and then. They are no more perfect than you or me.

Finally, this book is not intended as a primer for WitchCraft, Wicca, or any Pagan path. However, please note that the rituals, spells, and explanations of these religious/magickal practices are accurate. Some of my explanations may not fit your particular tradition, but you should remember that your explanations might not fit mine either.

And, yes, some of the Magick is "over the top." But, like I said in the first paragraph, this is fiction…

Dearly beloved, avenge not yourselves, but rather give place unto wrath: for it is written, **Vengeance is mine; I will repay, saith the Lord.**

Romans 12:19
Holy Bible, KJV

Mind the threefold law ye should,
Three times bad, and three times good.

Couplet twenty-three
The Wiccan Rede
Lady Gwen Thompson
First Printing, "Green Egg #69," Circa 1975

Thursday, January 10
St. Louis, Missouri

PROLOGUE:

White video static raked itself across the barely-focused television screen in a free-for-all wrestling match with overblown chroma and luminance. The brightest spot on the tube fell somewhere near the center where the thick dust had been haphazardly wiped away by a bare hand. As if actively seeking this small porthole, the oddly hued video flickered in random bursts through greasy fingerprints to create angry shadows dancing throughout the confines of the small room.

Splotchy stains washed across the walls, illuminated by the swiftly shifting silhouettes. Most of them had long ago been rendered unidentifiable by the growing layers of filth. They now competed for attention with their more recent counterparts. Some of them looked as though they could be the remnants of foodstuffs, possibly hurled in anger or disgust. Others bore more than a passing resemblance to various bodily excretions better left unconsidered by those easily sickened—or in at least one instance, horrified. Still others might simply be nothing more than the result of water damage from the sieve-like roof. Whatever they had each been in their individual existences, they now blended to become a single stomach-turning mosaic.

The canvas for this nauseating mural was the paint that covered the crumbling sheetrock. It might have been pale blue in a previous incarnation, but the color, much less the particular shade, now defied any positive recognition. Dirty grey did not even come close to describing it, and the patina of grime did nothing to lend even the smallest clue.

"It's now six seventeen a.m., and here's Jennifer to fill you in on what to expect for your morning commute." A muddy voice rattled outward from the speaker on the geriatric television set. "How's it looking out there, Jen?"

A higher-pitched voice buzzed through as the hand-off was taken in a smooth segue. "Not so good, Skip."

The screen switched to what might have been a chroma-keyed map being gestured at by what might have been a somewhat attractive woman—it was hard to say through the blur.

She continued. "Traffic is at a standstill at Forty-Four and Two-Seventy extending all the way back to Bowles Avenue due to an earlier accident, so you might want to avoid that area this morning if at all possible. And a reminder, police and MoDot crews are still on the scene of an overturned tractor trailer on I-Seventy, just east of Bermuda…"

The rushing sound of water in conjunction with a hollow, porcelain-throated burp echoed from a curtained corner of the room to drown out the thick audio of the TV. A steadily increasing whine followed, punctuated by a deep thud inside the walls as the plumbing complained. The familiar wet hiss of a toilet tank automatically refilling fell in behind—the pronounced noise droning unmuted for lack of a lid.

"Thanks, Jen." The news anchor's voice once again projected into the room from behind a faux woodgrain plastic grill. "In local news, the Saint Louis Major Case Squad is still looking for leads in the disappearance of Tamara Linwood. You will remember Eyewitness News was first to bring you this story when the twenty-seven-year-old grade school teacher was reported missing over one week ago after not showing up for work. Her locked car was found abandoned on the parking lot of the Westview Shopping Mall.

"Authorities suspect foul play but have declined to comment on a possible connection with the case of Sarah Hart. Hart disappeared from the same parking lot just under one year ago. Her badly decomposed remains were found several months later in a wooded area along the Missouri River. Anyone with information should contact the Major Case Squad at the number on the bottom of your screen."

Eldon Porter was paying little attention to the prattle of the reporters. They were nothing more than background noise filling the small motel room. He listened with only passing interest to the periodic weather updates and even less concern for the actual news.

Pipes sang a pained lament once again as he twisted the faucet handle on a rust-stained basin that barely clung to the wall—supported more by the deteriorating drain pipe beneath than the corroded lag bolts that were supposed to be doing the job. He frowned at a cracked rectangle of glass mounted on the wall over the canted sink, peering into a kidney-shaped section where the silver had not yet peeled from the back. With no more than a sigh, he automatically set about the task of washing his right hand. There was a time in his life, not that long ago, when he would have washed his hands. Not the singular, hand. But the plural, hands—as in two.

However, there is no reason to wash something you almost never use, and that is how it had been for almost a year now.

Ever since that night on the bridge—ever since the warlock, Rowan Gant, had tried to kill him with something so mundane as a bullet.

Of course, Gant had been left with no other choice than to turn to such a commonplace method of attack to save himself. Eldon's devotion had prevailed, and he had not been taken in by the sorcery and tricks. He had seen through the chicanery that masked the true depravity of the Satan-spawned heretic. The mundane was all that was left, for he was immune to the mystical. Had he only realized that the warlock would be carrying a pistol, he would have been triumphant.

Instead, he had failed in his task. Still, his righteousness and loyalty to his God's mission had protected him from death that night—but not from the hardship of injury.

Perhaps a skilled surgeon, or even a back alley quack for that matter, could have repaired some of the damage that had rendered his hand so useless. Perhaps yes, perhaps no. The point was moot now, as it had been then, for he could ill afford the risk of being caught.

Not as long as the warlock, Rowan Gant, was still alive.

Eldon looked down at his left forearm. The monstrous pink and white depression extended from just below his wrist to a point halfway up to his elbow where the bullet had ripped away a tunnel of flesh. It might not have been so severe had it not been for the raging infection that almost instantly made a home in the wound, killing off even more of the ragged tissue. The resulting fever had seared his brow for days and was quelled only after he had been able to muster enough strength to break into a pharmacy for antibiotics and dressings.

He'd done as little damage as possible when breaking in, made a guess about what might work, took only what he needed, and then begged his Lord to forgive him for the sin of theft. He knew his absolution had been granted when the fever finally broke three days later, and he had remained free.

Unfortunately, his penance had come in the form of lameness. The severity of the bullet's cruelty, combined with the infection, had left his hand a shriveled and useless claw and his forearm a misshapen appendage that was still visited by constant pain. Considering what the outcome could have been, in some small way he counted himself fortunate.

Gazing at the mostly healed wound, he noticed that the flesh surrounding the scar was reddish and swollen. The infection was gaining a hold again, as it had done several times now. He would need more antibiotics soon. Something different, stronger this time, because obviously what he had was no longer doing the job.

"…So if you haven't pulled out your snow shovel yet, you might want to think about it, because this front is definitely going to bring frozen precipitation with it this afternoon and evening. Most likely in the range of three to six inches." Yet another, different feminine voice squawked from the television in the corner.

"There's no way we can get a reprieve from that?" the anchor joked.

"Sorry, Skip, I don't make the weather, I just forecast it," the woman returned with a good-natured lilt in her voice.

"Meteorologist, Tracy Watson. Thanks, Tracy. It's six twenty-eight, and coming up in the next half hour of Eyewitness News this morning, health reporter Doctor Patrick Kennedy will tell us about some alternative treatments for back injuries."

"…And," the co-anchor chimed in on cue, "We'll have more on why the Major Case Squad has enlisted the aid of Saint Louisan and self-proclaimed Witch, Rowan Gant, to solve a bizarre homicide. We'll be back right after this…"

All that was within the small motel room came to a complete and abrupt halt.

The endless prattle that had in Eldon Porter's mind heretofore served only to chase away silence *now* had his full and undivided consideration. The mere mention of the warlock's name pealed loud and clear through the muddy audio, striking deep into his soul and bringing him to instant attention.

Water continued to sputter from the faucet as he turned to look at the flickering TV screen. He continued to stare, silent and completely motionless throughout all one hundred eighty lethargic seconds of inane commercials—advertisements for everything from fruit juice to car loans. Never once did he twitch or so much as even blink. In point of fact, he scarcely even breathed.

He had been in Saint Louis for over a week now and thus far had been completely unable to track down the warlock. On the surface, Gant's house appeared completely unoccupied. But, he knew it was not—not completely anyway. He knew this as he had been watching it carefully. Very carefully, because he also knew that he was not the only one watching.

Others were spying upon the house. In addition, others were spying from it. However, they were not looking for Rowan Gant; they were looking for him.

Eldon had begun to fear that the warlock had fled. That he was far removed from Saint Louis. Perhaps even from the state. It was this fear that had driven him to force the warlock's hand; that action had brought him here, to this room, to wait.

Now, his wait appeared to be over.

A tinny riff of music that intermixed with syncopated drumming noises suddenly spilled into the room to announce the resumption of the morning news broadcast. As it faded out, a dead-on shot of the anchors popped in to replace the station ID graphic.

"Welcome back to Eyewitness News this Thursday morning, it's six thirty-two, I'm Skip Johnson…"

"And I'm Brandee Street, filling in for the vacationing Chloe Winchell." The co-anchor dropped into the cadence with practiced timing. "At the top of the news this morning, peace talks are continuing…"

As per usual, the teasers that came before the station break were just that—teasers. Tidbits of information intended to keep you tuned in while the unimportant drivel is paraded before your eyes. Eldon held fast to his firm resolve and continued his frozen stance for yet another three-minute eternity.

"Greater Saint Louis Major Case Squad officials have confirmed reports that a self-proclaimed Witch is playing an important role in a murder investigation. Rowan Gant most recently aided the police in solving the murder of Debbie Schaeffer, the Oakwood College cheerleader who went missing late last year. He has now been called in once again to help with a bizarre homicide. Eyewitness News field reporter, Colin Kelso, joins us live outside city police headquarters. Colin…"

The screen switched to a video feed showing the image of a reporter clutching a logo-adorned microphone and staring stoically into the camera. Even with the extreme blur, his overly youthful appearance was evident. "Thanks, Brandee. As you stated, we have confirmed that self-proclaimed Witch, Rowan Gant, has been brought in to help with the investigation of a very strange and brutal murder. At around three a.m., police were summoned to an abandoned warehouse at the corner of Locust and Fourteenth streets. There they found the body of a man suspended by a rope from the roof ledge."

"Colin," the anchorwoman's voice cut in, "I understand that there has been some speculation that this crime might somehow be linked with another murder?"

"Yes, while authorities have not made an official statement, there has been speculation on that fact. Viewers will remember that two weeks ago, the body of Lena Duke was found hanging from a tree in Cherokee Park in Cape Girardeau, Missouri. The ritualistic manner in which she was killed bears a striking resemblance to this crime.

"Statements released earlier this week indicate that the Cape homicide may be somehow linked to the killing spree of Eldon Porter which occurred here in Saint Louis early last year.

"Right now, authorities are still being tight-lipped about this case. We will keep you updated as the situation develops. Back to you, Brandee and Skip."

The screen cut back to a headshot of the unnaturally honey-blonde newscaster paired with a smaller inset of the field reporter. "Colin," she spoke. "Has Mister Gant actually been to the scene of this particular crime?"

"I've been told by one detective that, yes, in fact Mister Gant was brought in early this morning. An interesting development, however, just moments ago Mister Gant was seen leaving the scene with Detective Benjamin Storm of the city homicide squad and a woman we believe to be his wife, Felicity O'Brien. Although we were unable to obtain a comment, we did get this footage showing some type of altercation."

The screen switched to show the wildly shaking image of a van, partially illuminated off and on by video lights. Unintelligible, but obviously heated voices could be heard in the background over the shouts of reporters and camera operators. As the centerpiece of the video byte grew larger and began to stabilize, a man shot into view from behind the open door of the vehicle, apparently rushing toward the cameras. In an instant he halted, then appeared to be jerked backward, disappearing into the vehicle.

"Any idea what was going on there, Colin," she asked as the video repeated.

"We were unable to obtain a comment from anyone on the scene at this time, I'm afraid."

"Okay, thanks Colin," she said, and the inset was replaced by a wide shot of the news desk, revealing both anchors as well as a third figure seated at the L-shaped return. "Keep us updated on this breaking story."

"Will do, back to you Brandee and Skip."

After a measured beat, the anchor continued. "So, how many of us have complained about lower back pain?"

"I know I have," chimed in Skip Johnson. "Joining us this morning is Doctor…"

Eldon finally blinked, and as he did he instantly tuned out the voices coming from the television, relegating them once again to muted background noise. He allowed a thin smile to pass briefly across his face, the only outward sign of the elation he now felt.

The warlock was still here.

He had just needed to draw him out, and his plan had worked even quicker than he had hoped.

He absently wiped his wet hand on his shirt as he took the few steps across the room to the broken down bed. The water continued sputtering and splashing in the rusty basin, melding in an off-kilter tune with the voices from the TV. On the scarred surface of a makeshift nightstand, a book was positioned with supreme care, as if on display. Eldon reached out with his good hand and lifted it reverently, then used the knuckles of his clawed left hand to open it and flip through the pages.

Near the back of the tome, he finally stopped, bringing his gaze to rest on a particular passage, his eyes darting back and forth as he read and re-read the words. Slowly, his lips began to move, and then eventually a whisper of sound began to slip between them. Finally, his gravelly voice spoke aloud to be heard only by him.

"For it is written, Vengeance is mine; I will repay, saith the Lord."

He continued to repeat the passage with growing rabidity, clipping the sentence until the only words spoken were "Vengeance is mine."

Three Hours Earlier

CHAPTER 1:

G raphical images of playing cards expanded in happy accordion patterns across the glowing screen of my notebook computer as the machine proclaimed me victorious in this latest game of solitaire. Unless I'd lost track, this one made six for me and something on the order of ten million for the machine, give or take. I wasn't actually keeping count, though. Well, not of the computer's wins, anyway.

I tucked my fingers back in behind my eyeglasses, forcing the frames to ride up on the bridge of my nose, then rubbed my eyes before directing my bleary gaze at the lower corner of the screen. I'd started this mindless activity at twelve and it was now 3:07.

That was a.m., mind you.

Of course, there wasn't much else to do. Watch TV, surf the web, read a book. None of these options were particularly appealing to me, not even the endless games of solitaire. What I really wanted to be doing was sleeping, but the way my head was throbbing, that wasn't about to happen.

The annoying thud that was pounding out a droning rhythm throughout the whole of my grey matter began early in the evening and had not subsided in the least. But, so far it hadn't grown any worse, for which I was thankful. Of course, I knew that wouldn't last. It would be getting *much* worse. I just didn't know exactly when.

I'd had this kind of headache before, more times than I cared to count, actually. It wasn't sinuses, and it wasn't just your normal stress related "take two aspirin and lie down for a while" kind of pain either. This was an ache born of unnatural influences. It was the pure physical manifestation of fear and dread. The kind of headache I experienced every single time I knew something horrible was about to happen, and there was nothing in this world I could possibly do to prevent it.

Unfortunately, for me, I tended to be afflicted by these damnable things way too often.

I ran my hand across the lower half of my face and felt the rough crop of stubble that, by now, was certainly shading my jaw line. Then I tugged at my goatee for a moment. The action prompted me to remember that I'd recently noticed the dark brown was being infiltrated by grey and white like a quickly spreading fungus. I absently considered a dye job for a moment then dismissed the idea as silly. I'd never been particularly vain before, so there was no reason to start now.

I reached behind with both hands and massaged the back of my head for a moment, hoping that it might help quell the ache.

It didn't.

Picking up my coffee cup, I took a swig of the remaining contents and noticed immediately that it had grown cold. I guess I'd been a little more caught up in solitaire than I'd realized. Oh well, it had kept my mind off the pain, at least a little.

I pushed back and quietly got up, then carefully hooked around the small dining table where I'd been seated. I aimed myself toward the orange glow of the light on the coffeepot, using it as a beacon in the darkness. Since it was presently residing on the counter in the closet-sized room that was supposed to pass for a kitchen, I gave little thought to this being a problem. However, since I still wasn't used to the layout of this apartment, in my single-minded quest for fresh java I cut my entry through the doorway far too shallow.

There was a loud thump, followed by me quickly listing to one side, and then the ache in the back of my head was pushed aside in favor of a new sensation. Of course, that feeling was a sharp, and far more extreme, pain in my toe.

I caught my breath, quickly swallowing the yelp that I'd managed to stop midway in my throat, and then fought to stifle a groan that quickly followed on its heels. A pitiful sounding mixture of the two managed to escape anyway.

Just for good measure, I stuttered a few random selections from the big book of four-letter expletives, passing them as quietly as I could through clenched teeth. Finally, I half limped, half hopped into the kitchenette and leaned against the counter.

I'd been propped there for no more than a minute when my muffled swearing was interrupted by a sleepy voice at the doorway.

"Row? Are you okay?"

"Yeah," I grunted with little conviction in my voice. "Yeah, I'm okay."

I hadn't heard her approach, not that I was surprised. I was a bit preoccupied to say the least, and besides, she was far more graceful than I would ever be. I grimaced, not so much from the pain, but because waking Felicity was exactly what I had wanted to avoid.

"What are you doing up?"

"Just attempting to break my toe," I muttered, turning my head and looking back toward her.

"What happened?" my wife asked, her voice a quiet blend of two parts sleep to one part concern, all underscored by a faint Celtic intonation. "You're sure you're okay, then?"

Felicity was second generation Irish-American, and she had spent an enormous amount of time in Ireland throughout her life. She was never completely free of the lilt, though it was most pronounced whenever she was overtired, under stress, or as in this case, half asleep. It almost always came bundled with a rich and colorful brogue to match.

"Yeah, I'm okay," I told her as I focused on her slight form. "Just stubbed it, that's all."

She had propped herself in the doorway, using the back of her hand for a pillow as she rested it against the frame. In the dim light, I could see that her eyes were closed as she yawned. A loose pile of fiery auburn hair sat atop her head in a Gibson-girlish coif. Whenever she let the cascade of spiraling tresses hang free, it would easily reach her waist. Her pale skin seemed to almost glow in the darkness.

She let out a heavy sigh and stretched slowly. She was clad in an oversized t-shirt, but her tight figure still managed to tug it into varying degrees of eye candy as she languidly arched her back. How she managed to look this good even when she had just climbed out of bed was something beyond my comprehension, but I certainly wasn't going to complain.

"Aye," she said as she reached out and switched on the overhead light. "So tell me why you're awake, then."

"Because I couldn't sleep?" I offered, squinting against the sudden infusion of brightness.

"Aye, don't be a smart ass now. You know what I meant."

"Would you believe I was trying to get some work done?"

"No." She shook her head.

"Getting a drink of water?"

"Rowan." She cocked her head and shot me a frown as she paused—effectively impaling me with her *I'm serious* look. "I'm half asleep, but I'm not blind. You've coffee on, and you've been playing solitaire on your computer. Quit screwing with me, then."

"Okay," I answered with a defeated sigh. "I'm waiting for Ben to call."

As absurd as it sounded, it was the truth.

It may be the middle of the night, but I knew beyond a shadow of a doubt that the telephone was going to ring, and Detective Benjamin Storm was going to be at the other end. For me, very simply, this was a foregone conclusion.

What's more, it was not because he happened to be my best friend and that he just felt like talking at an odd hour. It was going to be something I didn't want to hear but probably already knew. In any case, I knew it would be something that I had no choice but to deal with.

Felicity closed her eyes and let her head tilt forward, dropping her forehead into her hand.

"Nightmare?" she asked softly as she began massaging her brow. She was intimately familiar with the forms my precognitive intuition would sometimes take.

"Headache."

"Humph," she grunted, then asked hopefully, "Did you take anything just in case?"

"Not that kind of headache," I replied.

"You're certain, then?"

Her question was answered by the grating peal of the telephone vibrating against the walls of the small room before I could even utter the "yes" that now lodged itself in my throat.

My wife looked up at me with sadness in her jade-green eyes and then gave a slight nod to the coffeepot. "Aye, I'll go put on some clothes. Best pour me a cup of that as well."

I started to protest. "I don't think..."

"...That I should go?" she shot back, filling in my sentence and cutting me off. "Are you planning to stay out of it?"

I sighed and fidgeted at the sudden tension. She already knew what my answer would be.

"Aye, I thought so. We're not discussing this, Rowan," she continued with a stern shake of her head. "If you go, I go. End of story. Now answer the phone, then." She was already turning around the corner of the doorway on her way back to the bedroom as she issued the last command.

I knew better than to press my luck, especially on this subject. We'd beaten it beyond recognition already, and we were both too stubborn to give in. I took a step forward, picked the phone out of its cradle on the fourth ring, and then placed it to my ear.

"Yeah, Ben. I'm here" was all I said.

"Awww, Jeezus H. Christ, Row... Jeeeez... Goddammit..." He launched immediately into a string of curses, his voice a peculiar mix of relief, anger, and disgust.

Whenever my friend started a sentence this way, I knew that what followed probably wasn't going to be good. Of course, I'd known that before the phone ever rang, but there was always that small inkling of hope that I might be wrong. Judging from the baseness of Ben's first words, I knew that this would not be the occasion.

"Porter?" I inserted my question into the lull that trailed along in the wake of his outburst.

"Yeah," he returned, his voice slightly calmer. "But that was a given, I guess."

In an instant, the "probably" became an absolutely, and the "wasn't going to be good" was nothing less than a cold fact.

"Uh-huh. Truth is I'm surprised he waited this long," I replied. "It's been more than two weeks since he killed that woman in Cape Girardeau."

"Yeah." He paused. "So, what gives? You sound like you were awake already."

"Yeah. I was."

"So what's up? Don't tell me you were waitin' for me to call."

"Okay, I won't."

"Jeez, Row…" The note of resignation in his voice was clear. "So, did you have one of those nightmares or somethin'?"

"No. Just a headache."

"Bad one?"

"Bad enough."

"Regular, or was it one of those hinky, weird-ass, *Twilight Zone* ones that you get?"

"Something like that." I shook my head even though he couldn't see me.

Twilight Zone. That's what my friend liked to call it whenever I would engage in any form of psychic detection or supernormal communication. He was accustomed to the peculiar psychic events that had seemed to plague me for the past couple of years, but he still had his own unique branding for them. He had a whole handful of euphemisms—"la-la land," "out there," and even just plain "weird," but *Twilight Zone* remained his favorite. I guess I couldn't blame him for the interpretation though. Even I wasn't always comfortable with the paranormal excursions myself, but then, I also didn't always have control over them either. And, while a certain amount of mysticism comes along with being a practicing Witch, at times I felt almost as if I had plugged directly into the main switchboard of the "other side."

Disconcerting is just about the nicest word I could use to describe it. You don't want to hear the others.

"So why didn't you call me?" he asked.

"And do what? Tell you I had a headache?"

"Hasn't stopped you before."

"Actually, when I've called you in the past I've had a little more to say."

"Yeah. Maybe so."

"So, do you want me to meet you?"

"For what?"

"To go to this crime scene?"

"No, actually. I was just calling to make sure you were okay."

The meaning behind his words was quickly apparent to me. For a number of reasons, I was most likely at the top of Porter's hit list; not the least of which was the fact that I had shot him. Of course, he was trying to kill me at the time, so I didn't have much choice. However, since he had already tried once, we had every reason to believe that he would do it again.

This was exactly why Felicity and I had spent the past two weeks residing in a tiny, unfamiliar apartment in a secure building instead of our own home. We were in hiding, and it was starting to get on my nerves.

"So, the victim is male?" I asked

"That's what they said. I just got the call a few minutes ago."

"So where is the scene?" I pressed again.

"No way. Stay put, Row. Let us handle this."

"You know I can't do that, Ben."

"You don't have a hell of a lotta choice now do ya'?" he shot back.

"I'll just show up," I told him calmly. "I can find out where the scene is without your help."

"And I'll fuckin' arrest your sorry ass if you do."

"Ben…" I just allowed my voice to trail off.

"You know, Rowan, we ain't just a bunch of bumblin' idiots. Cops solve murders all the time without your help."

"I know, Ben, but this is different."

"Yeah, I know you think it is, but it's not. Why can't you just stay put where I know you're safe, and let me handle this?"

"Because I want my life back, Ben."

"Gettin' yourself killed would kinda defeat the purpose now wouldn't it?"

"We've had this discussion before, Ben."

"And I don't recall bein' convinced that time either."

"I need to do this," I appealed.

He huffed out a heavy sigh after an extended silence. "Fine. Jeez. Okay. At least if you're with me, I can keep an eye on ya'. I'll swing by and pick you up. But listen, Row, you'd damn well better tell Felicity before I get there. I don't have time for an argument like last time."

"Don't worry. She'll be coming with us."

"Both of you?" he groaned. "Sheesh. Lucky me."

"Hey, it's not my idea."

"Are you willin' to stay home and let me handle this?" he queried flatly.

"I thought we'd already established that as a no," I replied, somewhat confused by the question.

"Then quit tryin' to blame her. It IS your fuckin' idea," he huffed. "Meet me in the lobby. I'll be there in fifteen."

CHAPTER 2:

"This is fucked..." Ben spat, shaking his head in a display of disbelief and looking upward as he spoke. "This S.O.B is just plain sick."

It was just after four a.m. by the time we arrived, and we found ourselves standing in the middle of Locust Street downtown. We had signed in on the scene log with Felicity and me listed as consultants and allowed in only by Ben's graces.

Stepping onto the active participant side of the bright yellow strip of barrier tape that cordoned off the street was akin to entering another world. I glanced around, feeling both out of place and right at home in the same instant. In the past two years, I'd visited more active homicide crime scenes than many cops see in their entire careers, and I didn't even have a badge. Something seemed very wrong about that, but it was a fact I simply could not change. I didn't find it reassuring at all that I was becoming so accustomed to it.

Cold wind sliced in a linear gust down the thoroughfare, flaring the band of plastic tape as if to highlight the repeated imprint of block letters along its length. Bold strokes formed words that had become all too familiar to me—CRIME SCENE DO NOT CROSS. The temperature was settled for the moment at an even thirty-six degrees, but the computed wind chill pushed the overall feeling downward into the range of the mid-twenties.

There were a half dozen crime scene technicians milling about on the ground, while another handful could occasionally be spotted working on the roof of the building that was before us. The medical examiner's hearse had already arrived, and the area was illuminated by the visual insanity of flickering light bars on idling emergency vehicles.

When the street-level scene was taken as a whole, my friend's candid observation simply became a commentary that mirrored my own feelings. Unfortunately, he was talking about something far worse, for what was taking place on the tableau of the cold asphalt was only a supporting backdrop for the spectacle above.

My gaze followed Ben's, coming to rest between the second and third floor windows of the four-story, brick building. There, carefully directed spotlights illuminated the centerpiece of this nightmare. Garish shadows molded themselves in a shroud about the nude and blood streaked corpse of a man. Suspended by a rope tied about his ankles, he was hanging upside down. His head was obscured by an executioner's hood, and his arms were splayed out to the sides, perpendicular to the rest of his body, as if to form an inverted cross. The appendages were held stiffly in place by what looked like a two-by-four across his shoulders. At this distance, I couldn't be positive, but the piece of wood appeared to be held fast by something encircling his wrists and neck.

This, in and of itself, was macabre enough to make anyone believe that it could only be a Hollywood "slasher flick" in the making. If only that were true, for it didn't end there. From the victim's groin, downward to a point in his mid-torso, his abdomen was split open. There, protruding from the ragged tear like a grey-white serpent, his intestines cascaded across his chest to hang in a pendulum-like loop several feet beneath. Each time the wind would pick up, the sash of organ tissue would move with the breeze, undulating like heavy drapes next to an air vent. Blood still dripped at protracted intervals from the exposed viscera to plop wetly onto the dark stain that now graced the sidewalk below.

Behind us, a loud and very wet sounding splatter tore our attention away from the scene as a patrol officer involuntarily launched the contents of his own stomach onto the pavement.

I looked back over my shoulder in response to the sound and then glanced over at Felicity. She was clutching my arm tightly and staring upward while absently chewing at her lower lip. She had been to a few crime scenes before but had not been subjected to anywhere near as much of this grisly scenery as I had. Still, she looked stable for the moment, so I returned my stare to the three-dimensional horror show that was playing out in front of me. I swallowed hard, because to be honest, I was only a half step away from heaving myself.

"Ya'know, Doc Sanders told me once that the average adult has about thirty feet of intestines." Ben paused for a moment after reciting the fact. "Man, I've seen a lotta crap in autopsies, but I never really expected to see anybody's guts stretched out like that."

"Disembowelment was not uncommon during the Inquisition." I spoke quietly, struggling to keep my voice even. "Actually, it was a favored form of punishment and torture."

"You mean he did that to 'im while he was still alive?" Ben asked with a thin strain of disbelief in his voice.

"Oh, yes," I nodded as I spoke, then swallowed hard again. "Probably rather slowly..."

As I'd known it would, my headache was starting to get worse. The stark chill of fear climbed up my vertebrae and began clawing at the base of my neck. There was something unseen here that was begging my attention, and I wasn't entirely sure I wanted to give it.

"Jeezus..." He shook his head. "Guess I shoulda suspected that, considering..."

I knew full well what his unspoken words implied. Eldon Porter made a habit of torturing his victims mercilessly before finally bringing about their end. During his last spree, he had even burned two of them alive.

I allowed my gaze to fall away from the corpse as I turned my head, but I didn't have to let it fall far. I was of average height, but I still had to crane my neck back to look up at Ben's face; average in stature he definitely was not. His particular pencil mark on the doorjamb had hit six feet when he was in junior high school, and he had still proceeded to grow another six inches after that. He was no stranger to the weight room either, and the rest of his physique made a perfect match for his elevated height.

Formidable was a word that came to mind at first glance; when he had still been a uniformed officer, just plain scary tended to be the more accurate description.

He was looking back at me with dark, questioning eyes that peered out of angularly defined features and natural reddish-tanned skin—unmistakable visual evidence of his full-blooded Native American heritage. His large hand was tucked beneath a shank of collar length, jet-black hair, and he was slowly massaging the back of his neck. This was a common mannerism of his, and it told me that his mind was doing far more behind those eyes than simply waiting for me to say something.

I said something anyway. "Was there a Bible?"

While an outside observer might have found the question somewhat odd, it was something I was certain he had expected me to ask.

"Yeah, that's what they said when they called," he told me, giving a short nod to the affirmative as he spoke. "Bookmarked and highlighted."

"Passage?"

My friend stopped massaging his neck long enough to thumb through a small notebook then read his shorthand back to me, "At the mouth of two witnesses, or three witnesses, shall he that is worthy of death be put to death; but at the mouth of one witness he shall not be put to death. Deuteronomy seventeen, six."

"He's working from his list again…" I muttered. "When you ID this guy, he'll be someone that one of the original victims knew."

"Yeah," Ben agreed. "That's kinda what we figured."

The "he" I referred to was, of course, Eldon Andrew Porter. The list was exactly that, a list. It comprised the names of Witches, Wiccans, and various other Pagan individuals living in the Saint Louis metropolitan area. It was, of course, by no means a comprehensive census of persons engaging in what is often collectively referred to as alternative spirituality; however, the odds were that it wasn't terribly short either. Porter had compiled it himself by way of various sadistic tortures, such as the one displayed above us now.

A bookmarked Bible was his calling card and the highlighted passage, a message. What we were being told was the reason this particular victim had been chosen. His crime was that of being a Witch. We'd been here before, so that much was a given. And, just like the Bible verse said, he had been accused by more than one witness. There was never much reading between the lines necessary, for Eldon was nothing if not precise about the messages he left behind.

Basically, Porter was a single-minded killer. What made him unique was his highly particular criterion for committing murder. Put very simply, he executed Witches.

That was the short answer. The long answer went something like this: Porter was a highly suggestible sociopath with a mild paranoid psychosis. Several years ago he committed a crime, was caught, convicted, and sent to prison. That should have been the end of the story, but society simply wasn't that lucky. While incarcerated he had been deeply affected by a fire-and-brimstone prison ministry. Something called a "God Pod." Unfortunately, he completely missed the allegorical sense of biblical text and took much of it literally. In the end, what should have been a tool for rehabilitation had, in his case, created a serial spree killer.

The man literally came to view himself as a modern day equivalent to the inquisitors of fifteenth century Europe, and just two months shy of one year ago, he had started his own series of Witch trials here in Saint Louis, Missouri. Far removed from medieval Europe in a geographical sense, yes, but he'd gone to great lengths to adhere to the tortures and execution methods of that long ago era as prescribed in the *Malleus Maleficarum.*

Roughly translated from the original Latin, *Malleus Maleficarum* meant the *Hammer of the Witches.* In fact, the "hammer" was a book—an instructional manual written by a pair of inquisitors by the names of Heinrich Kramer and James Sprenger. In its day, it had been the one true and official guidebook for the persecution of accused Witches and heretics.

The language did not matter, however. Whether scribed in Latin or English, the tome was most definitely not my favorite piece of literature.

At the time of Porter's original killing binge, I'd been asked by Ben to consult on the case because of a symbol found carved into the flesh of the first victim. My own spiritual path and studies of various religious practices had helped my best friend solve a crime before, so I guess I had seemed like a natural choice at the time.

The truth is that unbeknownst to me, I was already being sucked into it by an ethereal beckoning. Once I became directly involved on this plane, those forces came to bear with a vicious intensity. After that, it had all been downhill for me.

Much to Ben's horror, I had even ended up becoming one of Porter's prey; on a very foggy night, on a pedestrian bridge spanning the Mississippi River, February last, the self-proclaimed "Hand of God" had almost succeeded in making me his seventh victim.

"Yo, white man, you okay?" Ben asked.

It took a moment for the words to register, and I realized that I was just staring at him. "Yeah, I'm fine."

"You don't look fine. You were kinda zoned there for a minute."

"Have you looked in a mirror?" I asked in retort.

"Yeah. Funny. Ya'know, I'm still not all that keen on you bein' here, Row," was his answer. "Felicity either."

"Yeah, you've told me that several times already."

"I'm serious," he added.

"I know you are."

"For one thing, it's only been a coupl'a weeks."

"I know." I nodded assent as I spoke.

The pair of weeks he was referring to amounted to the period of time it had been since I had played a fairly significant role in the capture of a serial rapist. In and of itself a good thing, except that due to various factors in the investigation—both seen and unseen—I hadn't been coming across as particularly stable lately. Of course, considering my gift—or curse, depending upon how you viewed it—it was the unseen that really caused the problems.

"And then there's..." he began, but seemed to purposely allow his voice to die away on the wind. I noticed then that he was staring past me and at Felicity.

What he left unsaid was the fact that the rapist had come after her, actually managing to effect a kidnapping if for only a few short hours. Even though we'd stopped him before he could go any further, in her case, it made it only slightly less traumatic. In light of those events, I could certainly understand his concern.

I looked over at my wife and saw that she was still staring upward, oblivious to our exchange. "I know, Ben. Believe me, I know."

"You know, Rowan, we set you two up in that apartment for a reason."

The point he was trying to make was simple: Porter was going to be after me, no two ways about it, and my friend didn't want me out in the open.

Of course, if your aim is to kill Witches, you might as well go after the real thing, and I definitely made no bones about being just that. Considering everything that had gone on in my life over the past couple of years, I was just about as far "out of the broom closet," so to speak, as one could be. Therefore, I was not very hard to accuse. I had already admitted it in public—which, by the way, Porter had been sure to remind me of as he pronounced my condemnation and attempted to throw me over the side of a bridge with a noose around my neck.

Thankfully, much of that night had now become a blur. I still had nightmares about it and probably always would, but they were finally starting to fade into two-dimensional representatives of what they had once been. Dulled and flattened, they were much easier to take than the full-blown, Technicolor reenactments. Still, I was looking forward to a future when they would be visited upon me with less frequency.

I knew that day wouldn't come as long as Porter was free.

Of the things I recalled clearly from that night, I knew that in my bid to escape I had shot him. I definitely remembered pulling the trigger, and there was even a blood spatter at the scene that provided physical evidence that I'd hit him. Nevertheless, when the police arrived, there was no body to be found.

No lifeless remains.

No hard and fast proof of his demise.

I had blacked out at almost the same instant the handgun had discharged, so I was no help in the eyewitness department. At the time, Ben had been convinced that Porter had fallen from the bridge to a certain death in the icy river below. The other members of the Major Case Squad on the scene concurred.

For them, it was all over but the paperwork—one of my friend's favorite clichés and one that I'd heard him quip several times before.

But for me... Well, I was the proverbial odd man out. I held the one dissenting opinion in their clutch of optimism. Something in the back of my head told me that Porter was still alive, that the wound I'd inflicted was not so grievous as to take his life, and that he had disappeared into the fog—not the water. That inkling had eventually become an issue of extreme contention between Ben and me—to the point where I finally just kept my nagging intuition to myself.

Well, for the most part anyway.

Unfortunately, when all was said and done, I was the one with the correct answer to the sixty-four thousand dollar question: Eldon Andrew Porter was alive and still just as demented—if not more so— than before. It had merely taken him ten months to come out of hiding.

Now that he had surfaced, I found myself wishing that I had been a better shot.

"It's a bit of a climb," the patrol officer ahead of us said over his shoulder. "We have to go up to the fourth floor, then over to the roof access."

My eyes were still adjusting to the darkness inside the building as we climbed the debris-strewn concrete stairs. The faint nasal bite of urine, both stale and fresh, joined in a pungent reek with feces and rotting trash to foul the gelid air.

"Careful there," he warned, directing the beam of his flashlight on a crumbling step.

We picked our way around the hazard, single file—Felicity in front of me and Ben bringing up the rear.

"There're a lot of homeless that crash here, what with the ministry across the street handing out free lunches and all," the officer continued, offering up an explanation for the background stench. "Actually smells quite a bit worse over at the freight elevator shaft."

"Any of 'em in here when you arrived?" Ben asked.

"No, not when I got here," he answered. "Stockton was first on the scene though."

"He up there?"

"No, he's the green one downstairs tossing his cookies."

"Friggin' wunnerful," Ben spat with more than just a note of sarcasm. "He say if he saw anyone?"

"Just the dead guy."

Ben grunted his displeasure before moving on to his next question, "Who's runnin' the scene?"

"That would be Lieutenant Albright."

"Whoa." Ben all but halted on the stairs. "Not Barbara Albright... Tell me you're not talkin' about 'Bible Barb.'"

The uniformed officer stifled what might have been a knowing or perhaps a nervous laugh. Maybe even both. It was hard to tell. "Yeah. That's the one."

"Shit! What the hell did I do to deserve this?"

"What's the problem, Ben?" I asked back over my shoulder as we began ascending the next flight of stairs.

"Well, I know ya' know Arthur McCann with the county police," he offered.

There wasn't a Pagan in St. Louis who didn't know McCann. He was a devout Christian with a badge who claimed to be an expert on occult religions, and he used his position within the police department to preach his own brand of intolerance and hatred. I'd had more than one run-in with him myself.

"Yeah, sure," I answered.

"Well, stick him in a skirt and give him a little authority and you've got Barbara Albright."

A loud burst of static sounded ahead of us, overcoming the background chatter that had been issuing from the officer's radio. The tinny hiss was followed by a questioning voice, "Unit Fourteen?"

The officer thumbed his microphone and answered, "Fourteen."

"Fourteen, Lieutenant Albright wants to know if Detective Storm has arrived on scene yet. Over."

"That's affirmative," he returned. "I'm bringing them up right now. Over."

"Fourteen, be advised that Lieutenant Albright is requesting that Detective Storm come up alone. Copy."

"Say again?"

"Fourteen, switch up."

The officer reached to his belt and twisted a control knob on his radio, changing to a clear frequency, then spoke again. "Yeah. Go ahead."

"Yeah, Shelton, she doesn't want any civilians up here," the voice answered.

"Tell him they're consultants," Ben instructed. "They're logged and cleared for the scene."

"Yeah, Detective Storm says they are consultants, and they're cleared," the officer relayed into his microphone.

A short burst of static followed then was replaced by silence. We had halted midway up the second set of stairs when the original call came over the radio, and we now waited in the cold darkness a half dozen steps below the second floor.

The pop and crackle of interference once again broke the silence and the disembodied voice of the other officer audibly sighed before continuing. "Shelton, here's a direct quote, 'tell Storm to leave his devil worshipper downstairs where he belongs.'"

Ben's own words came in a slow drone directly behind the echo of the radio. "Fuuuuck me. Just fuuuuck me."

Chapter 3:

I protested, but it didn't do any good. This time it was out of Ben's control, and no amount of complaining from me was going to accomplish anything positive. Besides, he was on my side, or at least that is what I thought. In the end, he continued up the stairs, and we were escorted back out onto the street.

The wind had picked up as a storm front rolled in, so we were waiting in my friend's van with the engine running and the heater on. He had been somewhat reluctant to relinquish the keys, and I guess I could understand why, since he had just gotten it back from the shop a week ago. I'm sure the fact that I was the one responsible for putting it in there to begin with was a big stumbling block for him as well—but that was another story.

I suppose that is probably why when he finally gave up the keys it was to Felicity instead of me, which also was why she was sitting in the driver's seat.

"You've been pretty quiet." I leaned back in the passenger seat and let my head roll to face her as I spoke. The vehicle's heater had not yet defeated the chill, and my words vented outward on an opaque cloud of frost. "Are you doing all right?"

Felicity looked back at me with a flat expression. It was apparent that she was tired, but more than that, it was plain to see that she was overwhelmed. "Aye, that would depend on your definition of all right, wouldn't it, then?"

"Pick one," I offered.

She took a deep breath and exhaled heavily, then reached to the dash and clicked the controls to dual-duty—vent and defrost. The warm air slowly started clearing the fog that had formed on the inside of the windshield. "I'm not going to throw up if that's what you're asking."

"That's a start."

"What about you?" she asked.

"I'm fine." I shrugged, rolling my head back to face out the window. I watched as the arc of clarity inched its way up the glass from the bottom. "Still have the headache, but I expect that will be with me for a while."

"Any worse yet?"

"Yeah. Still tolerable, but it's ramping up."

She reached out and laid the palm of her hand across the back of mine. After a moment she spoke, "Aye, you're well-grounded for a change. And without my help."

My ability, or lack thereof I should say, to center my energies and maintain a solid connection with the Earth had been a concern as of late. In the psychic realm, grounding was your first line of defense and one of the most basic of all abilities. During the past year, Eldon Porter's attempt on my life had taken its toll, leaving me just about as grounded as a runaway helium balloon. It was only recently that I had recaptured the simple ability.

"Can't stay dependent on you forever, can I?" I shot her a tired grin.

Our impending moment was interrupted by a sharp rap on the passenger-side window. I turned to see my friend's face staring back at me. Even though the frost had all but completely cleared from the windshield, I hadn't noticed his approach. His brow was entrenched in a deep furrow and his jaw clenched so tight it made my headache worse just to look at him.

I quickly rolled down the window. "What's the story?"

"Don't ask," he returned with a curt shake of his head. "You don't wanna know. So, listen, you think you can come up with somethin' off this scene?"

"That's why I'm here," I replied, somewhat puzzled by the question.

"You're sure?"

I shook my head and stammered for a second, searching for the words to form an answer. "Well... Ben... You know I can't say that. You know as well as I do, that's not how it works."

He shook his head vigorously and held up a hand. "Just friggin' tell me if you can get somethin' off this scene or not."

"Maybe." My voice took on a defensive tone. "I won't know until I try."

Ben rubbed his eyes then sent his hand back to massage his neck and muttered, "Shit."

"What's going on, Ben?" I asked again.

After a moment, he began shaking his head as a decision visibly fell upon him and his shoulders drooped.

"Not here," he said, then shifted his gaze over to Felicity. "You better get in the back unless you're drivin'."

"Okay, I give up. What's going on?" I asked. My frustration had finally festered to a point of eruption.

"Settle down," Ben ordered with a hushed voice and a stern glance.

The drive had been short but conspicuously wordless. In complete silence, we had traversed slightly more than a mile of block-long jaunts and eleventh-hour ninety-degree turns. Fortunately, less than five minutes passed before we arrived at our final destination, which turned out to be a small diner at the intersection of Seventh and Chouteau. Still, even five minutes can seem like forever when you are sitting next to a taciturn cop who outwardly appears to be pissed off at the world, you included.

I was no stranger to "Charlie's Eats," and neither was Ben. In fact, this is where he had first shown me the case file that proved Eldon Porter's identity. But, that wasn't its only distinction. With its proximity to police headquarters, officers frequented it at all hours.

There was even a pair of parking spaces on the lot designated specifically for patrol cars. The standing joke was that, other than the food itself, "Chuck's" was probably the safest place in the entire city to have a meal.

Joking aside, the truth was that while the fare was far from four-star gourmet, it was good, with sizeable portions, and reasonably priced. Anything from a doughnut to a cheeseburger, or even the house specialty—appropriately dubbed "The Kitchen Sink Omelet"—was available 24/7. On top of that, everything on the menu came complete with a bottomless cup of coffee.

"Look, Row," my friend continued after I reluctantly followed his instruction and sat back in the booth with deliberate heaviness. "I know where you're at, really I do, but you gotta listen to me for a minute."

"I'd like to, but you haven't been saying anything," I fired back.

"Jeez, Felicity, could you kick 'im or somethin'?" He aimed his glance at my wife as he made the rhetorical statement.

"Aye, I doubt it would do any good," she answered anyway.

"Heya, Storm," a bear-like man with a wild bush of a red beard called to Ben from the other side of the counter then nodded in my direction. "Rowan."

I dipped my head in acknowledgement and did my best to replace the frown I knew I was wearing with at least some semblance of a smile.

"You ever go home, Chuck," Ben asked the man.

"What for?" The man chuckled as he re-tied the string on his stained apron. "This your wife, Rowan?"

"Felicity, meet Chuck." I made the introduction. "Chuck, Felicity."

"Nice to meet you," my wife said with a lilt, following the words with one of her winning smiles.

"Same here," Chuck agreed.

"Little slow this morning?" Ben asked.

Chuck cast an eye at the clock and shook his head. "Nah, shift change comin' up. Just the calm before the storm. Heh-heh," he chuckled. "But I guess the 'storm's' already here, huh?"

"Yeah, Chuck." Ben shook his head. "Friggin' hilarious."

"Gimme a break, it's early. So, can I get youse guys anything?"

"Just coffee," my friend told him.

"Make that two," I said.

Felicity added, "Three."

Chuck reached under the Formica-sheathed counter, and when he withdrew his large hand, a trio of ceramic coffee mugs were hooked on a single index finger. He set them down, then in a swift motion snatched up a full Pyrex globe of java and filled them all with a single practiced pour.

Ben slid partially out of the booth and in a pivoting motion ferried the steaming mugs to our table.

"Youse gonna be here for a bit?" Chuck asked.

"A while, probl'y," Ben returned. "Why?"

The large man behind the counter hooked his thumb over his shoulder. "I gotta go in the back and check in a delivery. Wendy oughta be here in a bit. You wanna yell back there if someone comes in before she gets here?"

"We can do that."

"I 'preciate it." Chuck nodded as he turned, then called back over his shoulder before disappearing into the back of the diner, "If youse want any more coffee, help yerselfs."

A quiet lull ensued, broken randomly by the noise of Chuck shifting boxes in the back room and Felicity stripping open packets of sugar. The static-plagued tune of the *Talking Heads "Psycho Killer"* fell in behind the duet as it wafted from the speaker of a tinny radio behind the counter.

Considering what was happening a few blocks away, I suppose the song was appropriate.

"Can you tell me what's going on now, Ben?" I finally appealed.

"There ain't no other way to say this. You've been banned from any investigations involving the Major Case Squad."

I blinked. I waited for him to tell me he was kidding. He didn't, so I spoke. "Excuse me? Banned? Why?"

"Listen," he started again. "That's what I was gettin' ready to tell ya'. With Bee-Bee runnin' the show, there's not a hell of a lot I can do."

"Who's Bee-Bee?" I asked, shaking my head. "I thought somebody named Albright was in charge."

"That's Bee-Bee. Bible Barb," he explained. "Lieutenant Barbara 'fuckin' holier than thou' Albright."

"But, I thought you were running this investigation," Felicity said.

He shook his head. "I'm just the investigating officer of record for the original case."

"Well doesn't that carry any weight?" I asked.

"For gettin' me outta bed in the middle of the night, maybe, but that's about it. It's pretty simple. She lieutenant, me lowly detective, and that's the size of it."

"Banned?" I repeated again.

"Yeah, Row. Banned."

"Aye, but you seemed to be running things before," Felicity interjected.

"Yeah, well it doesn't usually happen that way. It did then, but only because I was originally assigned the case, and the powers that be gave me some breathing room."

"So why aren't they now?" I asked.

"Well, let's see..." He rolled his eyes and huffed out a breath. "For starters, the lieutenant I reported to with the Major Case Squad retired."

"And this Albright woman is the replacement?" my wife half asked, half stated.

"Exactly."

"Correct me if I'm wrong," I posed, "but I was under the impression that lieutenants were basically management and that they didn't get that directly involved in investigations."

"Yeah, pretty much," he agreed with a nod. "But not always. Some of 'em get involved. As it happens, Bee-Bee is a real hands-on, stir-the-shit type."

"So can't you go over her head?" I pressed.

"Not really. I dunno if you missed it, but in the past year we've gotten a new mayor and a new police chief in the city."

"Yeah, so?"

"Yeah, so, there's been a change in management my friends, and I'm not exactly considered a model employee right now."

"Why is that?" Felicity asked.

"Does a little nocturnal incident at the morgue a few weeks ago ring a bell?" he asked.

Unfortunately, it did. During the hunt for the serial rapist, I had convinced Ben to get me into the medical examiner's office to view the remains of a victim from an overlapping investigation. Normally, this wouldn't have been a problem, except that I had talked him into doing so in the middle of the night. The chaotic psychic events that ensued from there had caused quite a bit of commotion in this realm and my friend a generous share of trouble at the time. Apparently, they still were.

"Well, what if I had a talk with her?"

He scrunched his brow and looked confused. "What about?"

"About me and what I can do to help."

"Were you just not listening?" he asked incredulously. "The woman flat out said for me to 'leave my devil worshipper downstairs where he belonged.' News flash, Kemosabe. She was talkin' about you."

"I realize that, Ben, but she doesn't know anything about me."

"Oh hell yes she does," he returned. "At least she thinks she does anyway."

"How can she?" Felicity chimed in.

"Neither one of you is particularly low profile," he answered.

"You mean the papers?" I asked.

"...And the TV." He nodded.

"But that's just media hype," I told him in a dismissive tone. "That's not going to tell her anything."

"Well, guess what?" he chided. "She's read 'em and watched 'em all, and as far as she's concerned, they're gospel. And she didn't get the nickname 'Bible Barb' for nothin'. She's drawn her conclusion, white man. You're the wicked Witch, and that's all there is to it."

"But that's just her," I objected.

He countered with a statement I hadn't expected, "And a few others."

"Who?" Felicity asked. "Arthur McCann?"

"He's one, obviously. But there're more... A handful of uniforms. Couple of detectives... Couple of the higher-ups, including the new chief..."

"What about my track record?" I asked.

He started shaking his head again, "I got news for ya', Row. Your track record has a few potholes, which is another reason why you aren't scorin' any points. Right now you're kinda looked upon as a loose cannon."

"What?"

"Yeah," he continued. "Chasin' after Porter on that bridge, the thing at the morgue..."

"What about you?" I asked with a nod in his direction. "What do you think?"

He fell silent for a moment, looked away, then sighed before bringing his eyes back to meet mine.

"After what you did a few weeks back, I think maybe you might be a bit of a danger to yourself, yeah."

He was talking about the fact that I had deliberately run his van through a set of plate-glass windows in order to get inside a building.

"That was different, and you know it," I argued. "The sonofabitch had Felicity in there."

"Yeah," he rebutted. "And that's the only reason I let it go, white man. If you'll remember correctly, I lied about what really happened on my report."

I didn't have a comeback for the comment because I knew he had done exactly that.

"Listen, Row," he started after an uncomfortable silence. "You've still got friends in the department, and I'm one of them."

"Even though you think I'm a danger to myself," I volunteered with a slightly sarcastic edge to my voice.

"Yeah, even though," he echoed. "Cut me some slack here. I know what you can do. I've seen it first hand. And I'm even willin' to trust you if you wanna know the truth."

"Trust me to what?"

"To help stop this bastard."

"That will be hard to do if I'm cut off from the investigation."

"I know."

My friend turned to stare out the window, and I allowed my gaze to follow his. Our muted reflections stared back from the pane of glass, mirroring our weariness like an overexposed snapshot. The darkness of night was still holding its ground and seemed in no hurry to relinquish its position. A quick glance at my watch told me that there was a pair of hours yet to go before the morning would ooze in above the heavy clouds.

"So, where do we go from here, then?" Felicity piped up again.

"Back to the beginning. Back to what started this whole conversation." He turned his gaze to her, then to me. "Do you think you can come up with somethin' worthwhile off that crime scene?"

"That's kind of a moot point isn't it?" I shook my head as I asked the question.

"No. No it's not," he replied.

"But you said I was banned from the investigation."

"Officially you are."

"Aye." My wife cocked her head to the side and raised an eyebrow. "What are you saying?"

"What I'm sayin' is that if I'm gonna take a chance on losin' my badge, I need to know it's gonna get us somewhere."

I never got a chance to answer my friend's question.

CHAPTER 4:

T he muffled electronic wail of a pager began sounding from
somewhere across the table. By the time it had completed its
second demand for attention, it was joined by the steadily rising trill of
a cell phone vying for the same.

"Jeeeez…" Ben complained aloud as he pulled the beeper from
his belt and fumbled with it until he managed to switch it off and then
peered at the display while sending his other hand to rustle through his
coat pocket. "It's Albright," he told us as he laid the pager on the table
and withdrew the screaming phone.

Before he could thumb the button on the second device to
answer the call, the beeper began pulsing once more, prompting him to
clumsily stab at it again.

"Yeah, Storm, hold on…" he barked into the phone while
struggling to mute the pager.

The device was swallowed by his large hand, and his searching
fingers were no match for its relatively diminutive size. Felicity finally
reached out, snatched the noisemaker from his palm, and pressed the
appropriate button. He quickly mouthed the word "Thanks" in her
direction before turning his attention to the voice at the other end of
the cell phone.

"Uh-huh, yeah, I'm here," he said as he sent his free hand on
another fishing expedition, withdrawing it from his pocket a moment
later and laying his notepad on the table. "Yeah… Yeah…"

My friend held his pen poised over the paper as his eyes closed,
and his face noticeably slackened. He dropped the pen and sighed
heavily.

"Yeah, okay. You're sure? Uh-huh. Yeah, great… No, I'll take
care of that. Jeez, I don't fuckin' need this… Yeah, I know. Okay.
Yeah." He picked up the pen, and his hand began moving as he
scratched out a jumble of letters that were legible only to him. "Can

ya' spell that? Yeah…Yeah…Uh-huh…t-i-g-k-e-i-t. Yeah. Two S's? Okay…Got it.

"Okay, yeah. You sendin' someone?" He shook his head as he spoke into the phone. "Yeah. Yeah. No problem. He's with me now. We'll be there in about ten. Yeah. Later."

He pulled the device away from his ear and immediately began stabbing at buttons in an ordered fashion.

"What's going on?" Felicity asked.

"Just a sec," he told her as he tucked the phone against the side of his head once again. "Yeah, Osthoff, it's Storm… Yeah, tell me about it. Listen, there's a file folder in my desk, middle drawer. Yeah…Yeah…Got it? Good. So there's a list in there. Yeah. So, I need you to call Ackman and feed him the numbers. Yeah, yeah… It's not good. No, he's with me. Yeah, I know. No, he's on scene so call his cell. You got the number? Great. Thanks. Yeah, I'll tell him. Bye."

The cell phone beeped as he pressed a button to end the call and then stared across the table at us with an eyebrow arched and a pained frown deepening the fatigue lines in his face.

"What?" I finally asked.

"I'm thinkin'" was his reply.

"Uh-huh," I returned. "Now tell me something that isn't obvious."

"Chill, Row." He reached up and rubbed his forehead. "This ain't good."

"What is it, Ben?" Felicity asked, her voice carrying far more concern than had mine.

"Well, that was Ackman back at the scene. Albright had him call. Looks like she wants you there after all."

"Why the change of heart?"

"Seems Porter left you something."

"What?"

"A note. But they aren't sure quite what it says. Well, not all of it, anyway."

"What do you mean?"

"Well, it's apparently a page from a book," Ben explained. "Or a copy of a page. His handwritten note reads 'Gant—your wife has lovely hair.'"

"What the hell is that supposed to mean?" I shook my head and frowned.

"Beats me, but the rest of the printed text is in German, so until it's translated we won't know much. Albright did recognize a few words; apparently, she took German in high school or somethin'. *Prossneck, Deutchland, Folterung, Hexefertigkeit* and the year sixteen twenty-nine."

He stumbled over the pronunciations, but I'm not sure I could have done much better.

"According to Bee-Bee they roughly translate as *Prossneck*, Germany, torture, and WitchCraft."

Felicity audibly caught her breath and jerked, dropping her coffee cup in the process. Hot java splattered across the table, spilling over the edge. The ceramic mug bounced once from the wet surface before falling to its demise on the tile floor. Ben jumped back in his seat and instantly began extracting handfuls of paper napkins from the metal holder next to the window. In his haste, he sent the salt and pepper shakers spilling into the seat and a bottle of catsup rolling toward me. The condiment-filled vessel came to rest against my own coffee cup with a sharp plinking noise, which is fortunate, because I wouldn't have caught it. I was otherwise paralyzed by the words my friend had just recited.

"You okay, Felicity?" he asked as he began mopping up the spill.

My wife's normally pale complexion was washed to stark white as she sat frozen, staring across the table at Ben. Her green eyes were wide, and it didn't take a Witch to literally feel the fear coming from her.

"Felicity?" Ben called her name again and then shifted to me when she didn't answer. "Row? What the hell? What's going on?"

The throb in my head moved up the scale a pair of notches, instantly becoming far more than a nuisance. Fear-induced nausea welled in the pit of my stomach and sent a bitter burn into the back of my throat. I slipped my hand along the edge of the table until I reached Felicity's and then clasped her fingers tight.

"It's not going to happen," I said, fighting to mask my own distress.

"What?" Ben pressed as he threw more napkins onto the puddle of cooling liquid. "What's not going to happen?"

I turned my gaze to him but continued to hold Felicity's hand tightly. "The page is most likely from a book by Wilhelm Pressel," I recited. "It's pretty obscure, but most anyone who's studied the Witch Trials of the Burning Times is familiar with it. It didn't dawn on me at first, but the minute you said *Prossneck*, Germany, well, that's a bit of a giveaway. Anyway, if it is in fact a page from *Hexen und Hexenmeister*, then the text is an actual accounting of the first day of torture inflicted upon an accused Witch in the year sixteen twenty-nine."

"Okay. That's the kinda thing that would fit with this wingnut's profile. But, what's with the comment about Felicity's hair?"

"The first thing the hangman did to this woman," I explained, "was to bind her hands, attach her to a torture ladder, and cut her hair off." I swallowed hard before continuing. "He then doused her head with alcohol and set it on fire to burn the rest of her hair off down to the roots."

"Aye," Felicity muttered quietly as she regained her voice. "And that was only the beginning."

"He's taunting me," I stated as anger began to creep into my voice. "The sonofabitch is telling me what he plans to do to my wife."

"Jeezus… Goddamnit…" Ben whispered. "And I thought I was takin' the easy out. So much for breakin' it to you gently."

"You couldn't have known," I offered with a shrug.

"No," he returned. "But the note is only half of it."

"What else," I asked with a grimace.

"Aww man, Jeez..." He rested an elbow on the table then dropped his head into his hand and closed his eyes. "They ID'd the victim..."

The portent in his voice was unmistakable, and it struck both Felicity and me with no less force than a physical slap across the face. I could almost guess what was coming, and I am certain Felicity could as well.

The ache inside my skull took on the properties of root canal sans anesthetic. I braced myself for the news, not truly wanting to hear it but unable to escape its reality.

"Oh, Gods..." Felicity murmured into the silence between us, audibly broadcasting her dread.

"Yeah," Ben returned. "Randy Harper. He took out a member of your Coven."

"Dammit," I spat the curse. "Isn't this how I got involved in all this shit to begin with?"

My reference wasn't lost on him. The first investigation I'd helped Ben with had been the murder of Ariel Tanner. She had been one of my students in The Craft as well as a good friend. Moreover, she had been the priestess of the Coven Felicity and I had since adopted.

"Yeah. Déjà vu and all that crap," Ben returned.

"Gods..." Felicity moaned, and her eyes grew wide. "What about everyone else? If he knew about Randy..."

"That was the second call," Ben said as he nodded. "I've kept a list in my desk since this all started. Ackman is going to contact them, and we'll go from there."

"What about Nancy?" my wife appealed. "Someone should be with her. Unless..."

She caught her breath as the thought struck. She didn't have to voice it for us to know what it was.

"Don't panic," Ben told her. "Ackman is making the calls. We don't know anything yet, so let's just assume that she's okay."

Felicity closed her eyes and took a deep breath as she nodded affirmation. I gave her hand a squeeze but wasn't certain how reassuring it would be. I knew she could easily sense that I was just as worried as she was. I dropped my chin to my chest and stared at the table as a solemn hush blanketed our little corner of the diner. Even the radio behind the counter was spewing only dead air.

"I've had enough nightmares this decade," I finally muttered. "Will someone please wake me up."

"Here she comes." Ben canted his head toward me and whispered, "Play nice and keep the *Twilight Zone* stuff to yourself."

It was obvious that we had not only been expected but that our arrival on scene had been announced. We had just barely topped the metal stairs leading to the roof access of the warehouse a few seconds prior to his comment. Before we could get our bearings, we were greeted by the sight of a woman wearing a heavy trench coat walking purposefully toward us from several yards away.

The assortment of circumstances combined with the raging pain in my skull had centered my mood somewhere between foul and just plain pissed off. "What if I don't?"

"I'm not kidding here, white man. She'll kick your sorry ass outta here," he snarled under his breath. "And I'm damn liable to help her. Got me?"

"Listen to him, Rowan," Felicity demanded as she squeezed my arm. "This isn't the time. Not now."

"When will it be the time?" I asked, my voice flat. "Tell me that."

"I don't know. But not now. Please."

She was still frightened, and I couldn't blame her. The written threat was enough by itself, but backing it up by torturing and killing a member of our own Coven drove the point past home. It fueled the horror and urged it across the line that separated intimidation from violence. Omen from action.

While I still felt some of the same fear that enveloped my wife, mine was rapidly turning to calculating anger. Still, they were both correct. I needed to keep myself on an even keel, or I wasn't going to get anywhere.

"Yeah," I muttered. "Okay."

"I'm friggin' serious here, Row," Ben said.

"I know. I know."

Lieutenant Barbara Albright reminded me of someone's mother. She didn't resemble anyone in particular, actually. She just fit the appearance of a generic, prim and proper, sixties sitcom mom who had been strategically updated to fit the style of the decade—but only where absolutely necessary. She was slight of figure and wore her white hair in a shoulder-length coif that was just traditional enough not to be out of vogue but wasn't exactly riding the cutting edge either. She looked to be in her mid-fifties, but that, in and of itself, could have been an illusion. She was very simply just that nondescript.

The one thing that stood out about her appearance was the thin-lipped expression she now wore. According to Ben, it was how she always looked. At any rate, it was the kind of mask a card player would kill for, and I was betting she knew exactly how to use it.

"Mister Gant, we need to get some things straight right now." She started talking three steps before she reached us. "I am not exactly sure what went on during my predecessor's time in charge, but I know for a fact that I do not like the things that I have read."

She came to a halt directly before us and took a firm stance before thrusting her gloved hands into her pockets. She stared at me with glacier blue eyes, unblinking and unwavering, never taking a moments attention away from my face nor acknowledging the presence of Ben or Felicity. At the V where the lapels of her dark grey trench coat overlapped, a yellow-gold, cross pendant stood out against her sweater in a blatant display.

"I also do not like you or what you represent," she continued her speech. "Your involvements in previous investigations were a travesty and an embarrassment to the Major Case Squad. It is only by the grace of God Almighty that no officers were injured or killed because of your antics. You should also know that I am of the opinion that had you stayed out of it and allowed us to do our jobs, there would have been far fewer victims. Not to mention that Eldon Porter would now be incarcerated."

"Exc..." I started to make an objection, but the first word was cut off by Felicity's instantly tightening grip on my arm. Even in the midst of her apprehension, she was remaining logical and level headed, something at which she was very practiced, until you pressed the correct button, of course. If that occurred, well, let's just say that your only hope would be if your deity of choice happened to be listening.

"Yes, Mister Gant?" Lieutenant Albright cocked her head and frowned even more, which is something I hadn't thought possible.

"Nothing," I answered flatly.

"Now then," she started again. "You need to understand that you are here only because Porter left a message specifically for you. Otherwise, I would have you arrested if you came within a mile of a crime scene. The truth is that I want you to see what you have caused through your interference, and I am not the only one who sincerely hopes that it haunts you for the rest of your days."

"Lieutenant, you don't even begin to know," I returned with a cold edge in my voice.

She ignored my comment. "Be aware that any further involvement you have in this case will be at my discretion, and you can rest assured that I will exercise it to the fullest extent. I intend to keep you on a very short leash, Mister Gant. VERY short. Am I making myself clear?"

I stared back at her for a long moment, remaining mute. The temperature atop the building seemed even colder than it had down on the street, but that was most likely an effect of the company rather than the climate. The expectant lull was filled with forlorn sighing noises as the wind weaved its way through broken windows on the floor below us then gushed up the stairwell and out through the open door.

In my head, I flipped through several responses for her question, but unfortunately, not one of them was particularly appropriate, given the circumstances. They would have made me feel better, most definitely, but would have served only to get me cuffed and processed just for good measure. I finally decided on a one-word answer. I took a deep breath and fought to ground my ire, or at the very least, keep the brunt of it out of my voice.

"Perfectly," came my response.

"Good," she returned. "I am glad to know that we understand one another. Now if you will kindly go back downstairs, I am going to have Detective Storm here escort you to the medical examiner's office. I will meet you there in due course."

"Wait a minute." I shook my head and blinked as I felt my forehead automatically crease from the sudden feeling of confusion. "Aren't we going to look at this crime scene?"

"We have been looking at it, Mister Gant," she told me as she turned on her heel. "You, however, are not."

I started toward her as she began walking away, and felt not only Felicity's grip tighten, but also Ben's barrier-like forearm thud across my chest as I ran into it.

"Then what the hell did you call me up here for?" I shouted after her.

She stopped in her tracks and stood with her back to us for a measured handful of seconds before twisting slightly and looking back over her shoulder at me.

"I thought we had already established who is in charge here, Mister Gant" was all she said before turning and continuing on her way.

CHAPTER 5:

"I can't believe she did that!" I punctuated the angry comment by slapping my open palm hard against the side of Ben's van. The force of the impact joined with the frigid sheet metal to send a loud thump in one direction and a jarring sting up my arm in the other. I instantly regretted the action but did it again anyway. In fact, I did it twice more and would have continued had my friend not circled his hand about my wrist and stopped me mid-swing.

"Calm down," he barked. "My friggin' van didn't do anything to ya'."

I turned to face him, my infuriation seething outward in hot waves. "Dammit, Ben, she called us up there just so she could try to intimidate me."

"Yeah," he nodded. "That's her style. Whaddaya want me to tell ya'? Now shut up and quit makin' a scene."

I took quick notice that my outburst had, in fact, attracted attention from some nearby uniformed officers and crime scene technicians, but I didn't really care.

"Who the hell does she think she is?!" I demanded as my voice rose well above any necessary volume.

A sudden swath of blue-white light fell across us, struggling to fend off the darkness and expose us to the world. It slashed drunkenly back and forth, growing brighter with each pass. The varied sounds of interested commotion blended with frenzied footsteps at an ever-increasing volume.

Ben shot a startled look over his shoulder and declared a staccato string of expletives that ended with "I really don't need this shit."

With a quick jerk, he yanked the passenger door of the vehicle open and shoved me at the opening as he ordered, "Get in."

"Hell no!" I exclaimed. "They want a story, I'll give them a story!"

I shuffled back and sidestepped him as he reached for me again. I don't know how I pulled it off, but I somehow feigned a quick shift in position that left my friend grasping at air and me skirting quickly around him and the open door. The television reporters were almost upon us, and I was aiming myself toward them with fire in my throat and a vitriolic commentary on my tongue.

Before I managed to take a second step, however, the front of my coat laminated itself to my chest and forced the air from my lungs. I could no longer feel the ground beneath my feet, and my stomach fluttered with the butterflies of momentary weightlessness as I literally arced backward in flight. I stumbled once more to the ground, remaining upright only by the grace of the large hand that was twisted into the back of my coat.

I was stiffly swung in a shallow half circle, and after that I didn't see much of anything other than the seat of the van rushing headlong toward me. I twisted and fought to step upward into the vehicle as I was propelled at it and in the process raked my shoulder hard against the frame. The door was already being slammed behind me as I fell in a twisted heap with my torso lying across the engine cover. Toward the rear, I heard the side door groan in a discordant harmony with my own as it was quickly forced open. The rush of activity was instantly followed by Felicity climbing in and slamming the opening shut.

I pushed myself up from the shadows and into a sitting position, twisting in the seat as I rose. The stark lights now filled the interior of the Chevy from the front and sides as video cameras were brought to bear on it. I squeezed my eyes tightly shut and twisted my head, throwing up my hands to shield my face, but I still saw spots from the brief glance into the man-made suns.

We were parked outside the cordoned area of the crime scene proper, and therefore, fair game. Now that I had called down their unrelenting attentions upon us, we had become the main course.

The muffled exterior noise jumped in amplification as the driver's side door of the van opened, and a chaotic mix of voices began ricocheting around us.

"I said, NO COMMENT!" I heard my friend shout over the unintelligible questions as he folded his large frame in through the opening and levered the door shut.

The intensity of the clamor was once again suppressed, but the beams of garish light still sliced through the shadows. If they were to be denied a sound byte then they were intent on fighting like a pack of wild dogs for the best clip of video.

"Thanks, Rowan," Ben snarled at me with thick sarcasm in his voice as he thrust his keys into the ignition and started the van. "Thanks a whole hell of a lot. Just what the fuck did you think you were doing?!"

"Giving them what they want!" I barked in return.

"Have you lost your goddamned mind?! Where the hell do ya' think that's gonna get ya'?!"

"Someone has to tell them what's going on."

"That's for the public relations officer to handle, not you."

"I'm talking about that bitch upstairs! Someone's got to tell them what she's doing!"

"Don't you get it?!" he declared, thumping his fingertips against his forehead and gesturing angrily. "Have you suddenly gone stupid on me or somethin'? You run off at the mouth about Albright, and you're screwed! Like it or not, in this situation, you're the odd man out. They'll spin the whole fuckin' thing to make you look like a freak, and the way you're actin' right now it wouldn't be hard!"

It took a moment for what he said to sink in, but I knew he was correct. I was as out of control as I had ever been.

"I'm sorry," I exclaimed. "But there was no call for what she did. It was a power play, and you know it."

"Yeah, it was," he admitted as he pulled the gearshift down into drive and pounded his fist twice on the horn before letting off the brake. "I told ya' how she was..." He took a moment to direct an exclamation toward the windshield. "Get outta my way you friggin' asshole, or you're gonna get run over! Jeezus!"

My friend twisted the steering wheel and nudged the vehicle slowly forward through the group of reporters and camera operators as they began parting. As he brought the van around and rotated the wheel back toward center, he shot me a quick glance.

"Listen, Kemosabe, I had no idea that was what she had planned, but it doesn't surprise me. I told you what she thought of ya'."

"But that whole exercise was done for no other reason than to get under my skin." I asserted.

"Uh-huh," my friend grunted. "That's how she plays the game."

"Well, her rules suck."

"Aye, but that doesn't matter," Felicity said from behind me. "She succeeded in exactly what she set out to do. Look at yourself, then. I've never seen you lose your temper like this."

"Yes you have," I shot back as I turned in my seat to face her. "You just don't remember it because a sick sonofabitch had you drugged up on Rophynol."

"Aye," she answered with an uncharacteristic hardness in her voice. "He did at that, but I remember more than you know, Rowan Linden Gant. More than you know."

As she slumped back in her seat, she continued to stare at me with a cold fire in her jade green eyes. I knew at that moment that I had flipped the wrong switch.

I hoped my chosen deities were listening.

In keeping with the theme set forth by Lieutenant Albright, the security guard at the Saint Louis City Medical Examiner's office had been phoned about our impending arrival. He let us in while on his way out the door to grab a smoke. He had been instructed to tell us to wait in the lobby until she arrived. Another tactic on her part, obviously, but there was nothing we could do. The door that led farther into the building was locked. I knew, because I succeeded in raising Ben's anger a notch by ignoring his vehement instructions not to check it.

Remnants of the recent holiday season still visibly occupied the reception area of the office. Customarily, the room was bland and functional, so the ornamentation was quick to conjure a "what's wrong with this picture" feeling.

Intertwined silver and gold garland still hung in shallow swags along the edge of the counter with a dozen or so holiday cards folded over them and on display. The screen saver on the computer behind the desk offered a snowy scene, complete with an inviting-looking log cabin and a twinkling Christmas tree. Here and there, other decorous attentions to detail could be picked out—a coffee mug emblazoned with a picture of Santa Claus; a wreath on the door leading back to the offices, also locked; and even a half-depleted bowl of festively-wrapped candies. All of them came together to form the whole: an unlikely clutch of cheer in the midst of a place that seemed overwhelmed by depression. I didn't know about anyone else, but it just wasn't working for me.

I'd seen the inside of this building too many times, not only in my waking hours but in nightmares as well. I had grown to despise its plain façade over the past couple of years. Still, as much as I hated it, I couldn't escape. If it was nothing more than morbid fascination that brought me here, at least I could seek help, but I wasn't fortunate enough to have a sickness to blame. I had become a permanent satellite inextricably gripped by the gravity of circumstance; my erratic orbit inevitably intersecting with an occupied autopsy suite. As often as not, I felt compelled to bring about the collision myself, and right now, I was at ground zero of yet another impact. Even though I was not at fault this time around, the ever-associated migraine was looming like a dark shadow over me.

This place was always a seething well of pain for me, and this morning was no different; of course, my irascibility factor being off the scale as it was didn't help matters at all. I had started hearing the voices of the dead—screams mostly—the moment we turned onto Clark Avenue. Staving them off became a somewhat violent internal struggle as soon as we entered the building.

I sought refuge from the ethereal by embracing the mundane. I occupied my mind with trivial tasks in order to erect a mental barrier—anything from mutely reciting the alphabet in reverse to intensely pondering a shadow on the wall. At one point, I even found myself wondering about the holiday cards. Considering that the clientele of a morgue are normally beyond any need for celebration, they seemed out of place to me. I reached down and flipped one of the greetings partially open to reveal the inscription, which showed it to be from a sales rep at *Stryker Corporation*, a well-known maker of medical implements. I checked another and saw that the sender was a local wholesaler of surgical supplies.

I guess I had been over thinking the situation. Of course, in my agitated state, perhaps I was not truly thinking at all.

Unfortunately, seeing the names of the companies led me to dwell on such things as powered bone saws and stainless steel scalpels, which in turn brought back memories of post-mortems I'd witnessed first hand. Fearful cries from the other side rose in volume for a brief moment as I rushed to switch channels on my thoughts before they could suck me in.

"Aye, Ben. How long do you think we'll be waiting, then?" Felicity asked aloud, her voice thankfully snatching my attention away from the place I'd been heading.

There had not yet been enough time for me to redeem myself, and I was still firmly entrenched on her bad side. She hadn't spoken directly to me since my offhanded comment over half an hour ago, and it wasn't looking like she intended to change that any time soon.

I looked over and focused on her. She was seated in a chair across from us, her leather jacket unzipped and revealing the stylized logo of a previous year's Kansas City Pagan Festival that adorned the front of her sweatshirt. Her legs were crossed, and one foot was bobbing in time with music only she could hear.

I absently pondered the wisdom of the logo on her shirt being visible, given the current situation. For the first time in years, I was actually considering not being quite so open about my spirituality. Of course, once you've taken as many steps out of the broom closet as we had, getting back in was almost impossible, so the idea was moot. Still, calling attention to it might not be the best course.

She looked up from her wristwatch and gazed toward Ben with an expectant expression that barely masked the fatigue showing in her face. "It's been almost twenty minutes now."

He pushed away from the counter then looked out the doors and through the glassed-in foyer. "Who knows? Bee-Bee probably wants Row to stew long enough to do somethin' stupid."

"Like he hasn't already?" she volunteered.

"Yeah, well I'm talkin' stupid enough to give her a reason to arrest 'im."

"Hey!" I declared. "I'm standing right here you know."

Ben looked at me. "Yeah, and?"

"Yeah, and, you two seem to have a bad habit of talking about me like I'm not here, that's what. You do it all the time."

"Not all the time. Just when it's for your own good."

"That's subjective."

"Uh-huh. Two-way street, Row. You aren't exactly the pinnacle of objectivity yourself."

As much as I hated to admit it, he had a point. Of course, that didn't mean I had to like it. "Well, it's still annoying."

"Yeah, well so's when you talk to dead people the rest of us can't hear."

Felicity piped up, a matter-of-fact tone permeating her voice. "Aye, Ben's right."

"What do you mean?" I scrunched my forehead as I spoke. "You've ventured over to the other side yourself as I recall."

"Not about that." She dismissed my comment with an impatient shake of her head. "About your giving Lieutenant Albright a reason to arrest you, then. If you don't calm down, you're going to do just that."

"You're not gonna win, Row," Ben offered. "Especially if you play 'push me-shove you' with her. She'll knock your ass down and kick you while you're there."

"Whatever happened to the whole 'to protect and serve' thing?" I asked.

"Number one," he returned, "you've been watchin' too much TV. And number two, never pull the 'taxpayin', law-abidin' citizen who pays your salary' crap with a copper. Trust me, it just pisses us off."

"So, it's okay for her to treat me like a criminal?"

"How many times have I gotta tell ya', Row? This is reality. She's holdin' the cards here, not you."

"Yeah, I know," I grudgingly admitted. "But she's still getting to me."

"That's YOUR problem, then," Felicity said. "You know how to get around that. Ground and center yourself."

"Yeah, yeah, you're right," I said as I pulled my glasses off and rubbed my eyes, lingering for a moment as I pinched the bridge of my nose between my thumb and forefinger.

"How's your head?" Felicity asked, her voice still edgy but softened by a few degrees of concern.

"Killing me," I answered.

"*Twilight Zone*?" Ben asked.

"Yeah," I nodded slightly. "And we're already hell and gone past the signpost."

CHAPTER 6:

L ieutenant Albright breezed in through the front doors of the medical examiner's office just over twenty minutes later. True to what Ben had told me earlier, her gelid expression had not changed in the least.

"Mister Gant," she said as she entered, cracking what might have passed for a pleasant smile had there not been so much sarcasm affixed to it. "I am surprised to find you here in the lobby as I asked. Apparently you CAN obey the law if you try hard enough."

"The door is locked," I answered coldly. "You know that."

"Of course." She nodded. "But that sort of thing has never stopped you in the past."

I caught an acidic response in my throat and choked it back down, turning my head to the side and closing my eyes as I did so. I heeded Felicity's advice and took an audibly deep breath in through my nose, then exhaled slowly through my mouth as I opened my eyes and turned back to face Albright. I could feel energy flowing along my spine and coupling with the Earth in a solid ground. It was as tangible to me as a hot and neutral lead on an electrical outlet. Still, it didn't bring complete calm, and simply being in this woman's presence made me bristle.

"Look, Lieutenant," I began. "You've made your feelings perfectly clear. I have no desire to continue down this path with you."

"And which path would that be, Mister Gant?" she asked, feigning ignorance.

"I'm telling you that I am not going to allow you to bait me any longer, Lieutenant," I replied. "I'm here, just like you asked. I'm just waiting for you to tell me what it is you want from me."

I cannot say that she was visibly disappointed by my stance, but I definitely had the feeling that some of her steam had instantly become just so much condensation. There was a short period of silence while she considered what I had just said. I fully suspected that she was using the time to regroup and plot her way around the obstacle I had just placed before her.

"Mister Gant," she proceeded with a tilt of her head. "What I want, you cannot possibly give."

"How so?"

"No matter what powers you may claim to have, you cannot change that which has already happened. I firmly believe that the man on the table beyond that door is there because of you. There is nothing you can do to bring him back nor any of the other victims for that matter."

"No. No I can't," I agreed in a quiet tone.

"Now, just a little while ago I had the unpleasant duty of phoning Mister Harper's wife to ask that she come down here to identify his remains, and..."

She didn't get a chance to finish the sentence. Like a banshee wail, Felicity's voice pierced the air between us, rendering everyone mute. "You what?!"

"Excuse me?" Albright turned her hard stare on my wife.

"Aye," Felicity began as she stood and moved forward, bringing herself eye-to-eye with the lieutenant with no more than a pair of steps between them. "You told Nancy that Randy was dead, over the phone?"

"And what would you have had me do, Miz O'Brien?" she shot back.

"Send someone to tell her in person."

"That is not how it is done."

The one word response that my wife uttered next surprised everyone, including me. "Bitch."

The thick calm that enveloped her as she spoke was something I had seen only once before and was in no hurry to see again. The button that had now been pushed was well up the column from what I'd done earlier. I wasn't sure if there were enough Gods to create a pantheon that was capable of quelling the fire that had just been ignited.

I actually saw a wash of surprise flow across Lieutenant Albright's features as she stared back at the redheaded tempest in front of her. It was obvious that Felicity's outburst had blindsided her.

"What did you just say?" she asked.

"I think you heard me, then," my wife answered with frigid purpose in her voice as she cocked her head to the side and glared. "But I'll be more than happy to repeat it for you if you'd like."

The door on the back wall of the lobby clicked loudly and then whooshed open just as Albright started to open her mouth. A pale young man with a stoic expression and scraggly goatee poked his head through the opening and regarded us with general disinterest. After a moment, he pushed the door wider and held it open with his back against it.

"Doc says for you to come on back" was all he said.

Albright swung her gaze from the young man back to Felicity and shook her index finger perfunctorily as she mustered a menacing tone. "We will finish this discussion later."

"Aye," my wife retorted as she gave her a curt nod, but still never broke eye contact. "I'll be looking forward to it, then."

"Johnathan, could you please turn that down?" The medical examiner on duty called out to the diener who had led us back to the autopsy suite, raising his voice to be heard over the music that filled the room.

On the opposite wall, the young man was standing at a stainless steel sink performing what must have been some daily routine considering the mechanically adept way he was approaching it. Whatever it was, it involved angry-looking medical implements that appeared as though they would be more at home on the set of a horror movie.

Aphrodite's Child's "Four Horsemen" was blaring from the speakers of a compact stereo nestled on a shelf in an out of the way corner. Considering the tune was one that came from my generation, it was not the type of music I would have expected to appeal to someone as young as the assistant, but to each their own.

He wordlessly abandoned his task for a moment to step over and spin the knob on the bookshelf sound system. He dropped the volume out of our range of hearing just as the chorus was about to inform us as to the color of the fourth horse.

It didn't matter. Like most anyone, I already knew the color and what it represented. I found no particular amazement in the coincidental symbolism either. It was the sort of thing that seemed to be happening to me constantly these days, and I'd grown jaded to it.

"Thank you," the M.E. stated aloud, the tone sounding as though the words came more from habit than actual courtesy.

We were standing next to a metal table in the tiled room. The form resting atop it was zipped partially into a body bag that could be seen at the foot. From the vicinity of the waist upward, it was also covered by a white sheet, a necessity because of the two-by-four that was still attached to the corpse.

The weathered length of wood jutted out on either side, exposed for all to see. Randy's pale hand was twisted into a pained claw, his wrist mottled purple and swollen where several circlets of bailing wire held it fast to the wood. Frozen blood streaked the appendage and glistened wetly as it thawed.

I stole a glance at Felicity. She was holding her eyes tightly shut with her fist pressed against her lips. Her visceral anger had been replaced for the moment by bitter anguish.

I took a deep breath of the frigid air in the suite as I struggled to maintain control, myself. The smell of death and raw meat stung my nostrils, and I choked back the desire to vomit. The fact that a good friend was lifeless beneath the shroud made this experience different from any other. Even when I'd helped investigate Ariel Tanner's death,

I had never been in close proximity to her corpse as I was now with Randy. I wasn't entirely sure I could handle it.

If the increasing throbs inside my skull were any indicator, I would have to say no.

The doctor turned his attention to us. "Now then, we won't be starting the post until later this morning…"

"Is Doc Sanders doing it?" Ben interjected, referring to the chief medical examiner for the city.

"Doctor Sanders is on vacation right now," the M.E. replied.

"What about calling her in," my friend pressed. "She's familiar with the way this wingnut operates, and I'm sure…"

"I am certain Doctor Friedman can handle the task, Detective," Albright announced with a thread of agitation in her voice, cutting him off mid-sentence.

"I'm afraid she is unreachable." The doctor was obviously miffed but offered the explanation anyway. "If I remember her itinerary correctly, she is on a cruise ship somewhere in the Bahamas."

"When's she get back?" Ben forged ahead.

"Storm!"

"Yeah, okay, sorry Doc. You were saying?"

The M.E. sighed and then continued, "We won't be starting the official post until later this morning; however, I assume you are all aware of the condition of the body, so the cause of death is not likely to be much of a mystery."

"How did you ID him?" I asked

"His driver's license," Lieutenant Albright answered for him.

"He was nude when I saw him hanging from the building," I ventured. "Where did you find that? With the note?"

"Not exactly," she replied. "Doctor?"

The M.E. looked surprised. "Lieutenant, since Mister Gant knew the deceased, I am not certain that…"

"No, Doctor," she returned. "I insist. Mister Gant needs to see this."

Doctor Friedman glanced at me with an apologetic shake of his head. I had met him before, and this was the closest I'd seen to real compassion from the man. That made me fear what I was about to see even more.

His sudden attack of humanity was well placed, but he just didn't have the backbone to stand up to Albright. Without another word, he pulled back the sheet, hesitating initially before finally executing the deed.

"Awww, Jeeeez..." Ben exclaimed. "Lieutenant..."

"Shut up, Storm," she cut him off yet again.

Eldon Porter wanted no mistakes made in identifying Randy Harper. In point of fact, he had gone out of his way to be certain of it.

Bile rose in my throat, and I began to physically tremble from the sickening mixture of sadness, pain, and overwhelming anger as I stared at the horror before me.

Felicity yelped, and I heard her behind me as she began to sob, but she was soon drowned out by the thick noise of blood rushing in my ears as my pulse began to race.

The means of identification was just what Albright had said it to be—a Missouri driver's license. What she hadn't warned me of was the fact that it was firmly affixed to the center of his forehead by a framing nail driven deeply into his skull. Judging from the lack of severe trauma, Porter had probably used a nail gun.

I probably would have stood there transfixed by the appalling sight, eventually falling into ethereal sync with the final violent moments of his life had it not been for the anguished scream that suddenly sliced through the room.

CHAPTER 7:

My muscles tensed as the unconscious fight or flight response took over. I instantly flinched, and the action sent a stab of pain through the shoulder that I'd earlier bounced off the doorframe on the van. The sharp ache crawled up my neck and bore straight in to join with the rank and file of my preternatural migraine. It didn't help either that I immediately followed the wince by jerking my head up from the grisly horror on the autopsy table and shooting a startled glance over my shoulder in the direction of the scream.

At least I thought it was the direction of the scream.

The piercing wail glanced once again from the tiled walls before folding itself into a fading echo that melded with pained whimpers. I twisted slowly around, searching for the source of the noise, but found none.

"What's wrong, Row?" Ben asked.

"Did you hear that?" I answered, asking the question of myself as much as of him.

"Hear what?"

"That scream," I explained. "Someone screamed."

Under most circumstances, I was perfectly capable of distinguishing between the real and the ethereal, and this scream definitely sounded like the former. However, with no one in the physical realm to whom I could attribute it, and since it was apparently audible to no one else, I could only assume that it had originated on the other side. But, something didn't feel right about it. I couldn't explain why, but it didn't fit. It was just too real.

I shuddered as I tried to wrap my thoughts around it. For a split second it made me itch all over.

"You goin' *Twilight Zone*, white man?" he asked with sudden concern as he nudged my wife. "Felicity, do that thing."

She was still choking back a sob. "What thing?"

"That thing where you make him not 'zone out,'" he stated urgently. "Ground 'im or short 'im out or whatever."

"Please, Mister Gant," Lieutenant Albright spat as she tilted her head and shot me a disgusted stare. "Spare us your theatrics. This is neither the time nor the place."

"I wish I could, Lieutenant," I answered as I leaned to one side in order to look past her at the door. "But trust me, I'm not that good an actor."

"Come now, Mister Gant. You have obviously fooled Detective Storm for some time now."

"Lieutenant," Ben started. "There's more to this than you know."

"I don't think so, Storm," she answered without looking at him. "I know exactly what is going on here, and to be honest, it bothers me that an officer attached to my unit can be taken in by such blatant chicanery."

"I'm not bein' takin' in by anything, Lieutenant," he returned.

"Of course you are, Storm. This man is nothing but a charlatan, and you are blinded by misplaced loyalty. You have been bewitched by his lies."

"Don't go there, Lieutenant," he responded with more than a mere hint of anger in his voice.

Benjamin Storm was capable of taking a level of personal abuse that would set off the most even-tempered of individuals, and yet he would remain perfectly calm. However, he had his own set of triggers, among them being an almost fanatical devotion to his friends and family. Albright's treatment of me had been wearing on him with each sardonic jibe she made, and it was finally beginning to show.

From the corner of my eye, I happened to catch a thin smirk that passed across the lieutenant's features and knew that this was exactly what she wanted. Without missing a beat, she seized on the trigger and squeezed.

"How does it feel to be personally responsible for this man's death, Mister Gant?" she asked.

"Back off, Lieutenant," Ben instructed before I had a chance to respond.

"It's okay, Ben," I said.

She ignored both of us—or pretended to at least. "This is the second acquaintance of yours to meet a violent end, is it not? It would appear that being your friend is rather hazardous."

"I said, BACK OFF, Lieutenant!" My friend's voice raised a pair of notches in volume and filled the room to capacity.

"Or what, Detective?" She placed heavy emphasis on his title as she turned to face him.

"Let's you and me go have a talk," he instructed, jerking his thumb over his shoulder in the direction of the door.

"I think perhaps we should," she retorted. "You seem to be forgetting who is in charge here."

He stepped back and aimed a hand at the exit. "After you."

As Albright brushed past him, he turned to the medical examiner who had been shuffling about in silent discomfort during the entire exchange. "You wanna get them outta here, Doc." The words were more a command than a question. "I think they've seen enough."

Doctor Friedman nodded and muttered a quiet "yes" in acknowledgement. Ben then brought his eyes to rest on us and pointed at me. "You stay on this side of the never-never-land county line, got me?" He shifted his gaze to Felicity without waiting for me to answer. "And you make sure he does. I'll be with ya' in a few minutes."

"Ben, it's not worth…" I started.

He cut me off as he turned and stalked after the lieutenant. "Just go with the doc, and do what I tell ya' for a change. This ain't gonna take very long."

Ben's voice carried.

Even with several walls and closed doors between us, it carried, and it did so beyond anything I'd expected. It rode up and down as if someone was repeatedly twisting a volume knob back and forth just to see what it would do. You couldn't really make out everything he was saying, but at the peaks, you definitely picked up on the expletives. He even used a few that I wasn't sure I'd ever heard before, but I was positive I wouldn't be attempting to repeat.

Lieutenant Albright's stern voice fell into the low volume valleys between, inching up an octave or so in pitch but never even beginning to approach my friend's elevated level of animated expression. There were enough snippets of both voices to get the general gist of the argument and that it was yours truly who sat at the center of the conflagration. No big surprise there, but still, between the both of them, within the past five minutes my name had been mentioned seventeen times. Actually, a more accurate statement would be that it was mentioned by Ben and taken in vain by Albright.

"He's screwing up his career." I tossed the comment out as nothing more than an idle observation. I didn't really expect an answer.

"Aye, but better him than you," Felicity replied, giving me one anyway. "At least it is his choice this time."

We were sitting in the lobby of the medical examiner's office, occupying a pair of seats against the wall opposite the reception desk. Doctor Friedman had not seemed entirely sure what to do with us once Ben and Albright left, so he had parked us here for lack of a better place.

"What's that supposed to mean?" I asked.

"It wasn't all that long ago that you were ready to do it for him, then. Remember the reporters?"

"Oh, yeah, that," I replied with mild embarrassment in my voice. "I wasn't really thinking about the various consequences at the time."

"We noticed."

"That would have been manageable, though," I offered. "He could have done some damage control. Thrown it all on me and distanced himself."

"Aye, Rowan, we're talking about Benjamin Storm," she outlined. "He'd never abandon you like that. The man is more loyal than a Saint Bernard."

"You're right," I acknowledged. "I think he still could have found a way around it though. But this, I don't know…"

"Aye, maybe so, but I'm betting it's moot now," she said.

She tilted her head back and closed her eyes, then let out a heavy sigh. Her face was still flushed from her recent bout of weeping as well as the attempt to contain it. Her composure had returned for now, but the emotional burden remained, for both of us.

"Probably," I muttered, then finally asked, "So, what about you and me?"

"Aye, what about us?"

"I had the impression that I pushed a button or two earlier."

"You did," she acknowledged.

"So?"

"So, that was before the bitch in the other room got under MY skin."

"Not wanting to choose between being the pot or the kettle?"

"Aye, let's just say I gained a thorough understanding of how you felt."

We fell quiet as the argument down the hall continued for another round. I rolled my arm up and pushed back the sleeve on my coat to glance at my watch. I frowned when I saw that the bezel was shattered, and what I could make out of the display was mostly a darkened splotch where the liquid crystal had cracked and burned out. I looked at it for a moment, puzzled by what I saw. I quietly shifted in my seat, slightly twisting left then right as I mentally reenacted being forcibly shoved into the van.

Without a doubt, I remembered my left shoulder striking the doorframe, but I couldn't recall anything happening on the right. Still, it was the only explanation, and cliché as it was, it had all happened too fast for me to remember for sure.

"What are you doing, then?" Felicity asked.

She must have sensed my gyrations in the seat because her eyes were still closed.

"Trying to figure out how I broke my watch."

"Aye, it probably happened when Ben tossed you into the van."

"That's kind of what I was figuring."

She lifted her arm and held it out to me. I reached up, pushed back the cuff of her leather jacket and looked at the timepiece that encircled her delicate wrist. I found myself stopping to think about the jumble of lines on the display before remembering to mentally flip them over. The lack of sleep was catching up with me.

"Remember to subtract fifteen," Felicity reminded me about her penchant for setting her watch fast, ostensibly so she would always be on time.

I didn't bother to point out to her that she was still habitually late.

The calculation worked out to the time being 8:15 a.m. It had been a little over four hours since we'd first arrived at the crime scene with Ben, but it already felt like it had been a week. Unfortunately, I knew from experience that it was only going to get worse. One of these days I hoped to be able to experience the other side of that coin—the one where it actually got better after the getting worse part.

I lowered my wife's arm back to her lap and turned my head to look out the entrance foyer. The sun had officially peeked over the horizon something around an hour ago, give or take a few minutes. Still, the cloud cover that layered itself over the city wasn't about to relinquish its hold. The muted light that managed to filter downward took on the grey pallor of dusk and oozed in to bring illumination, though not necessarily to brighten the landscape.

I heard my wife rummaging in her pockets as I stared through the windows at a wintry morning in Saint Louis. From where we sat, I could see the upper edge of the city hall parking lot on the opposite side of Clark Avenue. Cars were already filling the spaces as people went about their routines, oblivious to the horror going on behind these walls. To them, Randy Harper was no more than an unnamed victim of an atrocity that had been reduced to a ten-second breaking-story byte—and even that was only for those who actually caught the morning news.

A part of me wanted to be angered by their apathy, but for once this morning logic prevailed, and I knew they couldn't be blamed. Still, it hurt. It was a throwback to the whole "misery loves company" thing. I was in mourning. In my heart, I wanted everyone else to mourn as well.

What pained me even more, however, was the fact that I wasn't entirely certain that Lieutenant Albright was far off the mark in hanging me for the crime. Perhaps I was an unwitting accomplice in some bizarre, convoluted sense of the concept. People were dying; friends were dying. Moreover, for all the horrors I saw in my mind, I was powerless to stop it. In fact, I seemed to be at the center of it.

Felicity was still shuffling around behind me, and I finally heard her soft voice filled with deep concern, "Nancy?"

Silence filled the lobby. Even the argument between Ben and Lieutenant Albright had fallen to a level easily muffled by the walls. I could faintly hear the frantic sobbing coming from the earpiece of the cell phone my wife had to her ear.

"I know, I know…" Felicity murmured. "Is someone with you? Good."

I closed my eyes and slowly massaged my temples while listening to the local side of the conversation. My wife was possessed of an intense maternal instinct. Ever since we had adopted this young Coven, they had become like foster children to us. In many ways, that feeling ran even deeper for her.

"Aye, I know dear, I know. Put Cally on, then," she continued. "Cally? How are you making it? Is Nancy okay? Aye… Aye… I know. Have you spoken to anyone else? Aye, that's good. Gather them. She needs her friends with her. Good. Yes. That's where we are now…"

I looked back over my shoulder to see my wife nodding gently as she spoke, sadness woven through her pretty face and eyes glistening with tears that she was barely holding back.

"No honey, don't bring her down here," she instructed, as the gentle nod of her head became a semi-vigorous shake. "Not yet. She doesn't need to see him like this."

I reached over, covered Felicity's free hand with my own, and gave it a reassuring squeeze. I didn't envy her at the moment, but I respected her devotion to the Coven and loved her even more for it.

"Aye, make her a strong cup of chamomile and willow bark tea. Aye, keep her grounded, and just listen to her... I know... I know... Yes, Rowan and I will be there as soon as we can... I don't know, dear, I don't know... Aye, it's not good, then... Aye, we'll see you soon, I promise... Remember—just listen to her... Aye, goodbye."

The phone issued a forlorn peep when she disconnected, and she sat there mutely staring at the device in her hand. A tear broke loose from the well in the corner of her eye and began rolling slowly down her cheek.

"How is she?" I asked.

"Hysterical," she answered softly. "Cally is with her."

"Yeah, I kind of picked that up. What about everyone else?"

"On the way. They'd been contacted by the police already, just like Ben said."

"Good." I nodded.

"How did..."

She anticipated the question. "Nancy was out of town on a business trip. Training seminar or something like that, then."

"Okay."

"This is wrong, Rowan," Felicity made a quiet, almost emotionless declaration. "It is just wrong."

Silence rushed back into the room, filling the void as the words faded out. I squeezed her hand once again and tried to think of something to say but failed. I knew exactly how she felt, but we had fallen out of sync.

At this particular moment, I was shifting out of the early stages of grief and rushing headlong into anger.

CHAPTER 8:

"A ye, where are we going?" Felicity asked from the back seat of the van.

Ben hadn't rubbed more than two words together in the same breath since he'd come through the door and into the lobby of the medical examiner's office. The best we'd gotten was a short "come on" coupled with a jerk of his head as he continued past us and out the front doors. He already had the Chevy started and was waiting impatiently for us by the time we caught up with him.

Now, we were heading through the city, him brooding behind the wheel and paying even less attention to traffic signals than usual. The turns he was taking formed no discernable pattern and fell in place with no particular destination I could imagine. The only thing that was obvious was that we were heading away from the M.E.'s office at an accelerated clip. It seemed, very simply, that he couldn't widen the gap between himself and Lieutenant Albright fast enough.

"Dunno," he muttered in return, keeping with his current trend toward one-word responses and grunts.

Thus far, I'd kept my mouth shut, but I was about to lose what little control over my tongue I had left. Knowing Ben as well as I did, I was fully aware that it was best to just leave him alone when he was like this, and he would open up when he was ready. Right now, I didn't consider that an option. I had more than enough on my mind without piling this on top of it. I felt responsible for whatever had gone on behind those doors, and selfish or not, I didn't have time for that guilt to be getting in my way. I was going to clear this slate, and I was going to do it right now.

"All right, out with it," I demanded.

My mood was darkening at a thoroughbred's pace; I had already bypassed coldly succinct and moved full bore into rudely abrupt.

"With what?" he shot back without looking in my direction.

"Whatever you've got going on in your head," I returned. "I know you probably want to yell at me, so just do it and get it over with."

"What the hell are you talkin' about?" he asked.

"That whole deal back there with Albright," I pressed. "It's not like we couldn't hear the explosion."

"If you were listenin' in then what the hell are you goin' on about?"

"Aye," Felicity interjected, using her voice to drive a wedge between us before the situation could become any more volatile. "We weren't exactly eavesdropping you know. We could hear voices but couldn't make much out, then."

My wife had placed her hand on my shoulder, and I could feel her acting as a lightning rod, forcing me to discharge at least some of my welling anger.

"Yeah," he huffed as he released the wheel with one hand and smoothed back his hair before allowing his fingers to come to rest on the back of his neck. "Yeah, I know. Got kinda loud, didn't it?"

"Aye, just a bit," she agreed.

"So fill us in," I asked when at least a modicum of calm had crept into my voice.

"Well, I'm not workin' this case anymore if that's what you're askin'."

"But, do you still have a job?"

"Yeah, for now," he answered. "But I dunno how long that'll last."

"So she didn't suspend you?" I asked.

"Nahh," he shook his head as he spoke. "She can't. Not directly anyway. But, she can pull strings, and you can bet she's makin' those calls right now. The other thing she CAN do is kick me off the Major Case Squad, and she did that before I even opened my mouth."

"I'm sorry, Ben," I sighed. "Man, I'm so sorry."

"What're you apologizin' for?"

"For doing this to you, of course." I shook my head. "This wouldn't have happened if you hadn't been defending me."

"Is that why you think I wanna yell at ya'? Fuck that." He screwed up his face and gave me a dismissive wave. "This was just the sprinkles on the icing for her. Albright has had it in for me from the git-go."

"But..."

"But nothin', white man." He cut me off. "You aren't responsible for this, so give it up."

"Aye, what if she gets you suspended, then?" Felicity asked.

"Then I get a vacation," he offered with a shrug.

"Are you sure about that?" I asked.

"At this stage of the game, yeah," he nodded. "I haven't done anything to get myself shit-canned yet. Reprimanded, yeah. Transferred, maybe. But it's nothin' I can't live with."

"Then why did you come out of there so pissed off?" I questioned.

"Hey, Kemosabe, I was in there with Bible Barb. I seem to recall you losin' it yourself a little earlier. You wanna re-think that question and ask it again?"

"Yeah, I guess you're right."

"Besides," he ventured. "She said some shit about you that really got to me."

"Like what?"

"No way, man. I'm not gonna repeat it." He shook his head. "But let's just say the bitch is lucky I won't hit a woman."

"I'm so glad that you're here," Cally told Felicity as she hugged her tight. "Nancy's upstairs in the bedroom. She just fell asleep a few minutes ago."

"Aye, dear." My wife returned the embrace and spoke in a comforting tone. "That's good then."

We were standing in the entryway to Randy and Nancy Harper's two-story home on Arkansas, just a block off Grand Avenue in the city. We'd been here several times before when they'd hosted circles for the Coven. Those happier recollections now seemed to dull against the painful sharpness of this new memory in the making.

I glanced around and noticed a small, wheeled suitcase, which was parked at an angle against the wall, pull-handle still extended. It had obviously been forgotten in light of the current circumstances. In the opposite corner, a bentwood coat tree stood at attention beneath a crush of winter outer garments. Next to the stairs, a small, antique telephone table sat with a pile of mail strewn across its top. A digital answering machine occupied one corner, its green power indicator glowing in the muted light of the hallway. I absently wondered why, at times like this, the normally insignificant things around us would stand out in stark contrast to everything else. Without warning and for no apparent reason, they would become illuminated details in a darkened tableau. It was more than just curious to me. In a sense, it was almost disturbing.

"Oh, Rowan..." Cally let her voice trail off for a moment as she released Felicity and wrapped her arms around me. "The police were just here. They looked around for a while and asked a few questions."

I gave her a reassuring pat on the back as I returned the hug, feeling her conspicuous anguish connect with my own purposely subdued emotions. "It's okay, Cally. It's okay. They have to do their jobs."

"She's been asking for both of you," she told us as she pulled away.

"Aye, we're here now," Felicity said. "But let her rest. She'll be needing it."

"Everyone else is here," Cally continued. "They're in the back."

"Go ahead." I nodded to them. "I'll wait for Ben."

"Detective Storm?" the young woman asked.

"Aye, he brought us."

"He's finding a place to park the van," I added.

"He'll be along in a bit," Felicity told her as she took her arm and guided her back down the hall.

I watched them disappear through a doorway at the end of the corridor, then turned and opened the front door as I heard a familiar voice and shuffling feet on the other side. Ben had just raised his hand to knock as I swung the barrier open and moved to the side.

"How'd you know I was there just now?" he asked as he stepped in through the opening.

"You mean besides the fact that we arrived together?" I asked, not really expecting an answer to the sardonic question.

"Don't be a smart ass. I mean how'd you know I was there right at that moment? You doin' that hocus-pocus stuff?"

"Nothing quite so ethereal," I answered. "I heard you talking."

He seemed almost disappointed. "Oh. Okay."

I cast a glance outside before swinging the door shut and noticed a uniformed officer getting back into his patrol car, which was parked on the street in front of the house. Moderately sized flakes of snow were beginning to float down from the grey sky, drifting at ever changing angles on the gusts of cold wind.

"Starting to snow," I said, announcing the observation for lack of anything better to say.

"Yeah." Ben nodded as he shrugged off his coat, keeping his voice low. "Gonna get bad out there. They're callin' for three to six inches."

"They were saying just one to two last night."

"Yeah, well you know how it is," he answered while looking around the foyer. "Nice digs."

I took his coat and hung it from an available hook on the dark, bentwood tree, then slipped out of mine and did the same.

"Randy is..." I caught myself and reformed the sentence. "Randy was a real estate agent," I continued the explanation as I turned back to my friend. "He picked this place up back when property down here was going for pocket change. Gutted it and rehabbed it himself. Kind of like you and Allison did with your place."

"He did a hell of a job."

"Yeah. Yeah he did." I frowned as I nodded. The past tense references were sickening reminders of why we were here.

"So," Ben spoke after a moment of awkward silence, still keeping his voice at low volume. "How's she doin'?"

"Nancy?" I raised an eyebrow. "She's asleep upstairs. Everyone else is in the back."

"Probably good for 'er," he replied.

"Yeah, for now," I agreed before proceeding into voicing a worrisome thought. "Cally said someone from the department was already here. They aren't going to descend on this place and turn it into a circus are they?"

"Nahh." He shook his head. "They shouldn't anyway. Copper outside said it was Murv from the CSU and Osthoff from Homicide. Matter of fact, we just missed 'em. They couldn't find anything though. Looks like Porter didn't grab him from here."

"A clue would have been nice," I said. "But in a way, I'm glad they didn't find anything. Here anyway. Nancy doesn't need them crawling all over the house right now."

"Yeah. Prob'ly not," he agreed.

"So is the officer outside going to hang around or what?"

"He's stayin' put. There'll be someone assigned to watch these kids 'round the clock."

"That's good."

"Ya'know, Rowan." Ben reached up and massaged his neck for a moment. "You once told me that there's a huge number of Pagans in Saint Louis…"

I gave a vigorous nod as I confronted his unspoken comment. "There are, but I suspect that they will be safe this go around. For now, anyway. Porter is after me personally, and the only reason he killed Randy was to bait me."

"Yeah, that was kinda obvious. So, I don't wanna sound crass or anything, but considerin' your track record, couldn't he have just killed any Pagan on his list?"

"Yes and no," I answered.

"You think he's really plannin' all this that deliberately?"

"I don't know. He's not stupid, Ben. I'm betting he's done his homework. He knows that re-initiating the spree he went on a year ago would draw me out, but I think he wants more than that."

"Yeah, he wants you dead, white man."

"Exactly, but just getting me out of hiding isn't going to make that happen. He has to get me vulnerable and unprotected."

The look on his face told me that my comment was merely verbal corroboration for his own theory. "So killin' Randy was his way of tryin' to piss you off then. Just like the note about Felicity."

"And knock me off balance. That's how I see it, anyway," I agreed and then continued with an explanation of Coven dynamics. "Groups like ours are literally a family unit within Pagan culture. There is a bond within a core of a Coven that can often times be stronger than blood relation. Going after any one of these kids is the same as going after one of my own. It's the difference between killing a stranger and killing a family member."

"Yeah," he sighed. "I had a feelin' that's what this was all about. I just wanted to hear it from you before I opened my mouth."

"Glad I could help," I replied, my voice short on emotion.

"You're right," he told me. "He's not stupid. You came after him by yourself once, so he figures he can make it happen again."

"Yeah. Simple as it sounds, I'd have to say that's his plan."

"Well, he's screwed 'cause you ain't gonna do that, white man."

"That remains to be seen."

My friend took on a hard expression and thrust two fingers stiffly against my chest. "That wasn't a question, Row. It was a statement of fact. You're NOT doin' it. Not this time."

"Okay," I returned in order to appease him.

"I'm serious as a heart attack, white man," he detailed, still trying to keep his voice low as it developed a stern edge. "This ain't Hollywood. The sonofabitch wants to kill you."

"Trust me, I'm well aware of that, Ben," I told him.

"Yeah, well we're not talkin' videogame dead here, Row. We're talkin' about the real thing. For keeps."

"Yeah, Ben. I know," I answered, my hackles raising a bit at once again being treated like a child.

He splayed his hands out in a gesture that visibly told me to stop and that it was the end of the discussion. "Listen, don't make me lock your ass up just to keep you outta this."

"Okay, fine," I answered curtly. "You win."

Thick tension hung between us for a measured beat, eventually softening but never really dissipating entirely.

"So is there anyone else we should know about?" Ben finally asked. "Former Coven members? Anyone like that?"

"No, not that I can think of off hand." I shook my head as I ticked off the points. "No one has left this group since Felicity and I adopted it. I've practiced solitary most of my life. And, the only other Coven I was truly a member of dissolved a long time ago."

"Any of the members still around?"

"Not in Saint Louis," I replied. "It was a fairly small group, and we only split because everyone but me ended up moving out of state."

"What about family? Like your old man?"

"He's out of town right now. Besides, he won't go after a non-Pagan. Not intentionally."

"You sure?"

"Pretty sure."

"'Pretty sure' don't cut it." He reached up to massage his neck, and was obviously pondering something. After a moment he seemed to make a decision and spoke again. "Well, if your old man is out of town, we're covered there. What about your sister?"

"Ironically, she's in Germany right now. Her husband is stationed there with the Army."

"Okay, well I think we should have someone keep an eye on Felicity's family just to be safe."

"Shamus will love that," I muttered sarcastically.

My wife's father was not exactly what you would call a big fan of mine. Truth was, he believed that I had corrupted his daughter and diverted her from Christianity. He refused to take into account that she was already walking a Pagan path when I met her. At any rate, my dealings with the Major Case Squad investigating occult-related crimes were nothing less than fuel for his disdain. This would just stoke that fire.

"Yeah, well he'll just have to live with it," Ben returned.

The muffled but cheerful warble of a ring tone started behind me, and my friend reached around to his coat and searched through a pocket. I stepped to the side as he withdrew his cell phone, quickly perused the display, then stabbed it on and stuck it to his ear.

"Yeah, Helen, thanks for calling back," he spoke into the device.

The name struck a chord, and I knew immediately that the individual at the other end had to be his sister, Helen Storm. She was a psychiatrist and probably one of the most understanding individuals I had ever met. Ben had talked me into making an appointment with her just recently when the nightmares about the horrors I had seen started becoming too much to handle. I had made that first visit under duress but quickly struck up a friendship with her.

Unlike her brother, Helen fully embraced her Native American heritage. While I was never able to pin her down on anything, something told me there was more to the woman than just the framed diploma on her wall—something mystical, in fact.

"Uh-huh, I'm afraid so," Ben continued. "Yeah, that was us. They didn't waste any time gettin' it on the air, did they?... Yeah, I know... No, he's okay. For the time being anyway... Yeah... Well, he's in the middle of it whether I like it or not, so there's not a lot I can do... Uh-huh, that's what I'm thinkin'... Yeah... Uh-huh... So, what's your schedule lookin' like today? Any chance you could come over?...

That'd be great... Yeah... In the city, on Arkansas. 'Bout a block off Grand... I can give ya' directions... Okay, lemme check..."

My friend twisted the phone away from his mouth and shot me a questioning look. "She wants to know if Nancy is gonna be okay with havin' a shrink show up? Whaddaya think?"

I started to open my mouth to answer but never got that far. My lips froze as I shuddered, every nerve ending in my body jangling as though each was connected directly to an electrical wall socket. The involuntary jerking motion was immediately joined by an excruciating pain that lanced sharply through my head. The rush of blood in my ears rose and fell, only to be replaced suddenly by the violent sound of a horrified scream.

The muted light in the entryway strobed to unbearable brightness then collapsed in on itself. Color faded, leaving the scene before me a grainy black and white representation of its former self, depicted in overblown cartoon contrast.

I heard my friend's concerned voice call my name in a long, slow-motion drone as I began physically slipping downward.

My knees announced their displeasure with the situation as they thudded on the hardwood, and I continued to literally vibrate. I could feel my fingernails cutting into my palms as my hands involuntarily twisted into clawed fists. I was gnashing my teeth, and I could taste blood in my mouth from where I was repeatedly biting my tongue.

However, at this particular moment, any concerns I had for those problems gave way to the fact that the floor was now slamming itself hard against my face.

CHAPTER 9:

I wasn't sure what the noise echoing in my head actually was. It was struggling to be heard over the blood rushing in my ears, which in and of itself, was already in heated contention with an unnatural ringing sound that permeated my skull. At any rate, my violently distorted thought processes attempted to assign a familiarity to it.

One possibility presented itself as the rumble of a weak earthquake. Another was that it was a small explosion. There were several others, but in retrospect, those two were the only ones that came close to anything even remotely possible. What I later found out was that it hadn't been any of the above. In reality, what it had been were the frantic steps of several feet thudding against the hardwood flooring as everyone ran to the front of the house.

Right now, however, as far as my brain was concerned it was an unsolvable and very perplexing mystery. The vibration rolled toward me down the hallway, growing in intensity as it traveled through the polished surface. Upon reaching me, it joined with my cheek, made its way inward through some bizarre osmosis, and reverberated throughout my skull. The final effect was that of turning the sound into a tactile sensation as much as an auditory one.

I could feel myself being rolled over as my back arched and my muscles stiffened once again. Pain I can only describe as a full body leg cramp assaulted me, and I felt my breath catch in my throat. The physical sensation was accompanied by an elevation in my mental confusion—an elevation a full order of magnitude beyond anything I had experienced thus far.

In that moment, the source of the noise no longer mattered.

Then, as suddenly as it began, the seizure reached its zenith then plunged immediately to an anticlimactic end. My body fell limp, and the hot air that had been trapped in my lungs expelled in a violent rush. I wheezed loudly as I sucked in a fresh breath, at once gasping and then choking on the coolness.

Light flared in a kaleidoscope of colors and then slowly began fading back to muted normalcy. A tangle of voices competed for attention as my short-circuited neurons reset and began processing sensory input once again. Heavily contrasted shapes were moving around me, and I struggled to focus in on them.

"Rowan?" Ben's voice bled in behind the rapidly declining rush in my ears. "Rowan? You okay?"

Felicity's concerned tone mixed in with his. "What happened? Ben? Rowan?"

"Is he okay?" Cally was asking from somewhere above me.

A male voice I recognized as R.J. weaved its way between the others. "What's going on?"

"Oh no..." Shari's voice began a different sentence.

"...is he okay?" Her twin sister Jennifer finished it.

I was surprised that I was able to understand any of the words, much less make any sense of them, considering that they were all speaking at once. However, I was at least able to pick out those few fragments. I blinked hard and willed my eyes to adjust to the dim light of the hallway. It still seemed darker than it had before the seizure had overtaken me, but as clarity returned, I found myself staring at the reason.

Everyone but Nancy was huddled in a tight circle above my prone body, blocking out what little illumination there was within the corridor. I felt a quick wave of claustrophobia but managed to suppress it as I focused on their faces.

"Rowan, are you okay? What just happened?" came Ben's voice once again, firing the words in a rapid staccato.

"I'vff fallen and I canth geth up?" I croaked the first thing that popped into my head. My tongue was filled with a series of sharp pains, and I took notice of the fact that when I spoke my pronunciation was thick and blunted.

"Jeez, Row," my friend admonished as he screwed up his face. "This ain't the time to be crackin' jokes. What's goin' on here?"

"Aye," Felicity added. "Ben's right."

"Thorry," I told them as I pushed myself up on one elbow and used my other hand to massage my jaw where it had impacted the floor.

I opened my mouth and touched my fingertips to the end of my tongue. When I pulled my hand away, it was wet with saliva-diluted blood.

"You're bleeding," Cally gasped.

"I think I bith my tongue," I said.

"Yeah, no kiddin'," Ben spoke again as he offered me his hand. "That still doesn't explain what just happened."

"I donth know," I answered as I gripped his forearm. "Buth I think I know whath an epilepthic seizure feelth like now, and ith not pleathant."

Everyone in the group shuffled back as I stood. I didn't have to exert myself much as Ben did most of the work, levering me upward with a steady pull. Felicity stepped forward the moment I was upright and touched her hand carefully to my face, moving it from side to side as she inspected it. I wasn't sure, but I thought I heard a frantic voice calling out in the distance. I listened hard, but my ears were met only by the ambient noise of the house.

"Was it some kinda *Twilight Zone* thing?" my friend asked.

"I donth know. Maybe. Probably."

"Well shit, white man, what DO you know?"

"I know my fathe hurths."

"I'm not surprised," he returned. "You tried to dent the floor with it a minute ago."

"Aye, into the bathroom with you then," Felicity ordered with a slight nudge then directed her attention to the others as she assumed command. "Shari, do me a favor and grab some salt and a glass from the kitchen, please. Cally, you go check on Nancy. The commotion may have disturbed her, and she shouldn't be alone if she's awake. The rest of you go on back to the dining room, and I'll see to Rowan."

"I'm fthine," I objected.

"Aye, so you say, but I'll be the judge of that, Rowan Linden Gant," she returned.

"So, was it one of those visions or something?" Ben threw out the question.

"In a minute, Ben," Felicity instructed him as she made a shooing motion with her hand. "Let him at least rinse his mouth out with some salt water, then. Go ahead with everyone else, and we'll be along shortly."

The group split apart, and Cally headed up the stairs. Shari hurried several steps ahead of the rest of us on her way to the kitchen at the back of the house. As Felicity took my arm and started guiding me along, I heard the faint voice again. This time, I could actually make out the words, and unless I was mistaken, the disembodied vocalization was calling Ben's name.

"Didth you hear that?" I asked as I halted and cocked my head sideways.

Felicity continued for a half step past my sudden stop, then looked at me. "Aye, hear what?"

Again, tinny words floated into the air, "Hellllooooo! Benjamin! Talk to me!..."

I slowly turned back to my friend who was bringing up the rear. Without a doubt, the sound was coming from his direction.

A look of embarrassed realization washed across his features as he stared back at me then down at his hand and muttered, "Dammit."

I followed his gaze then gave him the answer to his earlier question. "Thtell her I think ith'll be fine."

As Felicity and I continued down the hall, he had his cell phone pressed against his ear and was both apologizing to Helen and explaining what had just transpired.

I spit a mouthful of salt water into the washbasin for the fifth time. The first go around it had been bright red, but this time it had only a slight pinkish tinge. I wiped my mouth with the back of my hand then poured the rest of the solution down the drain and twisted on the faucet. After rinsing out the basin and washing my hands, I took a seat on the closed lid of the toilet.

Felicity offered me a hand towel, and I took it. She reached up and pulled the free strands of her hair away from her eyes as she stood over me and inspected my face once again. With extreme care, she tenderly pressed the tips of her fingers around my cheekbone until she hit a spot where I winced noticeably.

"Aye, nothing broken, but you're going to have a bruise," she announced as she cocked her head to one side. "Tongue."

"What?" I asked.

"Show me your tongue, then," she directed.

I opened my mouth and did as she told me; I knew it wouldn't get me anywhere to argue. She leaned a bit closer and squinted for a moment then nodded. I closed my mouth and peered back at her.

"So, what's the verdict, 'Doc O'Brien'?"

"You chewed on it pretty good, that you did," she answered. "Still bleeding a bit, but not too bad."

"Yeah. I figured as much."

"Your speech has cleared up."

"That's a plus."

"Aye, it is. So what did happen out there?"

"Like I told Ben." I shook my head as I spoke, "I don't know. It just hit me out of nowhere."

She took a step back and crossed her arms, regarding me silently for a long moment before speaking again. "So, are you thinking it might have been Randy trying to communicate with you?"

"Don't know. Maybe," I answered. "There was that whole thing back at the M.E.'s office."

"Aye, I wondered about that."

"You and me both."

"What really bothers me is that you still seem to be well-grounded, then. You shouldn't be affected this way."

"You won't get any argument from me there. This is kind of weird too. Usually I 'see' something or get sucked into an empathic experience; even if it is usually pretty obscure."

"So?"

"So there's been none of that this time. Just a nondescript scream and now this seizure thing."

She raised an eyebrow. "Do you think it's something else then?"

I shrugged. "Believe me, I'm just as confused by this as you."

"Aye, but remember, you did start out with one of those headaches this morning."

I nodded. "Yeah, I did."

"Did you have any nightmares to go with it?"

"Never really got to sleep." I shook my head. "So there was never much of a chance for one."

"How is that, by the way?"

"What, the headache?"

"Aye."

"No better I'm afraid. Actually, a bit worse I think."

She stepped forward and swung open the right side of a tri-fold mirror over the sink. After a quick glance, she closed it and moved on to the center. A moment later, she was twisting the cap from a plastic bottle and shaking some of the contents into her hand. She tilted the container back and let the pills rattle back into it, deftly retaining three rust-colored tablets in her palm. She shoved the heavy dose of ibuprofen into my hand then filled a glass halfway with water and held it out to me.

"Go ahead, then, take them."

"You know this won't do anything for this kind of headache," I said in a puzzled tone.

"Aye, that I do." She closed her eyes as she nodded. "But they aren't for that. They're for your face. It will be hurting soon enough, and you don't need that on top of the headache."

"Oh, yeah, okay."

I popped the trio of pain pills into my mouth and took the glass of water from her. Unfortunately, the medicine was only midway down my throat when, for the fourth time this morning, a bloodcurdling scream pierced my skull.

CHAPTER 10:

The ibuprofen tablets lodged sideways in my throat as I involuntarily jerked at the sound. I sputtered and gagged for a moment, then thumped my chest hard with my free hand, forcing the lump of pills to continue along their way. With a quick gasp, I wheezed in a lungful of air. My eyes were watering, and I coughed to expel the water that had ventured down the wrong pipe.

I looked up, fully expecting Felicity to be gazing back at me and wondering why I was suddenly choking. Instead, I found that she was wearing just as startled an expression as I'm sure was plastered to my features. On top of that, she was looking toward the open door. Before either of us could utter a word, a second cry echoed through the house sounding vaguely like the word "no." As it faded, it became an anguished sob, supported on all sides by sympathetic words uttered softly by a second voice.

"Aye, that would be Nancy, I'm afraid." Felicity turned to me and spoke in a hurried voice as she rested a hand on my shoulder, "Are you okay, then?"

The earlier stampede was already being repeated as everyone came back up the hallway, passing by the bathroom on the way.

"I'm good," I choked out as I coughed once again. I was still sitting on the toilet lid and leaning against the washbasin. I motioned at the door with one hand. "Go. I'll be along in a minute."

I didn't have to tell her twice. In fact, she was already moving in the direction of the doorway as I answered her. I watched her go and then pushed myself upward. My muscles were already feeling the leading edge of soreness from the convulsive attack they'd endured. I rinsed out the glass and set it to the side before taking a handful of the cold water running from the tap and gingerly splashing my face. I lingered for a moment at my eyes, letting the coolness soak in as I rubbed. They felt tired and gritty, and that was only one of the many unpleasant sensations coursing through me.

I dried my face with the hand towel and stood for a moment, my expressionless countenance staring back at me from the vanity mirror. My cheek was already swelling noticeably, and my eyes were bloodshot. I desperately needed a shave, and my goatee could have stood a trim as well. It seemed as though every time I looked into a mirror lately I would see just that many more grey hairs.

"Hell gettin' old, ain't it?" Ben's quiet voice came from behind me as he voiced the observation.

I glanced over my shoulder at him then back to the mirror. "Do you need to get in here?"

"Nah," he replied. "Just checkin' on you."

"Old," I muttered with a sigh as I gazed back at my less than flattering reflection. "I'd be inclined to agree with you, but the problem is, according to my driver's license I'm only forty."

"It's not the years, Kemosabe…"

I finished the cliché bromide for him. "…It's the mileage. Yeah, I know."

"Cheer up. You got a few left in ya', white man," he said.

"I don't know, Ben. I'm feeling like a bad re-tread right now."

"So, like maybe you need to do that groundin' thing you and Felicity are always talkin' about," he offered. "Ya'know, so the creepin' ooga-boogas can't fuck with ya' so much."

"That's the other problem," I said. "I'm already doing that."

"For real? You ain't just sayin' that to get me off your ass?"

I guess I'd lied to him about my condition too many times for him to take my word for it right off the bat.

"Yeah, for real. You can ask Felicity if you want."

He pondered my answer for a moment before speaking. "So, that's not a good thing then, huh?"

"No." I shook my head. "No, it's not."

"So, whaddaya gonna do about it?"

I tucked the hand towel across the bar on the wall then turned to face him and leaned back against the vanity. "I don't know," I told him as I shrugged. "I haven't figured that out yet."

"Can't you cook up a potion or wear some garlic around your neck or *somethin'*?"

"What was that you told me earlier?" I answered. "I think it was, 'you've been watching too much TV.' Besides, garlic is for warding off vampires."

"Does it work?" He grinned back at me.

I couldn't help but allow myself a small chuckle. "I don't know, Chief. I've never met one."

The sobbing noises that were filtering down the corridor had diminished for the moment. They had actually been sliding up and down the scale ever since they began, and this appeared to be one of the low points. More soft voices, including the unmistakable Celtic brogue of my wife, could be heard joining the first in an attempt to shore up the explosion of grief. I needed to get out there myself, but I didn't know that I was ready to face it; not quite yet, anyway. I felt a bit selfish, hiding away and wallowing in my own problems, but there was far more to this than just Randy's death. And, since I was at the center of it, I was bearing a disproportionate load that was getting heavier all the time.

A small tickle had been working on the back of my head for a good part of the morning, and it was now resurfacing. This time it bypassed its normal annoyance stage and leapt directly into a nagging question.

I furrowed my brow and pursed my lips for a moment as I mulled the query over. I wasn't entirely sure why it mattered, but for some reason it was begging an answer.

"You got that look," Ben announced.

"Excuse me?"

"You know, that look like you're confused about somethin'."

"Maybe a little puzzled."

"Okay, so spit it out."

"I don't really know if it's important."

"Yeah, so spit it out anyway."

"Okay. You wouldn't happen to know where Porter is originally from would you?"

"Not off the top of my head, why?"

"Because of some of the choices he's made lately," I explained. "Using the page from *Hexen und Hexenmeister* for one. The nail for another."

"I thought the nail was pretty obvious," he said.

"On the surface, yes, but he could have guaranteed that we could ID the body in a lot of other ways. The nail has symbolism of its own..." I let my voice trail off.

After a moment, Ben spoke up. "Okay, so you wanna enlighten us mortals?"

I was so caught up in pondering the query that I just gave him an offhanded answer. "Witches aren't immortal, Ben."

"Yeah, whatever. You wanna fill me in please? What about the nail?"

"What?"

"The nail, Rowan. You're obsessin' about the nail, and I'm kinda lost."

At some point while I was staring off into space, he had retrieved his notebook from his pocket, and he now appeared poised to record any pearl of wisdom I may utter. I was afraid he was about to be disappointed by a cheap, plastic imitation.

"Oh, that. Nails are a major component of Witch jars and have been long thought by certain cultures to act as a deterrent to magickal forces and WitchCraft. Kind of a protective talisman of sorts."

"Do I wanna know what a Witch jar is?"

I shrugged. "It's just a version of the talisman. I can give you details if you want them."

"Is it important?"

"I don't know."

"You don't seem to know a lot today."

My reply was laced with sarcasm. "Thanks a lot."

"Just an observation." He shrugged then continued. "Okay, so anyway, two plus two equals what? Thirty-seven?"

I furrowed my brow deeper and shook my head. "What are you talking about?"

"I'm tryin' to figure out where you're headed with this. You're just talkin' about nails and the Hex Meister book. What's that got to do with where Porter comes from?"

"Like I said, the whole nail mythology fits in very well with particular cultures, such as the Pennsylvania Dutch. Add in the book which is German…"

The distance-muted jangle of a telephone floated down the corridor and came to us through the doorway.

"So what you're sayin' is that you think Porter might be from Pennsylvania."

"Maybe. Maybe not. It's just a thought."

"And it tells us what?"

"That's what is puzzling me. I don't know."

"I see." He flipped his notebook shut with a frown and stuffed it back into his pocket. "Well that was a waste of time."

"Cut me some slack, will you, Ben," I stated. "You're the one who asked."

He held up his hands. "Yeah, yeah, you're right. I'm sorry. It's been a long one for all of us I guess."

I heard R.J. pick up the phone on the fourth ring and answer it with a solemn "Harper residence."

Ben glanced up the hallway from his position leaning against the doorframe of the bathroom, then looked back at me, and cocked his head toward the front of the house.

"Looks like they're gettin' ready to bring 'er back this way," he told me. "Guess we'd better make an appearance."

"Yeah," I nodded. "You're right."

"Hey, Rowan." A young man with long dark hair poked his head around the side of the door. "How are you doing?"

"I'm okay, R.J.," I told him with a slight smile.

"Good," he nodded quickly. "So, like, the phone's for you."

"For me?" I asked, "Who is it?"

"I didn't catch his name, but he said he was a cop." He shrugged. "He just asked if he could speak to Rowan Gant."

"I'm with Ben already. Why would the police be calling me here?" I puzzled.

"Albright's probably got a copper checkin' up on you," Ben offered. "It'd be just like her."

"Great." I rolled my eyes. "Just what I need. Okay, R.J., I'll be right there."

"'Kay."

The young man disappeared behind the wall, and we heard him moving back up the hallway.

"Be just your luck she'll get on the phone and start chewin' on you again," my friend offered.

"This wouldn't be a good time for that," I returned.

"Hey, at least I warmed her up for you."

"Thanks, Ben," I said with something nearing good-natured sarcasm rimming my voice. "Thanks ever so much."

Everyone had moved back into the dining room before I ventured into the corridor and made my way to the front of the house. Ben tagged along behind me, ostensibly to lend some moral support if I was about to be verbally worked over by Albright yet again.

My left shoulder was beginning to ache, and the pain was going out of its way to make itself known. I'd had trouble with the joint ever since Porter had rammed an ice pick into it that night on the Old Chain of Rocks Bridge, especially when I was faced with a change in the weather like today. Not to mention, bouncing it from the doorframe on Ben's van had only served to aggravate the old injury. I took a moment to rotate it in the socket and felt a grating pop, which just made it worse. I winced and hoped the ibuprofen would be kicking in soon.

"You okay?" Ben asked.

"Shoulder," I told him.

He nodded then leaned his back against the wall opposite me. "Yeah, sorry about that."

"Uh-huh," I grunted. "I'll get you back."

"So, don't worry too much," he continued, keeping his voice low. "If they want you to come in, I'll go with ya'."

I nodded acknowledgement back at him as I picked up the handset from the telephone table and pressed it against my ear. "Hello. This is Rowan Gant."

I was greeted with the hollow sound of static that told me the phone was definitely off hook at the other end, but there was nothing else. For a moment, I thought that I might have been placed on hold. However, as I listened I was certain that I could hear the thready sound of breathing intertwined with the semi-silence issuing from the earpiece.

"Hello?" I spoke again. "Anyone there?"

"You must excuse me," a painfully familiar voice returned. "It is not every day that I speak with the spawn of Satan."

CHAPTER 11:

I froze.

There wasn't much else I could do.

The voice sounded hollow and distant, but there was no mistaking to whom it belonged.

The pain in my shoulder erupted from a smolder to an intense blaze, just like a fire suddenly fed by a back draft. The sharp ache coursed down my arm, searing every nerve ending in its path before ricocheting from my fingertips and driving back upward into my skull. I closed my eyes and sighed heavily as the burning spasm tightened my scalp and opened the gates for the dull throb that had been sequestered in the back of my head.

What I wanted to do at this very moment was to explode with anger. Instead, I forced myself to remain grounded and keep my voice even. I opened my eyes and turned to face Ben as I spoke, "Hello, Eldon."

My friend had been slouched against the wall, and he now came fully to attention, his face masked with a look of incredulity as he stared back at me.

"Porter?" he mouthed the question silently, holding his hand to emulate a telephone as he placed it to the side of his head.

I nodded slowly in response.

"You would have been proud of your disciple, Gant," Porter was telling me. "He maintained his allegiance to you right up to the end."

"What do you mean?" I asked.

"And the great dragon was cast out, that old serpent, called the Devil, and Satan, which deceiveth the whole world: he was cast out into the earth, and his angels were cast out with him."

"Book of Revelation," I offered. "I already know you can quote the Bible, Eldon. Why don't you stop hiding behind someone else's words?"

"Hiding? You are the one hiding, Gant. I am walking in the light of God."

"You'll excuse me if I have a little trouble with that, Eldon," I offered. "I seem to recall your God saying 'Thou shalt not kill.'"

"He also states that there is a time to kill. Ecclesiastes…"

"…Three, three. Yeah, I've heard. So why don't you tell me what you really meant?"

Ben had become a flurry of activity, moving with a choreographed swiftness as he stepped forward and checked the caller ID display on the telephone's base unit. He quickly retrieved his notebook, scribbled something, and then motioned to get my attention and mouthed, "Keep him talking."

I felt like I was in the middle of a movie about a kidnapping and that I had been selected to take the call making the ransom demand. I nodded and tried to concentrate on what Porter was saying.

"…remained impenitent."

"I'm sorry, Eldon," I returned. "There must be some static on the line, I didn't catch that first part."

"There's no static," he answered calmly. "You were distracted by Detective Storm instructing you to keep me on the line while he gets this call traced."

My first inclination was to assure him that his comment was untrue, but that's what always happens in the movies, and it's always a lie. I decided to go for broke. "You're right, but can you blame us?"

Ben had taken a few steps down the hall to get out of earshot and was now whispering into his cell phone as he read off something from his notebook. I glanced down at the caller ID display and noticed that it said "PAY PHONE," and gave the number. I couldn't place the exchange other than that it was definitely a Saint Louis number.

"No, I suppose that is the sort of thing you would do," Porter replied, an eerie flatness to his voice. "His loyalty to you is misguided, but he will soon see the truth."

"What truth is that?"

"Your devotion to Satan, of course."

"I think you have me confused with somebody else."

"Lest Satan should get an advantage of us: for we are not ignorant of his devices."

"Second Corinthians, chapter two, verse eleven," I told him. "Nice try, but you aren't the first person to take it out of context and throw it in my face."

I knew my comment could very possibly serve to antagonize him, but I didn't care. He'd already done his share to anger me—and he had succeeded in spades.

"Set thou a wicked man over him: and let Satan stand at his right hand," he told me.

"Psalm, one-oh-nine, verse six. Come on, Eldon, you didn't really call here to recite the Holy Bible to me did you?"

Ben was nodding as he continued whispering into his phone. He looked up in my direction and motioned at me to keep Eldon on the line.

"Did you get my note?" the voice asked.

The only other time I had spoken to Porter was when he had pronounced my sentence the night he tried to kill me. Then, as now, his voice was cold and emotionless. This last comment was a sudden and unexpected exception. He sounded almost gleeful.

I felt a wave of heat flush through my face as my blood pressure rose. My free hand clenched into a hard fist, and I fought to maintain my composure. Unfortunately, my stolid silence gave him exactly what he wanted.

"I've been doing some more reading, Gant. Research mostly. Historical…"

"Good for you," I muttered, barely able to contain my anger.

"Oh yes," he replied. "It is very good for me. You see, it seems that I've been far too narrow in my scope when it comes to extracting confessions."

"I hadn't noticed."

"Take your disciple for instance. He was my first disembowelment. I thought it went very well."

I sucked in a deep breath through my nose and let it slowly out through my mouth, steeling myself before answering him in a cold tone. "I thought you said you weren't able to break him?"

"Oh no, you misunderstood. He confessed. He just never told me where I could find you."

"That's because he didn't know," I spat.

"It doesn't matter. I've found you now."

I looked over at Ben, and he once again waved his hand, indicating that I should keep Porter talking. I frowned hard. I wasn't sure how much more I could take before I completely lost control.

"Maybe you just think you have," I said.

There was a long silence at the other end, and I thought for a moment that he might have hung up, but then his voice issued once again from the earpiece. "You never did tell me if you got my note."

"You know I did."

"I made that selection specifically for you. What did you think?"

"I think you are a sick bastard."

I thought I heard him actually laugh before settling once again into his emotionless voice. "Your wife is very lovely, Gant. For a heretic. I suppose you are aware that the inquisitors of the fifteenth century sometimes found it necessary to, shall we say, 'have their way' with the women they interrogated?"

My fragile pane of composure shattered into jagged shards. The heat that had earlier flushed my face now consumed my entire body. I could feel myself shaking, and I was gripping the handset so tight that my fingers were beginning to numb.

"Listen to me you son-of-a-bitch," I spoke evenly into the mouthpiece. My voice started at a low volume, but with each sentence it grew along an ever-increasing upward arc. "This is between you and me. No one else, got me?! You had better start praying to your God right now. You'd best pray that the police get to you first, because I'm coming after you. I'm coming after you, and I'm going to kill you! DO YOU HEAR ME GODDAMMIT?! I'M GOING TO FUCKING KILL YOU, YOU BASTARD!"

I was holding the phone in front of my face, screaming into it. Adrenalin was pumping through me, and I was shaking uncontrollably. I felt a hand clamp on my shoulder, and I wheeled about, swinging the handset like a club. My hand was suddenly engulfed by Ben's own. He pushed me against the wall and held me there as he ripped the telephone away with his free hand. He brought it up to his ear and listened then frowned before dropping it onto the table beside the base and snatching up his cell phone.

"It's clicking, like maybe he hung up," he fired his voice into the device. "Tell me you nailed the bastard... Yeah... Yeah... Okay, I'll hang on..."

My friend looked at me with a mixture of concern and what looked as though it might have been fear in his eyes. He was still holding his cell phone to his ear, but he twisted the mouthpiece down out of the way. "Jeezus, Row... Calm down... 'Kay?"

I was still shaking, but Ben had me stiff-armed against the wall; I wasn't going anywhere. I sucked in a deep breath and glared back at him as I spoke, "The motherfucker just told me he was going to rape my wife!"

I heard a gasp, and when I looked to the side I realized that my outburst had attracted the attention of everyone else in the household. The worst part was that the look on Felicity's face told me that she'd heard every word of what I'd just said to Ben.

I stared back at her pained expression, watching as her earlier fear visibly resurfaced. I mutely chastised myself for losing control and tried to find something to say to her that would quell her uneasiness but came up empty.

"Yeah, yeah I'm here," Ben began speaking again as he twisted the cell phone back into place. "He what? You've gotta be kiddin'... Shit... Okay... Yeah..." He let out a heavy sigh. "Yeah... I'll be here... Thanks."

I turned back to face him and found his concerned gaze still locked on my face as he switched off the phone and stuffed it into his pocket. The thick silence in the corridor rose to a crescendo and was then replaced by his almost apologetic voice. "You okay now, Row?"

"They didn't get him, did they?" I asked.

"No. No, they didn't." He shook his head as he spoke. "So, can I let you go now?"

I was still tensed and shaking, but the sight of my wife behind him had forced me to calm quicker than I would have otherwise. I nodded to him, and he tentatively relaxed his stance, waiting a short moment before releasing me entirely.

As soon as I was free, I stepped past him and wrapped my arms around Felicity. She laid her head against my shoulder and held tight.

"Aye, it was him," she whispered. "He called here, then."

"It's okay," I told her. "It's okay."

Looking past her I could see the rest of the group milling about in the corridor, staring at us with their own brand of fear on their faces.

"They had the number to the pay phone from the caller ID." I spoke aloud to Ben without turning; my tone was just short of an accusation. "It's not like they had to trace it. What went wrong?"

"That wasn't the problem, Row," he answered. "They pinpointed the location right away and dropped every copper in the area on it like the friggin' sky was fallin'."

"So what happened?"

"Jeezus, Row, this bastard is a piece of work..."

"What?"

"He had two pay phones stuck together with duct tape, white man."

"Awww, Gods..." I brought one hand up to massage my forehead as I closed my eyes. "That's why it sounded so hollow. He relayed it."

"Yeah. Not exactly the most high tech. All you gotta do is call one pay phone, tape it to the one next to it, and then dial here with that pay phone..."

"Doesn't really matter, it worked, didn't it?" I spat.

"Yeah. Unfortunately it did. They're lookin' at the computers now, tryin' to trace it back, but since he was nowhere around, odds are he was talkin' to ya' on a cell. He was hell and gone from the scene the minute he dialed the fuckin' number."

CHAPTER 12:

"I really don't want to monopolize your time," I said as I leaned against the deck rail and looked out across the back yard.

"You are not monopolizing anything, Rowan," Helen Storm answered in the clear and carefully worded fashion I'd grown accustomed to since our first meeting less than one month ago. "Besides, I was ready for a cigarette."

Ben's sister was a self-described chain smoker, and she supported her claim easily. To me it seemed like an odd habit for a psychiatrist, but then, she was also human. We all had our vices—for instance, with me, it was cigars—so I was not about to make a judgment.

In the physical features department, Helen bore more than a passing family resemblance to her brother; the obvious exception being that she stood just shy of a foot shorter than he was. Other than that, they shared the same mysteriously dark eyes and characteristic profiles. Her thick, black hair hung in a straight fall that pleasantly contrasted her softly angular features. It was streaked here and there with strands of grey, which was the only visual indicator that she was the older of the two siblings.

I shrugged inside my coat, giving a slight shiver against a random gust of wind that managed to infiltrate its folds and then tugged the zipper up another pair of inches in self-defense.

Yellow-brown stands of decorative grasses ringed the inside of the yard, each clump angling upward in shallow arcs to peek just inches over the top of the privacy fence. Snow was now falling in heavy waves, drifting downward, slipstreaming sideways on the wind and then tumbling to rest on the dormant carpet of Zoysia.

"Nancy probably needs you more than me," I said while looking down and absently inspecting the burning cigar I was twisting between my thumb and forefinger. "She's the one who just lost her husband to a psychopath."

Helen exhaled a stream of smoke and tapped the ash from the end of her cigarette before gesturing. "Look there, Rowan."

I looked up then swiveled my head and followed her finger with my eyes. A sturdily-caged bird feeder sat atop a post in a nearby section of the yard with a pair of black-capped chickadees flitting in and out of it. A much larger bird, speckled along its brown back, hung from the side where a suet cake had been affixed.

"That is a northern flicker," she announced.

"Avoiding my question?" I asked, looking back at her with a slight smile.

She shrugged as she spoke. "No, not really, Rowan. I am simply fascinated by birds. Besides, you did not ask a question. You made a comment." She returned the smile as she paused and took a drag on her cigarette. "Now, if I were to treat your comment as a question, first I would point out that Eldon Porter is a sociopath not a psychopath."

"Touché," I answered.

"Secondly, I would tell you that Nancy has exactly what she needs, given the circumstances. Family. As she advances through the stages of grief, her family will be the most effective support system she could ever need. She will talk to me when and if she feels ready to do so. Perhaps she will never need me. I cannot say one way or the other at this stage. That is something that is peculiar to the individual. You can rest assured, however, that she is not yet ready."

I returned to staring out into the yard as she spoke. The seasonally barren branches of trees twisted in the air, their grey-black bark collecting cottony traces of the falling precipitation. As I stared at them, they began to look as though they were spindly arms reaching out in some agonized death throe—all in all, a visual metaphor for my own tortured mood.

I took a hard drag on the end of my cigar. I normally reveled in the spicy taste of a good, Maduro-wrapped smoke, but at the moment it wasn't bringing the pleasure I hoped. I allowed the blue-white smoke to stream out slowly between my teeth, making a futile grab for some modicum of enjoyment and finding none.

"Ben asked you to come here for my sake, didn't he?" I asked.

My matter-of-fact tone didn't faze her. "Of course, Rowan, but you knew that already."

"Yeah, I guess I did."

"I am certainly willing to be here for all of your friends as well," she added.

"I'm sure they would appreciate that."

"Under the circumstances, however, you are the primary concern."

"I'm okay," I told her.

"I am certain that you are," she replied. "However, I sense that you have concerns of your own."

"Don't we all?" I asked the question in an easy, rhetorical sense. I wasn't looking to be difficult, and I didn't want to come across to her that way.

"Of course," she answered in her own comfortable tone. "Your concerns, however, are far less... shall we say 'mundane', than most."

"Yeah," I agreed. "Guess so."

"Benjamin told me you had some type of seizure earlier."

"You could call it that."

"Do you think that it was something else?"

I looked over at her. "What do you mean?"

"Your comment." She shrugged. "It implies that you think of the episode as something other than a seizure."

"Oh, that." I nodded then shrugged. "I'm not really sure what it was. I know it wasn't very pleasant, but other than that..." I allowed my voice to trail off as I pondered the event.

"Do you feel that it might have something to do with Eldon Porter?" she asked.

"Maybe."

She shuffled for a moment and then looked up at the grey sky. "I love snow. It carries with it such a simple purity."

"It's frozen water crystallized around any number of impurities it picks up in our polluted atmosphere." I stated the fact. "Not sure how that qualifies in the purity department."

She regarded me with a slight chuckle. "I see that you are not in the mood for philosophical metaphors today, Rowan."

"Guess not."

She nodded as she fished out a fresh cigarette and lit it from the smoldering butt of the first. After discarding the spent smoke in the sand bucket, she cocked her head to the side and watched me for a moment.

"How has Felicity been holding up?" she finally asked, shedding her initially adopted clinical air.

"Okay I guess. But, you probably know more about that than me."

I based my observation on the fact that my wife had recently taken advantage of Helen's offer of therapy in the wake of the kidnapping and attempted rape she'd experienced.

She clarified the question. "I meant in light of what has happened today."

"She's frightened," I offered with a shrug. "Natural reaction if you ask me."

"I should think so." She nodded. "Porter's threats are coming on the heels of a very traumatic experience for her. She is feeling terribly vulnerable right now."

"How deep does that vulnerability go is the question," I said aloud.

"Meaning?"

"I don't know," I sighed. "I guess I'm lamenting my own feelings."

"Would you like to share those feelings, Rowan?"

"Like? No. But, to be honest, standing here talking with you, I have to say that I feel compelled to, yes."

She let out a small, musical laugh. "Compelled? Oh my, Rowan, I truly wish that all of my patients were as easy to work with as you."

"You mean you don't have this effect on everyone?" I smiled.

"Believe me, my life would be much easier if I did," she returned.

"Probably be boring though," I offered.

"Perhaps, however, you are certainly not boring in any sense of the word, Mister Gant." She puffed on her cigarette and watched the large woodpecker as it continued drilling away at the suet cake. "So, you were saying?"

Her casual attitude had put me at ease as usual, and suddenly my emotional baggage seemed much easier to unpack in front of her.

"I can't help but wonder if part of the vulnerability she is feeling might stem from a lack of confidence in my ability to protect her." I offered the thought to her and waited patiently for her analysis. The wait was short.

"What is it that would lead you to believe such a thing?"

"I don't know." I shook my head. "Just a feeling."

"Is it really a feeling, or is it something you have conjured in your imagination?"

"Full of questions today, aren't you?"

"It is my job, Rowan," she returned with a smile and cocked her head to the side. "Now, do you happen to have answers for my questions?"

I raised an eyebrow as I looked back at her. "I get the impression that I do whether I know it or not."

"You catch on fast."

"I can probably find a few people who would dispute that," I returned with a grin.

"We all have our critics," she answered then brought her free hand up and began tapping her index finger against her pursed lips as she deepened a crease in her brow. After a moment, she spoke again. "I am confident that I would not be breaking a doctor-patient trust by telling you that your feeling is incorrect. Felicity has no lack of confidence in your ability to protect her."

I sighed heavily as I weighed the information I'd just been given. "I'm sure that should make me feel better, but unfortunately it doesn't."

"Why do you think that is, Rowan?"

"I suspect that the logical answer would be that I am the one who lacks the confidence."

"That would be the logical answer, yes."

"But not the correct answer?" I asked.

"I am certain that it is a part of it, Rowan, but I believe we both know that it goes somewhat deeper than that."

"Okay. How about, I'm afraid?" I said simply.

"What is it that you fear, Rowan?"

"It isn't obvious?"

"Why don't you tell me? Is it so obvious?"

"Well, I think it is," I shrugged as I spoke. "I'm afraid of Porter."

"Are you really?"

Again, I raised an eyebrow and regarded her silently for a moment. "Yeah, I'm pretty sure I'm afraid of him. I mean, the bastard is out to kill me, and he doesn't seem interested in giving up on the idea."

"I am not so certain that you are being honest with yourself, Rowan."

"Okay, I'll bite."

She drew her lips into a thin frown for a moment, her expression telling me that she was obviously in search of the words to express what was on her mind. It didn't take her long to track them down.

"As I recall, you are the man who purposely drove a van through a set of plate glass windows, climbed injured from the wrecked vehicle, and then headed straight into a situation where you could have been ambushed by a killer."

"What does that have to do with anything?"

"It does not sound like the action of a fearful man to me."

"No," I agreed. "It was the action of a desperate man. The son-of-a-bitch had kidnapped my wife."

"All right, perhaps that was not the best example for you. How about this...Do you remember a conversation we had a few weeks ago, Rowan, when I asked you why you had chased Eldon Porter out onto that bridge by yourself instead of immediately calling the police?"

"You mean the conversation where you refused to tell me why YOU thought I did it?" I asked with good-natured sarcasm in my voice. "Vaguely."

Helen smiled back at me. "You have been thinking about it then."

"You could say that."

"Have you reached any conclusions?"

"You mean other than the fact that it was a stupid move on my part?"

"I would not necessarily call it a stupid move, Rowan. You were ill prepared, perhaps, but not stupid. That is, however, a matter of opinion."

"I'd have to say that you are in the minority with that opinion," I told her.

"Be that as it may, you still have not answered my question."

I huffed out a breath and brought my cigar up to my lips but hesitated without taking a puff. Instead, I watched the feathery snow as it threw itself against the ground in gathering clumps, quickly overcoming the landscape with its whiteness.

"I've heard a rumor that I did it because I have a 'heroing complex' and that I'm suicidal," I finally responded.

"That would be a psuedo-scientific term coined by an amateur psychiatrist, I assume?"

"You tell me. You're the one with the sheepskin."

"Let me ask you this. When you have placed yourself in harm's way, have you done so in order to seek glory and recognition?"

"No."

"Do you want to die?"

"Not particularly."

"Then, were I you, I would ignore that diagnosis."

"I'll give it a try."

"Good. Now, you are still not answering my question, Rowan," she pressed with gentle firmness. "What I want to know are the conclusions YOU have reached about why you did it."

"I'm not sure that I have, Helen," I told her then took a long drag on the cigar and rolled the smoke around in my mouth. I still wasn't enjoying it.

She sighed heavily and then joined me in silently watching the forming snowscape. This sudden inconsistency in her otherwise calm demeanor was probably the closest to impatience I'd ever seen in her. Still, her annoyance didn't seem to be directly with me although I am sure I played some role in it. What I felt from her was that she was struggling with a decision that on an everyday basis she would have easily snubbed out of principle. After a full measure of heartbeats, she spoke again.

"The situation you currently face has placed an unfair imperative upon you, Rowan. Normally, I would feel it best to continue guiding you along your path until you reach a logical resolution. However, I fear that in this case I may need to take a more active role, and because of these extraordinary circumstances, I am going to break one of my own rules."

"You're going to tell me I'm a fruitcake?" I looked back at her with a smile as I cracked the joke.

She ignored my thin attempt at levity and locked her eyes with mine in a coldly serious gaze. "You are not afraid of Eldon Porter, Rowan. You are afraid of yourself."

CHAPTER 13:

I blinked.

I thought about what she had just said, and then I blinked again.

"I'm afraid of myself?" I repeated the comment back to her as a question.

"Yes, Rowan. You fear yourself. You harbor a deep-seated fear of the things you are capable of doing."

"You mean the nightmares? The channeling? That stuff?"

"That is a part of it, yes," she explained. "But in reality, those are simply talents you possess which fuel your turmoil."

"I'll admit the nightmares tend to be pretty scary, but..."

"No, Rowan," she interrupted. "Open your eyes and see beyond the surface. You recently told me that you felt as though you were on the inside looking out but could see only darkness, did you not?"

"Yeah," I nodded. "I remember something like that, and as I recall, you told me to use that darkness as a mirror."

"Yes." She smiled and gave me a curt nod to the affirmative. "Now what I want you to do is look into the reflection, not merely at it. For you, understanding lies within the depths of the image."

I tilted my head forward and removed my glasses then rubbed my eyes for a moment before sliding the spectacles back onto my face and returning my gaze to her. "Helen, your wisdom is starting to sound like the mystical advice of a little, green swamp creature from the sci-fi movies we all know and love."

"Really? I rather saw myself more as a drifting Shao-Lin monk." She allowed herself a small chuckle as she made the reference to the old television show.

I continued with the theme. "So, should I pluck the pebble from your hand now?"

She returned a brief smile then in almost the same instant fixed me with a hardcore seriousness in her eyes as she gazed at my face.

"Levity aside, Rowan, you should heed what I am telling you, for I cannot give you the full answer. With only a very few exceptions, I can merely guide you. In this case, guiding has become a bit of a shove, yes, but I dare not do anything more lest you lose sight of that which you need to see."

"So, what you are saying is that I still have to learn the lesson the hard way."

"If you are to learn it and not simply hear it, yes."

"Okay," I replied. "I'll buy that. But what if I've already learned the lesson, and you just think I haven't?"

"All right, then." She looked back at me with an even gaze. "Enlighten me, Rowan."

I blurted out my conclusion, "You think I'm afraid that I might be capable of killing Eldon Porter."

"Do I?"

I halfway expected her non-committal response. "Yes."

"Then I believe you have missed my point entirely."

My overblown confidence in the statement was immediately deflated. "Excuse me?"

She shook her head. "Like I have told you before, Rowan, it is not about what I think. It is what YOU think that is important."

"Okay." I played along, couching the comment differently in an attempt to regain my position. "Then, I'm afraid that, given the opportunity, I might kill Porter."

"Are you?"

I tilted my head and endeavored to take a puff on my cigar, only to find that it had gone out. "You were supposed to say, 'Correct, Rowan, now pass go and here is your two hundred dollars.'"

"That prize is not going to come from me, Rowan. It is an epiphany that will come from inside of you."

"Helen, you're making my head hurt."

She smiled and chuckled once again. "I am sure that this is not the first time I have done so, Rowan, and I suspect that it will not be the last."

"Thanks." Sincerity permeated my voice.

Helen finished lighting a fresh cigarette and allowed herself a deep drag then exhaled before looking out across the yard and answering me. "For what, Rowan?"

"For putting up with my hard-headedness, I guess."

"You are most welcome."

I rummaged about in my pocket for a lighter and then knocked the dead ash from the end of my cigar. I turned my back to the wind and shielded the end of the smoke as I brought fire to it once again, twisting it carefully to keep the ember even. While I stuffed the lighter back into my pocket, I turned the stogie around and gazed at the glowing coal as I blew on it, inspecting for runs. Satisfied, I tucked it back in the corner of my mouth and puffed as I leaned forward on the deck railing.

"So, back to Felicity," I finally said. "She's seemed kind of edgy—even before she was kidnapped, I mean. You're sure she feels safe?"

"I never said that your wife feels safe, Rowan," she answered in a no-nonsense tone. "I said that she does not lack confidence in your ability to protect her."

"Okay, call me dense, but I don't see what the difference is."

"She has her own fear, Rowan."

"Has she been any better at recognizing hers than I am at mine?"

"Yes, as a matter of fact, she has."

"Any chance you could share?"

"No, Rowan. That is something for her to express if she is to come to terms with it herself."

"You do know that she's a Taurus, right?"

"Then I suspect that when she decides to express her feelings, you will be hard pressed to miss her point."

I nodded as I stared out into the falling snow. "Yeah, but will I end up impaled on it is the question."

"I thought Albright took you off this case?" I asked Ben, keeping my voice low.

My friend had just finished telling me that he'd been in touch with the officers searching the area where the phone call from Porter had originated. Unfortunately, they were coming up empty; of course, I had expected that to be the case.

"Yes and no," he answered, keeping his voice hushed as well. "I'm not involved in the investigation, but I just got officially assigned to you and Firehair."

We were standing in the kitchen, both of us working on steaming mugs of coffee. It was probably the best cup I'd had in a month and most certainly the best I'd had today: a rich, flavorful brew derived from freshly ground Kona beans with just a hint of cinnamon and hazelnut in the background. We owed this small pleasure to the fact that Nancy had always been the connoisseur of the drink within our group; therefore, her pantry was always fully stocked with the finer makings of java.

"Bodyguard duty?" I asked before taking a sip of my drink.

He nodded. "Somethin' like that, yeah."

"So maybe she had a change of heart," I offered. "She knows that we're friends."

"Dream on, white man." He shook his head and frowned as he spoke. "She wants ta' make sure she can find us. It's her way of keepin' me under her thumb."

I nodded in understanding. "If you're watching us then she knows where you are at all times."

"Where we ALL are," he added. "'Zactly."

I gave him a quick shrug. "Could be worse."

"Yeah," he sighed. "At least this way I can keep my finger in without raisin' too much suspicion."

"You know, Ben," I began. "If your connection with me is going to screw up your career…"

"Haven't we talked about this before?" he interrupted.

"I'm just saying…"

He held up his hand and gave his head a quick shake. "Forget it. My career, my decision, end of story."

Looking past my friend for a moment, I watched as Felicity refilled her own cup. She was standing in the pass-thru alcove between the kitchen and the dining room.

Just by looking at her, you couldn't tell that she was worn out, but I knew better. We were all running on adrenalin, caffeine, and extended second winds; at least *she* looked good doing it, which was more than I could say for myself.

The comforting sounds of a fire crackling in the fireplace on the other side of the alcove provided the ambient backdrop to the quiet conversations scattered throughout the dining area. The earthy scent of the burning wood filled the air. Outside, snow was continuing to fall in steady curtains of white. Were it not for the circumstances, this just might have been a perfect, laid-back day to sit and visit with friends.

"Helen seems to be fitting right in then." My wife voiced the observation as she sidled up next to me and leaned her head on my shoulder.

"Yeah, that's my sis for ya'," Ben returned as he cast a glance back over his shoulder.

As my friend turned back to us, his cell phone began warbling. He plucked it from his belt and inspected the face. "Fuck me, it's Bible Barb," he muttered aloud as he glanced around then cocked his head in the direction of the hallway. "I don't wanna disturb anyone, so I'll be up front."

I nodded. "Okay."

He was already answering the phone with a curt, one word admission of his last name as he exited.

"It's a good thing," I offered to my wife as I watched Ben leave.

"What is?" she asked.

"Helen fitting in so well. She can lessen the burden on you."

"Aye, that she can, but I'm their Priestess. It is MY job to be there for them."

I frowned with concern. "You don't resent her being here do you?"

"Not at all." She dismissed my question. "It is just that I have a responsibility to them. It is something that comes with the title High Priestess, you know."

"Yes, I know, hon, and you HAVE been there for them," I soothed. "But you need a break too, and Goddess knows I'm not much help in this department."

"Aye, you aren't," she sighed the matter-of-fact statement. "On top of that, you're just another worry for me, in and of yourself then."

Her voice held a slight hint of animosity at the end, leading me to believe the second half of her statement was what bothered her most. I was only slightly taken aback by her brutal honesty. I'd grown used to it over the years.

Back up the hallway, I heard the faint treble of Ben's cell phone ringing yet again.

"Sorry," I said.

"No need to apologize," she told me. "I'm not angry with you. Not about that anyway. I know you've as much to deal with as I."

"But you're mad at me about something else?"

"Aye, but this is neither the time nor place to discuss it then."

"Felicity, I know how you are," I said. "If you don't let it out, you'll just build up resentments."

"Don't you worry then," she instructed. "I'll get over it."

"You say that now, but I have a feeling I'll pay for it at some point."

She agreed with a purposeful nod. "Aye, that you probably will."

"Well, don't sugarcoat it." I offered the comment with its own thin lacquer of sarcasm.

"Aye, I won't."

"Uhmm-Hmmm!" The sound of Ben clearing his throat intervened before our conversation could dip any closer to the danger zone. "You two want me to get you some gloves and ring the bell?"

"No," I said in a quiet tone, chagrined that our verbal discontent had been witnessed.

Felicity simply shook her head.

"That was quick," I said.

"Yeah. No reason to drag it out. So listen," my friend began as he reached up and massaged his neck. "There's been a bit of a change in plans here."

"She didn't pull you off this completely, did she?" I asked, shunting my un-quelled annoyance off to another target.

"No," he returned. "No, she didn't. Believe it or not, she actually wants you and me to go look at somethin'."

Felicity immediately pushed away from the countertop next to me and started from the room. As I reached out for her, she shrugged away from my hand and turned. She raised a finger and stared back at me, cold fire in her green eyes. A single tear was advancing across her cheek, and she held her rigid position for a weighty measure of time before she finally spoke. "Aye, go. You go, but you'd best come back."

With the unmistakable instruction given, she turned on her heel and strode through the pass-thru into the dining room.

"I didn't say I was going to..." My words trailed off almost immediately as I realized they were falling short of reaching her; not that she would have been paying attention if they had.

"Dammit," I muttered as the lightning bolt of realization struck me square between my eyes. "I'm not sure, but I think I might have just figured out what your sister was trying to tell me."

"She's good for doin' that kinda shit to people," Ben affirmed.

"Yes, she is."

"So, is Felicity gonna be okay?" he finally asked.

"Yeah, eventually," I told him.

"Should you maybe go talk to her?"

"Not now." I shook my head. "I've been married to her for a long time, Ben. Trust me, this is something that will play out later when we're alone."

"You sure?"

"Oh yeah," I guaranteed him. "I'm sure."

"How 'bout you? You gonna be all right?"

"Yeah." I was still staring after my wife. "Yeah, I think so. I'm just not sure how I feel about being a matador."

"Do what?"

"Nothing. Forget it." I reached up and rubbed my temple for a moment. "So what's the deal? What's so important that Albright needs us to look at it right now?"

"Well, so anyway," he stumbled over the words a bit, "so what happened is the phone company managed to peg the number Porter used. It was a cell just like we thought."

"Well, that's good, right?" I asked.

"Not for the guy it used to belong to," he replied.

"You mean he killed someone else already?"

"Not exactly." He shook his head. "More like before."

"Before?"

"Yeah." He visibly grimaced as he spoke, both looking and sounding as if he really didn't want to tell me. "We've actually known about this guy for a few days."

"A few days?" I almost couldn't believe what he was saying. "What do you mean you've known about him for a few days? Why haven't you said anything?"

"Look, Rowan," Ben huffed. "The Major Case Squad doesn't report to you, you know. There was no reason to get you involved."

I was more than just slightly angered by what I had just been told, and my voice came out as a thin hiss. "But if this happened a few days ago, maybe if I had gotten involved THEN, Randy would still be alive!"

He glanced through the passage into the dining room then back at me with his eyes wide. "Keep your voice down, Rowan," he ordered in a strained whisper through clenched teeth. "There were reasons you weren't called."

"They'd damn well better be good ones," I hissed back. "Because I lost a friend today and if I could have prevented it…"

"You couldn't have, so drop it," he interrupted with the stern instruction.

I took a deep breath and let it out slowly as I glared back at him. I knew I had to trust that what he was telling me was true, but the reality was a hard lump in my throat, and I was finding it hard to swallow.

"Look, Row," he sighed. "We need to move on this. Carl Deckert from county homicide is waiting for us at the scene right now."

"Why now?" I demanded, barely managing to keep my voice even and low.

"I don't know." He shook his head. "Bee-bee has a bug up her ass about this all of a sudden, and she's already got Deckert waitin' for us."

"I couldn't care any less about what she wants right now, Ben," I told him.

"Yo, Kemosabe," he appealed. "I'm on your side here, but let's go have a look-see. This is a damn sight better than being banned from the investigation. Maybe you can do some hocus-pocus or somethin', and we can nail this fuck before anyone else gets killed."

"So you're going to let me go at this my way?" I was demanding as much as asking.

"I didn't say that," he returned. "I'm not lettin' you put yourself in danger over this."

"What about Felicity?" I asked. "I'm not so sure I want to leave her right now."

"Because of that little deal a minute ago?"

"No, because Porter obviously knows where I am, so I'm sure he knows she's here too."

He shook his head and waved me off. "I know what you're sayin', but it's covered. There's a copper out front and one in the alley."

I started to object, but he held his hand up to stifle me before continuing. "Let me finish. If that ain't enough for ya', Mandalay is on her way over with another Feeb, and they'll probably be here any minute."

There were very few people besides him whom I would trust with Felicity's safety, and FBI Special Agent Constance Mandalay was one of them. I'm certain he was playing that fact as his trump card to my impending objection.

"You're sure?" I pressed.

"Yeah, I'm sure," he told me. "I talked to her right after I got off the phone with Albright. They'll probably be pullin' up about the time we head out the door."

Back up the hallway, the doorbell chimed as if cued by some ethereal director.

"Well?" My friend looked at me expectantly and gave a quick nod as if to say, "told you so."

"Okay," I agreed. "Okay, I'll go. Just one thing: How are you going to stop me?"

"Stop you what?"

I didn't explain. I just closed my eyes and rubbed my forehead as my ever-present migraine sidestepped any attempts to keep it at bay. Even worse, it began inching up the scale. "Nothing. Don't worry about it."

CHAPTER 14:

"Kass-perzik-somethin-oww-ski, according to his driver's license. First name, Joseph." Ben looked at me and shrugged. "I dunno how the hell to pronounce it. Starts with a K and it's got some Z's and W's in it."

The ambient temperature inside the house wasn't much different than it was outside. In fact, it was probably exactly the same. The only thing that made it feel warmer was the shelter itself and thus a reprieve from the wind chill factor.

"So how is it spelled?" I asked as I buried my hands in my coat pockets and worked my fingers to jump-start the circulation.

"Why?"

I shrugged.

He pulled out his notebook and flipped through it for a second. "Shit. Can't read my own handwriting. Hey Deck," he called across the room. "You got a spelling on the victim's name?"

Saint Louis County Homicide Detective Carl Deckert was best described as everyone's grandfather. He was a thick, round man, aged somewhere in his mid to late fifties. A trimmed crop of fine, grey hair covered his head, and that was often sheltered beneath a fedora with the brim neatly snapped over his brow.

His attitude, forged in a different time, was one filled with manners and kindness. His eyes never lacked the mischievous twinkle of a youngster nor his ruddy face a friendly smile. He usually had something good to say—even under less than perfect circumstances.

His overall appearance and demeanor had to be advantageous in his line of work, because to be honest, if I didn't already know him, I would never suspect he was a cop. Even if I did, he still came across as someone to whom you could bare your soul.

Presently, he was several feet away from us with the virtually omnipresent fedora pushed up high on his forehead as he carefully studied the room. At his side, he held tight to a bag that might have been a sack lunch. I didn't ask.

"K-A-S-P-R-Z-Y-K-O-W-S-K-I." The older county detective offered the string of letters from memory. "You pronounce it, kasper-kush-kee."

I mentally aligned the letters and then silently repeated the name back to myself, placing the proper "ksh" emphasis on the ZYK combination and allowing the W to remain silent. "Slavic, obviously," I said aloud.

"Yeah," Deckert agreed. "It's Polish. Means something like 'the place of Kasper's son.'"

"You get that from the next of kin?" Ben asked.

"Still haven't found any yet," Deckert told him with a shake of his head.

"Nobody?"

"Nope. Not so far."

"So, what's up with you and the genealogy lesson? You been eatin' a bunch of kielbasa or somethin'?"

"My *babcia* was originally from Poland."

"Your what?" Ben asked.

"Grandmother," he explained. "She was a first generation immigrant." He then gave his head a quick tilt to the side before adding, "But since you brought it up, she did make a pretty mean kielbasa and kraw."

"What's a 'kraw'?"

"Sauerkraut."

"Oh, okay. I love that stuff, but it kills me every time I eat it."

"Yeah, me too."

"Hey, she make those pierogie things too?"

"Yeah." Deckert nodded. "Pierogies, kluski, golabki, krupnik, you name it. *Babcia* was a hell of a cook."

"That what's in the bag?"

"I wish."

"Too bad. Jeez, I guess we better stop talkin' about food," Ben said. "I just realized I haven't had anything to eat since dinner last night."

"Hey," I interjected. "Is this really the appropriate time and place for this discussion?"

I suppose there was some level of disdain in my voice that was readily apparent because both of them looked at me with somewhat apologetic expressions on their faces.

"Coppers do this shit, Row," my friend told me. "You know that. It's how we keep from goin' nuts."

"Yeah, I know," I replied. "Sorry... I'm just... I don't know."

"It's okay, Rowan," Deckert offered.

Ben shifted the subject back to what had originally led down the culinary path. "So why were you askin' about his name anyway, white man?"

"Curiosity I guess," I told him. "Trying to make sense of everything."

"Well I hate to sound crass." Ben tossed in his two cents, "But his name could be Smith. Doesn't really matter. He's dead."

"You're right," I returned. "But he was alive once."

"Uh-huh. 'Bout two weeks ago," Deckert offered and then explained. "According to the M.E., he'd been deceased for approximately a week when he was found, and that was a week ago itself."

I nodded. "So I've heard."

The wholly unmistakable funk of death still lingered on the gelid air, and the lag time between death and discovery Deckert just mentioned explained it. Fortunately, it was faint as there had been some time for the place to air out; which also explained why every time I spoke I could see my words as well as hear them. Still, it was nowhere near as bad as it could have been.

I let my eyes roam and slowly scanned the area around me, getting a visual feel for the place. We were actually standing in the partially finished basement of a house that sat just inside the municipality of Wood Dell. Recently hung sheet rock formed a wall to our right and was marred at intervals by wide vertical swaths of joint compound. Bare studs to our rear formed a half-wall return that separated one section from the next. At the far end of the room, a doorway led deeper into the basement and presumably the ongoing remodeling project.

My gaze eventually came to rest on the centerpiece we'd surrounded—a set of well-seasoned sawhorses, age-greyed and paint-spattered, that were occupying the middle of the room. A hardwood one-by-ten was stretched across them with the beginning of a decorative edge routed into one side. The smoothly tapered cut ran for approximately ten inches then suddenly degraded as the careful craftsmanship vanished into an arcing gouge that hop-scotched across the surface of the wood.

On the bare, plywood sub-floor beneath, a chalked outline stood out against the sawdust and construction detritus. At a bulbous point in the scribed profile that was obviously where the man's head had been, dried blood stained the wood a rusty brown. It had pooled in a haphazard pattern that in a bizarre sense resembled a fuzzy map of Italy, morbid as that observation was. Additional stains spread outward from what had probably been the early stages of purging and putrefaction.

The coppery scent of the old blood blended with the nasal bite of sappy lumber, adding themselves to the potpourri of odors. Even as faint as it was, in the back of my mind I wondered if I would ever be able to forget the sharpness of this smell.

My friend took notice of where my focused stare had fallen, and he cleared his throat.

"You slippin' into la-la land?" he asked.

"No," I returned, breaking my intense gaze away from the outline and turning to Ben. "Just thinking."

"Coroner's report says he bled out," Deckert told me as if he felt a need to explain the bloodstain. "Looks like the wacko came in while the guy was working, picked up a hammer, and jacked him in the head.

Poor bastard just laid there and bled to death. Of course, he probably would've ended up being a vegetable if he hadn't."

"Lesser of two evils," I muttered.

"Something like that," he agreed, then continued. "Anyway, from what we found it looks like the asshole might have lived here for at least a couple of days after he killed him. Maybe a week."

"So Porter's been in town for at least two weeks?"

"Yeah," Deckert answered. "Looks that way."

"I still don't understand why you didn't tell me about it until now," I contended.

"Albright was already running things, Row," Ben spoke. "She made it pretty clear that you weren't to be involved."

"But you called me this morning about Randy, and that was before you even knew who the victim was."

"Yeah, and I got my ass chewed for it too."

"Earlier you said there were reasons I wasn't told," I continued. "Reasons means more than one."

"Yeah, it does."

"Would you like to expand on that?"

"You won't like it."

"So what's new about that?"

Ben paused and stared at me for a moment. "Truth?"

"I would hope."

"It wasn't just Albright. Deck, Mandalay, and I recommended that you be left out of it so we could keep your sorry ass from showing up here unescorted."

"That seems to be a theme with you lately," I returned.

"So sue me," he answered.

"Maybe later," I told him for lack of anything better to say.

My friend circled back to the original topic once again. "Well anyway, considerin' the name and the evidence, I'm bettin' this guy wasn't a Witch."

"You can't base it on his name, Ben. WitchCraft crosses several ethnic boundaries, and there is such a thing as Slavic Paganism," I answered then gave him a nod. "But you're right. I don't think that this victim was Pagan, and that's what bothers me."

Quiet fell in the room while I stood pondering the unheralded death of a man I never knew. I could feel my face hardening into a frown as I mulled over the facts I'd been given.

"Whatcha' thinkin' about now, Row?" my friend finally prodded.

"Why would Porter do that?" I asked aloud, talking to myself as much as to him.

"Do what?" Ben asked.

"Deliberately kill a non-Pagan individual."

"Hell, Rowan, who knows?" Deckert shrugged and shook his head. "Covering his tracks probably."

"But it just doesn't make sense," I said. "Porter's thing has always been killing Witches. The last time around he even had a crisis of faith when he accidentally killed a non-Pagan."

"As I recall," Ben offered, "he ended up blaming you for that."

"That's how he came to terms with it, yes," I assented.

"Yeah, well, I think Porter's made it clear that it's not just about killin' Witches anymore, Row. He's got it in for YOU."

"Yeah, I know," I replied. "So why am I here?"

I knew my words sounded more like a demand than a question the moment I heard my own voice, but I couldn't help it. The dam had finally broken on my headache, and it was ramping up at an ever increasing rate. On top of that, I had an anxious feeling slithering around inside me that I just couldn't shake. I didn't know if it was fear, nerves, or something ethereal. I couldn't even pinpoint if it had to do with me or someone else. All I could say for a fact was that I didn't feel right, and this excursion was beginning to come across as an exercise in futility.

"Whaddaya mean?"

"I mean exactly that. What am I doing here? What does Albright want me to look at?" I waved my arm in a semicircle to indicate the scene before us. "Surely not this."

"Well, there's more in the back," Deckert offered then held up the brown paper bag. "But she also said she wanted you to see this."

"So that isn't your lunch?" I asked, fighting to keep the sarcasm out of my voice and only partially succeeding.

Fortunately, Carl ignored it.

"Hell no," he replied as he set the bag on the end of the board that was resting across the two-by-fours and then proceeded to unfold the top. "I don't know what it is."

Deckert reached into the now open bag, and when he withdrew his hand, he was holding a somewhat old-looking and dirt-smeared mason jar. From where I stood, I could see that the ring holding the lid on was rusted and weathered. A winding or two of black electrical tape encircled the rim and neck of the glass vessel. It appeared to be approximately half full with various shapes; some large, some small, some dark, some light, and some were even shiny. Pale liquid made up the remaining volume to within a pair of inches from the sealed top.

"Where did you find that?" I asked.

"Flowerbed next to the front porch," Deckert replied. "One of the Crime Scene guys noticed that the mulch had been disturbed. He found this buried about a foot or so down."

"Yeah," I nodded. "That would be about right."

"So you sound like you know what it is?" he half-stated, half-asked.

Ben had reached out and taken the container from Deckert and was holding it up in the dim light. He inspected it intensely, holding it close to his face as he twisted it then announced, "There's nails and fishhooks and razor blades and all kinds of other shit in here."

"Probably some screws, broken glass, pins, needles, and anything else sharp you can think of too," I added. "That's a Witch jar."

"THIS is a Witch jar?" Ben asked.

"What's a Witch jar?" Deckert wedged in his question.

"It's a protective talisman from a long line of folklore." I offered the same general explanation I'd given Ben earlier. "They are used to repel Witches and especially magick. Sometimes they're called Witch bottles. Porter probably made it and buried it out front in order to protect himself from me."

"So when you mentioned these things earlier, I asked you if it was something I needed to know about," Ben said, still inspecting the container.

"Actually you asked me if you WANTED to know about them," I replied.

"Same difference," he shot back.

"Hey, I'm sorry," I apologized with a somewhat defensive tone in my voice. "I was just speculating at the time. I didn't know that he'd actually leave a Witch jar somewhere."

"Yeah, I know, but what I'm sayin' is that you made out like it was something weird and all. I don't see what the big deal is. It's just a bunch of nails and shit in a jar of water."

"That's not water, Ben," I told him. "It's urine."

He sat the jar back onto the board in a quick flurry of motion and then began wiping his hand on his pants leg as he screwed up his face in disgust. "What the fuck?! You mean he pissed in it?"

"Yeah," I nodded. "That's how you make a Witch jar."

"Jeezus, white man. That's just gross."

"Hey." I shrugged. "I told you that you probably didn't want to know."

"Well hell, I can see why they would work," Ben, announced. "I'm repelled by the damn thing myself."

"That's not exactly the intended use, Ben," I told him. "It's not the 'disgust factor' that does it; besides, now that it's no longer buried it's pretty much useless."

"It has to be buried?"

I canted my head in a quick nod. "In order to work, yes."

"So it's just a jar of piss?" he asked.

"Pretty much." I nodded. "With sharp objects in it."

"So was it like some kinda magic or spell or somethin'?"

"More or less."

"Well, there's a WHY for you. If Porter is so dead set on killin' Witches then why would he do something like this?"

"For the very same reason he wants to kill Witches," I explained. "Superstition. Like I said, a Witch jar is something drawn from folklore."

"So if it's just a superstition then how can it work?"

"Have you ever heard of a self-fulfilling prophecy?"

"You mean like when you get yourself so worked up worrying about something that you actually make it happen?" Deckert asked.

I nodded my head. "Exactly. It's the same concept. That's the thing about magick. If you believe in it enough, you can make it real."

"Okay, but this thing is still gross."

"I'm not going to debate that with you," I replied as I motioned to the vessel. "But, now you know what a Witch jar is."

"Wunnerful," he muttered. "I feel sufficiently educated now."

"So, Carl, you said there was something in the back?" I ignored my friend's sardonic tone and directed my question to Detective Deckert.

"Yeah." He pointed to the doorway at the other end of the divided room. "He got a little artistic on the walls back there."

"Monogram of Christ?" I mentioned the wreath-encircled X bisected by a P because it had been one of Porter's calling cards the last time he had gone on a killing spree. I had even been on the receiving end of a series of ethereal stigmata of the same shape each time he claimed a victim. Unconsciously I reached my right hand over to massage my left forearm, as it had been the canvas for the bloody signs. Fortunately, there were no indications of a repeat performance at the moment.

"Yeah, there's a couple of those." He nodded affirmation as he spoke. "But there's some other stuff. Star kinda things. Not sure what they're s'posed to be. You'll just have to look at 'em."

I shuddered for a moment and looked around as the hairs on the back of my neck rose painfully to attention. The tickle of gooseflesh serpentined down my spine and spread out from there, making me tense my muscles in pure reflex.

"You okay, white man?" Ben asked.

"I'm not sure," I replied without looking at him. "I feel…"

I allowed my voice to trail off very simply because I couldn't find words to describe the feeling that had come over me.

"You feel what?" my friend pressed after a moment of expectant silence.

The tingle that was prancing about on my skin oozed down my arms and welled in my hands, making them feel as though circulation was only now returning after an extended absence. Painful pricking sensations needled my fingers in a rapid-fire assault. I looked down at my hands and rubbed my thumbs against my fingertips. The pain intensified with each pass, and my hands began to burn as if they were on fire.

I've never been a big fan of Shakespeare, so I don't quite know why I picked his work to quote other than the fact that it seemed to fit. I looked up at them, and the line of prose exited my mouth before I could even think. "By the pricking of my thumbs, something wicked this way comes."

CHAPTER 15:

"That's Shakespeare, ain't it?" Ben asked.

"*Macbeth*," Deckert offered. "Act four, scene one."

Ben looked over at him and raised an eyebrow.

"Gimme a break, Mona's a high school English teacher." Deckert shrugged as he referred to his wife. "I've seen the play a few hundred times."

Ben turned back to me. "So is this some kinda *Twilight Zone* thing, Row?"

"Yeah," I said as I nodded. "You could say that."

"Okay." He gave me a questioning gaze to match his tone. "What's it mean?"

"How many times do I have to tell you..." I began.

"Hold on," Deckert interrupted and motioned for us both to be quiet. "Did you hear that?"

"Hear what?" Ben asked.

"I don't know," he replied. "It sounded like it was coming from upstairs."

Ben shook his head. "I didn't hear anything."

We stood in relative silence, gazing up at the drop ceiling over our heads and listening intently. Detective Deckert still held his hand up, frozen in place as we waited.

"Listen." His eyes grew wide as the noise filtered down to us. "There it is again."

To me, it sounded akin to a screaming hiss, coupled with a dull roar, and occasionally punctuated by a popping sizzle. It was muffled by the walls and ceiling above us, but it was definitely growing louder by the second. There was something frighteningly familiar about the sound, and I was searching my memories as fast as I could, trying to place a cause with the effect.

Before I managed to make the connection, my friend spoke up. "Hear something hell, I can smell it."

He wasn't the only one. The acrid bite of burning wood and synthetic materials now mixed with the earlier odors in the basement and wafted through on a thin layer of smokiness.

"Seems a bit strong to be someone's fireplace," I observed.

Suddenly, the piercing wail of a smoke detector lanced its way through the basement from the direction of the stairs.

"Holy Jesus, Mary Mother of God," Deckert muttered.

Ben skipped past any semblance of muttering and went directly to exclamations. "Sonofabitch!"

He was already moving when he bellowed the expletive, hooking around me and heading for the stairs. Deckert and I followed close on his heels.

This particular staircase was positioned such that it formed a steep angle diagonally against the far wall. Due to the structural design of the foundation, in order to keep that angle from being far too oblique, it reached a small landing near the bottom, then made a ninety-degree turn, and continued down for another short flight of steps. The stairwell, in and of itself, had been a part of the remodeling project and was now enclosed by thin sheets of paneling applied directly to the wooden studs.

Ben was several steps ahead of us and hit the bottom stair at full speed, launching himself past the other two and onto the landing. By the time we reached the opening, we could hear him bounding upward and coughing violently.

Deckert urged me ahead, and I stumbled for a moment, raking my shin against the edge of the stair. I groped for a handrail and found none, so I pushed off and started upward again, ignoring the pain in my lower leg. As I hit the landing with the older detective puffing hard behind me, I made the turn and was immediately enveloped in a thick haze of smoke.

The detector in the stairwell was still screaming at full volume, echoing from the paneled walls and drilling an intense pain deep in my ears.

The cloud of smoke was increasing at an alarming rate, and it easily began to overtake the narrow space as it billowed in from beneath the door. I came to a sudden halt as my eyes began to water and burn. Partially blinded, I held my arms outstretched, trying to feel my way up the staircase, and lurched forward.

My heart was racing, and I involuntarily sucked in a deep breath of the polluted atmosphere then immediately hacked it outward, sputtering and choking as I fell once again on the stairs. I could hear Ben up ahead of me barking out his shallow breaths and then the heavy sound of a body against solid wood as he threw his weight against the door. The thud was followed by my friend's choking voice. "Owwww! Shit! Jeezus! Goddammit!"

I pulled the neck of my shirt up over my nose and mouth and dragged myself upward. Deckert was immediately to my rear, and he grabbed my arm in an attempt to help me up, but he was already breathing so hard when we hit the landing that the sudden rush of smoke was taking a far quicker toll on him.

The din of the fire was echoing from the walls, and dangerous sounding creaks and groans were now beginning to insinuate themselves into the fray.

I squinted hard in the darkness of the thickening atmosphere and saw a pinpoint of reddish-orange appear above me. It started to grow, and I realized that I was standing directly beneath it. I threw myself backwards, barreling into Deckert, and propelling us both into the wall at the bottom of the landing. The slab of paneling that angled up over the stairs suddenly erupted as flames ate through, fed by the noxious gases the treated laminate was expelling. The smoke detector began to warble sickly as the blaze lapped at it with an arcing fan of orange. A moment later, there was a loud snap followed by a crash as the sheet of paneling broke apart and fell across the stairs.

Bright orange light illuminated the cloud of smoke in the stairwell as the roar of the conflagration announced its arrival. I thought I could see the silhouette of my friend moving at the top of the stairs. I started upward amid the rush of heat and began kicking the flaming pieces of pressboard off to the sides in order to make a path.

I was still working at the task when he started down through the maelstrom. My ears were met by the cacophony of a repetitive thump, and before I could look up, I collided with my friend.

"Down!" he croaked, grabbing me by the shoulder and twisting me around. "Back down!"

I pushed forward, taking hold of Deckert's arm as I went and pulling him back down the stairwell with me. The three of us stumbled back into the basement hacking and gulping at the less tainted air. I looked back and could see the smoke now curling along the ceiling at the mouth of the stairs, stretching grey tendrils to undulate languidly along the acoustic tiles. The paneled wall along the stairs was starting to bow and discolor, and in the amount of time it took me to suck in another breath, yellow flame began to pry open the seams.

"It's fuckin' blocked or somethin!" Ben sputtered the words and then coughed hard before continuing his frenzied explanation. "I couldn't budge it. Besides that, it's hotter than hell."

"There's got to be another exit," I appealed.

"In the back," Deckert wheezed. He had lost his hat in the rush, and his hair was sticking out in disarray. He seemed to be having even more trouble breathing than Ben or me, and he was fingering his tie in an attempt to loosen it.

"Carl, are you okay?" I reached over and worked the knot loose for him as I stared into his face.

He managed to spit out a response. "Yeah, yeah, I'm okay."

He was lying. His face was pale, and I could see that his left hand was clenched into a fist.

"Come on," Ben urged, hooking a hand under one of Deckert's arms as I took hold of the other. "We gotta get outta here before…"

The fluorescent fixtures in the ceiling buzzed loudly and immediately doused, throwing us into almost complete darkness. The smoke was now rolling into the room behind us, and it was no longer content with hanging in wispy cloudlike formations around the ceiling. It had taken on a life of its own, and it was intent on filling the room to capacity with its airborne virulence.

A wave of heat was pushing through the room, chasing away the earlier frosty atmosphere that had plagued me. We started forward across the darkened basement, aiming for the dim light of the doorway some forty feet away. We had taken three steps when from behind us there came a noise unlike any I'd ever heard.

The initial sound hammered into my ears and drove directly into my skull, jarring every bone in my body. It was followed immediately by a dull roar that swelled in pitch to a persistent ring, all underscored by my ears feeling as if they were full of water.

I remember being lifted off my feet and flying forward through the air, only to be deposited onto the plywood sub-floor a pair of yards from my original position. My face did a quick double bounce from the hard surface, and my arm twisted as it folded beneath me, driving a harpoon of pain into my already tortured shoulder.

I groaned and rolled to the side then began pushing myself upward. An out-of-control spill of orange flame rolled down the stairs and waved its angry arms upward, instantly igniting the rectangular foam ceiling tiles. Black smoke from the burning polymers joined its dingy grey sibling to push deeper into the room, at the same time adding a layer of toxic fumes to the haze.

"Ben?! Carl?!" I could hear myself inside my head, but to my ears, the words were a muffled tangle of syllables.

My friend was already dragging himself upward, but Carl was motionless between us. I struggled to my feet and stumbled for a moment. I touched my face, and it felt sticky. My nose and cheek were aching, and my shoulder felt like it had just gotten in the way of a freight train.

I don't know that Ben could hear me any more than I could hear him. His lips were moving, and I thought I could pick out something resembling his voice. In any event, we both took hold of Deckert and pulled him to his feet. We half dragged him toward the doorway as he began to come to then he started moving with us as we rushed for the opening.

I cast a glance over my shoulder and saw that the wall along the stairwell had already begun to collapse, bringing the melting tiles and grid work of the drop ceiling with it. The flames were arcing in violent bursts, swinging monkeylike from panel to panel as they consumed anything they touched. When I returned my gaze forward, I realized that it had crowned over us in the open space above the tiles and was now burning through in our path.

Directly in front of me, a molten dollop of foam ceiling tile dripped to the floor, pulling a stream of flame with it. I shifted hard to the right, slamming once again into Carl and pushing him into Ben. We careened around the synthetic lava flow and slammed against the wall then ricocheted back onto a zigzagging course and covered the last few feet to the doorway.

The ringing in my ears had subsided to a low whistle, and I could now hear the roar of the holocaust around us. Ben shoved Deckert through the opening then clamped his hand on my shoulder and pushed me in. The plywood sub-floor had ended at the threshold and dropped a few inches to the original concrete, so I tripped as I went through. Ben followed and faltered as well.

The smoke was now hanging in the entire basement from the waist up, and we were hunched over in search of cooler, cleaner air. The only source of light in the room, other than that of the flames behind us, was a small, glass block window above us at ground level.

We began scanning the room with frantic urgency, battling the thickening smoke for visibility. The caustic fumes were beginning to overtake us, and each breath was coming at an even higher cost.

"Where's the door?!" I heard Ben almost scream the question. "Where the fuck's the door?!"

CHAPTER 16:

Angry flames had all but caught up to us, casting sharp fingers of orange past the doorframe. The fire had become a hungry cat, and the three of us were mice cowering in a hole. I searched for a door to close on the opening and found only bare hinges where it had been removed. I jumped and backpedaled to the center of the room as the claws of the monster made a desperate grab for me, singeing my hair in the process. For a moment, the arc of the blaze retreated as if it had been sucked back into the realm of hell from which it had originated. Unfortunately, as with any storm, it was merely a false calm. The pause lasted no more than a breath before a second explosion rattled through from the opposite end of the house, forcing a blast of flame, heat, and burning debris in upon us.

We danced about, avoiding the flying detritus as best we could. All the while, we were struggling for each and every breath as a fresh supply of smoke billowed into the room. Carl hit the floor with a heavy thud, and I rushed over. He was kneeling, and I came down even with him. Although my eyes were burning and blurred, I could still see that he was looking worse by the moment.

"How are you doing, Carl?" I felt myself yelling just to be heard through the thickness in my own ears.

"Goddamn... Chest... Fricking... Killing... Me..." He wheezed in a breath between each word.

I wasn't qualified to make a diagnosis by any means, but I'd seen this before, and the only thing that entered my mind was heart attack. I didn't say it aloud, but I could tell by the look in his eyes that he was thinking the same thing.

"Do you have a handkerchief?" I raised my voice once again.

He nodded and began trying to reach into his pocket. I took over and rummaged through his coat until I found the large cotton square. I gave it a quick fold then pressed it over his nose and mouth.

"Breathe through this," I instructed him. "And try to relax. We're going to get out of here."

He pressed his right hand up over the makeshift mask and nodded.

I climbed to my feet and began feeling my way clockwise around the room, keeping as low as I could in search of breathable air. I still had my shirt pulled up over the lower half of my face, but it was being overwhelmed by the ash content of the atmosphere. I could see that Ben was moving on the other side of the room, engaged in the same search from the opposite direction.

"Back wall," Deckert croaked, barely audible over the din of the fire.

"Where?!" Ben screamed.

Deckert motioned with his right arm as he sputtered and coughed, repeating, "Back wall."

I tried to move quickly in the direction he had indicated and nearly fell as I bounced from a stack of boxes. I was almost reduced to being on my hands and knees, so I sucked in a halting breath then half stood before propelling myself forward. I made it three steps before hammering face first into something that felt cold and metallic. I let out a yelp as my forward motion was immediately impeded and the air forced from my lungs. I groped through the harsh smoke, feeling my way in the darkness as I lowered myself down to the floor. I blinked hard and gulped in a breath, holding my hand against the metal for fear of losing it. I was just getting ready to yell that I had found the door when my eyes focused on the old refrigerator to which my hand was plastered.

"Over here!" Ben's strained voice pierced through the roar.

"Where?!" I screamed out in return.

"On your right!" came his reply.

I twisted my head and could see him kneeling down next to the wall. On my hands and knees, I scrambled across the concrete floor toward him. Carl was still several feet away, and though he was still kneeling, I could see that he had propped himself against the waste pipe that jutted upward from the floor in the center of the room.

Before I reached my friend, he had gulped in a fresh breath of air and was now standing again. I could hear him thumping against the door, the hammering noises coming as punctuation to the high-pitched groan as yet another section of the drop ceiling grid crashed to the floor in the next room.

Ben dropped back down beneath the billowing haze. His face was smeared with soot, and his lower lip was bleeding. I struggled to focus on him and suddenly realized that my glasses were missing. Still, even with that handicap, I saw what could only be fear in his dark eyes.

"Metal door with a deadbolt," he told me, his voice hoarse but raised in order to compete with the conflagration. "Fuckin' keyed on both sides."

Keyed on both sides; that was definitely not the kind of news I was wanting to hear. There was no way to open the door, and finding a key in this holocaust was unthinkable even if there was one to be found.

"What are we going to do?" I screamed the question, unable to keep the terror out of my voice. "Can't you shoot it or something?!"

"This ain't a goddamn movie, Rowan!"

"Do you have a better idea?"

Desperation, the greatest motivator of all, overtook Ben and became the deciding factor. With it as an impetus, it took him less than a second to seriously consider my idea. He clutched my shoulder and pushed me away as he ordered, "Move back! Get outta the way!"

I followed his instruction as if I had any choice, dragging myself backward as quickly as I could. As I watched, he reached inside his coat then withdrew his hand. In it was clutched a nine-millimeter Beretta.

"This is gonna be loud," he screamed at me. "Cover your face 'cause shit's gonna fly!"

With the instruction given, he stood and felt about on the door for a moment. I watched the blurry scene playing out before me, as he settled on a spot then raised the handgun until it disappeared into the thick haze of smoke. I saw his legs move as he took a measured step backward.

A bright flash of yellow-white erupted within the billowing cloud, coupled with a sharp sound of the muzzle report as it echoed from the walls. My ears popped and filled once again, feeling as though they'd been punctured by ice picks, and then a tinny ring settled in for good measure.

At the same instant, something hard, hot, and sharp hit my cheek and sent a sting through it. I reached up and felt it protruding from the skin, and even more blood began to run in a warm rivulet across my face. My arm automatically flew over my eyes just as the next flash of light and controlled explosion made themselves known. The second was followed by a third and that by a fourth. By the time Ben had snapped off the sixteenth and final round from the semi-automatic pistol, the sound seemed to me to be no louder than the pop of someone clapping hands.

I peeked out from beneath my arm and saw that a small shaft of light was streaming in to illuminate the cloud of smoke. Ben dropped himself downward and wheezed in a deep breath. As he came fully into my field of vision, I could see that his hands and face were cut and bloodied from the blowback of the shrapnel.

I couldn't hear him, but I could see him laboring for a breath as he moved himself to the door. The shaft of light flickered as he reached up and tugged at the barrier. It didn't budge.

My heart fell, and the acidic bite of terror forced its bitter taste upon the back of my tongue. A gelid finger ran up my spine before chilling the back of my brain, and I swore I heard the sigh of the Dark Mother calling me. In the front of my mind, I saw my wife's tense face and clearly heard the echo of her voice, *"Aye, go. You go, but you'd best come back."*

I continued to watch as my friend worked his finger into the hole and then seemed to struggle with it for a moment. His hand jerked as if something had given way, and he pulled hard.

Suddenly, he fell back, and the door swung inward allowing the light to grow from a small shaft to an enormous beam. Coldness spilled in across the floor, and the smoke punched upward for a second then began rushing outward through the opening as more flowed in from behind. Fresh air hit us low, and we gulped at it as we crawled across the floor. Unfortunately, it also provided a new source of oxygen for the insane combustion behind us.

The orange flames that had been clawing at the doorway now paled to a bright yellow as they expanded. The wooden doorframe that had until this point only charred and smoldered now offered itself up for sacrifice as fully involved fuel. In an instant, the remaining bits and pieces of drop ceiling crashed downward and swung in through the blaze-encircled opening.

I scrambled up from the floor, making a half step-half leap into the space between Deckert and me in the process. He was still leaning against the waste pipe but was now slumped and unresponsive to his surroundings. I covered the short distance fast, but the flaming debris had a head start.

I landed just short of Carl, and a single heartbeat after, a piece of burning acoustic tile impacted his back and set his coat ablaze. I scrambled to my knees and pulled my bare hand up into my coat sleeve, slapping at the flames to keep them away from his head as I struggled to pull his coat off. Ben was immediately on the other side, hefting him up and extracting his right arm from the sleeve. With a quick twist, we wrenched Deckert out of the lined trench coat and threw it across the room.

Ducking under his limp arms and draping them over our shoulders on either side, we supported him between us and rushed headlong for the now open door. The cold air embraced us as we stumbled through the opening, me going first. Ben supported Deckert's weight from below as we struggled up the concrete stairwell, slipping and sliding on the fresh snow.

Ben pushed upward, and I shouldered more of Carl's weight as he moved up the stairs. I twisted to increase my support and slipped from the edge of the step, tumbling backward. Ben caught Deckert and held him as I grabbed frantically for the handrail. I managed to grip the cold metal at the last moment, keeping myself from crashing at the bottom but ending up a pair of steps below the two of them.

I started back upward, and a heavy "whump" sounded behind me. A rush of hot air and smoke pushed past through the door and into the exterior stairwell, forcing us to choke on our breath once again. Flame licked past me on the right, and I ducked my face into my shoulder as I continued to move. Fear kicked in once again, and I scrambled up the stairs, ducking beneath Deckert's shoulder and taking the lead once again.

The frozen precipitation was coming down hard above us, forming its own brand of haze in the atmosphere, and our labored breaths puffed out like bursts of steam escaping from an old locomotive. The frosty air filled my lungs only to be vomited back out in a violent sputter. I hacked violently and felt myself going lightheaded. I pushed hard, the muscles in my legs burning with the strain. We had to get away from the house, and Ben wasn't going to be able to drag both of us. I gulped in another deep breath and willed myself to hold onto it.

I topped the stairs and pushed out, trying to pull the dead weight behind me, all the while hoping that the "dead" part would remain a figure of speech. I found my footing as I stepped into the yard and pressed forward. A split second later, Ben crested the flight of steps, and we limped away from the danger of the house, trudging through a good two inches of icy, white fluff.

We were stumbling almost drunkenly across the yard, traveling in no particular direction other than away. The sound of a distant siren tickled the inside of my ears, thrusting itself past the ringing that had been left in the wake of the close-proximity gunfire.

I hoped that it was on its way here.

My cheek was beginning to throb where the shrapnel had impacted it earlier, and I remembered that it was probably still protruding from my face. The fog in my brain was starting to clear, ushered away by the quick dose of adrenalin my body elected to inject into my bloodstream at the bottom of the stairs. I realized that I was aching in more places than just my cheek, and I was going to have to take inventory at some point.

However, at this particular moment, Deckert was my primary concern. I released the breath to which I had willed myself to cling and drank in a new volume of the clean atmosphere, continuing to press forward. Even though we were heading away from the house at a wounded trot, the stench of the fire remained with me as if I was still standing in the basement. I was afraid to look back at the house because I feared that I would see the monster chasing after me. I could still feel the heat at my back.

I continued on my trajectory in the opposite direction of the burning house, not exactly sure where we should go. I only knew that we needed to get far enough away that we would be safe, and then we could use a cell phone to call for help.

I was just about to look up and try to gain my bearings when the dull pain of a full-force tackle tore into my back. I was twisted away from Deckert by the blow, and pitched forward. An unintelligible banshee wail soaked through the curtain of semi-deafness in my ears, and someone rode me to the ground, flailing madly all the way.

CHAPTER 17:

The utter shock of being tackled took a moment to set in. Initially, my face was filled with snow, and I was blinded to what was going on around me. That, combined with my still diminished hearing, left me in a surprised daze. All I knew was that someone was on top of me, and I thought that I was being hit repeatedly. Whoever was attacking me was also yelling something, which to me was, for all intents and purposes, unintelligible, coming across as nothing more than a jumble of excited noise.

I was pinned in place and stunned into immobilization. As the bewilderment wore off, however, I could definitely feel the thumping against my back. I started to wince as the next blow fell and then realized that it didn't really hurt all that much. My mind raced as I tried to reconcile the absence of serious agony in connection with the blows. Unfortunately, the equation simply didn't work out for me.

I finally decided that either I had already taken so much abuse while in the house that it just didn't matter any more or that the adrenalin in my system was dulling the pain for the time being so that it could spring it on me later. Whichever it was, my attacker was having very little effect at the moment other than just generating some general discomfort.

I suddenly felt myself being rolled to the side, and it crossed my mind that maybe I could seize the opportunity. I clenched my fists, preparing to fight back against the mysterious combatant. As my right shoulder rotated upward, I pulled my left arm in and slid it beneath my rising chest. By the time I was on my side, I had twisted it free, and I tensed my muscles in preparation. Using the supplied momentum to roll myself the rest of the way over, I swung my left arm in a wide, roundhouse arc.

Fortunately for both of us, the firefighter kneeling next to me jerked back just in time to cause me to miss.

"Whoa, sir!" she shouted as her hand came up and deflected my arm.

Her voice was just audible enough for me to make out what she had said, and the sight of her brought my tension back down to a manageable level. I allowed myself to relax, and my head fell back into the snow. "Carl..." I wheezed. "Heart..."

Her lips moved, and I shook my head.

"He's right here." She raised her voice and repeated the comment as she fought the zipper on the front of my coat with a sense of urgency. "The paramedics are already with him. Are you having trouble hearing?"

"Yeah. Explosion. Ringing." I sputtered once again as my breathing started to come under control for the first time in what seemed like forever. "He okay?"

"He'll be fine, sir," she told me.

"Ben?"

She pointed above and to my left, so I twisted my head to have a look. My friend was remaining staunchly by Deckert's side as the paramedics were loading him onto a backboard.

Ben pulled a clear, plastic oxygen mask away from his face and sputtered, "I'm here, white man."

I made out what he was saying more from reading his lips than actually hearing him.

"Can you walk, sir?" The firefighter was talking to me again.

I turned my face back to her and managed a weak grin. "I was before you tackled me."

She smiled back. "You didn't give me much choice. We were coming around the back to vent the structure, and the first thing we saw was the three of you running like maniacs. We couldn't seem to get your attention though."

"Well, there was this fire you see..." I let my voice trail off.

"Yeah, that's what I hear," she answered with a grin. "So, we need to get this coat off of you."

I swallowed hard and looked back at her as if she had lost her mind. "You did notice that it's snowing out here, didn't you?"

My wry comment was peppered with small fits of coughing.

"Yes," she nodded as she spoke. "But apparently you DIDN'T notice that you were on fire."

The abrupt tackle suddenly made all kinds of sense. The light must have snapped on behind my eyes because she just looked back at me and grinned.

"I thought someone was attacking me," I offered.

She nodded. "I pretty much got that from the roundhouse. Can you sit up?"

I pushed myself up and felt half the joints in my body pop and creak as I did so. I winced and continued until I was fully upright. The firefighter gingerly extracted my arms from the heavy winter coat, and without hesitation, the cold air wrapped itself around my sweaty body, bringing an instant chill. The snow beneath me was already melting from my body heat and soaking into my pants, leeching the warmth from me. Sitting there, I started to realize just how miserable I felt.

The firefighter worked her fingers through the elastic strap on another oxygen mask and pulled it over the back of my head then adjusted the business end over my nose and mouth.

"Just breath normally," she instructed.

I nodded as I sucked in the fresh oxygen then spit out a quick cough.

"I know it's hard, but don't gulp it," she told me again. "Just breath normally."

I stared across the yard at the back of the house and saw that with the exception of the smoke billowing from the basement door, the outer structure seemed relatively intact. Of course, I had no idea what the damage was like from the front. In any case, the blurry scene before me sat farther in the distance than I had expected. Apparently, we had been covering ground at a pretty good clip when we escaped.

"You're lucky," my rescuer told me as she shuffled around and draped a blanket across my shoulders. "It looks like your coat took it all, except maybe…"

"Except maybe…" I started to ask then pulled the mask out from my face for a moment. "Except maybe what?"

"Did you happen to have a ponytail?"

"Yeah, I do."

"Well… Not so much anymore."

The front of the house was a somewhat different story as compared to the back. Although it could have looked far worse, it was obvious upon first glance that the structure had been involved in a fire. A portion of the roof had been burned through, and all of the windows were broken. Smoke still streamed out of any open orifice, mixing itself with the falling snow to form an eerie curtain of haze.

Firefighters were still entering and exiting the home, attacking what remained of the blaze with hoses that trailed in through the front door as well as around to the back side. Still, from outward appearances, it didn't look anywhere near as bad as it had been on the inside.

Being mid-afternoon on a weekday, there was a noticeable absence of onlookers; something I'm sure made life easier on the professionals trying to do their jobs. One of the firefighters had told us, however, that a news crew was on the scene.

Ben and I were presently parked in the back of an ambulance, watching the goings-on through the open back door. Carl Deckert had already been rushed from the scene in a different life support vehicle, siren blaring and emergency lights strobing. The last thing we had been told was that he had gone into a full-blown cardiac arrest but that the paramedics had been able to defibrillate his heart. He certainly wasn't out of danger, but he had a strong, regular pulse and was stable for the time being.

My cheek was throbbing where an EMT had extracted a piece of shiny, brass-colored metal about the size of the nail on my pinky finger. From the look of it and the circumstances of it embedding itself there, we decided that it was probably a piece of the collar surrounding the deadbolt.

Ben was seated across from me in the back of the ambulance. He had been far from immune to the flying shrapnel himself. He was presently slouched forward with his elbows on his knees, quietly staring out the opening in the back of the vehicle. His hands were wrapped in loose windings of gauze that were stained bright red in the spots where blood had soaked through, and he allowed them to hang limp.

I hugged the blanket tighter about myself and reached around to carefully feel the back of my neck. There was some minor soreness but nothing worse than one would get with a mild sunburn. However, just as the firefighter had told me earlier, where there had once been eight inches of hair gathered into a ponytail, my hand felt a singed stump of bristles.

"You needed a haircut anyway, white man," my friend said with little emotion as he glanced in my direction.

Neither of us seemed to be able to muster much feeling other than exhaustion. My hearing had begun to return although my ears still felt stuffy, and there was a faint ring in the background. Ben complained of the same, but at least we were able to carry on a conversation without shouting at one another.

The ambient noise of thrumming diesel engines on the emergency vehicles drifted in low, and we could hear radios and various voices of the firefighters on the scene.

"Maybe so," I returned. "But I can think of an easier way to have gone about it. How are your hands?"

"Fuckin' killin' me," he answered in a flat tone. "How 'bout your face?"

"About the same."

One corner of his mouth turned up in a weak attempt at a grin. "Yeah, it ain't doin' me any good either."

I shook my head. "You must be feeling okay. You've still got your sense of humor."

"I'm alive," he agreed. "So are you. So's Deck... For now... That's somethin'."

"He'll make it."

"Yeah."

My shoulder was throbbing, and I reached my right hand up to massage it. The over-the-counter painkiller Felicity had dosed me with earlier had long since dissipated from my system, and I was starting to wish for something a bit stronger. I had all but forgotten about my ethereal migraine when the situation in this plane of existence had demanded my full attention; however, now that I was beginning to relax, it was starting to rap on the back of my skull, insisting that it be permitted entry.

"Really, Ben. He'll make it. It's not his time."

"You got some hocus-pocus goin' on there?" He raised an eyebrow.

Under different circumstances, he would have looked pathetic. He still had soot streaking his face although one cheek had been cleaned where he had an abrasion. His lower lip was swollen, and his reddish skin peeked out around his mouth where the dirt had also been wiped away. There were rings around his eyes. The whole picture came together with fuzzy edges due to my missing spectacles, and when he arched his eyebrow, I had the overwhelming need to chuckle.

"What're you laughin' at?" he asked.

"You should see yourself," I offered.

"Yo, Kemosabe, you got an Al Jolson thing goin' on yourself."

"Yeah, so I guess we're both a sight."

"Prob'ly. So, you never answered me. The thing with Deck. You got some inside info from the great beyond?"

"Just a feeling." I shrugged.

"I hope you're right."

"We just have to believe that I am," I offered.

He fell quiet for a long measure and stared at the floor of the ambulance. When he finally spoke again, his voice was heavy—weighted with a level of seriousness that made me listen intently.

"Ya'know, cops get that too."

"What's that?"

"Feelings. Kinda like intuition or somethin'."

"Everyone does to some extent," I replied.

"Yeah, I guess." He nodded then looked up at me. "I ever tell you about Chris?"

"Wasn't he your partner when you first got out of the academy?" I asked. "The one that…"

He finished the sentence for me. "…Got killed, yeah, that's him."

"You've never really talked about it to me, no."

"He was a good guy. Big S.O.B. Biggern' me. Good copper. You knew you could count on 'im to have your back. I learned a lot from 'im."

I just nodded acknowledgement and let him talk.

"Anyway, the night he was killed we were workin' third. He was actin' pretty nervous, real squirrely like. We stopped to grab some coffee, and he finally opens up and tells me that he's got a weird feelin' like it's his night or somethin'. Like he's wearin' a target. He said he'd had it all day and that when he left his house, he turned around and went back in twice to call in sick, but didn't do it 'cause he felt guilty.

"I didn't think much of it at the time, but he'd told me before that you develop a kinda sense about stuff. Told me not to ignore my gut, 'cause it was one thing a copper had that could save his ass. Anyway, half an hour later we responded on a liquor store holdup. He was hit the minute we got outta the car. He was wearin' a vest, but it didn't matter 'cause he got hit in the neck. Last thing he said to me was 'I shoulda stayed home today.'"

I watched him as he fell silent, and then I finally asked, "Have you talked to someone about this?"

"Hell yeah," he returned, slightly more life in his voice than there had been during the morose reminiscence. "Helen got me through it a long time ago. I'm just sayin' that coppers get those feelings too."

There was still a strange undertone in his voice. Something told me that there was more to this story than just an idle observation. It took a moment to dawn on me, but when it did, it struck me like a hard slap.

"Did Carl say something to you?" I asked.

"When we got here," he finally said with a nod. "Told me he had a weird feelin' like maybe he shoulda stayed home today."

CHAPTER 18:

"And how are you gentlemen doing?" The paramedic asked almost cheerfully as he climbed into the back of the ambulance with us and levered the door shut.

"Horrible," Ben answered.

I felt like adding "and terrible" as my answer to the question, but I really had no complaints that he could help me with, so I elected to keep my mouth shut. My migraine had returned full force, and it seemed to have inextricably attached itself to the pain in my shoulder. The alliance that was formed was executing a battle plan that included a full-scale invasion of every nerve ending between the two points. While something in the way of a nice analgesic sounded like a good idea, considering the source of the ache, I wasn't sure that it would do any good.

"What seems to be the problem?" he asked my friend, taking on a concerned tone.

"Ignore him," I offered, wincing as I turned my head. "He's always like this. Have you heard anything about Detective Deckert's condition?"

"Not yet, but we can check on him," he told me.

"We'd appreciate it."

"So how long are we gonna sit here?" Ben interjected.

"We're getting ready to transport you both to the hospital in just a few minutes," he told us.

"Guess I'd better call Felicity," I said aloud.

"Sucks to be you," Ben told me.

"Thanks," I gave him a sarcastic retort as I sent my right hand toward my coat pocket only to realize that I no longer had one. "Dammit! My cell phone was in my coat. Do you still have yours?"

"Yeah," he said as he nodded at me. "I think so. Lemme see…"

He began to gingerly slip his gauze-wrapped hand into his own coat pocket while looking over at the paramedic who was making some notes on a clipboard. "So what's the holdup?"

"The police are doing a little crowd control right now," he answered without looking up.

"Crowd?" I asked.

"Well, not really a crowd," he explained. "But we got a few onlookers, and one of them has a vehicle blocking the street."

"Roads gettin' that bad?" Ben asked.

"Yes and no," he answered, holding his hand out and giving a little side to side wiggle. "This guy's got a big van, and he's having a little trouble turning it around."

"How hard can that be?" Ben spat. "What's he like a moron or something?"

"Ben!" I admonished.

"He seemed like a nice enough guy," the paramedic shrugged. "A little weird, but hey, live and let live."

"Weird how?" Ben asked.

"You know," he returned. "One of those religious types. When I walked by, he was saying something about the Lord and consuming a fire or something like that."

The combination of words caused a twinge in my brain, so I mentally sifted through the various Bible verses I'd committed to memory over the years.

"Was it something like, 'For the Lord thy God is a consuming fire, even a jealous God,'" I said aloud. My words were slow and even. A slight note of fear rode in the crest of my voice as I finished.

"Yeah, that was it," the paramedic confirmed.

I looked across the aisle at Ben. "Deuteronomy four, twenty-four."

My friend was already rising as he spoke, "Tell me this asshole isn't tall with white hair."

"Yeah." He was nodding vigorously. "Did you see him out there or something?"

"You stay here, Rowan," Ben ordered as he started to push past the paramedic.

"Detective Storm, I think you should..." he began to object.

"Save it," Ben shot back.

I spoke up. "Ben, you're in no shape to do this."

He had already eased the ambulance door open and was peering out the narrow gap.

"Goddamit," he muttered. "I can't see 'im. You got a radio?"

"No, sorry," the paramedic answered.

"Shit!" Ben spat again and then turned to him. "Okay. Get out there and tell the first coppers you see to stop that van. Tell 'em it's on my authority and that there might be an armed suspect in the vehicle. Got me?"

"Yeah, but what's going on?"

"I ain't got time to explain it," my friend returned with an impatient bite in his voice. "Now get out there and do what I told you to do."

The paramedic didn't argue, and Ben pressed himself back against the built-in cabinets of equipment and supplies to make room for him to exit. Ben caught the door with his hand and continued to hold it slightly open so he could watch what was happening.

"Do you really think that it's Porter?" I asked.

I had already stood up and moved over next to him, but I couldn't get any kind of a vantage point where I could see anything more than a small sliver of the street and the house next door to the one from which we'd escaped.

"Somebody torched that house while we were in it, Row," he offered. "The door at the top of the stairs was blocked by somethin', I'm sure of it. And besides, the friggin' place went up too quick. Way too quick. My money would be on Porter."

"But if it IS him then that would mean he had to have followed us here from Randy and Nancy's place." I tossed out the observation.

"Yeah, prob'ly," he agreed.

My voice began to ramp up in pitch, audibly noting my panic. "But that would mean he knows where Felicity is…"

"Calm down!" Ben shot back, stopping me before I could implode. "Mandalay is with Felicity. She's safe. Besides, if the fucker followed us here then he's obviously leavin' her alone and comin' after you."

His logic headed off my sudden run toward hysteria and brought me back down to a controlled level of fear. I took a deep breath and let it out slowly. "Okay. You're right."

"There they go," he muttered as he pushed the door open a few more inches and cocked his head to the side.

I winced as a sharp pain burrowed into my shoulder and culminated in a grating ache throughout the joint. It felt something akin to a knife blade—or perhaps an ice pick—being thrust directly into the bone.

"It's him," I said aloud.

Ben glanced back at me, "*Twilight Zone?*"

I nodded. "Yeah. *Twilight Zone*. It's him."

His lips formed a grim frown; he nodded at me and then looked back out the gap in the door. "Jeezus H. Christ!" he exclaimed almost immediately, slamming the door completely open and leaping out the back of the vehicle. "Stay here!"

I could hear the roar of an engine being gunned as I followed Ben out the opening, completely ignoring his command. My brain was beginning to adjust to my uncorrected vision, and while detail was still muddy, I could easily make out the white panel van as it backed toward us with a quick lurch. The rear corner of the vehicle slammed hard into the police cruiser that was sitting diagonally in the center of the street no more than forty feet away from us. The high-pitched tone of metal deeply creasing blended with the hard sound of the crash and the hailstorm rattle of broken glass as it spilled onto the street from the car's headlight.

Out of reflex I jumped backward as the patrol vehicle moved several feet toward us and rocked up at one corner. Toward the front of the sedan, a uniformed officer lay in a heap on the slush-covered pavement as if thoughtlessly tossed aside. I could only assume that he had been hit by the van and that was what had prompted Ben to reveal his presence.

The familiar sound of a handgun popping nearby combined with the simultaneous metallic thump of the rounds impacting the side of the panel van. The handful of onlookers who had gathered on the perimeter were now screaming and scattering from the scene. The firefighters and paramedics in the immediate area ducked for cover near rescue vehicles.

The driver's side of the large van was angled toward me, and I stood there mesmerized by sudden slow motion that affected the scene. I could hear my own measured breathing echoing in my ears as the cacophony surrounding me became a muted background roar. There was a tingle in the back of my head, and my face felt hot and flushed. I looked up from the prone officer and turned my head to stare coldly at the open sliding door on the cab of the van. I didn't need my glasses to recognize the face staring back at me nor to see the hatred burning in his eyes.

The underlying roar rose in volume and was lacerated by the high-pitched grind of manual transmission gears as the extended moment fast-forwarded into real time. I heard Ben screaming my name as he crossed in front of me and pushed me back toward the waiting door of the ambulance. The wrenching groan of metal tearing apart scraped through the air once more.

I stumbled and slid on the icy pavement, catching the door to steady myself as I continued to watch the action play out. The van was already moving forward as Ben's arm whipped up from underneath his coat, his bandaged hand wrapped around his Beretta. Eldon Porter was still glaring at us from the open door of the vehicle, and I stared back with morbid fascination as my friend took aim.

An ye harm none. The snippet of the Wiccan Rede passed through my mind as I watched. It was the simplest of instructions and a covenant by which I endeavored to live my life. But now, it was something I was unable to embrace. I wanted Eldon Porter to be dead. I wanted Ben to empty his handgun into the bastard just as he had done with the lock on the basement door. I wanted him eradicated from existence, and the hatred I felt for him burned inside me hotter with each passing second.

From where I stood, the shot was clear. Ben was even closer. I started to breathe a heavy sigh of relief because I knew that at this distance my friend could not miss. It was all about to be over. The nightmare was coming to an end.

I jerked my head quickly to the right as several shots sounded from the opposite side. I saw the uninjured Wood Dell officer firing once again into the panel van as it lurched forward, allowing the patrol car to drop back down on the front corner.

I heard an almost anguished expletive to my left and whipped my gaze back. When my eyes fell on Ben, he was standing there slapping a fresh magazine into his weapon and jacking the slide back without having fired a single round.

I screamed, "What happened?!"

The tires on the panel van had bit through the slush and were now making a wet squeal against the pavement as the vehicle sped away.

"Goddammit!" my friend exclaimed once again, as he centered the muzzle of his weapon on the van and tracked it. However, the immediate opportunity for a clear shot had passed as it was already rounding the corner. "Goddammit!"

He lowered the handgun and then slipped it back into the shoulder rig as he turned. "Empty!" he shouted. "I never fuckin' reloaded after we got out of the basement!" His face was contorted in a painful mask of self-loathing.

I didn't blame him for what had happened, but I was infuriated. Porter was getting away, and we had missed a prime opportunity to stop him.

"Jeezus, I don't believe this!" my friend screamed as he ran toward the disabled police cruiser.

I released my grip on the ambulance door and chased after him, dodging a paramedic who was racing for the downed officer. I fought for steady footing on the grey slop that covered the street and slipped several times before making it the thirty-odd feet to where he was standing. He had cranked the passenger door open on the patrol car and was speaking into the microphone of the police radio.

I listened as he identified himself and then began describing the van. The last thing I heard him tell the dispatcher was the direction the vehicle had been headed and the street on which it was traveling.

I didn't hear anything else because I was lying on my side in the icy slush with the metallic tang of electricity coating my tongue and my body tensed in a violent seizure.

CHAPTER 19:

*I*t's dark.

It's cold.

I try to move, and then I remember that I cannot.

How long have I been here? I can't remember. It seems like forever. A day? A week? A month?

I'm confused.

I'm trying to think. Where am I?

Where am I? Hell, who am I?

My head hurts. My whole body aches.

Fear grips me, and I don't know why.

What is it?

Why am I afraid?

The feeling passes, and I just forget. It seems easier than trying to remember. It doesn't hurt as much.

I'm uncomfortable sitting here.

I try to move again.

That's right, I can't move. I wonder why.

My hands wriggle, but when they do, my wrists hurt. They are sore.

I can move my feet. Not much, just a little. My ankles hurt just like my wrists.

I hear water splash, and I can feel it on my feet.

Why are my feet in water?

Good question. Where am I again?

I listen.

It is quiet here in the dark.

Almost too quiet.

I don't like it.

I wait.

I listen.

Footsteps.

I hear footsteps. Heavy. Deliberate.

I keep listening and try to remember who I am.

T...

Tee?...

Tuh?...

Tay?...

Two?...

Two times two is four.

Two times three is six.

Two times four is twelve.

Twelve?

That's right, isn't it?

Two times four is twelve.

Two times twelve is sixteen.

Sixteen?

I'll start over. Two times two is eleven.

No, that's not right.

What was I trying to remember?

I give up.

My mouth tastes funny. Metal. Weird. Hmph. I can remember what metal is, why can't I remember what time it is?

It sure is dark.

There's that sound again. It's like a motor running. I wonder what it is?

Fear.

Cold terror.

Muted sirens were warbling in a frantic bid for attention, and they were filtering into my ears. I was cold, and I felt myself physically shiver. I was laying flat on my back, and there was something resembling a thin layer of permeable warmth draped over me. It felt like it might be a blanket, but it definitely wasn't the one I had on my bed at home.

So if I wasn't at home in my bed, I guess that ruled out this whole day being a nightmare.

My shirt felt damp along my right side and across my shoulders. My pants weren't much better. The chill seemed to seep in deeper and even drop a few degrees lower in the places where the wet clothing touched my skin.

I twitched and felt a fork of pain spread from one end of my body to the other. My head was pounding. My shoulder was aching. My knees hurt. My face was sore… And, it didn't stop there. I finally gave up on taking inventory once the individually identifiable aches and pains advanced past ten.

A familiar metallic tang had parked itself somewhere in the region of the back of my tongue. On the front half, my taste buds were being assaulted by the unmistakable woody flavor of a tongue depressor. All of it was underscored by the salty taste of blood.

Quiet voices and the crackle of a two-way radio eased in beneath the sirens, and an occasional thump or bump would fill in the gaps. There was an overwhelming sense of motion vibrating through my prone body, and I decided that I must be in the back of an ambulance. It was a new experience for me, and I had nothing to compare it to, but it seemed logical considering the sensory input I was working with.

I heard myself groan and then felt my stomach turn a quick flip as my body pitched to the side. At first, I thought I was going to fall, but then I felt myself pressed against straps that crossed my chest and legs. My muscles tensed anyway, and I paid the price as my various aches snapped to attention, letting me know beyond any doubt that they were still intact and intent on continuing to produce the agony for which they were conceived.

I groaned again.

"You awake, Row?" I heard Ben's gravelly voice over the mélange of sounds bouncing around the inside of the vehicle.

I started out by slowly opening one eye and rolling it around until I found his face. Then I opened the other and gained at least some sense of depth perception. I focused in and just stared back at him mutely.

My friend looked pretty much as he had when I'd last looked at him. Soot streaked and well worn. He peered back at me with a tired expression. "You gotta stop this shit, white man," he told me.

"What?" I croaked, my voice just as raw as his.

"Floppin' around like a fish outta water," he said.

"Yeah," I agreed softly. "I think you're right."

"Was it one of those outta body things?"

"Yeah."

"Just checkin'. You weren't sure last time."

"I'm pretty sure this time."

"Get anything from it?"

"Bad taste in my mouth," I replied.

"I would too."

I didn't bother to explain that my comment wasn't intended as a metaphor.

"Mister Gant?" A different voice called my name.

"Yeah?" I grunted. "Who wants to know?"

"Mister Gant, my name is Rick," the voice returned. A pair of surgical-glove-sheathed hands came into view and were followed by the face of a paramedic. "How are you feeling?"

"Are you serious?" I asked.

"Are you having any trouble breathing?" he continued, ignoring my sardonic query.

"No," I returned.

He adjusted a plastic tube beneath my nose then stole a glance at his watch. After a few seconds, I realized that he had taken hold of my wrist. Once he finished taking my pulse, he scribbled something on a clipboard. "Try to relax Mister Gant. We're only about seven minutes out."

"Yeah, sure," I answered.

I rolled my head slowly to the side and brought my eyes back to Ben. He was sitting on the bench across from the gurney, still holding his bandaged hands limply in his lap. He had leaned back against the wall and had his eyes closed. His chin was tilted up, and his jaw was set tight. I watched as he reflexively reached up with his right hand and started to smooth his hair back then winced before dropping the appendage back down. He let out a heavy sigh and frowned even harder.

"Porter got away, didn't he." I finally made the matter-of-fact statement.

"Yeah," my friend answered dully. "Yeah, he got away."

"Any leads?" I asked.

He shook his head slowly and then opened his eyes as he lowered his chin and looked over at me. "He dumped the van five blocks away. They're doing a house to house, and they brought in a canine unit, but nothing yet."

"He's not stupid," I offered. "He had an escape plan this time around."

"Yeah, I know."

"What about the officer he hit?"

"Broken arm and prob'ly a concussion. Looks like he's gonna be okay."

"Good."

"Asshole wants you in a bad way, Row. And he doesn't care who gets hurt in the process. Not this time."

"Yeah," I muttered.

It was bad enough that I had to live my life under a rock because of a demented killer, but everyone around me now seemed to be at risk. Pagan or not. It definitely was not a good feeling.

"Any word yet on Carl?" I asked.

His voice had a distant quality when he answered. "No. Not yet."

"Sometimes feelings can be wrong, Ben," I offered.

"Let's hope you're right."

"We'll be at the hospital in just about five minutes," Rick offered as a lull fell into the halting conversation.

"I never did call Felicity," I lamented.

"I called 'er," Ben told me.

"What did she say?"

"You don't wanna know."

"Is she mad?"

"You wanna think about that question and ask it again?"

"Stupid question, huh," I grunted.

"You said it, not me, but yeah, stupid question," he returned. "Gotta give her credit though, she seemed like she stayed pretty calm considerin'."

"That's a plus."

"Yeah, I guess, but she didn't sound too good, white man."

"What do you mean?"

He shook his head. "She just didn't sound good, that's all."

"Is there something you're not telling me?" I pressed.

I waited, but he didn't answer.

I moved on to the next question. "So can you get someone to pick her up?"

"Mandalay's already bringin' her," he offered. "The way Constance drives they're probably already there."

I tried to chuckle and it hurt. I winced, then coughed, and then winced again.

"What're ya' laughin' at this time?" Ben asked.

"You talking about Mandalay's driving," I told him as I forced myself to relax in an attempt to deal with the aches. "Which one are you, the pot or the kettle?"

"Gimme a break." He rolled his eyes and then sat quiet for a moment before taking on a serious tone once again. "So listen, Kemosabe, I need to talk to you about somethin'."

"I'm sorry," I told him. "I didn't mean to insult your driving."

"Not that." He scrunched his face and waved a gauze-covered hand at me. "I think we need to get you and Felicity outta town for a while."

"You mean you think I should run from this," I said.

"The wingnut's on a mission, Row," he returned. "I think it would be the best way to go. Not just for you but for Felicity and everyone else too."

I was chagrined. "So, it's more like you want to get me out of the way before someone else gets hurt."

"Yeah," he admitted. "Maybe. I guess that's part of it. But mostly it's for you and Firehair."

"What aren't you telling me, Ben?" I asked.

"Man…" he let his voice trail off for a moment. "Row,… Jeez… Listen to me, Felicity's with Mandalay so she's safe, okay?"

I couldn't keep the sharpness out of my voice. "Tell me what's going on Ben."

"The S.O.B. had already called Felicity's cell phone when I got ahold of her. He told her you were dead and that she was next."

CHAPTER 20:

I suppose it was a good thing that I had been strapped to the gurney. Not that anyone in the immediate vicinity was in any physical danger from me, of course, especially considering the shape I was in; but what my friend had said produced a result similar to that of mixing fire and gunpowder.

By the time it was all said and done, I couldn't begin to remember everything I had said—or to be more accurate—screamed. What I could recall were several targeted expletives and a devout promise that I would kill Eldon Porter as soon as I had the chance. My rant lasted from its inception in the back of the ambulance, through the lobby of Emergency, and right on into the treatment room. It had finally taken the threat of sedation to get me to calm down.

In reality, all the threat did was get me to shut up, because calm I definitely was not.

"Jeezusaychchrist!" Ben made the exclamation in an almost monosyllabic burst as he jerked away from the doctor who was treating him. "Do ya' think you stuck that damn thing in there far enough?!"

My friend had not allowed himself to be separated from me. He insisted that we be treated in the same room and had staunchly refused to have his sidearm secured anywhere other than within his immediate reach. As long as Porter was loose, he didn't plan to take any chances, and he was less than trusting of the hospital's security staff. In fact, he publicly referred to them as rent-a-cops, and he didn't mean it in a good way. Not that it was any great consolation, but so far, he hadn't been doing any better at making friends than me.

He was currently sitting in a chair with his hand resting on a small, wheeled table. The doctor was seated across from him and peering at the appendage through a magnifying lamp while working with a pair of tweezers. Fortunately, for Ben, those were the least dangerous looking of the stainless steel implements he had laid out on the side. Of course, that is probably one of the reasons that until his most recent exclamation, Ben had kept his eyes focused on the door instead of the procedure in front of him.

I was sitting on the end of the examination table watching the pair with only passing interest. Truth be told, I wasn't really paying that much attention. I was still stewing about Porter's call to my wife, and my brain was splitting its time between formulating a plan for revenge and processing the sensory input. Neither one seemed to be winning out, and all I was truly accomplishing was making my headache worse.

Just in case that wasn't enough to deal with, for some reason there was a song playing in the back of my head, and I was having a hell of a time attaching a name to it. I knew I'd heard it before, but the title, artist, and everything else was escaping me.

I thought for a moment that if I gave up trying to place it then it would probably come to me. That's how things always seemed to work. Unfortunately, the more I thought about not thinking about it, the more I dwelled on it. Once again, a prime example of how things always seemed to work.

I staved off another twinge of pain from somewhere around the back of my grey matter and decided to ignore the tune. For the moment, paying closer attention to the goings on before me seemed the most logical way to do so.

I watched as the intern regarded the industrial-sized Native American in front of him with an exhausted gaze and then took hold of his hand once again. "Detective Storm," he stated. "You are the one who refused to have a local anesthetic. Perhaps you would like one now?"

"I already said no," Ben answered.

"Then I suggest you find a way to deal with it."

"I don't like needles," my friend muttered.

"Not many people do," he returned. "But it would hurt a lot less if you had the local."

"No."

"Fine, if that is your choice. However, you are going to have to stop flinching. You still have some metal fragments in your hand, and we need to get them out."

"Well don't you think you can be a little gentler or somethin'? I mean do you have to dig around like that?"

"Detective," the intern began, clearly at the limit of his patience. "I don't tell you how to do your job, please refrain from telling me how to do mine."

Personally, I thought the doctor was handling the situation well considering that this outburst had made something on the order of the fifth time Ben had jerked his hand away—and, that's not to mention that he hadn't shut up either.

During their exchange, the door had swung open, and a nurse entered, armed with some fresh gauze and washcloths. She had been assisting with both of us earlier, and she now set about cleaning the area surrounding the wound on my cheek. I simply tilted my head to the side without a word, shifting my gaze between her and the floorshow. I couldn't help but notice that she wore a bemused expression as my friend bickered with the intern behind her.

"So much for bedside manner," Ben huffed. "Freakin' Marcus Welby you ain't."

"Marcus who?" the intern asked in an absent tone.

My friend raised an eyebrow and cocked his chin down as he stared at the doctor. "How old are you?"

"I don't really think that has any bearing on your treatment, Detective."

"Doctor Drew may be young," the nurse offered aloud without looking away from her task at hand, "but he knows what he is doing, Detective Storm."

Ben glanced over at the back of her head and then returned his gaze to the doctor. "You really don't know who Marcus Welby is?"

"No, I don't," he replied.

"Jeez. What's this world comin' to?"

"You said it yourself earlier, Ben," I offered in a flat tone, speaking for the first time since I'd been threatened with a hypodermic full of sedative. "We're getting old."

"Yeah, well, old is one thing," he agreed, "but that's no excuse for…"

The repetitive electronic refrain of his cell phone interrupted him, and he reached around to his belt with his free hand. He fumbled for a moment since the appendage was securely wrapped in fresh gauze but managed to grasp the small device. As he brought it up, he gestured at me and then to the intern with the stubby antenna while it continued to trill. "It's no excuse for him not knowin' who Marcus Welby is." He finished the admonishment then thumbed the phone to life and put it to his ear. "Yeah, Storm here."

"Is he always like this?" the nurse asked in a quiet voice as she swabbed my cheek with cold antiseptic. A light, southern lilt underscored her words.

I grimaced as the sting set in and tried not to flinch then shifted my eyes over to her. "Pretty much. Don't let it bother you though. He's really a good guy."

My own voice still sounded rough, and its tone remained emotionless and tired. I realized when I heard myself that I didn't sound particularly convincing.

"I'll have to take your word for it, Mister Gant," she returned with a smile.

"No, really, he is." I tried to sound more sincere. "And please call me Rowan. Every time I hear 'Mister Gant' I think my father is here."

She chuckled. "All right then, Rowan. You can call me Dorothy. I am afraid, however, that I will still have to take your word for it on Detective Storm."

"He grows on you," I offered.

She pressed something to my cheek that I later discovered was a butterfly closure and then inspected it closely. "There. All done."

"Thanks."

"No problem," she told me. "Doctor Kirkman will be back in shortly. He wanted to go over a few things with you."

"That's fine," I said then shifted to look at her. "Oh, my wife is supposed to be here."

She nodded. "Detective Storm told us. Someone will bring her back as soon as she arrives."

"Thank you." I tried to inject some enthusiasm into my still flat voice. "I really appreciate it. And there's just one more thing."

"Certainly," she said as she cocked her head to the side and gave me a questioning look.

"Another officer was brought in ahead of us. Deckert, Carl Deckert. We've been trying to get an idea of his condition for a while."

She nodded. "I'll see if I can find out something for you."

"Thank you," I told her again.

"You're welcome." She flashed me a quick grin and nodded in Ben's direction while turning to go. "You know, maybe you can teach some manners to your friend over there."

"I heard that!" Ben called after her as she exited the treatment room, but she was already gone.

My friend looked back over at me and shook his head. "Jeez."

I gave him a tired shrug in return.

"So, was that Allison?" I asked as I dipped my head at the cell phone in his hand, referring to his wife.

"What? Oh, no." He shook his head and clipped the device back onto his belt. "It was Ackman callin' to give me an update."

"Good news?" I asked hopefully.

"Not really," he returned. "Still haven't found Porter. The weather's not helpin', and it's gonna be dark in a few hours."

"Is it really that late?" I asked as I pulled my hand up to look at my watch, only to remember that it was broken when I saw the shattered face. I don't know why I hadn't just taken it off. I glanced around the room and found the face of the wall clock. It was fuzzy, but it was large enough for me to be able to read it without squinting too much. The position of the hands told me it was just past two p.m. This time of the year the sun was gone by five.

"You didn't sleep last night, did you?" Ben answered me with his own query.

I closed my eyes and massaged my forehead for a moment, then carefully laid myself back on the examination table. "No. Not much anyway."

The tune was moving itself back into the forefront, and its eerie chords sent a fearful shiver racing up and down my spine. Each note seemed to carry with it a tiny pinprick of terror that grew exponentially as the melody wove itself through the even rhythm.

"How long you been up?" His voice sounded hollow and distant.

I did a protracted mental calculation that should have taken no more than a second or two then finally answered. "Pushing twenty-four at least, I think."

"Jeezus, white man."

"He's got nothing to do with it," I mumbled.

"Who?"

"Jesus." This time my voice was almost a whisper.

The song was all but completely filling my ears now and sounding creepier by the second. If it were not for the level of exhaustion I was battling, I think I might have been overcome by the intangible fear. At the moment, even my earlier anger was falling by the wayside, and darkness was becoming a comfortable blanket. The fatigue broke through my defenses and began to batter me with its weapon of choice—sleep. I made a half-hearted attempt at fighting back but quickly found that I was hopelessly outmatched. With a final, heavy sigh, I surrendered.

The beginnings of a distant echo came from the other side of the room. "Dammit, Rowan, you know what I…"

I didn't hear the rest.

CHAPTER 21:

The only thing I really remembered about the trip home was that it was dark and that the back seat of the car was cold. Prior to that, there were some dreamlike recollections of unintelligible voices, a feeling like I was sitting up and floating down a long hallway, some fuzzy streaks of white passing through muted light, and of course, that damnable song playing in an endless loop between my ears.

It was still echoing there even now.

With more effort than I expected it to take, I let out a heavy sigh and tried to relax. After failing at that task, I reached down and reluctantly shut off the water in the shower. Then, I just stood there for what seemed like a good half hour. In reality, I think it was more like five minutes. The steam was dissipating quickly and water was dripping from my tortured skin. I tingled with a self-inflicted rawness on my face, neck, hands, and forearms where I had scrubbed to remove the soot and grime left over from the fire. I was still afflicted with a cough that would attack me without warning, but at least the episodes were becoming fewer and farther between. The doctor had told me it was an after effect of the smoke inhalation and that it would most likely work itself out in a day or two; as far as I was concerned, the quicker the better.

For a moment, I considered turning the water back on and just continuing to stand there motionless as I had for the last third of the shower. The warmth felt good, and it went a long way toward soothing the aches and pains that were once more answering a roll call throughout my body.

I started to reach for the chromed knob but hesitated as I heard the door open and then close, followed by Felicity's concerned voice. "Row, are you okay?"

I'd been in here for close to an hour, and she had already checked on me twice before now. Three was the charm I suppose.

"Yeah," I replied in a lazy voice as I reached up and slowly slid the shower curtain aside. "Yeah, I'm okay."

"I'm making you some tea, then," she told me, leaning her back against the door as she spoke. "Are you hungry?"

I had actually been expecting her to break out the verbal cat 'o nine tails on me over everything that had happened, or at the very least give me her particular brand of silent treatment. I knew that she was angry, but thus far, she had not shown that side. In fact, she had not even displayed any visible distress over the call from Porter. What was happening instead was that I was on the receiving end of her maternal instinct, which had evidently locked into overdrive.

"Not really," I shook my head.

Actually, I was, but my tongue was sore, and I didn't feel up to dealing with any additional pains that I might be able to avoid.

I watched my wife's expression and decided that she was simply doing a good job of hiding the fear that I knew she had to be feeling. I was just too far out of it right now to pick it up on an extrasensory level. Moreover, as to the subject of her wrath, I was sure it would be coming at some point. There was no doubt in my mind about that. Based on what I had seen staring back at me from the mirror, my guess was that I just looked so pathetic to her that there was no way she couldn't give me a stay of execution.

"Aye, are you sure?" She gazed back at me with even more concern. "You haven't eaten all day."

"I'm sure." I gave her a shallow nod. "Ben might want something though. You know how he is."

"He's already gone." She shook her head then reached up and pushed a loose strand of auburn curls back behind her ear. "Constance made him go. She's going to stay with us tonight instead."

I started to reach for a towel, and she quickly stepped forward to get it for me.

"That's good," I told her. "He needs some rest too."

"Aye, now." She shook her head and widened her jade green eyes. "Do you really believe that Benjamin Storm will be resting?"

"Probably not." I agreed with what her words implied. We both knew how Ben had a tendency to push himself until he dropped. "Not unless Allison makes him."

"Exactly."

"Maybe she will," I mused.

"We can only hope," Felicity said. "He did say he was going to go home and get cleaned up."

I began drying myself slowly, gently patting at my face with the fresh cotton towel. "Any word on Carl?"

"Aye. Ben said to tell you that the reason you two were having trouble finding out anything is that Carl was taken to a different hospital. He's in the cardiac care unit at Christian. He's stable at the moment and they're planning to run some tests in the morning."

"So he's going to be okay?"

"I hope so." She shrugged. "I'm afraid that's all they would tell him."

I nodded. "Okay. At least he's all right for now."

The multi-toned harmonica whistle of a Chantal teakettle started low and rose in volume on the other side of the door. Felicity wasn't a big fan of microwaves when it came to making tea, or much else for that matter, so the kettle was one of the few cooking implements we had brought along with us. Since the bathroom in this apartment backed up against the kitchenette, even with the door closed, the not-quite-harmonious chord was loud.

My wife stepped back toward the door and allowed her fingers to rest on the lever-like handle. "I found your spare glasses and put them on the dresser in the bedroom... And I laid out some fresh clothes for you on the bed. Are you sure there's nothing else I can get for you?"

"I'm sure, honey," I told her. "Thanks. I'll be out in a few minutes."

She opened the door and started through, then stopped and looked back at me with what could have been sadness in her eyes; or perhaps it was relief, I wasn't exactly sure. "I love you, Rowan Linden Gant. You know that, don't you?"

"Yeah, honey, I know. Same here."

"Feeling better?" Special Agent Constance Mandalay asked, looking up from her coffee as I trudged into the room and eased myself into a chair.

Mandalay was petite and wore her brunette hair in a stylish, shoulder-length crop. Still in her late twenties, on the surface she appeared to be just a fresh-faced youngster. She looked as though she would be right at home on any college campus, chasing after a handful of letters to park behind her name, or waving pom-poms and cheering the home team on to victory. Descriptors such as pretty, cute, and perky immediately leapt to mind in conjunction with the young woman.

To me, her youthful countenance sometimes made it hard to believe that she already possessed a law degree from Cornell and had joined the FBI right out of school. However, I knew all too well that beneath the façade there was a hard-nosed femme fatale packing a forty-caliber Sig Sauer along with the finely honed skill to use it.

"Yeah," I answered her. "About as much as I can at the moment."

"That's good, because you look like hell," she offered with a sweet smile.

"Thanks, Constance," I returned with an amused grin. "Nice to see you too."

We had first been introduced to Agent Mandalay when she had exerted her federally bestowed authority to assume the helm of an investigation Ben had been leading. The initial contact between the two of them had been just short of explosive; as for me, well, I was on the top of her list from the get-go. I'm not talking about the good list either. The adversarial interaction between us all had continued right through to the very end of that case.

Fortunately, various events from the investigation—negative though they were at the time—served to enlighten her as to my usefulness as a consultant even if my methods tended to run perpendicular to the established norm.

Since that time, our relationship had grown beyond the boundaries of work. In fact, we had all actually become very good friends. Even Ben, who regarded the FBI with great disdain, habitually calling them "Feebs," and vocally lamenting their involvement in any investigation he was connected with, had come to treat her like any other cop.

"Here you go," Felicity said as she set a large ceramic mug in front of me. "Drink it all, and I don't want to hear any complaints about the taste."

I slowly waved my hand in a circular motion over the top of the mug, wafting the steamy aroma upward to my face. I still had the smell of burning wood and plastics embedded in my nose, but I was able to pick up a few recognizable odors from the pungent brew.

"Willow bark... Ummm... Valerian root... And something else," I offered aloud. "I'm not sure what."

"Chamomile," Felicity returned.

I easily recognized the analgesic and calmative properties of the herbs that comprised the tea. "I'm already tired, sweetheart," I told her. "You don't really need to sedate me, you know."

"Aye, I'll be the judge of that now," she replied. "I've some honey if you want a spoonful or two to mask the taste."

"No, that's okay."

"You're sure, then?"

"Felicity, please." I shook my head. "You've got to be exhausted yourself. Sit down. Relax."

"I will in a minute," she answered. "I need to put a fresh pot of coffee on for Constance."

"Don't worry about that, Felicity, I can do it," Mandalay offered, starting up from her seat.

"You sit down, then," Felicity instructed her. "I'll see to it."

"Her maternal instinct gland is stuck in the on position," I said to Mandalay as an offer of explanation. "She gets like this sometimes."

"I can hear you, Rowan," my wife called back from the kitchenette behind me. "Shut up and drink your tea."

I arched an eyebrow at Constance and silently mouthed, "See what I mean?" Then I raised my cup and took a small sip. The tea was still too hot for me, considering the condition of my tongue after the two seizures. I blew on it for a moment then set the mug back on the table to let it cool.

"So, how did you get elected to be babysitter tonight?" I asked.

"I volunteered, actually," Mandalay replied. "After I got a look at Storm, it seemed like the thing to do."

"What about our Coven? Porter might go after one of them again."

She shook her head as she reassured me. "Don't worry. All taken care of. Between federal agents and local police, there's no way he can get to any of them."

"You're sure?"

"Trust me, Rowan. It's covered."

"Okay," I said. "It's just that... Well, what with Randy and all..."

"Don't worry, I understand. It's okay."

"Well, I want you to know that I appreciate it. Especially you staying with us."

"It's not a problem, Rowan," she shrugged as she spoke. "It's my job."

"Maybe so, but after today..." I hesitated for a moment, feeling awkward at voicing my weakness to her. "After today, I think I'll sleep better knowing that you're here."

We sat in silence for a moment then I spoke again, a hint of embarrassment in my voice, "I guess that sounded pretty corny, huh?"

She shook her head. "No."

I tilted my head down and looked back at her over the rim of my glasses for effect. "This is me here, Constance."

"Okay, yeah," she smiled. "It sounded corny, but I know what you mean."

"Well thanks for not laughing."

The telephone on the wall in the small kitchen trilled, and I slid my chair back.

"I'm laughing on the inside," Mandalay replied with a smile.

"Yeah, I figured as much."

Felicity called out to me as I stood up. "Stay put, Rowan, I'll get it."

"I'm not an invalid, Felicity," I responded as I turned and reached around the corner, snatching the phone from its cradle just before my wife's hand reached it.

I shot her a tired grin, and she rolled her eyes at me before stepping back to the counter and sliding the freshly rinsed coffeepot into its base.

I tucked the phone up to my ear and said, "Hello?"

There was no formal greeting in return. Just a cold, familiar voice reciting in monotone, "If a man abide not in me, he is cast forth as a branch, and is withered; and men gather them, and cast them into the fire, and they are burned."

CHAPTER 22:

M y face was hot in an instant, and I could literally feel my heartbeat thumping in my ears as I flushed with anger. My first inclination was to explode, lash out as I had done earlier in the day. My emotional reaction bolted from its corner and landed a solid punch on the jaw of logic as the bell sounded. The contest had begun.

Hateful words formed on my lips, and I clenched my teeth to keep them at bay. Blood rushed in my ears as I took a deep breath, searching for a solid ground to which I could attach. The opposing sides of my brain were engaged in an all out brawl with the prize being control of what would come out of my mouth in response to his selected verse.

It all came down to a fight between my overwhelming compulsion to explain to him in minute detail exactly how little regard I held for his life and the need to remain rational. I have to admit that rationality was looking very weak at the moment.

The pause was lethargic, and my mute struggle continued as I simply stood there with the phone pressed against my ear. I was just about to spew a stream of vile adjectives into the mouthpiece when he spoke again.

"I know that you are there, Gant," he said. "I can hear you breathing."

Again, his voice oozed into my skull from the handset. The very sound of it made me feel physically ill, and I swallowed hard to push back the column of bile I felt climbing up my throat.

The mouthful of expletives rammed against the back of my teeth in an attempt to break free, and I drew my lips into a tight line. I started to tense then felt myself connect to the ground I had sought. I don't know how I managed it, but I wasn't about to refuse the link. A calm washed over me, and I let my hot breath out in a slow stream. My logical half rallied and landed its own sucker punch to my emotional side then took over—for the time being, at least.

My first rational thought was to appeal to his sense of morality, as much as it existed within the confines of his malformed psyche. We had already established that he had not exhibited the same restraint regarding the safety of those he perceived as guiltless as he had during his last spree. Still, it was worth a try.

"You almost killed an innocent man today, Eldon." I turned to face Agent Mandalay as I spoke, clenching my fist and concentrating on keeping my voice even.

Her eyes widened as she immediately picked up on the cue. Behind me, I heard Felicity gasp, and I turned quickly, trying my best to paint a reassuring mask onto my face.

"Detective Deckert?" he asked.

"Yes." I held my initial reply to a single syllable lest I lose what little control I was exerting over my temper. Accomplishing that, I forged ahead with an entire mouthful. "Or even Detective Storm for that matter. Neither of them are Witches."

I could hear Mandalay in the background as she pushed away from the table and began whispering into her cell phone.

"Both of them are your friends, aren't they?"

"Yes they are."

Porter actually chuckled at my answer before saying, "Then for you to claim that they are innocent is ridiculous."

"Guilt by association then?"

"Of course," he replied. "If you are not part of the solution, Gant, then you are part of the problem."

"I don't remember that from the Bible, Eldon," I offered.

"But now I have written unto you not to keep company, if any man that is called a brother be a fornicator, or covetous, or an idolater, or a railer, or a drunkard, or an extortioner; with such an one no not to eat." He laid heavy emphasis on the word idolater as he recited the passage.

"You don't think that you are taking that out of context?"

The earpiece chirped once, and the phone went to hollow silence punctuated by distant clicking. I pulled it away from my ear and turned back to Agent Mandalay.

"He hung up," I told her. "Or we got cut off, I don't know which."

"He's on a cell," she told me as she twisted her own away from her mouth. "The signal dropped before they could pinpoint it on the grid."

"Dammit," I spat. "How did he get this number anyway? How did he know where we are?"

"Believe me, Rowan, I'm wondering the same thing myself," she told me. "But don't worry, we'll... What?" She stopped abruptly and twisted her phone back up to her mouth then looked at me and held up a finger. "Hold on a second."

I nodded, then turned back, and dropped the handset back into its cradle on the wall. I looked over at Felicity and saw that her fear had now surfaced and was evident in the form of a hard edge stricken across her soft features. I was just opening my mouth to reassure her when the phone rang again.

I snapped my head around and stared at the device. On the second ring, I picked it up and placed it against my ear without a word.

"I was beginning to think you planned on leaving the phone off the hook all night, Gant," Porter said.

"What happened," I asked with a heavy note of sarcasm. "Did you go through a tunnel?"

"Don't try to play that game with me, Gant. I know you've figured out that I'm on a cell phone. I'm not stupid."

"I didn't say you were, Eldon."

"Then you know that the reason we were cut off is that I hung up. I know how this works."

"So you think you can't be tracked," I spat back. "Good for you."

"You know better than that, Gant," he instructed me. "I know that I am being tracked. I hung up so that Agent Mandalay would at least have a challenge."

I turned to Constance and motioned her over.

"Enough of that, Gant," Porter continued. "Let's get back to our little talk. What I follow is scripture. There is no context, only truth."

"Don't you mean that you are simply being self-serving and ignoring the context?" I contended.

I grabbed a notepad from the countertop and looked frantically for a pen. Coming up empty I glanced over at Constance and snatched one from her breast pocket then scribbled "he knows you are here" on the top sheet and handed it to her. She looked back at me with a surprised expression and then nodded affirmation.

Porter was still talking to me. "...So you see, the ends justify the means."

"That's pretty narrow-minded of you, Eldon," I said. "But then, I don't suppose I should expect much from someone of such a limited scope."

His voice hardened. "I thought we'd established that I'm not stupid. I was expecting something a little more eloquent. Insulting my intelligence is beneath you, Gant."

"What about killing you?" I asked. "Is that beneath me?"

"Why, Gant," he took on a tone of mock surprise. "You sound angry. What happened to your little claim of being good and nature loving? What is it you always say? An ye harm none. You don't sound like you are practicing what you preach."

"I asked you the same thing regarding the commandments of your God," I replied.

"My path is clear." He fired his response back with an audible thread of anger playing through it. "Is yours?"

"Where it concerns you, yes it is."

"And what of YOUR commandment to 'harm none'? Or is that merely another of Satan's tricks?"

"It doesn't apply here."

"So why don't you tell me who's ignoring context now?"

My temper was on the edge of flaring, and I had to pause for a moment before finally answering, "I'm not interested in arguing semantics with you, Eldon."

Once more, the phone chirped and went dead. I shot it a disgusted look then slammed it back onto the cradle before glancing back over to Mandalay.

"He hung up again," I told her.

"He's using multiple cell phones," she explained. "The first call was on the one he used earlier today. They're still tracking the ID on the second one, but it was definitely a different signal."

"Guess he doesn't feel like taping any more pay phones together," I volunteered with a tinge of sarcasm. "This is insane. First Randy and Nancy's number, then Felicity's cell, now here. How is he getting this information?"

"Well, the Harper's number is easy enough to explain," Constance volunteered. "He probably got that one from Randy or something he had on his person. What about your cell, Felicity, is that a published number?"

"Aye, it's on my business cards," Felicity acknowledged from behind me, trepidation thick in her voice.

"Are those readily available to the public?" Mandalay asked.

"Aye," Felicity said. "I'm freelance. Every camera and photo supply store in Saint Louis has a stack of them for referrals."

"So that would explain that," Constance said in a thoughtful tone. "Either he got Felicity's number from a business card or maybe even that came from Randy as well. But, the number here is private and unpublished. There should be no way he could get his hands on it. Did you give it out to anyone?"

I looked back at her then closed my eyes as the obvious answer bludgeoned me with my own stupidity. "Randy," I said quietly. "Randy had it."

"Yeah." She shook her head and frowned. "I'll lay odds that is your answer."

Felicity's tense voice brought us back to the situation at hand. "Do you think he's going to call back?"

"I don't know." I shook my head as I turned. "But it's going to be okay."

"Okay? Rowan, he knows where we are!" she appealed.

I was so accustomed to Felicity's strength that I was taken aback by the growing intensity of her fear. The still fresh horror of the kidnapping and attempted rape had bruised her deeper than either of us had realized, and her façade was beginning to tear away.

I reached for her. She stepped forward and fell into me, burying her face against my shoulder and wrapping her arms tightly around me. Before I could utter a single word, the phone pierced the room with its metallic jangle for attention.

I twisted slightly, keeping one arm securely around my wife and snatched up the telephone with my free hand. I consciously released my temper from its mental prison and began speaking the moment I brought the handset to the side of my head.

"You're really starting to piss me off, Eldon."

"Good," he replied.

"I'm going to hang up now," I spat.

"Before you do, there is something you should know."

"What? That you're a sick, twisted sonofabitch?" I barked. "I already know that."

Instead of the sarcastic reply I expected from him, I heard a thin hissing noise mixed with the sound of a car engine. There was a scratchy, rustling noise followed by what sounded like a faint squeal.

I snarled into the phone again. "What? No comment you sorry ass…"

I stopped short as the squeal repeated, this time sounding far more like a distinct, nasal whine. This time it was followed by a high-pitched whimper.

Bile rose once again in my throat as I fought my stomach's urge to evict anything it might currently contain. Gooseflesh prickled along the back of my neck and terror swelled in my chest. I continued to listen in abject horror as a sobbing, feminine voice choked out two faint words, "Help me."

"Thou shalt not suffer a Witch to live, Gant," Porter's voice issued once again from the earpiece.

"What are you doing, Eldon?" I almost pleaded.

"Her judgment is at hand," he continued speaking as if he hadn't heard me. "Are you willing to be responsible for it?"

"PORTER!" I screamed, but there was nothing more than the hollow sound of the disconnected line to answer me.

I slammed the phone back into the cradle once again. The mechanical bell rattled out a muted ding that was mixed with the bang of plastic against Formica. The excess force caused the device to jump back out and clatter across the counter before bouncing from the floor and swinging pendulum-like from its spiral cord. I didn't bother to pick it up. I just closed my eyes and held Felicity tight.

"What, Row?" she said, her voice muffled as she spoke into my shoulder. "What did he say?"

I couldn't speak. My mind was racing as I tried to move all of the pieces together. There was something vaguely familiar about the woman's voice, and it had now displaced all of the other nagging bothers that were dancing about in my brain.

Agent Mandalay spoke up from across the room. "The second and third calls came from the same phone, but we couldn't pinpoint a grid location before we lost the signal."

"You got a name though, didn't you?"

"What?" Mandalay asked with a faint note of confusion.

"The owner of the cell phone," I explained. "It's a woman, right?"

"Yeah," Her puzzled tone blossomed. "How did you know that?"

"Because he put her on the phone just before he hung up," I told her.

"So she's still alive?" she asked.

"For now."

"Dammit!" she snarled as she began stabbing at the buttons on her cell phone once more.

"What's her name?" I asked.

"Millicent something," she answered, dividing her attentions between dialing the phone and checking her notes. "Millicent Sullivan."

Felicity tensed against me as she heard the name. Pain stabbed into the center of my brain, and I damned myself for being so careless.

"Dear Mother Goddess..." I moaned. "How could I have let this happen?"

"Rowan, what's wrong?" Mandalay asked.

I squeezed Felicity tighter as I felt her begin to tremble.

"Rowan, talk to me," Agent Mandalay pressed again. "Do you know this woman?"

"We know her as Starfyre," I answered quietly. "She's being considered as a dedicant in our Coven."

"But I thought everyone was..."

"They were," I cut her off. "We were still just considering her. She hadn't been taken into the fold yet, so no one would have thought to call her about any of this."

CHAPTER 23:

"So explain to me again why we weren't watchin' this Sullivan woman?" Ben smoothed back his hair and then winced. He pulled his bandaged hand away and then stared at it as if it was the first time he'd ever seen it. I didn't give it long before he did away with the bandages altogether in a fit of frustration.

Apparently, he had only just gotten out of the shower when Mandalay contacted him about Porter's call. Even though she assured him that she had things covered on our end, he insisted on returning immediately. No amount of explanation from her was going to convince him otherwise. Judging from his rumpled appearance, he had probably still been getting dressed on the drive over.

We were assembled in the living room of the small apartment. Ben occupied one end of the sofa and Mandalay the other. Felicity was parked in the chair, cradling a cup of tea between her dainty hands; but me, I couldn't begin to think about sitting. I had too much of an infusion of nervous energy. I was standing at the sliding doors, holding the heavy drapes partially open, and looking out across the snow-covered balcony to the parking lot several floors below.

"She was only a dedicant," I replied without turning.

It had been just slightly over an hour since Porter had called, and my anger was still fresh. My jaw had now added itself to my list of aches due to the fact that I was unconsciously grinding my teeth. I kept catching myself in the act, but I didn't seem to be able to stop. I was still fighting a case of the jitters that was born of the creepy tune looping in the back of my head; so, I wasn't sure if the teeth gnashing was an effect of the anger alone or a combination of rage and anxiety. Whatever the cause, it was beginning to get very old.

"And that means she's like what? A non-person?" He splayed his hands out in a gesture of helplessness.

I shook my head sharply and allowed the drapes to fall closed as I turned. I was frustrated that I had to explain something that I perceived as trivial common knowledge especially in light of my current emotional state. I took a deep breath and huffed it back out, trying to keep in mind that Felicity and I were the only ones in the room familiar with Coven dynamics and order. "I really didn't mean for it to sound like that," I told him. "Basically, a dedicant is someone who has made a conscious choice to study a particular religion, or most often, religious path. What we often refer to as a tradition. They take an oath to study and learn the tradition."

"So it's like making a pledge or a promise. Somethin' like that?"

"Aye, exactly," Felicity chimed in.

"So this isn't something unusual then?" he asked.

"Not within the confines of a Coven, no," she answered again. "Not at all."

"So what you're really sayin' is that she wanted to join your study group?" He simplified my answer as he looked back and forth between us.

"Something like that, I suppose, yes." I nodded. "At any rate, she had approached Cally about joining our Coven some time back. We met with her on a couple of occasions, and we discussed the possibility of her dedicating. What you have to remember is that taking someone into a Coven is not something you do lightly, so we took some time to mull it over. We were actually planning to bring her in at Yule, but she was out of town."

"So she wasn't actually a member of your group yet?"

"No. Not officially." I shook my head. "She would have been brought in at the next Full Moon meeting."

"Well, Porter obviously chose her because of her relationship to you," Mandalay offered. "He didn't just get lucky. How would he have found out about her if she wasn't actually a member?"

"I don't know." I shook my head and shrugged. "My best guess would be Randy, but I can't be sure. It could be that Porter asked him for names when he tortured him. We pretty much know that's how he started compiling his list of victims originally. Or it could be that Randy had her name and some notes in a day planner or a PDA."

"Notes?" Ben asked.

"Established Covens take bringing someone new into the fold very seriously," Felicity offered as explanation.

Ben sighed heavily then brought his other hand up to massage his neck, only to repeat the wince and stunned stare.

"Dammit," he muttered as he shook his wounded mitt and then lowered it back into his lap.

I began to slowly pace. "I blame myself for this," I announced. "I should have considered it as a possibility."

"Aye, I think not," Felicity asserted. "I'm their High Priestess. I am as much at fault as anyone, if not more."

She had regained her composure quickly. Still, I knew by looking at her that it was a defense mechanism. What she had done was nothing more than a temporary patch job on her exterior demeanor. Inside, there was still a swirling ball of gut twisting terror, but she had no intention of letting any more of it show; not in front of Ben and Constance at least.

"Neither one of you is at fault for anything," Mandalay returned. "There was no way you could imagine that Porter would go this route."

"Believe me, Constance." I gave her a quick nod. "I can imagine a lot out of this whack job. I've got scars to prove it."

"Mandalay's right," Ben interjected. "Beating yourselves up about all this isn't doin' either one of ya' any good. Not to mention that it ain't gonna get us anywhere."

"Well, what IS being done?" I asked.

"Right now, there's a CSU team on their way to Sullivan's apartment. Her car is listed on the hot sheet, and every copper on the street is lookin' for it."

"We don't know that he has her car," I objected.

"We don't know that he doesn't," Ben returned. "Look, Row, let us do the cop stuff, it's what we do. Like I've told ya' before, we actually solved a few crimes by ourselves before you came along."

I closed my eyes and put my palms up to my temples, squeezing my head between my hands and roughly massaging at the same time— as if I could will the pain away. "I'm sorry," I muttered. "I don't mean to be arguing with you about this. I'm just kind of at the center of it, and I'd give just about anything to be somewhere else."

"That's understandable," Mandalay said. "You've been through a lot today."

I shook my head. My eyes were still closed, and my fingers were now working at my scalp. "Today is just the beginning," I said aloud. "There's an end coming. I don't know when or where, but I'm not sure I want to."

The moment the words exited my mouth, I felt a wave of dread hit me. If that wasn't enough, I could physically feel my wife's startled gaze instantly burning a hole in my back as I stood there.

"What's that s'posed to mean?" Ben asked.

"I don't know," I answered. "Forget it. I'm just rambling."

"You sure?" he pressed. "That ain't some kinda hocus-pocus la-la land thing you're spoutin' is it?"

Mandalay offered her observation. "Yeah, Rowan, that sounded a little on the morbidly prophetic side, especially coming from you."

"Really. Forget it." I waved a hand at them. "My head is killing me, and I'm just running off at the mouth."

The truth was that I didn't actually know what the comment was supposed to mean. I didn't even know for sure why I had said it. I only knew that there actually was more to it than just idle rambling and that it sounded just as bad to me as it did to them.

"You need to take somethin', Kemosabe?" Ben asked.

"Wouldn't do any good," I sighed. "So anyway, go on. You were telling me what the plan is…"

"CSU, car…" He ticked off what he'd already said. "Keepin' an eye on public places since he seems to have a penchant for exhibiting his kills."

"By then it would be too late," I contended in a flat tone.

"Believe me, Row, we know that," he returned. "But it's somethin' that has to be done."

"We're also watching for the possibility that he might use one of the two cell phones again," Mandalay added to the list. "If he does, we'll be on top of it, and maybe this time we can get a grid location."

"What about me?" I queried.

Ben feigned ignorance. "Whaddaya mean? What about you?"

"Don't play dumb, Ben." My voice once again took on a note of annoyance. "You know damn well what I mean. Porter killed Randy, and now he has Star, and he's going to kill her. You've already said that he's choosing his victims to get to me."

"Yeah, I know where you're headed but don't go there." His tone was adamant.

"What do you mean, 'don't go there?'" I couldn't help but raise my voice a step. "There's no place for me to go, Ben. He's bringing it to my doorstep!"

He addressed me with deadpan seriousness in his voice and a hard expression forming across his features. "Listen, Rowan, I'll be honest with you, Albright already said something about this."

"Screw Albright," I spat. "If she wants to ban me from something else, tell her to go ahead."

"No, you don't get it," he snarled. "She's all about using you for bait."

"Will wonders never cease," I said, injecting the words with as much sarcasm as I could muster. "She and I finally agree on something."

"Rowan! No!" Felicity yelped.

Out of the corner of my eye, I caught the startled expression on her face, and as I turned to look at her, she slowly stood.

"I can't let him kill Star," I told her as if the conclusion was obvious.

"Aye, I won't allow it," she proclaimed.

Ben glanced her way then back at me as he spoke. "Well don't worry, Felicity, cause it ain't gonna happen."

"Why?" I demanded.

"Because it's not how we do things, Rowan. This isn't a cop show. We don't use civilians as bait for crazed serial killers."

"Yeah, well maybe it's time to change your rules."

"I can't listen to this," Felicity blurted with a mixture of both fear and anger in her voice.

I looked over at her, and she was trembling. She stared at me with her eyes glistening, and I knew there were tears behind them begging to be released. I took a step toward her, and as I reached out to touch her, she backed away and sidestepped. I stopped, immediately feeling the torment that now afflicted her. She put her hand to her mouth and then shook her head again. With that, she turned and disappeared down the short hallway and into the bedroom.

The door made a dull sound as it slammed.

"Jeezus, white man." Ben shook his head.

"You should probably go talk to her," Mandalay offered softly.

I was torn between running after her and pleading my case. Choosing between the woman I loved more than my own existence and the life of someone I barely knew was the last thing I needed at the moment. I mutely pled for guidance from The Ancients and met only with silence.

I started toward the bedroom door and hesitated. I felt damned no matter which direction I went. I took another step then turned and stared at Ben.

"Listen, apparently the whole idea isn't out of the question or Albright wouldn't have brought it up," I finally countered.

"Why the hell do you think she was all over your ass back at the morgue, Rowan?" He stood there looking at me with his eyes wide and questioning.

"Because she doesn't like me?" I answered.

"Exactly. And because she doesn't like you, she was trying to get you worked up so you'd do somethin' stupid, Row."

"I thought we'd already established that."

"I mean as in stupid like going after Porter. She wants to let you throw yourself out there as bait, and if you get killed in the process, oh fuckin' well, too bad so sad."

The revelation struck home, knocked me down, then kicked me a few times just for good measure. I stood there mute, wondering how I could have been so totally oblivious to her intentions.

"Am I that stupid?" I finally asked, an uneasy calm in my voice. "Have you known this all along?"

"No." He shook his head. "Don't feel like the Lone Ranger, I didn't catch it either. I just found out on the way over here."

"How?"

"A call from one of the coppers on the case," he answered. "He overheard a phone conversation she had, and he thought I should know."

"Recklessly endangering a civilian on purpose?" Mandalay sounded incredulous when she asked the question. "Have you gone to IAD about this?"

"That'll be my next move." Ben nodded. "But I want to make sure I can count on my source and get something a little more concrete before I make an accusation like that. Right now it's just hearsay, plus there's someone else involved, and I don't know who."

"Let's give her what she wants," I muttered.

"HELL No!" Ben stood and thrust his hand at me as he made the exclamation. "You just forget that shit right now! Hear me?"

"Look, Ben." I focused on him with as much intensity as I could muster. "This sonofabitch is playing this out like some kind of contrived, low-budget movie. He's going to torture and probably kill an innocent woman just to get me out in the open. I can't let him do that."

"We don't plan to," he shot back.

"You can't stop him." I shook my head. "He is going to keep killing until he gets to me."

"You don't know that we won't get him, Row," Ben said.

"Oh yes I do," I nodded and spoke with absolute certainty.

"You wanna tell me how?"

I just stared at him. The silence in the room grew thick and charged with a frightening energy that made my skin prickle.

"Dammit, Rowan, stop this crap. Just get in there and talk to your wife."

"I can't yet," I said with a disconcerting calm.

"Why the hell not?"

"Because that's him now."

Ben shook his head and gazed back at me with confusion creasing his forehead. "Him now what?"

The startling ring of the telephone answered the question for me.

CHAPTER 24:

Ben followed me all the way into the kitchenette, spouting instructions as he made himself my shadow. "If it is him, then don't explode on 'im, Row. You've gotta keep the bastard talkin' until we pin him down."

"I know, Ben," I returned.

"I'm serious, white man," he said as he continued to reinforce the mandate. "After this afternoon, I can easily see you losin' it here. You gotta keep your temper under control."

I rounded the corner of the doorway and turned, placing my hand on the telephone as I stared wordlessly back at my friend. On the fourth ring, I lifted the receiver and placed it against my ear, then spat, "What the hell do you want this time, Eldon?"

Ben moved his head through a frustrated gyration as he grimaced, closing his eyes and then opening them again as he came back to face me. He settled his stare on me with a thin-lipped frown cutting a deep gash beneath his angular nose.

I continued to watch him as he held the obvious question in his eyes.

"So you ARE going to answer the phone, Gant." Porter's voice poured out of the speaker, blended throughout with self-righteous arrogance. "I was beginning to wonder if you had run back to Hell where you belong."

I gave my friend a quick nod in the affirmative to his visual query.

"Without you?" I asked into the handset, my tone a fountain of dark sarcasm. "Never crossed my mind. I want to make sure you don't miss it."

He actually chuckled, something I hadn't expected. The very sound of his voice was already sickening to me, but the theatrical measure of forced laughter made me want to turn and vomit in the sink.

"Well, Gant," he replied. "When I am finally called by the Lord, unlike you, I will have the pleasure of living in his divine presence."

"Yeah, well, we will have to see about that," I snarled. "So while I've got you on the phone, why don't you answer something for me."

"She's still alive," he returned. "For now."

"Slow down, Eldon. That wasn't even the question."

"Really?" He seemed almost surprised. "Okay. I'll play along. What did you want?"

I watched Ben carefully as I spoke. "You see, what I want to know is this: If I'm such a big, bad minion of Satan like you say I am, then what exactly makes you think that I am going to give a damn about some insignificant woman's life?"

My friend's eyes widened, and he glared at me as he made a grab for the phone. I had anticipated the reaction and easily ducked his hand as I stepped backwards.

"You see, I should expect you to say something like that. It's exactly what Satan would say. But, it's not her life that I think you are worried about," he replied with undaunted surety in his words.

"Sounded that way to me," I prodded. "Maybe you should explain it to me so I understand."

The fact that I still had Porter on the line appeased Ben for the moment, and he started to calm even though he still kept a suspicious eye cast in my direction.

Porter chuckled again. "Be serious, Gant. We both know that it's her soul you want."

"You think that's what it is?" I asked.

"Of course. Tempting the weak is what you do—corrupting their souls and recruiting them into Satan's army. This is what keeps you in his good graces. If you can't succeed then you will fall from favor with Satan."

"What? You actually think that I am recruiting a satanic army?" I returned. "You're crazier than I thought you were, Eldon."

"So you are admitting your allegiance to Satan, then."

"No. I don't even believe Satan exists, Eldon. Not that you are going to believe me, no matter what I say."

The speaker on the telephone issued a forlorn plink then shifted into the hollow thrum of a disconnected line. I stepped forward and dropped it carefully into the wall cradle.

"He says that Millicent Sullivan is still alive," I said as I leveled my gaze on my stoic friend.

"He hang up?" Ben asked.

"Yeah," I returned.

"Row, I asked you not to go ape-shit on the SOB," he began to admonish.

"He didn't hang up because of anything I said, Ben," I told him. "And he's going to call back any minute."

"That's not exactly what I mean," he said. "Hold on a sec." He frowned hard then turned away from me and called back into the living room. "You get anything, Mandalay?"

"He was using the Sullivan woman's phone," her voice echoed back to us. "They're tracking the... What?... Hold on for a second Storm... Okay, go ahead..."

She shifted attention back to the conversation on her cell phone once again.

Ben twisted his head back to me, "Listen, Row, you've got to calm down. If you antagonize the sonofabitch, he just might kill the woman."

I shook my head. "No. Not yet."

"How can you be sure of that?" He cocked his head to the side as he looked back at me. "This 'effin wingnut is just about as off kilter as you can get. You don't know what he's gonna do."

"I won't dispute the first part," I told him. "But the fact that she's still alive tells me that she is his bargaining chip. He's got my attention, so now he's going to use her to get me out in the open."

"How do you know she really is still alive?" he pressed.

"Because he would have gloated about it if she wasn't."

"I dunno about this, white man. You'd better hope you're right."

"We've got him crossing between two cells," Mandalay's voice came from almost immediately behind Ben.

My friend stepped to the side and turned to look at her. "Where?"

"Near Interstate Two-Seventy and Highway Forty," she answered.

"Troop C headquarters is just west of there off of Forty." Ben referred to the highway patrol.

She nodded briskly. "The field office has already notified MHP and County. I was just getting ready to call in to the Major Case Squad and let them know what's going on."

"Good deal." Ben reached up to his neck but caught himself. Judging by the look on his face, he apparently managed to do so just before flexing his hand enough to bring on any real pain. He dropped his hand back down and continued. "Maybe we can put an end to this whole thing right here and now."

"It's not going to be that easy," I told him as I shook my head.

He held up his hand to stop me and then huffed out a breath as he stared at my face. He was looking for something in my expression but wasn't finding it. "Look, Row," he said. "Do you think that maybe you just might be wrong this time?"

"You have no idea how much I'd like to be," I retorted. "It's not like…"

My sentence was truncated by the telephone pealing for attention once again. I snatched up the handset and brought it to my ear.

"What took you so long, Eldon?" I chided. "I was beginning to think you'd lost my number."

"I am her absolution, Gant," he said in a measured cadence, but this time his voice held more distraction than arrogance. "And you will be witness when she is released from her darkness and given unto the glory of God Almighty."

"Let me talk to her," I demanded.

He continued, ignoring my assertion. "You will know when it is time. Vengeance is mine."

Flat resonance issued from the speaker for yet another time as the connection was unceremoniously ended.

I took in a deep breath and let it go in a heavy rush as my shoulders dropped. I rested the handset back onto the hook and looked up at Ben and Constance.

"Well?" Ben appealed.

"He wants me to see him kill her," I answered.

"Jeezus..." my friend muttered. "He give you a place or somethin'?"

I shook my head. "No. He sounded a little preoccupied. I think he knows he was on the line too long the first time around."

"He's probably going to try getting off the main roads then," Mandalay offered as she began stabbing at the buttons on her cell phone.

I could feel the icy breath of the Dark Mother on the back of my neck, and I shivered inwardly. She was waiting in the wings for someone, and I had a bad feeling that the someone just might be me. There was simply no way that this was going to play out well.

Ben stared at me and furrowed his brow. "I know that look, Kemosabe. Whaddaya got chewin' on ya' now?"

"Nothing," I replied in an absent tone.

"You're lyin', Row."

"Am I under oath all of a sudden?"

"Awww, man, Row..." he started.

I moved past him with deliberate purpose. "I need to go talk to Felicity."

"Hey." I offered the word softly as I pressed my back against the door and felt it click shut.

It was quiet in the room. My wife was sitting on the edge of the bed, hunched over, with her arms encircling a pillow. Her back was to me, and I could hear her sniffling. Either she was still crying, or she had only recently stopped.

The only light in the room came from a reading lamp on the book table to one side of the bed. It cast a soft luminescence across the dark blue comforter, then dissipated, leaving Felicity in the muddy shadows just beyond its reach.

I waited for a long stretch and received no response.

"Do I need a white flag?" I finally asked.

I watched as she slowly moved, releasing her grip on the pillow and setting it aside. Her dainty hands slipped upward and pushed her mane of spiraling auburn back from her face. She continued to the back of her head, where she gathered it with a twist and pulled it into a fiery fall over her left shoulder then began to fiddle with it absently. The pale skin of her now exposed neck seemed to glow in the semi-darkness.

"Aye, it was him again, wasn't it?" she asked, her voice almost a hoarse whisper. "On the phone?"

"Yes," I answered, keeping my own voice low for fear of shattering the tenuous calm in the room. "It was him."

"Is Star dead?" she asked, the words catching in her throat.

I noticed after a moment that I was shaking my head even though she couldn't see me; I verbalized the answer. "No. She's still alive."

Silence filled the space between us and thickened as each second passed. The energy in the room was a chaotic mix of anger, sadness, fear, and resolve. It assaulted me on every level, igniting my nerve endings with cold fire. The physical atmosphere was warm—too warm—but I still fought off an overwhelming need to shudder as I pushed away from the door and stepped farther into the room.

"We need to talk about all of this, honey," I said.

She still hadn't turned to face me, but I could see her head bob in the shadows as she spoke. "Aye, we do."

I pressed on. "Star is still alive, for now, but he does intend to kill her."

"This shouldn't be happening," she muttered

"I know," I said. "Believe me, I wish it wasn't."

"What did he say to you?"

"No, honey," I objected. "There's no need for you to…"

"Dammit, Rowan," she half demanded, half pleaded. "Don't leave me out. The bastard called me this afternoon."

"Ben told me," I acknowledged. "I was going to talk to you about that later."

"He's sick, Rowan."

"I know that."

Another lull slipped through the room. I heard her take in a cleansing breath and watched the shadows as her shoulders moved upward then slowly fell when she exhaled. She pulled her hair upward and began working it into a loose pile on her crown.

"So what did he say to you?"

"Honey…"

Insistence permeated her voice. "What did he say, Rowan?"

I lowered my head in resignation. "He said that he was her absolution."

"What else?"

I sighed and moved another step toward the bed. "He said that I would be a witness to her release." I left out the "vengeance is mine" comment.

"So you are going to go save her, then" came her flat reply.

"I don't think I could live with myself if I didn't try."

"You could let the police handle it now." There was a narrow thread of hope woven through her voice.

"I will. If they can…" I let my words trail off.

She turned slightly, twisting her body and glancing over her shoulder. As she repositioned herself, she moved partially into the light. My eyes were finally adjusting, and I could see that her cheeks were flushed. Her smooth skin glistened with the dampness of her tears, and she reached up to wipe her eyes.

"Aye, you think they can't?"

"It doesn't feel very good," I offered.

"Aye, so you will sacrifice yourself for her, won't you?"

"It's not my intention."

"But you will if you have to." She offered the comment as a statement of fact and then paused before finally asking, "Won't you?"

I didn't answer her.

"Aye, what about me?"

"You'll be safe," I said softly. "Mandalay will be here with you."

"That's not what I mean, then, Rowan!" She turned farther into the light and glared at me sharply. "What of me? Why are you so willing to leave me alone? Don't you love me anymore?"

"Felicity!" I was stunned. "How can you even think that? Of course I love you. More than anything, you know that."

"Why do you want to leave me then?"

I moved forward and took a seat next to her on the bed. She leaned into me as I slipped my arm around her and pulled her close.

"Honey." I tried to soothe her. "I don't want to leave you."

"Aye, but you will," she said. "If you die…"

I didn't want to lie to her, but I didn't want to acknowledge the possibility either. I had nowhere to redirect the conversation, and I was beginning to share her pain.

"I have to do whatever I can to keep you safe," I finally said. "That is what this is about. I love you. I will always love you. No matter what."

She moved her head against me as she slowly shook it. "Aye, I am not ready to be without you."

"I'm not ready to leave," I told her.

"But you will…"

"If that is what it takes to keep you safe," I said. "Then, yes, I will."

"Do you really think that he would try to come here?"

"If he can't get me out in the open, yes I do. And I can't allow that to happen."

A siren sounded outside, muted by the walls, but audible all the same. I gave her a reassuring squeeze before standing up and moving to the window. I cautiously pulled back the heavy drapes and peered out through the hole then down across the parking lot. I watched the emergency lights of a squad car flickering in chaotic strobes as the vehicle accelerated down the street. The lights disappeared, and the wailing siren slowly faded in the distance. I allowed the insulated fabric to fall shut, and I turned back to face Felicity.

"You don't have to do this, then," she insisted, her Irish brogue thick from her ongoing distress.

"Yes I do," I answered, feeling a strange calm at the decision.

Her nervous fidgeting had been completed, and her spiraling curls now sat atop her head in a loose Gibson-girl. Her green eyes flashed wetly in the dim light as concern deepened the lines in her face. She'd run the gamut—anger, guilt, all of it. The tone in her voice brought everything back around to demands once again.

"What did Ben say," she contended as if the answer would somehow make a difference.

"The same thing you just said," I replied.

I took a deep breath as I ran my hand across the lower half of my face, brushing my bearded chin. I winced as my fingers grazed a still-healing wound on my upper lip—a leftover from my stunt with Ben's van.

Felicity took on a pleading tone as she gazed at me, "Then why are you doing it?"

"Because we can't keep living like this," I answered. "Because I want us to have our lives back."

"How can we have our lives back if you get yourself killed?"

I wasn't sure if the next words out of my mouth were the truth or a lie. I spoke them anyway. "I'm not going to get myself killed."

Tears were once again rolling across my wife's cheeks, and her voice cracked as she trembled. "Damn your eyes, Rowan Linden Gant, you'd better not, then. Aye, you'd better not."

Chapter 25:

"Stay right there" were the first words to issue from Ben's mouth as I walked out of the bedroom.

Felicity was still in the process of making herself presentable before coming out—her words, not mine—and I swung the door shut to give her some privacy. I wasn't paying all that much attention to what was going on up the hallway as I exited, but his voice was urgent and the instruction concise. The energy forming the sentence told me that I needed to pay heed.

I looked up and saw immediately that he had positioned himself at the opening of the short corridor. His back was to me, and his left hand was extended behind, motioning me to stop. I caught a quick glimpse of his right hand and saw that it was filled with his sidearm.

My heart fluttered and hardness filled my throat as my mouth went almost instantly dry. Unencumbered fear raced from my brain to my stomach and brought more life to the already churning bile. Each of my muscles tensed in unison as I froze, making my knees suddenly feel weak as they locked.

An insistent series of thumps sounded from the front door.

Beyond my friend, I could see Agent Mandalay—her hand wrapped securely about her forty-caliber Sig Sauer and her arm stiffly positioned to repel a close-quarter hostile entry.

I caught my breath as I felt the tension thicken. Ben raised his Beretta and assumed a solid firing posture in a single fluid motion.

"Tell Felicity to stay in the bedroom," my friend called over his shoulder, keeping his voice low.

My voice was caught in my throat, and I found myself unable to move. He glanced back at me quickly.

"Just stay behind me, Rowan."

I watched on as Mandalay reached out with her free hand, gripped the doorknob, and then brought her eye toward the security peephole.

Sharp pain arced through my body as my muscles executed the impossible task of tightening even more. I was holding my breath, and my chest was beginning to burn. I heard the latch disengage behind me as Felicity twisted the knob on the bedroom door and began to swing it open.

My immediate thought was to turn and push her back into the room, but I remained frozen. I heard the whoosh of air as she pulled the barrier farther aside, and I shot the hot breath from my lungs as I forced myself to act. I felt my arm unlock—first at the elbow, then at the shoulder. My waist broke free and started to twist as I began to move. Fortunately, I was still looking forward when Mandalay's shoulders fell to a relaxed position. I stopped myself and jerked as my muscles tensed again. Constance carefully holstered her weapon as she glanced away from the peephole and back to Ben, just as another knock sounded.

"It's your lieutenant," she said with a note of relief.

"Friggin' wunnerful," he muttered, but he still relaxed noticeably.

"Row? What's going on?" Felicity's voice came from behind me, couched with a slight hint of fear.

"Lieutenant Albright appears to be dropping in on us," I replied as my heart eased back to a normal rhythm.

Felicity screwed up her face in disgust. "Aye, that *saigh*? Do we have to let her in?"

"That what?" Ben asked.

"*Saigh*," she replied as if the Gaelic word was common knowledge. "You know. Bitch."

"No kiddin'?"

"Aye."

"Hmph, I gotta remember that one," Ben muttered then called back to her. "Well, trust me, Felicity, I'm not real excited about her bein' here myself."

Mandalay twisted the knob on the deadbolt and unlatched the swing bar security lock then swung the door open. Lieutenant Albright stood on the opposite side, a scowl on her face and her hand raised in preparation to knock once again.

"Just exactly what is going on in here?" she demanded as she breezed in through the open door, instantly locking her eyes on Ben. Her frown deepened measurably the moment she noticed he was in the process of stowing his sidearm in his shoulder rig. She didn't even bother to acknowledge Mandalay.

"We were just being cautious," the petite FBI agent announced to the back of the lieutenant's head.

Albright swung around to face her. Constance shot her a forced smile as she arched her eyebrows.

"Do I know you?" Albright demanded. "Which department are you with?"

Mandalay reached into her jacket and produced a folding leather case which she deftly flipped open with one finger. She thrust the badge and federal ID out at arm length and then made a great show of introducing herself. "Special Agent Constance Mandalay, Federal Bureau of Investigation." She smiled sweetly once again then as she snapped the badge case closed and slipped it back into her pocket she adopted a mocking tone. "We met this morning, by the way. I guess you were just too busy to remember."

I couldn't see the look on the lieutenant's face, but I made a mental note to ask Constance about it when this was all over because I am certain that it was priceless. I heard Ben stifle a snort and couldn't help but turn one corner of my mouth up in a partial grin. Even with everything that was going on, I still appreciated the underlying humor in the moment.

Albright snapped her head around at the noise and landed her frosty stare on Ben then moved it to Felicity and me.

"This is a secure building," she finally announced, moving farther into the room as she spoke. "Don't you think you were going a little overboard?"

"Not in my assessment, Lieutenant," Ben returned, his voice strained. "Porter got the phone number here somehow, so I'm not puttin' anything past 'im."

"I am well aware that he has the telephone number," she said. "However, that is a far cry from him actually showing up here."

Ben shrugged. "Judgment call."

"Which is exactly why I removed you from this case to begin with," she snorted. "Your lack of judgment."

She let out an angry breath and then looked him up and down as if inspecting a soldier in formation.

"You shouldn't even be here, Storm," she chided as she waved her hand at him in a dismissive gesture. "Look at you."

"I can still do my job, Lieutenant," he answered evenly.

"How long have you been on duty today, Detective?" she pressed.

"That's irrelevant."

"I am not authorizing any overtime for this you know."

"I don't remember askin' for any."

She wasn't getting the reaction she obviously wanted, so her anger grew with each sentence.

She glared at my friend and said, "I just want to be absolutely certain that you understand that. Am I clear?"

Ben spat his reply, "Crystal."

"Feel the love," Mandalay muttered just loud enough for everyone to hear.

Albright ignored her, but Felicity snickered, and my grin spread wide enough that I found it necessary to lower my head and turn it to the side in order to hide from the lieutenant's scrutiny. At this point, the stress had been so cloying, for so long, that the momentary release combined with our exhaustion had made us somewhat giddy. There was still a nervous overtone to the transpiring events, no doubt about that, but it was impossible not to be amused by Mandalay's sardonic observation. Of course, the lieutenant immediately put an end to it.

"Mister Gant," Albright snarled. "I do not think you are in any position to find this amusing. Nor you Miz O'Brien."

"Don't lecture me, Lieutenant," I answered. "I've had more than enough for one day, and I'm in no mood for it right now."

She unsheathed the sharp edge of her voice as she glared at me. "Gant, if I were you I would take a different tone. As it stands now, you will be very lucky if you are not charged with accessory to murder."

"Do what?" Ben barked.

I shook my head, and my eyes involuntarily squinted as obfuscation took control of my face. "Excuse me?"

"Your telephone exchange with Porter was utterly irresponsible," she detailed, pointing at me with a stiff index finger. "The comments you made regarding Miss Sullivan and the lengths to which you endeavored to antagonize Porter may very well cost that young woman her life."

"Awww, Jeez..." Ben muttered.

"What the hell are you talking about?" I demanded. "How do you even know what was said?"

Albright folded her arms across her chest and continued glaring at me.

"The phone's tapped, white man," Ben said aloud as he reached up to smooth back his hair. He caught himself once again, but this time he lifted his other hand and began tearing away the gauze wrappings just as I had earlier predicted. I was mildly surprised that it had taken him this long.

"Sorry, Rowan," Constance added. "We did it after he called the Harper residence. SOP. We didn't really expect him to call here, but we couldn't take the chance that he wouldn't. I was going to tell you, but we got sidetracked."

"Okay," I returned. "I guess I shouldn't be overly surprised by that. So exactly what is your problem, Lieutenant?"

"And I quote," she said. "'Then what exactly makes you think that I am going to give a damn about some insignificant woman's life,' end quote."

I stared back at her. "You're just as bad as Porter when it comes to taking things out of context, aren't you?"

"Don't you dare compare me to that sick individual, Gant," she ordered.

"Listen to me, Lieutenant," I took on my own hard edge. "When this SOB starts calling you and threatening your life, and more importantly the life of your spouse..." I paused to suck in a breath and try to temper my composure somewhat. "...Eviscerates and kills one of your friends, then kidnaps someone else you know and threatens to do the same to them, THEN you can say whatever you want to him. Until that happens, what you can do is get off my ass."

"You are pushing it, Mister," she threatened.

"Lady, the only one pushing it here is you," I barked. "Now get out."

Ben cleared his throat in a loud burst and then mumbled, "Calm down, Row."

Albright raised her voice. "Excuse me?"

"You heard me. Get out of here before I throw you out."

Ben cleared his throat again and shot me a warning glance. "Shut. Up. Rowan." He quietly voiced the instruction in a purposeful cadence, but it was too late. I was already well on my way over the line.

Albright cocked one eyebrow into a shallow arch, and from where I stood it appeared as though a thin smile passed briefly across her lips.

She held her voice even as she spoke. "Did you just threaten me, Mister Gant?"

"Threat, promise, whatever," I responded. "Take it how ever you want. What I can tell you for a fact is that if you were a man I'd be escorting you out, if you get my meaning."

Albright reached inside the open front of her trench coat and slipped her hand toward her back. When she withdrew it, there was a bright clink of metal against metal, and a pair of handcuffs rested in her tight grip.

"Lieutenant," Ben spoke up. "Don't do this."

She glanced at him with a look of contempt but didn't respond to the plea. Instead, she snarled, "Get out of the way, Storm."

With that, she fixed her stare on me and started across the room. She didn't have much distance to cover, and before I could blink, she was standing in front of me. In a quick motion, she took hold of my wrist and twisted. A searing lance of pain drove inward through my left shoulder as she wrenched my arm behind my back in a rough motion. I grunted at the discomfort as she continued to lever my forearm up until my wrist rested between my shoulder blades. I quickly turned my head in defense of my nose as she shoved me forward, and my face slammed against the wall.

Felicity had been elbowed out of the way, and my gaze met hers as my head turned. I could see that another bout of fear and anger was welling behind her tired eyes.

My wife quickly darted her head away and yelped, "Ben, do something!"

I could hear my friend behind me trying to soothe her. "Calm down, Felicity. We're gonna fix this."

She turned back to me, her eyes wild and then panned her glare on to the lieutenant as she launched into a violent-sounding string of Gaelic. "*Fek tú Saigh! Loscadh is dó ort! Damnú ort! Tú tuaireapach! An-duine! Tú stríopach! Go n-ithe an cat thú, is go n-ithe an diabhal an cat! Tú féad póg mo thóin saigh!*"

I only picked up a few of the words; considering what I actually did understand, it was for the best that she had chosen Gaelic for the diatribe.

"Felicity! Honey! It will be okay." I tried to reassure her as she spat the curses. "Call Jackie and tell her..."

Before I could get the instructions for our attorney out of my mouth, Albright barked, "Shut up, Gant!"

Felicity drew closer and launched another expletive-ridden sentence at her, *"An cac capaill, saigh! Go hifreann leat!"*

Thankfully, Ben took hold of my wife's arm and pulled her away, interposing himself between her Irish temper and the lieutenant before this could escalate to a physical level. I wasn't so certain that I would trade places with him at the moment.

That was, of course, until the real pain started.

Agony shunted into the center of my brain as my ears began to fill with the sound of rushing blood. My teeth clenched hard, and the horrid metallic tang from earlier in the day returned in force. I bucked against my body's sudden desire to posture and fall to the floor.

Sharp pain bit into my wrist as Albright slapped the edge of the handcuff against it. I focused on that sensation, using it to divert the inexplicable seizure I felt approaching. The sound of the metal teeth ratcheting grated in my ears as she snapped the circlet shut and continued to tighten the restraint until it pinched my flesh. Still holding me pinned against the wall, she grasped my free arm and yanked it behind my back as well.

Her hand pressed deep into my back, and her touch felt cold. I involuntarily seized on the sensation and immediately felt intense alarm. I gasped a startled breath and closed my eyes.

Distorted, three-dimensional shapes ricocheted through my brain, layering atop one another in jerky, freeze-frame motions. As they joined, I could begin to make out a defined image. In a sudden burst of light, I found myself staring at a contrasty countenance, inverted though it was. Hanging before me in the void was a woman seated upon an ornate throne. A crown rested atop her head, and her vestments were regal, those of royalty. Even though the image is inverted, her dark eyes seem to be looking down upon me imperiously. In her right hand, she is holding forth a shining sword.

I knew immediately that I had seen this image before. It was the face of a tarot card—specifically, the Queen of Swords.

My eyes snapped open and locked on the wall. Still, the afterimage floated in the empty space before me, in crisp focus, as clear as a framed photograph. All sound around me began to echo languidly in my ears as the light in the room flared then dimmed.

"You are under arrest, Mister Gant," Lieutenant Albright announced. Everything became surreal as I struggled to keep myself in this reality. Voices began to slur, and all sound took on the quality of mud. When she continued, her voice came thick and slow—the words blending into one another as they thudded against my eardrums. "Yooouuu haaaaavvve ttthheee rrriiiigggghhhttt tttoooo rrrreeemmmaaaiiinnn ssiiilleennntt. Ifff yooouuu gggiiivvvee uuuupp…"

CHAPTER 26:

I wasn't willing to let this happen again.

Not now. And, definitely not with Albright here.

I sucked a deep breath in through my nose and struggled to ignore the pains that seemed to be checking in from every inch of my body. I held the breath for a few seconds and then began allowing the air to flow out between my lips in a slow stream. Inside my head, I began my bid for control.

My snap decision was to counter whatever was happening to me with the simplest defense I could imagine. Mutely, but with great concentration I began to recite the alphabet, backwards.

I closed my eyes and focused a small part of myself on maintaining a steady cadence with my breathing. In through my nose, out through my mouth, repeat. Z, Y, X, W... In nose, out mouth, repeat... V, U, T, S... Breathe in, breathe out, repeat... R, Q, P, O...

What I was doing was simple. It was textbook, obvious. It was also something that in my off-kilter state, I had been forgetting to do. I was grounding and centering—this was Psychic Self-Defense 101.

The rush in my ears began to fade, and the Doppler distortion of sound accordioned in upon itself, collapsing everyone's words into tonal reality. For what had to be the first time today, I felt almost relaxed. Pains were still assaulting me from every corner of my being, but they were tangible pains and real aches—discomforts born of the physical realm instead of the ethereal. In a bizarre sense, I welcomed them.

"I believe you might want to re-think this action, Lieutenant." Mandalay's voice worked its way into my ears through the various commotions. As close as I could figure, she was somewhere behind me and to the right.

I opened my eyes and could see that Ben was still restraining Felicity with as much care as he could, considering her angered state. I could barely hear him talking to her—or trying to talk to her at least—as she continued to vent poignant comments in Gaelic, occasionally intermixed with colloquial Irish profanity.

"Stay out of this," Albright barked at Agent Mandalay, then pressed the other cuff against my still free wrist.

"I am very serious about this, Lieutenant," Mandalay continued, undaunted, raising her voice to be heard. "I think that you may be on some fairly shaky legal ground here."

"I don't think that..." Albright started to reply but suddenly shifted her attention to the side. "Storm! Can't you get her to shut up!"

"*FEK TÙ SAIGH!*" Felicity's voice rose sharply as she twisted around Ben and struggled to break free.

"Good Lord," Albright spat. "Cuff her, Storm."

"Leave her out of this!" I demanded as I tried to twist my head farther around, only succeeding in giving myself a cramp in my neck.

Ben answered harshly, "No way, Lieutenant. Not happenin'."

"Storm!" she snarled.

Felicity's angry voice pierced the atmosphere in the small corridor once again. "*FEK TÙ! Póg mo thóin saigh!*"

"Christ!" Albright exclaimed. "What is that gibberish anyway?"

I don't think she really wanted an answer, but I gave her one anyway. "It's not gibberish. It's Gaelic."

She barked at me. "You shut up, Gant."

I really wanted to spout off a comeback, but I wasn't entirely sure that it would be in my best interest. I quickly weighed my situation and, right or wrong, decided it probably couldn't get any worse. However, just to be safe I kept my comment near the middle of the road. "You're the one who asked."

She was not amused. "Did I not just tell you to shut up?!"

"I must have missed that," I returned with heavy sarcasm.

Albright took on a threatening tone. "All right, Gant, would you like to add resisting arrest to the charges?"

"Who's resisting?"

"Speaking of charges, Lieutenant," Mandalay started again. "Just exactly what would those be?"

"I can think of several," Albright shot back.

"That's interesting." Mandalay spoke in a professional but condescending tone. "Because I can't imagine a single one that would stick. However, I can think of several that Mister Gant can bring against you."

Albright had completed handcuffing me but continued to hold me against the wall as if I were some danger to her and everyone around me. My arms were starting to cramp, and I had lost feeling in one side of my face where my cheek was pressed into the wall. I couldn't see what was going on behind me, obviously, but it sounded as though Albright might have turned to face Constance before she spoke.

"I am not interested in your opinion," she snarled.

"Well, I'm going to give it to you whether you want it or not," Mandalay continued, unfazed by the older woman. "In short, that opinion would be that you are very close to violating Mister Gant's civil rights."

Albright let out a supercilious cackle that actually made me nauseous. "You Feds amaze me," she asserted. "Every single one of you thinks you know more about the law than any other cop, no matter how much experience they have. Does the Bureau issue the attitude with the badge, or is it learned behavior?"

"Actually," Mandalay said, not missing a beat, "I paid for mine."

"Excuse me?" Albright retorted.

"Oh yes. I just paid it off last year as a matter of fact." Mandalay adopted her own attitude in rebuttal. "Cornell Law, class of ninety-seven. Of course, you could be correct; I might not know what I'm talking about. I was only the salutatorian."

Edgy silence filled in behind the explanation. Even Felicity had stopped struggling with Ben, and for the first time since the altercation started, she was mute.

"He threatened a police officer," Albright finally declared, her voice filled with a tenuous confidence.

"I perceived no threat," Constance offered. "How about you, Storm? Did you see Rowan threaten the lieutenant?"

"Threaten?" Ben asked with mock surprise as he turned toward them. "No, I musta missed that."

"You're walking a VERY thin line, Storm!" Albright said.

My friend shrugged. "Sorry, Lieutenant. I must've been pre-occupied or somethin'."

Albright snarled. "You both know full well that it was a verbal threat."

"Sticks and stones, Lieutenant," Mandalay offered. "Sticks and stones."

Albright expelled an angry breath but remained mute.

"Back to what I was saying, Lieutenant." Mandalay began speaking again, completely in control of the situation. "You might want to re-think this action, and I'll tell you why. Let us just forget the civil rights violations, the inevitable lawsuits, and the bad press for a moment. Instead, let's look at some basic facts. One, you presently have Eldon Porter loose on the streets of Saint Louis. Two, Porter has abducted a woman with the intention of killing her. And most importantly, three, your one and only link to Porter is Rowan.

"Now, once again this is just my opinion." Mandalay added an infusion of sarcasm to the comment. "But I think you would be better served by releasing Rowan, bidding a hasty retreat, and allowing Detective Storm to act as your liaison."

Weighty tension flowed in to mix with the silence following Agent Mandalay's carefully worded suggestion. I was still making an indelible impression of my face in the surface of the wall, not of my own choice of course. My earlier mental exercise had done wonders for my inner self, but it wasn't accomplishing much regarding the physical aches and pains that were wracking my body. While I had somewhat welcomed them a few moments ago, I was more than ready for them to be gone.

The muscles in my arms were now approaching the full throes of cramping. If I was unable to change my position soon, the heightened discomfort I was currently battling was going to become searing agony. If that wasn't enough, Albright had not bothered to set the stops on the handcuffs—purposely I'm betting—and the metal bracelets were cutting off the circulation to my hands. The first one she had slapped the restraint around had already gone numb, and the second was well on its way.

Topping it all off, I was still dealing with the complaining nerve endings that surrounded my various injuries of the day.

I heard Albright force out another angry breath although this one sounded as if it held a bit of resignation as well. A moment later, the pressure against my back released and the jangle of keys met my ears.

"This is not over by any means, Gant," Albright warned as she unlocked the cuffs, taking little care as she did so.

First, one of my arms, then the other fell, coming down to my sides just as the initial wave of severe cramping was about to attack. I shook them loosely and then stretched.

"You had best hope that Porter does not harm that young woman." Albright continued to lecture me.

I worked my fingers in and out of my palms as I turned to her and then inspected my wrists. I stopped for a moment to rub the thick, red depressions that encircled them, biting my lip as feeling returned, taking the form of countless shards of broken glass and barbed hooks rattling about inside my digits.

"I doubt you'll be able to find anyone who is hoping for her safety any more than me," I echoed with as little anger in my voice as I could manage.

She simply glared at me, her jaw working as she clenched her teeth behind the thin gash formed by her intense frown.

"Storm," she finally snapped, turning to him. "Mark my words, Detective. Your days are numbered."

"Yeah." Ben half nodded. "I'll be sure to put it on my calendar."

Albright snorted haughtily then turned on her heel and stalked toward the front of the apartment. When she reached the door, she rested her hand on the knob and hesitated. After a brief moment, she turned to glare at the four of us.

"Yes, Lieutenant?" I asked, not sure what else to do.

"Just exactly what were you saying earlier, Miz O'Brien?" she queried in a demanding tone. "You kept repeating something."

Felicity glowered at the lieutenant as she crossed her arms beneath her breast. I could tell by looking at her that it was taking an immense amount of effort on her part to remain calm. My wife arched one eyebrow and spoke, her accent and brogue heavier than usual from the anger, "Aye, *Fek tù saigh,* maybe?"

"Yes," Albright snipped. "I suppose that is one of your Witch curses."

"Oh, nothing so eloquent as that, then," Felicity answered. "But, aye, it was a curse all right."

"What then?" Albright pressed.

I couldn't help but notice that she reached up and began fingering the small cross hanging around her neck. Unless I was misreading her, there was actually a small swath of fear in her face.

"Are you certain that you are wanting to know that, then?"

"I ASKED, did I not?" Albright barked.

Her voice cracked when she spoke, revealing for a fact what I had suspected. For all her verbal bravado, she actually harbored a fear of WitchCraft.

Felicity drew in a deep breath, cocked her head to the side, and then translated the phrase into carefully measured English. "Fuck. You. Bitch."

Indignation filled the lieutenant's face, but not before a barely noticeable wave of relief washed over it. If I hadn't been watching as close as I was, I never would have seen it. Nevertheless, I did, and I logged it away for the future.

She said nothing in return, but upon her exit, I would almost have to say that Lieutenant Albright gave my wife a run for her money in the door-slamming department.

CHAPTER 27:

"**D**amn," I muttered in the wake of the door's echo. "She's getting just as melodramatic about this as Porter."

"Yeah," Ben acknowledged with a heavy sigh. "She's got a real bug up her ass when it comes to you."

"You mean she's always like this?" Mandalay asked. "How does she keep her job?"

"Well, she was a lot worse just now than I've ever seen," Ben told her. "Usually she's just a Bible thumpin'... How'd you say that, Felicity? 'Sigh'?"

"Aye," she nodded. "*Saigh.*"

"Yeah, one of those," he continued. "But tonight, this was... Hell, I dunno what this was."

She looked at him and shook her head in disbelief. "Storm, you absolutely have to go to Internal Affairs about this woman. I hate to sound cliché, but she's a loose cannon."

"Yeah, you're right," he agreed. "I'm tight with a copper that moved over to IAD a couple years back. Maybe I'll drop in on 'im tomorrow if I have a few minutes."

"I think it would be advisable," Mandalay replied.

"Well," I spoke up. "I appreciate both of you coming to the rescue. Thanks."

Ben grunted, "Uh-huh. I'll prob'ly regret it. I'm bettin' I shoulda let her arrest ya' anyway."

"What for?"

My friend turned his gaze on Felicity. "Did you talk him outta puttin' his ass on the line?"

"No," she returned with a shake of her head. Her voice was still covered with a frost of anger.

Ben swung his head back to me and then jerked his thumb toward Felicity. "That for."

I expelled an annoyed breath, frowned at him, and then said, "We aren't going to go down this road again, are we?"

"Somebody's gotta chase after ya'," he replied.

"Look," Mandalay interjected. "Before you two start arguing, let's just see what happens." She rolled her arm up then pushed back her cuff to glance at her watch. You could almost see the quick mental calculation going on behind her eyes as she spoke. "It's just past seven. The last call from Porter was a little less than forty-five minutes ago, and they had pegged a grid location on him. We haven't heard a peep out of him since.

"We've all been a little preoccupied, especially with Lieutenant Albright. For all we know, this just might be a moot point by now."

"Yeah." Ben nodded in agreement with what she was implying. "The S.O.B might be cornered somewhere right now. Or, if we're really lucky, maybe they're stuffin' his ass in a body bag. I'll check with one of the coppers that I know who is on tonight. Mandalay, why don't you call the Feeb house and see if they have anything."

Constance gave her head an annoyed shake. "Field office, Storm. Can't you just say field office? You should know we aren't exactly fond of the nickname 'Feeb.'"

He returned an innocent, questioning stare. "What? I didn't call YOU a Feeb. I LIKE you."

She rolled her eyes at him in answer then reached into her pocket and extracted a cell phone. She flipped the cover on the device open with a quick snap.

"So Mandalay," Ben said as he fumbled his own cell from his belt with his wounded fingers. "Thanks for the backup with Albright."

She continued looking at her cell phone as she keyed in a number. "No problem, Storm. Even with all your faults and overabundance of testosterone, I like you too."

"I think I might have just been insulted," Ben quipped.

"Give me a break," she returned. "Just take it in the spirit it was intended."

"So lemme ask you somethin'."

"What's that?"

"You really salutatorian of your class at Cornell?"

"Actually no," she replied as she hovered her thumb over the send button and glanced up. "I was valedictorian. I just didn't want to sound too pretentious."

"Jeezus, Mandalay."

"What?"

"Nothin'."

"WHAT, Storm?"

"Well, it's just that you're a pretty good copper." He gave her an embarrassed glance and half shrugged as he spoke. "And, sometimes, like when you fix yourself up... Well, you're kinda hot."

She squinted one eye and shook her head at him. "Storm, are you hitting on me? Because if you..."

"Hell no!" He scrunched his face and gave her a dismissive wave as he rushed to cut her off. "I'm just kinda surprised to find out you're a nerd too."

Mandalay rolled her eyes then turned her back to him as she dropped her thumb on the keypad and headed out into the living room.

"I'm going to check the television," I announced as Ben began fat-fingering his own cell phone.

"Yeah," he called over his shoulder absently. "Friggin' media is prob'ly interviewin' the bastard on every channel as we speak."

I gave Felicity a nod, and we skirted around the massive Native American obstacle. He sidestepped as I gently nudged him, moving against the wall and allowing us to pass. We rounded the corner at the mouth of the small corridor and moved into the edge of the living room.

An earlier thought pushed itself up into view from the swirling tumult of my overtaxed brain, and I faltered for a moment before coming to a halt.

"*Caorthann?*" Felicity called my name in Gaelic, her voice threaded with mild concern. This was a pet name she'd had for me back before we were married, and I hadn't heard it in a long while. "Are you okay, then?"

"I'm fine, honey." I reached over and gently took hold of her arm. "What does the Queen of Swords mean?"

"The tarot card?" she answered. "I'm not sure. Mourning isn't it? Feminine sadness? The tarot is really not my strong point, but that's what I seem to recall from the little white book."

The little white book; I hadn't heard that one in a while. It was an affectionate nickname given to the booklet of definitions provided with what had to be one of the most widely known decks on the market—the *Rider-Waite* tarot.

"I know, mine either," I told her as I felt my brow crease with concentration. "I think you're correct, but it just doesn't feel right."

"Aye, where did you see this card?"

"When Albright had me up against the wall," I explained. "When she was touching me, I saw a vision of the card."

"Aye, you're sure it was the Queen of Swords, then?"

"Pretty sure," I nodded to her as I answered. "I had to really concentrate on it since it was upside down."

"Upside down?" she echoed. "Inverted, then. That would change the meaning, wouldn't it?"

"You're right," I said.

"I still can't be sure, but I think that reversed it means something like malice."

I reached up, pinched the bridge of my nose between my fingers, and let out a sigh. I was still grounded, but something out there was knocking at the ethereal door leading into my brain, and it was being very insistent. I had a feeling that it was going to call for reinforcements soon.

"You're sure that you're okay?" Felicity asked again.

"Yeah," I looked back at her with a slight smile. "Just tired."

"Aye," she returned. "I'll be right back."

She turned to the side and started away from me with a determined stride.

"What…" I began.

"The door," she answered without waiting for the rest of the question. "It needs to be locked."

I personally didn't feel that the task was an imperative with both Ben and Constance here, but I didn't disagree with her. If the simple act of setting the deadbolt would make her feel better, I was all for it. Besides, it was easily possible that she was picking up on things that I wasn't. It wouldn't be the first time.

I glanced around and saw that Mandalay had paced her way into the dining area, so I headed directly for the coffee table and scooped up the remote. Aiming the controller at the corner, I pressed the power button. The screen on the television flickered to life, and I immediately thumbed the volume down a few notches just in case.

I brought my gaze up and saw that Felicity had one hand on the knob for the deadbolt and one on the swing bar, pressing it tight against the door. Her head was down, and her shoulders relaxed noticeably. Apparently, that small measure of security had meant more to her than I realized.

Looking back to the television, I saw a tight aerial shot of what appeared to be an old multiple-story, warehouse-and-office type of structure. The front side of the building filled the screen, but any details that might have been present were all but faded into the background.

The scene was dark, but emergency lights were painting predictable swaths of red and white as they flickered from the tops of squad cars. I watched intently as they strobed, revealing a level of decay that told me the building was probably abandoned, or at the very least, had been vacant for quite some time. The setting was generic enough that I couldn't place exactly where it was, but it did appear to be somewhere near the riverfront.

The vehicles in the foreground were angled haphazardly across the partially cleared street, nosed into piles of snow along the curb. The tableau looked, at first, like toys left in disarray by a child in the midst of an imaginary game. Closer inspection showed that there was some amount of method to the madness, in that they formed a rough, staggered barrier.

Between the patrol cars and the building, a dark-colored sedan sat with the corner of its front bumper against the wall of the building. The car's headlights were still burning, slicing into the darkness to illuminate a small section of the structure's brick face. At the moment, it seemed to be the primary focus of the officers' attention.

Across the bottom of the tube, a stylized graphic cut a colorful streak; culminating on the left in the station logo. Words were emblazoned across the stripe, spelling out in slanted block letters, BREAKING NEWS.

I felt Felicity next to me as she slipped her arm in around my own then interlaced her fingers with mine and squeezed. Her other hand slipped across and closed in an unrelenting grip on my bicep.

With my free hand, I clicked the volume back up a notch as we both stared at the event playing out on the screen.

"...Shortly after six this evening," the reporter's voice-over faded in as I continued to mash the button and brought the sound up to a more discernible level. "An apparent car-jacking led to a high-speed chase which involved officers from five separate municipalities, as well as the Missouri Highway Patrol, Saint Louis County, and the Metropolitan Saint Louis Police department."

"Car-jacking my ass," Ben muttered from behind us.

"The chase began in the county near the Interstate Two-Seventy, Highway Forty interchange and proceeded through several neighborhood streets before continuing on eastbound Forty at a..."

"They've got the bastard cornered," Ben spoke again, louder this time.

"Ssshh!" Felicity urged.

"...Sideswiped another vehicle, injuring the driver, before exiting Hampton to Highway Forty-Four. Metropolitan police attempted to stop the car as it exited at the riverfront on Memorial Drive. The suspect then literally crashed through a construction barrier at Third Street and Washington, narrowly missing pedestrians who were crossing the street on their way to Laclede's Landing.

"The chase finally ended here at this abandoned warehouse on Second Street where the suspect fled the vehicle with a woman who is believed to be a hostage, and they are currently inside the building."

"There are two agents on the scene," Mandalay offered into the lull that followed the reporter's words. "Porter is definitely inside, and he has Sullivan with him."

"He won't go down without killing her first," I said.

"They know that," she replied. "That's why no one has entered the building yet."

"Osthoff just told me they have a SWAT entry team standing by," Ben told us. "They should be rolling any minute.

"I've been in there," he added. "It's at Second and Ashley. Back when I was in uniform, I chased this little prick into it after he had tried to break into a place a coupla' blocks over on Broadway." He shook his head and noisily sucked on his teeth as he pondered the screen. "There's a whole lotta places to hide in there. And in the dark on top of it? Shit…"

Ben's cell phone pealed, and he turned it up in his hand to inspect the display. With a disgusted grunt, he stabbed the device with his thumb then placed it against his ear. "Yeah, this is Storm. What can I do for you, Lieutenant?"

The languid pace of the drama on the television screen prompted the station to cut from the scene and back to the studio. The transition was a sudden switch to a groomed man behind the news desk who was staring at an angle off camera as he began speaking.

"We will now return you to network programming…" The reporter did a quick double-take motion with his head and then suddenly shifted a quarter turn toward the live camera with only a slight stutter.

I ignored the segue back to the sitcom and focused my attention on the side of Ben's conversation that I could hear.

"Yeah, we've got it on the TV right now," he said into the phone then waited.

Constance, Felicity, and I watched him as he frowned and rocked in place. He brought his free hand up to smooth back his hair, winced, shot it a disgusted look, and then went ahead with the mannerism anyway.

"Yeah, well I don't really think you can blame Rowan for you bargin' in here," he said with a note of irritation. "You wasted your own time, Lieutenant, not him.

"Uh-huh…Yeah…Uh-huh… Well, trust me, we weren't plannin' on goin' anywhere at the moment anyway, so I don't think you've got anything to worry about."

"That woman is a real piece of work," Mandalay muttered.

"Aye, I was thinking more like she's an *òinnseach*," Felicity remarked.

"What's that?"

"An idiot."

Mandalay smirked at the insult. "I'll agree with you there."

"Yeah, well, you can…" Ben barked suddenly and then paused for a moment to regain his composure before continuing in a restrained tone. "Yeah, well you'll just have to tell him that yourself. Yeah. Fine."

My friend ended the call without ceremony and then terminated the connection with a pair of clumsy thrusts from his thumb against the keypad. He looked up at us while shaking his head in an animated arc. "Jeezus H. Christ on roller skates!"

"What did she say?" Mandalay asked him, then added, "Like we can't guess."

"Well," he huffed. "She started out by blaming Row for her wasting time here, but I guess you prob'ly caught that. Other than that, she told me she's en-route to the scene and has officially *ordered* us to stay put until we hear from her."

"What are you supposed to tell me?" I asked.

"Let's not go there, white man."

"Ben…"

"Just the same shit, Row," he growled. "She's all about saying that you're responsible for whatever happens to Sullivan."

"Well," I returned, "I am."

"Look, Row," he said. "What I was saying earlier, forget it. You went with your gut, and you kept him on the line long enough to peg a location. You made the right call, and you aren't responsible for what this wingnut does."

"I won't argue it with you, Ben," I answered. "I know what I have to own up to in the end."

"You won't have to," Constance offered. "It won't hold up in court. There's no way."

"That's not where I will have to face it. Anything you do comes back to you," I told them, then recited a snippet of the Wiccan Rede as explanation. "Mind the threefold law ye should, three times bad and three times good."

"Aye," Felicity spoke up. "Don't you start quoting like Eldon Porter now. The law of three would not apply here."

"I won't debate it with you, either," I told her gently. "I deliberately antagonized him, and I just might have made the wrong choice."

"Stop second guessing yourself, Rowan," Ben instructed. "Albright's wrong. That's all there is to it. End of story."

"That remains to be seen."

"Ain't no remains to be nothin'," he spat. "She's wrong, so drop it."

Across the room, the bell on the telephone sprang to life, jangling out an angry-sounding demand to be answered. We all froze, staring at one another with shared trepidation. I started to move toward the kitchenette just as the ringer belted out its noise for the third time.

Behind me, Mandalay's cell phone began to chirp. By the time I brought my fingers to rest on the handset in the kitchen, Ben's phone had added itself to the fray, forming a discordant trio of chaotic tunes.

CHAPTER 28:

My stomach was starting to churn as I lifted the receiver and placed it against the side of my head. Bouncing around inside my skull was a desperate fear that I was about to become wholly responsible for Eldon Porter taking the life of a young woman who was associated with me by only tenuous threads at best. The concept of guilt by association was abhorrent enough, but this was virtually a case of guilt by future association.

It didn't matter how much reassurance I was given by Ben and Constance; the fact remained, in my mind I would hold myself accountable. I would experience a threefold return for my actions; there was no doubt. It was a foregone conclusion. And, I knew that if nothing else, it would be self-imposed. If it came to that, the payback would be harsh, and worst of all, inescapable.

My brain tabbed through the possible greetings, both appropriate and not—several of which I desperately wanted to snarl. I wanted to scream each of them at Porter in unending succession, backed with every thread of anger I could muster; anger was something I had in abundance right now.

However, at the same time the fire raged inside me, I was fully aware that even a single one of the phrases might possibly seal Star's fate the moment it was uttered. I simply didn't know what would push him over into the red zone, and I didn't want to find out. I forced myself to draw in a deep breath and search once again for center.

I don't know how long I actually stood there with the handset to my ear, staring off into space, completely mute. What I do know is that the pause was long enough for my choice of greetings to become inconsequential. As a fleeting moment of calm passed before me, I reached out for it and made a desperate grab.

My shoulders involuntarily relaxed as the person on the other end of the line spoke.

"Hello?" A confused, feminine voice flowed into my ear. "Anyone there? Rowan? Felicity?"

"Yeah, Cally," I answered with a slow sigh. "Yeah, I'm here."

"Are you okay?" she asked.

"Yeah, I'm fine, Cally," I told her. "Listen..."

"Do you have the TV on?" She began her excited query before I could finish. "They've got someone trapped in a warehouse. It's on all the stations. Is that him?"

"Calm down, Cally," I told her. "I know. We've been watching. And yes, it's him. So, listen..."

"I knew it!" she exclaimed, barreling over me once again. "I could feel it. I told everyone here that it had to be him."

"Cally..." I started again.

She didn't allow me to get more than a single word in. "He's got a hostage. Do they know who it is? What are they going to do?"

"CALLY!" I stated her name with a closely guarded firmness. "Slow down. Now be quiet and listen to me."

She fell silent for a fleeting moment and then spoke again in a meek tone that carried with it an overtone of worry, "Rowan, what's wrong?"

"Rowan, that was the field office," Mandalay's voice came at me.

I looked at her, and she gave a curt nod to the phone in my hand. "Porter is on Sullivan's cell, and he's trying to get through on this line right now."

"Rowan? Rowan? What's wrong?" Cally's voice insisted in my ear.

I nodded back to Mandalay and then spoke quickly into the phone. "Cally, listen, I have to go."

"Rowan," her voice took on a desperate whine. "What's wrong? Oh Gods! He doesn't have Felicity, does he? He called her today..."

"CALLY!" I barked again, all at once struggling with impatience at the situation and sympathy for her turmoil. "Listen to me. He DOES NOT have Felicity. She's okay, but I have to go. I'll explain later."

I could hear her crying my name as I dropped the handset back into the cradle.

I shot a quick glance over to Felicity, and she gave me an understanding nod. "Aye, I'll call her on my cell."

The telephone on the wall had pipped out a half ring the moment it hit the base and was already jangling its first full measure as my wife spoke. I closed my eyes and dropped my chin to my chest, drawing in a cleansing breath and forcing myself to blow it out slowly through my mouth.

"Rowan…" Mandalay appealed as the phone gave a second full ring.

I opened my eyes and looked up, giving her a shallow nod of acknowledgement as our eyes met. I could literally feel Eldon Porter on the other end of the phone even though I had not yet answered it; even the sound of the ring was different, angry and more urgent. This time it was the real thing, and I knew I had no choice but to play this out on his terms even though I had no idea what they were.

My hand had never left the telephone, so I slipped it back out of the base in one smooth motion. As the mouthpiece came near my lips, I spoke in the calmest voice I could evoke, "Hello, Eldon."

"You haven't won, Gant, you know that, don't you?" He spat the question tersely.

I could hear rustling noises coming over the phone as he apparently moved about within the confines of the building. I could only imagine what it was like—dark, cold, and no visible escape. Even for someone as insane as he, desperation had to be oozing from every pore.

I didn't feel sorry for him in the least, but I did fear the dangerous edge the panic would bring forth.

He was breathing hard, huffing shallow breaths out, and wheezing them back in at an alarming rate. The situation had the potential to turn sour in a heartbeat.

"I know, Eldon," I told him. "You're right, I haven't won."

"Don't patronize me, Gant!" he screamed. "Your sorcerers' tricks won't work this time! You just got lucky, that's all!"

"Okay, okay," I said as a shiver traced itself up my spine. "Let's work this out, Eldon."

I carefully covered the mouthpiece with my free hand and looked at Constance. "He's really edgy," I said. "Nothing like he was earlier. He's losing control really fast."

She twisted her cell phone away from her mouth. "I know. They've got it patched in, and I'm listening. Look, Rowan, we're working on something…"

"What?"

"Just keep him talking," she instructed. "You're doing fine."

"Who were you talking to?!" Porter demanded in my ear.

I stiffened, feeling as though I had just been caught in the middle of some heinous act. I pulled my hand away from the mouthpiece and spoke. "I wasn't talking to anyone."

"When I called! I couldn't get through! You had to be talking to somebody!"

I relaxed but not much. "That was just someone calling to check on me, Eldon."

"One of your minions, I'm sure," he retorted.

"You're right, Eldon." I agreed with him out of desperation.

"Damn you, Gant!" he shouted. "I told you not to patronize me!"

"Calm down, Eldon, we need to…"

"Stop telling me to calm down! Do you hear me?! Stop it, stop it, stop it!"

I pulled the handset away from my ear as he screamed. His voice buzzed in the earpiece, achieving a state of frantic distortion as he repeated the order.

I watched Constance as she glanced to the side and gave a nod. I could hear Ben whispering around the corner of the doorway and assumed that he was conferring with her. About what, I didn't know, but I didn't have time to speculate. She had told me they were working on something, so I had to trust them.

I tried to adopt a generic voice. "Okay, Eldon, I'm not trying to be patronizing to you. I'm sorry if that is how it sounded."

"What is wrong with you, Gant?" he demanded.

"I'm not sure I understand."

"There's something wrong with you," he replied. "There's something wrong with you!"

"Tell me what you mean, Eldon," I pressed.

"You aren't the same," he answered me, his voice shaking with yet unreleased anger. "You... You aren't the same as when I talked to you before."

"I'm the same, Eldon," I told him.

"It's a trick! You're trying to trick me again!" His voice jumped a notch in volume as he fired the accusation at me. "I told you it won't work, Gant. It won't work, Satan! Do you hear me?! It won't work!"

The calm insanity I had always associated with him was gone. He was now coming across as someone with one foot tenuously planted in reality but ravaged by unimaginable delusions. He was escalating beyond anything I had imagined, and I was rapidly losing faith in my ability to contain this.

My mind raced as I tried to formulate a response that wouldn't push him any further than I had already managed. Agreeing with him definitely wasn't the way to go. Trying to stick to the middle of the road wasn't any better. It seemed the only thing that had kept him on an even keel thus far was when he felt like he had pushed my buttons. He was at his calmest when he had my ire raised.

I swallowed hard and started to open the stopcock on the mental valve that was presently holding back my anger. I figured I would start small. Let some of it creep into my voice and see what his reaction was. On the chance that it worked, I would take it a little further. If he wanted me to let loose on him, I would be more than happy to oblige.

I glanced up and saw that Constance was looking off to the side and nodding vigorously as she motioned to me. I could hear her saying something into her phone, but I couldn't make out exactly what it was. Ben was apparently still just around the corner, because his urgent voice hit my unblocked ear. His words were much easier to understand.

In a quiet voice, he was telling someone, "He looks okay, so go now."

Before I could put my hastily formed plan into motion, Porter began to scream into the phone, forcing me to pull the handset away yet again.

"TELL THEM TO STOP, GANT!" His distorted voice arced several inches from the earpiece as I held the phone away from my head. "YOU BASTARD, I KNOW THEY ARE MOVING! TELL THEM TO STOP, OR I'LL KILL HER NOW!"

"No! Eldon! Listen to me!" I blurted.

Constance was shaking her head and waving. I could hear the frenzy in Ben's tone as he asked, "Did they catch that?!"

She didn't respond quickly enough for him.

"Mandalay!" his voice jumped. "Did they hear that?!"

"I don't know!" she shot back with her own thread of panic. "I lost the signal!"

"Abort!" Ben immediately bellowed, presumably into his phone. "He made you! Abort!"

Throughout the tangle of frenzied voices, I could still hear Eldon screaming at me, as well as my own pleas for him to listen.

The next sound to reach my ears came from the handset in the form of an agonized scream drilling its way deeply through my inner ear. It was high-pitched and definitely female. The tortured sound was followed by a sharp, thudding noise and then a second pained wail.

"Oh Gods!" I stammered as I squeezed my eyes tightly shut. I balled my free hand into a fist and began thumping it against my forehead in a vain attempt to push the imagined horror out of my head. "Dear Mother Goddess, no!"

The floodgates opened, and my anger spewed forth. My skin grew hot, and my ears began to ring as my blood pressure set a new benchmark for the term hypertension. I brought the handset against my head and shouted, "PORTER!"

There was nothing at the other end. Just a random repetition of hollow clicks that indicated the call had been disconnected.

I swung the handset out and hammered it downward into the base then vented my anger at the first person to enter my sights.

"What the hell was going on?!" I screamed at Mandalay. "Did you know what they were doing?!"

"Calm down!" she shouted back.

"Calm down?" I demanded as I stepped toward her. "Screw you! Don't tell me to calm down!"

An immense column of Native American filled the space between Mandalay and me as Ben quickly hooked himself around the corner. He planted one large hand against my chest and pushed, thrusting me rearward at an angle until I was backed against the countertop. "Goddammit, Rowan! Settle down!"

I heard Felicity yelp, "Ben!"

"You knew!" I roared, incredulity underscoring my anger. "Dammit you knew what they were doing, and you fucking got her killed, Ben! What the hell were you people thinking?!"

"Rowan, you don't know that he killed her." Constance projected her voice over mine as she wedged herself around Ben and into the kitchenette.

"You were listening in!" I spat as I struggled against my friend. "What the hell did it sound like to you?!"

"Dammit, Row," Ben appealed, his voice a deep boom. "Don't make me cuff you."

Hot tears were beginning to roll down my cheeks, a product of both anger and despair. I glared back at my friend, fighting the urge to scream at him again.

"Rowan, please…" Felicity's voice came from behind him in an anguished appeal.

"Did you even know where he was in the building?" I asked, my voice even but hard.

"Every indication was that you had his attention, Rowan," Constance explained. "We were just trying to get a couple of men into the building so we could pinpoint him."

"Yeah," I shot back. "Well look what it got you. Just what the hell were you doing calling the shots anyway, Ben?"

"Rowan," Ben said. "Like Mandalay said, it looked like you had his attention."

"What?" I didn't want to believe what I was hearing. "You used me?"

"Dammit, Row," Ben lamented. "It wasn't my choice."

"You were our barometer, Rowan," Mandalay said. "The SAIC made the decision not to go on voice analysis alone. Ben and I were gauging your reaction visually and feeding the information to the scene."

"I can't believe you did that," I said, swinging my disbelieving gaze between them. "Why didn't you tell me?"

"We couldn't be sure that you wouldn't accidentally tip him off," she explained. "Besides, you were already on the line with him when the decision was made. I'm sorry."

"It was how it had to be done, white man," Ben told me, his voice apologetic.

"Well, how it had to be done sucks."

He continued to hold me against the cabinets, my torso bending back over the edge of the countertop. We simply stared at one another, neither of us quite sure what to say next.

A few steps across the room, the apartment phone began to ring.

An electronic chirp issued a half step behind it, and Constance immediately flipped her cell phone open. She tilted her head and pulled her hair back with her free hand as she tucked the device to her ear. "Mandalay."

The bell jangled again.

"It's him," Constance stated as she looked at me then cocked her head toward the phone on the wall. "He never actually shut the phone off, and they tagged him as soon as he dialed. They want you to go ahead and talk to him again."

Ben looked me over and apparently decided that it still wasn't safe to leave me unrestrained. He twisted at the waist, keeping one hand firm against my chest while reaching past Felicity with the other and snatching the phone out of the cradle.

He held the handset in front of my face, and I took it from him wordlessly.

There was no way to put my rage in check, so I skipped the initial phase of my plan and went straight for voicing my disdain.

"What do you want now you sorry bastard," I snarled.

"Don't let that happen again!" Porter demanded.

"Go screw yourself, Porter," I fired back.

Silence interrupted the flow of the short exchange as he fell mute. I listened carefully, searching for any ambient sound I could identify—any indication that Millicent Sullivan was still alive.

"I see you're back to your old self," Porter finally spoke, his voice suddenly far calmer than it had been ten minutes ago. Apparently, my idea was correct.

"So glad that you're pleased," I chided. "So you must not have killed her."

"What makes you think that?"

"Simple, Eldon," I explained. "You wouldn't have called back if you had. If you kill her, you no longer have a hold on me."

"So you have decided to admit that you need her soul?"

My fear ebbed, but the dip was shallow. I harbored no illusion that he hadn't at least done something to her that was too horrid to consider.

My tone remained sharp. "Yeah, sure, whatever, Eldon. Now, let me talk to her."

"I'd love to put her on, Gant, but she seems to have passed out."

"What did you do to her, you sick fuck?"

"And thine eye shall not pity; but life shall go for life, eye for eye, tooth for tooth, hand for hand, foot for foot."

CHAPTER 29:

The quote from Deuteronomy was a verbal harbinger of things unimaginable. Unfortunately, I knew how literally Porter interpreted the Bible. I shuddered with the fear that he had in fact made one of the aforementioned choices and that it was more than just a recitation of chapter and verse.

My mouth began to water as my stomach convulsed, working into a knot, and then slowly unraveling. The acrid bitterness of bile singed the back of my tongue, and I swallowed hard to force it back down. The breadth of his cruelty should have been no surprise to me by now, but this was getting to be more than I could take.

When I finally responded to his pointed selection, my voice was cold and hard. "Skip the verse, Eldon. Just tell me what you did to her."

As he had done earlier in the day, he seemed to be taking morbid pleasure in the horrors he was committing. His personality had made another one-hundred-eighty-degree shift, and even though he was trapped with no means of escape, here he was gloating. Flaunting what he perceived as his newly found control over me.

"You wouldn't happen to know whether or not she is right-handed or left-handed, would you?" he asked.

"You son-of-a-bitch," I muttered. "If you cut her hand off, she's going to bleed to death."

"Son of God, Gant."

"Not of any God I know," I spat. "How badly is she bleeding?!"

"Oh, calm down," he chided. "She's fine. She even still has both of her hands." He paused for a beat then added a sinister, "For now."

"Then what did you do to her?" I repeated the question with added hardness.

"Nothing yet."

I knew he had to have done something, or she wouldn't be unconscious. I wanted to press him for an answer but wasn't sure if that would just set him off again. I decided my best bet would be to take a different approach. "So why did you bother calling me then?"

"To find out if she is left-handed or right-handed."

"I really don't know, Eldon. Why?"

"Oh well, it doesn't matter all that much, I suppose," he spat. "When the time comes, I'll take her left, just like you did to me."

I closed my eyes, and the memories flooded in. Things I thought I had finally come to terms with bored into my skull and re-awakened my own viscid fear.

I could almost feel the cold and even the dampness of the fog. The forlorn sound of violins filtered into my ears from somewhere above me, straining out a lament as only they could. I stood there motionless as I felt my own arm going numb.

Mentally, I was once again dangling in the chilled air with a thin, nylon rope twined tightly about my forearm, suspended precariously over the side of the Old Chain of Rocks Bridge. A raving madman, bent on ending my life had his bony hand wrapped around my throat and was squeezing. My consciousness was fleeing in panic, and I was all but prepared to join it.

It didn't matter that this was only in my head because it had once been all too real, and right now, the high definition memory was making my heart race all over again.

I pushed my still shaking hand back up to my side then thrust my thumb beneath the nylon strap and pushed outward. With a dull pop, it released, and I immediately wrapped my hand around the grip of the pistol.

The miniscule piece of breath I'd been able to grasp was failing quickly, and my vision was darkening as my eyes started rolling back in my head. The abbreviated lesson in the use of the pistol flashed through my mind as just so much jumbled nonsense. I could find no way to apply the instructions to my present situation.

Being unable to aim, I centered on what was left of my strength and pressed the gun upward at an angle across my chest until it met resistance.

The panicked voices of various stringed instruments blended to a thick, disharmonious crescendo in my ears...

For a brief instant I considered the fact that my left arm was now completely numb, and I silently begged for the resistance I found to be his arm and not my own. Then, tensing my body, I pulled the trigger.

The muzzle flashed.

The explosion reported deafeningly in my ear.

The spent shell ejected directly toward me and transferred its searing heat to my cheek.

Thick blood spattered like heavy rain across the side of my face.

The cold fingers snapped open.

Something thudded heavily against me and fell away.

A tortured scream faded into the distance below.

A single violin cried into the night, fading with sorrowful purpose toward silence...

Everything went completely black.

I was on the verge of hyperventilating when I opened my eyes. The torturous snippet of my life was well over one year old, but it had impressed itself upon me with the clarity of here and now. Each detail was as crisp and terrifying as it had been then.

As it continued to replay in my head, I fought to focus on the situation at the other end of the line.

"So I took your hand?" I retorted, finding a morbid solace in having caused him harm. "I guess that's one for me, then."

"You shouldn't have done that, Gant," he snarled.

"You were trying to strangle me, Eldon," I said. "Just exactly what did you expect me to do?"

"Accept your sentence," he returned.

"I don't accept the judgment of a lunatic."

"Whether you accept it or not, Gant, you can't deny your guilt. You have admitted it freely."

"So why take her hand," I asked, trying to push past this point of contention. "Isn't it mine that you want?"

"Oh, Gant," he replied. "You know what I want from you."

"So, why her then. Do you intend to torture me by proxy?"

"Like I said, your sentence has been pronounced," he replied. "Don't you remember?"

He was intent on reiterating my sentence, most likely for those I am sure he knew were listening. It didn't matter what I said to him, he was going to bring it all back around to this.

"I wasn't paying that much attention to you, Eldon," I said with a note of impatience. "But I get the feeling you want to remind me."

His speech became measured and almost theatrical. "By this our definitive sentence we drive you from the ecclesiastical court, and abandon you to the power of the secular court, that having you in its power now moderates its sentence of death against you."

"Yeah, sounds vaguely familiar," I retorted. "But let's get back to reality here. What makes you think you'll be able to execute that sentence?"

"I almost did that night," he answered. "Now I'll finish what I started."

"Bullshit, Eldon," I retorted. "You made a feeble attempt and ended up losing a hand in the deal. And now you're hiding in an abandoned building that's surrounded by police. Give it up, there's no chance."

"Yes there is."

"How so?"

"Because I have this woman, and you can't bear to lose her soul," he stated without hesitation.

I steeled myself for what I was about to say and tried to sound convincing. "You can have her. I'll get another."

"No you won't, Gant," he said. "I know you better than you think I do."

"If you know me so damn well, then why don't you just tell me what you want and get it over with," I demanded.

"A deal," he replied. "Your life for her..."

The telephone made a grating, double click, then fell silent.

"Eldon?" I queried into the handset.

My ear received only a thick silence in reply, but it was different from the times before when he had hung up on me. There were no clicks in the background and no empty hollowness to echo back. This time the phone seemed to have literally gone dead.

"He hung up or something," I stated aloud, looking at Ben and then Constance.

Ben took the phone from my hand then turned and slid it almost gently into the cradle. As he did so, he slowly relaxed his hold on me.

"He didn't hang up," Constance said carefully.

Ben had turned back to face me, and he seemed to be waiting for something. I glanced over at Constance; suddenly perplexed by the way both of them were acting. "What's going on?"

"Now listen to me, Rowan," she began, maintaining her calm tone with an obvious degree of purpose.

"Oh Gods! What did you do now?!" My voice inched up the scale as I felt my anger swell once again.

"Shut up and listen, Row," Ben barked.

Something about the way his voice was edged made me take immediate notice and fall quiet.

"The line was interrupted by the hostage negotiation team," Constance continued her explanation. "They are taking over the contact with Porter."

"What?" I shook my head in disbelief. "Why now? I had him talking."

"You did great," she replied. "No one is saying you didn't, Rowan. However, where the rules of hostage negotiation are concerned, they had already blurred the lines a hell of a lot more than I've ever seen them do before. The only reason they let him talk to you for so long was so they could gather information and get SWAT into position."

"Dammit!" I yelped. "If they try to go in there again, he's going to kill her!"

"They know, Rowan, they know." She held up her hands and motioned me to settle. "Believe me, that is the last thing they want."

"Well, he told me what he wants," I returned. "Me for her. Why don't we…"

"Not happenin', Row," Ben announced in a stern voice, verbally inserting a period into my sentence well before I had planned to be finished with it. "Just forget that crap right now."

"That's one of the reasons the line was terminated when it was," Constance told me, adding a shake of her head. "He started to negotiate a deal with you, and that is something the HNT is not going to let happen."

"It's one of the commandments in the hostage negotiation bible, white man," Ben told me. "Thou shalt not trade one hostage for another. No ifs, ands, or buts."

"So where does this leave us?" I demanded. "He's just going to escalate if they cut him off from me."

"You don't know that, Row," Ben replied.

"The hell I don't!" I said. "I've talked to this sonofabitch more than any of you. I'd really appreciate it if everyone would just stop telling me what I do and don't know!"

"Rowan." Felicity's voice hit me at the same time she slipped around Ben and came into my view. Her eyes were damp with the tears she was fighting hard to contain. "Let them handle it. Please?"

I leaned back and closed my eyes. My headache was back, and it was hammering away with a vengeance, all the while making sneak attacks on parts of my brain I didn't know I had. Something—or someone—was still knocking around at my ethereal perimeter, relentlessly looking for a way in. My best friend was willing to handcuff me to something stationary in order to keep me out of a mess that, whether he liked it or not, I was already at the center of. I couldn't remember everything I had shouted at Constance, but I was betting I owed her an apology. Finally, and worst of all, my wife had every reason to believe that left unchecked, I would make her a widow.

Actually, I take that back. The worst part was that she was probably correct.

I don't know if I had left anything out, but the laundry list was already several items too long for me to be comfortable with, so I was in no hurry to add to it. I knew for a fact that I had definitely been on the receiving end of better days than this, and I was longing for one of them right now.

I heaved out a sigh and reached up to massage my temples. "Look, all of you, I'm sorry," I said. "You're not exactly getting to see me at my best."

"S'alright, Kemosabe," Ben replied. "We know you're under a lotta pressure. That's pretty much why I haven't decked your ass yet."

"How fortunate for me," I quipped.

"I'm thinkin' maybe, yeah, it is," he said with a grin.

"So what do we do now?" I asked.

"We relax and wait for this to all be over," Constance advised. "Then you try your best to forget this day ever happened."

"You know I can't do that," I replied.

"We can try," Felicity pleaded.

"Honey…" I reached for her, and she slipped past Ben to melt into me. Her own energy was a chaotic turmoil, and it blended easily with mine, leaving us both unbalanced and preternaturally askew.

"It's all but over, Rowan," Ben offered. "They're gonna take this asshole down. No two ways about it. He'll go out in cuffs or a body bag. His choice."

"I understand that," I told him. "But what about Star? What if SHE is the one who ends up in a body bag?"

"That's why HNT has the ball now," Constance answered. "It is their job to keep that from happening."

"But, they have to understand that I am who he wants," I returned in a matter-of-fact tone. "There's no other bargaining for them to do."

"Believe me, Rowan, they know that," she assured me. "But that is simply not how things are done."

Her phone chirped again. I had lost count of the number of phone calls coming in and out of this apartment throughout this evening, so this was just another to add on to the pile.

"Mandalay," she answered, speaking into the device almost as soon as she flipped it open.

We all stood there, gathered in the kitchenette as if seeking some type of comfort within our small clutch. Safety in numbers, shared empathy, I don't know. I couldn't tell if it was actually working or just feeding the tension.

The expectant silence grew, as our only access to even her side of the conversation came in the form of reflexive nods occasionally coupled with scattered "yes's" and "uh-huh's." After a trio of minutes, during which our edgy anticipation swelled into a thick bubble around us, she finally uttered something more than a monosyllabic response.

"Are you absolutely sure?" she asked whoever was at the other end of the line, her features creasing into a frown. "You want both of them? No, I'm sure he will be agreeable to it. Okay. Thanks, bye."

She closed the cover on the silver device and clipped it back to her belt before looking at all of us. Then she allowed her gaze to center on me.

"That was the HNT," she said. "The lead hostage negotiator wants us to bring you and Felicity to the scene."

CHAPTER 30:

A gelid rush of foreboding injected itself directly into my heart and spread quickly through veins and arteries with each successive beat. My entire body took on a frightening chill. Hollowness filled my chest, and after a moment, my brain pointed out that I wasn't bothering to breathe. I released my mental grip on the feeling of icy terror and allowed my autonomic reflexes to continue once again unimpeded.

Even though I'm certain that my heart had never actually stopped beating, I would swear that I felt it stutter a bit as it seemed to restart.

I looked at Agent Mandalay and then slowly shook my head. "Call him back and tell him I said no."

"Do what?" Ben asked with confusion in his voice.

"But, Rowan, I thought you…" Constance began.

"Me, yes," I cut her off. "Felicity, no way. She's not getting anywhere near that sick bastard."

"Rowan…" Felicity brought her head up as she spoke.

"Listen, Row, the scene is secure," Ben offered.

"I don't care," I returned. "What do they want her there for anyway?"

"To interview," Mandalay said. "The same reason they want you."

"Interview about what?"

"Porter," she returned. "He called her today, so she's had direct contact with him as well. You need to understand, Rowan, the HNT looks for every piece of information they can possibly use. No matter how insignificant you may think it seems, they want to know about it."

"Fine. Then she can tell them everything he said to her by phone if they want to know that badly," I asserted.

"Rowan," Felicity interjected again. "You'll not be going without me then."

"Honey, you know as well as I do what Porter has done. I'm not willing to take the chance."

"Aye, but I am."

I shook my head vigorously. "No, Felicity, I can't accept that."

"Rowan," Mandalay began, "I can understand your concern, but think about it. There are over two dozen police officers on the scene, and that isn't even counting FBI and SWAT. Now, where else could Felicity be safer?"

"Right here as far as I'm concerned."

"I'm going," Felicity announced.

"No," I stated in the most adamant tone I could muster. "If they want me there, fine, but only me, not you. Those are my terms, and they're non-negotiable."

Felicity had pulled back slightly and now fixed me with an unforgiving stare as she piped up again. "Aye, but they're not yours to dictate, Rowan. If you are going then I am going. Those are MY terms."

"Felicity…"

"No," she insisted, her glare hardening. "Best you not argue with me on this because you won't win."

"But…"

"Aye, *Caorthann*, I said no." The stern quality that filled her voice when she cut me off was as much magickal as it was earthbound, maybe even more so.

This time, her use of the Gaelic version of my name was coupled with an undeniable energy. She meant to drive home a point, and she did so with earnest. She was correct. I couldn't win, and continuing to argue was just a waste of time. My desire to protect her was being trumped by her desire to protect me. Any other cards I could play would only bring us to an impasse.

I frowned and brushed my hand across the lower half of my face then shifted my gaze back and forth between Ben and Mandalay as I spoke. "Okay, but I want her as far removed from this as possible."

"Both of you will be," Mandalay replied. "The HNT is just going to be interviewing you, that's all. So you definitely won't be in any line of fire."

"I'll get our coats," Felicity announced, pulling away from me and skirting around Ben as he shuffled to the side.

"It's gonna be okay, white man," my friend told me.

"I hope so," I replied. "I don't have a very good feeling about this."

"*Twilight Zone?*" he asked.

I centered on the anxious energy that was using my spine as a multi-lane thoroughfare and felt the ache rise inside my skull as my scalp tightened. "Yeah, definitely."

Constance tried to assuage my obvious fear. "It's going to be okay." She gave me a slight smile then looked over to Ben. "We can take my car. Where's your coat, Storm?"

"On the couch." He gave a nod back toward the living room. "Thanks."

"No problem," she answered as she stepped around him. "Just don't get used to it."

"Jeez, Mandalay, now you sound like my wife," he jibed over his shoulder.

Her voice filtered back to us. "I knew I really liked Allison for some reason."

Ben swiveled his head back and focused on me. He stared at me in silence for a moment then jutted his chin toward me in a quick gesture as he brought his hand up to gingerly smooth back his hair.

"You seein' somethin'?" he asked quietly. "One of those visions?"

"No. Just feeling some stuff right now."

He gave me a questioning look. "So can't you do some hocus-pocus or something?"

"I wish I could."

"What about tossin' some salt around?" he asked. "I've seen you two do that. Ain't that some kind of protection thing?"

"Yes it is," I replied. "But trust me, this apartment has already been salted enough to give an elephant high blood pressure."

"So there's nothing you can do?"

"Stay grounded," I replied. "That's about it, I guess."

"Well do that then," he instructed. "So does this have anything to do with all that floppin' around you were doin' earlier?"

"I don't know, Ben." I reached up and began massaging my scalp again. "Maybe. I still have no idea what that is all about. All I can say is that something about this just feels wrong. It's almost like it's a big puzzle, but there's a crucial piece missing that would bring it all together and let you see what the picture is. Do you know what I mean?"

"Well, I don't know about a puzzle, white man," he echoed. "It seems pretty straightforward to me."

I shook my head. "No. There's something hinky about all of this."

"Hinky how?"

"That's just it. I don't know."

"You ain't helping me here, Row."

"That's pretty much the theme of the day, isn't it?" I retorted. "I'm sorry. This is all just going pretty fast, you know?"

"Yeah." He nodded. "I know."

I started to glance at my watch out of reflex and realized that I hadn't put it back on after my shower since it had been shattered. I turned and looked over my shoulder at the automatic coffeemaker. The digital display shimmered a five into a six as I watched, displaying the time as 8:36.

"Is it really that late?" I asked aloud.

"Uh-huh," Ben grunted. "Long day, huh? You get much sleep earlier?"

"I got a few hours, I guess, but they weren't exactly quality."

"Yeah, I figured as much. So, maybe all this is just the exhaustion and stress." He offered the second half of his observation with a shrug.

"Maybe," I verbally agreed, although in my head, I doubted it. Then I gave him a serious stare. "Listen, I need to ask you a favor."

"What's up?"

"Felicity," I said. "I need to know she's going to be taken care of."

"You'll both be safe, white man," he reiterated. "We already told ya' that."

"That's not what I mean," I replied. "I mean if something goes wrong."

"You ain't talkin about what I think…" He let his voice trail off as he furrowed his brow.

"Yeah," I nodded. "If something happens to me, I need you to promise me that you'll take care of Felicity."

"Nothing is gonna happen to you, Rowan." He informed me with absolute conviction in his voice while thrusting his splayed hand at me for effect. "They're just gonna interview you."

"But just in case."

"Don't be sayin' this shit, Row," he demanded. "Because if you're not gonna stick to the plan, you ain't goin'. Hear me?"

"Just promise me."

"Awww, Jeez, Rowan," he said. "Tell me you're going to play by the rules here."

"Please, Ben?" I appealed. "I need you to do this."

"Okay, yeah," he returned. "You know we would anyway. You two are family to Allison and me. But, I'm tellin' you that nothing is gonna happen, and if you try to do something stupid, I'll cuff you to the bumper of a patrol car; AFTER I kick your ass. Got me?"

"Yes, Ben, I understand."

"I'm not kidding, Row."

"Yeah. Me either."

"Maybe I'm wrong here, but shouldn't we have some lights flashing and sirens blaring?" I asked.

We had just pulled out of the parking lot of the apartment complex and onto the main drag with Constance behind the wheel and Ben riding shotgun. Felicity and I were parked in the back seat of the sedan, with me positioned behind Mandalay since Ben's seat was pushed back as far as it would go. My petite wife had even shifted more toward center in order to have any legroom at all.

We were belted in, and I had been fully expecting a mad dash through the city as soon as we began moving. Instead, Mandalay accelerated smoothly into traffic and joined the ebb and flow with less urgency than would be attributed to a trip to the local shopping mall.

"No big hurry," she said over her shoulder. "We'll be there in fifteen or twenty minutes."

"What do you mean no big hurry?" I repeated the comment back to her, certain that I had misunderstood. "Did I miss something here?"

"It's all part of the 'game', Rowan," she explained. "The longer they drag this out, the better position they will be in to negotiate."

"Porter isn't playing by their rule book," I insisted, trying to keep my emotions from assuming control and forcing me to escalate as they had done before. "I think they might want to consider a different strategy."

"They know what they're doin', white man," Ben offered with a diagonal glance back at me. "It's their job."

I sat back in the seat and grumbled. "I'm telling you that they are wrong. This isn't the same."

"I know it's hard," Constance spoke again. "But you really need to relax, Rowan. Hostage scenarios don't typically resolve in a matter of minutes. You are usually looking at several hours. Sometimes even days."

"Not this one."

"If the situation changes, someone will contact us," Ben told me. "Unless that happens, there's no reason for a Code Three response. So just sit back and enjoy the ride. You're gonna be wishin' for a little solitude once they start grilling you. Trust me."

I crossed my arms and shut my mouth. I appeared to be locked into a no-win situation with everyone this evening, so I decided not to press any harder. It would only serve to get me riled up.

I hadn't heard a peep out of Felicity, so I looked over at her and saw that she was fidgeting with the memory card on a professional-series digital camera. She never went anywhere without at least some type of photographic device at her disposal even if it was just the high-end point-and-shoot she always kept in her purse.

I continued to watch as she stared intently at the display on the back of the piece of equipment while expertly stabbing at the controls with her thumbs.

She had once told me that looking at the world from behind a lens made her feel safe. She could remain detached while still seeing everything. Sometimes, by becoming one with that intensity of focus, she would transition beyond the frame. The camera would become a microscope for her third eye, bringing into view things unseen in the physical realm.

As she switched the camera off and stuffed it back into her equipment bag, I made a mental note to stay out of the way if I noticed her looking through it anytime in the near future.

Fifteen minutes into the trip, we were moving along in what passed for the center lane of the highway. We had actually been making good time considering the icy condition of the roads and obscured dividing lines. Fortunately, traffic had been light due to the weather and time of night.

That bit of luck seemed to be expended, however. Up ahead of us, brake lights were suddenly beginning to announce themselves in dusky pairs, and the congestion was rapidly increasing.

I was pressed back into the seat, my face tilted upward and my eyes inspecting the dark headliner for lack of anything better to do. I felt the vehicle beginning to slow and canted my head forward.

"What's going on?" I asked.

"Sshhh," Mandalay admonished as she reached over and turned up the volume on the radio.

"…And we have a report of a multi-vehicle accident with injuries on eastbound Interstate Forty-Four at Jefferson," an announcer's voice issued from the speakers. "All lanes are shut down, so you might want to avoid that area for the time being. Also, there are reports of black ice on…"

"Friggin' wonderful," Ben proclaimed. "Guess we better go ahead and exit pretty quick, or we'll get caught up in that mess."

"That would probably be best," Constance agreed. "If we take the next exit, we could cut over and take Market down to Memorial."

"Yeah, sounds like a plan," he replied.

Mandalay's cell phone had begun to sing its tune as Ben was answering her. She reached for it as she glanced over her shoulder to make a quick visual check before changing lanes. She canted the wheel and eased the sedan over to the right and then flipped the device open and put it against her ear.

"This is Mandalay," she said.

The swath of bright headlights that suddenly illuminated the cabin of the vehicle seemed horribly out of place to me. I squinted to block them out. I was still trying to wrap my brain around why such intense light was coming at me from the driver's side of the car when the world as we knew it fell apart.

CHAPTER 31:

The mournful shriek of metal against metal filled my ears directly behind the explosive crunch of the other car slamming into ours. I was tossed hard to the side, my arms flailing in front of me as I reached for something to hold on to but found only handfuls of air.

I heard Felicity screaming on my right as the inertia was transferred to the rear end of our vehicle, causing it to whip wildly around on an off-centered axis. The safety belt bit into my shoulder and constricted around my waist as I strained against it.

"Holy shit!" Ben's voice boomed from the front seat.

I caught a quick glimpse of Mandalay expertly throwing hand over hand to veer the sedan into the direction of the skid in an attempt to bring it back under control.

I threw my right arm up and across the seatback, stretching it behind Felicity as we continued to pitch to the right. Out of reflex, I hugged her tight and pulled my forearm up around her head just as the other vehicle made a three-quarter spin to clip us once again with its rear end.

The additional force of the second hit propelled us again to the right, threading me straight out of my safety harness as my wife and I hammered into the passenger side door. My reflex had come just in time as my forearm took the brunt of the strike instead of Felicity's head.

A third crash sounded immediately on the heels of the second, and I felt the car lift upward on its side as sheet metal folded and groaned in protest.

Over the din, I heard Constance scream, "Goddammit!"

I knew it couldn't be good if she was using expletives. I threw my other arm over my wife, covering her face as Mandalay's unsecured cell phone flew over the back of the seat and ricocheted from my forehead. The tires were slipping across the icy pavement, making the vehicle jump and jerk as their surfaces would randomly achieve some modicum of traction, only to lose it in almost the same instant. I was expecting to roll at any moment and braced myself as best I could.

The unmistakable sound of glass shattering ripped through the air, but I couldn't identify where it was coming from. I stayed low in the seat and held tight to Felicity as the sedan thudded back down onto all four wheels, jolting us hard when it bounced.

Momentum carried us along, and I could feel that we were still languidly spinning. As we came upon the halfway point, we found ourselves sliding backward down the highway, headlamps from now oncoming vehicles casting harsh shadows within the cabin.

A new crash sounded in the near distance, and I pushed my head up to peer out the window just in time to see a newly involved vehicle fishtail into the passenger side of our car then bounce away into another.

We were thrown to the other side of the car, and my hip impacted heavily against the door handle. Felicity's body crushed against mine, and the air forced its way out of my lungs in a guttural huff.

The insane screech of metal on metal continued to underscore every other noise as horns blared into the cold night. I felt another thud, lighter this time, but still enough to propel me back into the seat and toss me upward. My arm was ripped away from Felicity, and her body followed mine as we both returned to sitting positions.

We were still skidding backward, and I looked forward to see blue halogen headlights filling the windshield. Before I could catch my breath, yet another vehicle joined the insanity by marrying itself with great purpose to the front end of ours. I snapped backward amid the deafening crunch, watching with detached interest as the interior filled with a hazy fog, and the windshield was instantly obscured by the deploying airbags.

I didn't black out. At least I don't think I did. Still, I couldn't begin to tell you how much time passed or what actually transpired between this moment in time and my last clear recollection, which was the white fabric of the airbags filling my field of vision.

The shrill cacophony of a car horn was insinuating itself into the mix of other sounds, effectively pushing everything else into the background.

I opened my eyes and saw that I was pitched forward, almost doubled over, and now staring at the floorboard. I put my hand against the back of the seat in front of me and pushed, levering myself into an upright position. I could feel someone moving next to me and turned to find Felicity pushing herself up as well. I could tell by the way she was moving that she was completely disoriented.

She began reaching toward the passenger side of the vehicle as she cried out for me, "Rowan!"

I slipped my hand over to her, and she jerked toward me the moment I touched her leg. She quickly shifted direction and grabbed for me, struggling against the center passenger lap belt that still encircled her waist. Her lower lip was bleeding, and there was a gash over her right eye, but she seemed to be coherent and moving okay.

"Are you all right?" I shouted over the din of the vehicle's horn.

"Aye, yes, I'm okay," she cried. "Are you okay?"

"I'm fine, I'm fine," I reassured her.

"Felicity! Rowan!" Ben's voice cut through the noise.

I looked up to see him reaching across the back of the seat. His nose was bloodied, and he seemed to be favoring his right hand. Looking past him, I could see a spidery, circular shatter point on the windshield that looked like it would just about fit his large fist.

"Ben!"

"Are you two okay?" he screamed.

"Yeah, I think so. You?" I shouted back.

"I think my fuckin' hand is broke," he returned. "Mandalay's unconscious. I think she's hurt bad."

"Oh Gods!" Felicity exclaimed as she continued to struggle with the lap belt. "Is she breathing okay?!"

"Yeah, I think so!" he yelled.

"Don't move her," Felicity called back to him.

"I know, Felicity, I know!" he returned. "Can you two get out?!"

"I don't know," I yelled back at him.

I sent my hands in search of the latch on my own safety harness and managed to thrust my knuckles into it hard enough to make it pop free. Taking hold of the door handle, I pulled it up and pushed. The door gave outward slightly, but other than that, it didn't really budge.

Looking out the window, I could see that the side of the vehicle was caved inward at the center structural pylon. I looked over at Felicity. "Honey, can you move over a bit!"

I was shouting to be heard over the blaring horn, but mid-sentence, there was a dull pop as a shower of sparks exploded from the front of the car. The lights flickered and went black. The horn warbled sickeningly then faded to silence. The last half of my sentence resounded through the cabin, breaking the new found calm.

Felicity shifted as far as she could to the opposite side of the vehicle, and I scooted with her. Twisting in the seat, I drew my legs up and lay back with my head almost in her lap. I pushed my right hand against the back of the front seat and then levered my left elbow into the other for support. Pistoning my legs with everything I had, I kicked hard against the door. It bounced outward a few inches and then sprung back against me.

I could hear the pained groan of metal from the front of the vehicle, and the ambient noise of the exterior burst inward along with a healthy blast of cold air. I kicked outward again, and the rear door creaked as it pushed open a few inches farther and remained there this time.

I sucked in a deep breath of chilly air and tensed all my muscles as I continued levering pressure against the mangled door. As I groaned, I looked up through the window and saw Ben with his shoulder wedged into the scant opening as he joined me in muscling it wider.

The sheet metal complained loudly, and the hinge popped out audible complaints as the door started to move. I closed my eyes and forced out a guttural scream as I sent everything I had into my legs and pushed. The sound started slowly, creaking through a low pitch, rising along the way until it burst forth as a loud crunch. My legs pistoned outward against nothingness as the door popped past the sticking point and flung open.

Ben's torso was already through the opening, and his good hand was extended toward me. I released my grip on the seats and took hold of the offered appendage. With a smooth pull, he slid me out the opening and up to my feet. As I stepped forward I turned, but he was already tucked back inside in the process of extracting Felicity in the same manner.

"Is everyone okay here?" A voice met my ears, and I looked back around to find a uniformed city police officer staring back at me, detached concern in his eyes.

Over his shoulder, I could see two patrol cars parked in the near westbound lanes on the opposite side of the concrete barrier. The emergency lights on the vehicles were flickering madly, and passersby were already slowing to gawk.

"The driver is hurt," I declared in answer. "She's unconscious."

The officer nodded as he looked over my shoulder at Ben and Felicity. I noticed that his arm moved almost instantly, and his hand rested on his firearm. I glanced back and saw that my friend's jacket was pushed back, revealing the grip of his Beretta peeking out of its snug home in his shoulder holster.

"I'm a cop," Ben told him, taking immediate notice of his posture. "Detective Storm. My shield's on my belt."

Ben moved his left hand slowly across and pushed back his jacket to reveal his badge. The uniformed officer relaxed noticeably and shifted his hand away from his weapon. As soon as the immediate tension faded, Felicity stepped forward and took hold of my arm.

"The driver of this vehicle is injured, and she is an FBI agent," Ben added, shifting without hesitation into his professional mode.

The uniformed officer immediately keyed up his radio and began speaking. "Dispatch, Unit Twenty-seven,"

"Twenty-seven, go ahead," came the static-plagued response.

"Dispatch, Unit Twenty-seven, ten seventy-two multiple vehicle accident with injuries on Interstate Forty-Four just west of Exit Two Eighty-eight. I have a federal officer down, over."

The speaker hissed again. "Twenty-seven, repeat officer down, over."

"Dispatch, Twenty-seven. Driver of involved vehicle is unconscious. Has been identified as FBI. One passenger identified as Detective Storm with homicide. He's injured but conscious and lucid, over."

"Twenty-seven, dispatch, rolling paramedics your location, over."

"Ten-four, dispatch."

I was rattled. It took a moment for me to realize that I was just standing there staring at the scene around me. I counted a total of five cars resting askew across the eastbound lanes of the highway. Mandalay's vehicle sat at the center of a small cluster of three that comprised the crux of the accident. The other two were spread out like billiard balls, one canted against the center median, the other was farther back and pointing into the oncoming traffic.

To my left, another officer was igniting flares and tossing them to the pavement at various intervals to create a cordoned area. I glanced around and saw that the occupants of the other vehicles seemed to be in far better shape than us.

"Rowan?" Felicity's voice called to me. "Are you okay?"

"Yeah, honey, yeah, I'm fine."

"You're staring off into space, then," she pressed. "Did you hit your head?"

"No, really, I'm okay," I said as I brushed her hair back from her face and gently touched her forehead. "How about you? You've got a pretty nasty cut over your eye. Looks like you're the one who hit her head."

"Aye, I'm okay. I'm worried about Constance though."

I nodded. "Me too."

I heard an electronic peal dance through the air, growing louder with each note and noticed Ben struggling to pull his cell phone from his belt with his left hand. By the time the device started into its next chorus, he had managed to snatch it up and thumb it on.

"Yeah, Storm here," he said, then waited a moment. "Yeah, well excuse me for not hearin' it. Uh-huh… Well that would be because somebody decided to hit us. Yeah… Uh-huh… Yeah, as in car wreck. Yeah, fuckin' totaled. Yeah, I'm busted up and Mandalay's hurt pretty bad but they're okay. A little rattled but okay. Yeah… Uh-huh…"

I was just turning to watch the officer who was checking on Constance when I heard my friend bellow, "You've gotta be fuckin' kiddin' me! Awww, Jeezus! There's no way in hell I can get him there that fast!"

CHAPTER 32:

"**H**ell yes I know it's only four miles," Ben barked into the cell phone. "If the fuckin' highway was open… Yeah, exactly. Uh-huh… There's a pileup at Jefferson too. Yeah, we're at Grand and Forty-Four, just west of the exit ramp. Yeah, can't miss it, there's a big friggin' pile of cars and enough flares down to decorate my birthday cake… Yeah, we'll be waitin'. Bye."

"What's going on?" I asked him as he made a few clumsy attempts to hook the phone back onto his belt then aborted the task and shoved it into the first available pocket he could find on his jacket.

"You were right, white man," he confessed. "Porter went off the deep end."

My stomach fell. I had almost forgotten why I was even out here in this mess to start with.

Felicity tensed against me and muttered, "Oh no…"

"He didn't?" I asked, leaving the subject of the question a solid implication rather than a spoken reality.

"No. He hasn't done anything yet that they know of, but he's making the threats." He spilled the details. "They thought they had him under control after they cut the line, but he escalated all of a sudden, and they haven't been able to talk 'im back down."

Car horns were randomly sounding from the growing sea of impatient drivers, adding punctuation to the blend of noises issuing from running engines and passing vehicles. Police radios scratched out communications in bursts of intermingled words and semi-cryptic ten-codes to keep the officers updated on the ETA of the paramedics, fire/rescue, and countless other things.

Looking past Ben and back down the highway, I could see flickering red lights in the distance. Far off sirens warbled and provided a high-pitched background for the occasional burp of an air horn.

"I hate to say…" I started.

"…I told you so, yeah, I know." He nodded his head vigorously as he finished the sentence for me. "Better just keep that observation to yourself, Row."

"Yeah, I will," I agreed. "So what are they doing?"

He continued his explanation. "They haven't gone in because they still don't know where he's holed up in there. But he's keepin' tabs on them somehow 'cause he knows what's goin' on every time they make a move, no matter which side of the building they go for. They're thinkin' he's gotta have a police band radio or a portable scanner. Something like that."

To my back, there was a droning hum that continued to grow louder by the second, throwing itself into the chaotic fray of sounds against an underscore of echoing thumps. It was the familiar sound of a helicopter. In the back of my mind, I wondered whose it was. It seemed too soon for an air ambulance, and I wasn't sure the media would even bother responding to the pileup considering the drama that was playing out on the riverfront.

"Great," I muttered with heavy sarcasm.

"Tell me about it." He nodded as he raised his voice against the growing din. "Anyway, about fifteen minutes ago he started demanding that they bring you to the scene. Since you were already on the way, they had no problem consenting even though it was going to be on their terms."

"Aye, that's about when Constance got that call," Felicity interjected.

"Yeah, exactly," Ben said. "And right when we got nailed."

"So can't they just tell him that I'm still on the way?"

He shook his head. "They've played that out. It's not workin' anymore. He finally hit 'em with an ultimatum. Says if he doesn't see you in front of the building in ten minutes, he's killing Sullivan, and that…" He paused and glanced at his watch. "…Was about three minutes ago."

A heavy rush of icy wind whipped around us, lifting a cloud of loose snow and causing me to squint as my eyes watered.

"Ten... Seven minutes?!" I yelped, forcing my voice upward to compete with the sound of the helicopter overhead. "There's no way..."

"Can you fly?" Ben shouted.

"Ben!" I returned. "This is no time for joking around. You know damn well that whole thing about Witches is just a myth!"

"No! I mean do you have any problems with flying?" He bellowed over the roar as he took hold of my shoulder and urged me to turn. "Cause right there's your fuckin' broom!"

The machine-fabricated vortex bit into my face as I twisted around, forcing me to cock my head down and to the side. My ears were filled with an inescapable roar as I watched a Bell JetRanger hurriedly touching down on the pavement a little better than thirty yards away.

"We've got five minutes," Ben yelled into my ear. "They'll have us there in two!"

"What about Constance?!" I screamed back at him.

"The paramedics will be here any minute!" he returned.

"Aye," Felicity's voice rose in my other ear. "I'll stay with Constance, then. You go!"

I snapped my head around to look at her. "Are you sure?!"

She nodded with a quick flourish, eyes glistening and her hair whipping about in fiery tangles. "Aye, but damn you, Rowan Linden Gant, you come back to me!"

I felt like I was stuck in the middle of the year's biggest box-office thriller. The script was moving forward at a frenzied pace, and we had now arrived at the ultimate stage of climactic melodrama. The point where, just before he rides off to save the world, the hero bares his soul to the gorgeous actress who is playing the part of the love interest.

Had I not been in the middle of it, I think I would have been forced to laugh at just how contrived it all seemed. Instead, I threw my arms around her and squeezed, burying my face against her neck beneath a cloud of spiraling auburn. I didn't know for sure what was ahead of me, but I knew that something still felt very wrong. I didn't really want to make a promise that I might very well be about to break.

I suddenly found myself hating the Lord and Lady for putting me in this position, despising them for what had been heaped upon me so unceremoniously in the past two plus years. I knew that I was rushing headlong toward a choice that no one should ever be forced to make. Moreover, with knowing that an innocent life was inexorably linked to my actions, there was no escape for me.

I had no idea what I had done to bring about this amount of horror as a payback, but I was rapidly approaching a crisis of faith.

I choked back a lump in my throat and spoke directly into my wife's ear, mimicking her penchant for using my full name whenever she wanted to drive her point home. "Remember that I love you more than anything, Felicity Caitlin O'Brien."

"Come on, Rowan!" Ben was screaming at me. "We gotta go now!"

I barely managed to kiss her as my friend manhandled me away, pushing me toward the waiting helicopter. "I'll bring him back, Felicity!" he screamed to her as we started to jog. "Promise!"

The frigid gale slapped us about, plastering any bit of loose clothing directly to skin and forcing its way through. We broke into a half run as we hunched over, our bodies almost involuntarily seeking escape from the driving force that beat down upon us as we entered the circular envelope of the spinning blades.

"What about your hand?!" I screamed at Ben as we ran.

"WHAT?!" came his response.

"YOUR HAND!" I shouted again, gesturing to my own then pointing to his. "WHAT ABOUT YOUR HAND?!"

He shook his head impatiently. "FUCK THAT!"

I canted to the left to avoid a chunk of vehicular debris then made a slight misstep on the slushy pavement and slipped to the side. The muscles in my thigh strained as I fought to stay upright, sending a sharp lance of pain through my groin and down my leg. Ben quickly clamped a large hand onto my upper arm and yanked me into balance, driving me back onto course toward the aircraft. I glanced up to get my bearings as I limped and saw the logo of a local television station emblazoned across the side of the helicopter.

"THIS IS A NEWS HELICOPTER!" I shouted.

"I KNOW!" Ben yelled. "THEY WERE ALREADY IN THE AIR! THEY'RE DOIN' US A FAVOR FOR A CHANGE!"

We both slid to a halt against the metal and Plexiglas skin of the vehicle. My friend immediately levered the front door open and gave me a push as I started to climb aboard. Once I was seated, he slammed the door and wrenched the rear entryway open.

The pilot was pointing and gesturing, and I realized that he was instructing me with hand signals to fasten my seat belt. I twisted wildly about and found the webbed nylon strap on either side of the seat then fumbled to marry the two ends together.

I felt the rear door, as much as heard it, when it slammed shut behind me. I shot a quick glance over my shoulder and saw Ben planting himself into a seat and frantically trying to secure his own harness one-handed. Another figure slipped into view and began helping him.

I felt someone poking me in the shoulder and looked over to see the pilot foisting a set of headphones upon me. I took them and pulled the semicircle over my head, only to have the earmuff-like shells slip down onto my jaw line. I reached up, slid the springy, crescent-shaped headband downward to tighten them and then readjusted the padded cups over my ears. An armature ending in a microphone jutted out from one side to hang in front of my face.

The sound of the engine was muffled but still present as a thick hiss of background static filled my ears. I looked forward through the Plexiglas bubble and saw Felicity in the distance, standing exactly where I had left her. She had her arms wrapped about herself, hugging her coat tightly to her body. Her hair continued to whip about on the man-made wind, slapping across her face and back over her shoulder, but her gaze never wavered as she stared directly at me.

"Welcome aboard SkyCam Two, Mister Gant," the pilot's voice crackled in my ears.

"Yeah," I answered him absently, still gazing out at my wife. "Thanks."

"Are we okay back there?" his voice popped through again.

A new voice answered; feminine and familiar. "All good, let's go."

Even through the barrier of the headset, I heard the high whistle of the spinning rotor as the pilot adjusted the collective to increase the pitch of the blades. My stomach jumped as the aircraft lifted easily from the ground and floated a few inches above the pavement with a slight rocking motion. The scream of the rotors shot through several octaves as we continued to rise on the cushion of air. I watched Felicity as she turned her face slowly upward, following the progress of the aircraft.

The red emergency lights of a life support vehicle bathed the area below us as paramedics arrived on the scene. With a smooth tilt, the helicopter spun in a quick semi-circle, pivoting on its axis as it nosed forward and shot into the night sky.

"We have about two minutes before we arrive on the scene Mister Gant." The female voice filtered into my ears over the background static.

It was the next sentence out of her mouth that told me why she sounded so familiar. "Do you think you could answer a few questions for our viewers?"

CHAPTER 33:

B randee Street waited patiently for me to respond. At least, I assumed she was being patient. I couldn't actually see her face, and the only thing I could hear was an even hiss of the background static. Getting my story had long ago become a personal mission to her. It had started right from the first time I had ever helped the police with a murder investigation, in fact.

Ever since, and including our first encounter, I'd given her nothing more than a handful of "no comments."

"I really don't think that this is the right time for an interview, Miz Street," I replied.

I turned my head and looked out through the window at the night, trying to ignore her. Below, the building lights tossed harsh luminance into the blue-black shadows of the snowy landscape. A soft halo of light seemed to rise above the concrete and steel structures, forming a fuzzy dome of cyan and white, streaked here and there with pale yellow. From this height, it made Saint Louis appear almost as a garish pockmark on the land.

We were cruising in what felt like a straight line, floating over the inner crescent of midtown, thirty seconds away from downtown proper. Up here we were autonomous, shrouded by a sea of darkness. There was still a heavy cloud blanket even though the snow had tapered off to nothing more than flurries hours ago. Above us, there were no stars and no moon, only the dark grey underbelly of the low stratum, illuminated by the reflected light of the city beneath.

The gauges on the instrument panels were rimmed yellow-orange, bringing a tepid illumination to the inside of the helicopter. Out the window to my right, I could see the lights of the vehicular traffic on Interstates Forty-Four and Fifty-Five—red taillights snaking along toward the east and south, yellow-white headlamps streaking north and west.

"Just a couple of questions, Mister Gant." She tried again.

"Really, Miz Street…" I began.

"Look, Mister Gant, my day started at three a.m. filling in as co-anchor. I haven't even been home yet."

"Join the club."

"What I'm trying to say is that I wouldn't be right here, right now, if I didn't think this story was important. Can't you just answer a few questions?"

"Lay off, Brandee." I heard Ben's voice in the headset.

"I wasn't talking to you, Storm." Her voice switched from an appeal to a seething rebuff.

"Maybe not, but I'm telling ya' to back off," he snarled. "Just friggin' do something good for a change without expectin' a payback!"

"Damn you, Storm, I…"

"HEY!" I snapped into the microphone. "Both of you calm down."

My headache was rallying once again and every inch of my body ached. I had too much on my mind to cope with this sudden outburst of bickering, and I felt like my head was about to explode. Being a part of an investigation was one thing, but everything hinging on me alone was unnerving.

I took in a deep breath and closed my eyes. I could feel the aircraft roll slightly to the side, and I tensed in the seat. When I reopened my eyes, I could see riverfront now occupied the side window, and the bright, red anti-collision light atop the Gateway Arch was winking in measured pulses, warning us to keep our distance. We completed our veer through a shallow turn and then continued on a straight course.

"Listen," I continued speaking, now that they had both shut up. "Miz Street, I need you to do me a favor. Just get me to the scene, and I promise I'll give you guys an exclusive once this is all over."

"Rowan!" Ben admonished.

"Let me talk, Ben," I shot back and then continued with a qualification. "Whatever I can legally discuss with you, Miz Street, I will."

"An exclusive." She restated the words with an air of suspicion. "You'll talk to our station only?"

"I'll go you one better," I returned. "I'll talk to you and you alone. It will be your story. No strings attached. Deal?"

I could hear the combination of excitement and mild disbelief in her voice when she replied, "Are you serious, Gant?"

"You ever see the TV show *Bewitched*?" I asked.

"Sure, but what's that got to do with anything?" she asked.

I twisted in my seat and turned my face to her. When I was certain she could see me, I splayed out my left hand and placed the index and middle fingers on either side of my nose, pointing in toward my eyes, then said, "Witches honor."

"Here we are," the pilot's voice came over the headset.

I turned my eyes back forward and then immediately gripped the edges of my seat as the aircraft rolled up on its side without warning. We hooked around in a steep, semicircular turn before the pilot brought us back upright. With a smooth hover, we began settling earthward with the nose tilted slightly up.

While I struggled to force my stomach back into its proper place, I shot a glance over at the pilot and noticed for the first time that as years went he was wearing better than a decade more than I was.

"Vietnam?" I uttered the single word query as I felt the skids bump against pavement once again.

"One ninety-second AHC" was all he said.

The aircraft had come briefly to rest on a small, private parking lot for one of the riverboat casinos that occupied dock space in front of Laclede's Landing. The lot itself was an asphalt plateau situated between Second and Third Streets, ringed by a tall, chain link fence, and under normal circumstances, manned by a security guard at a glassed-in booth. Because of its location along the tiered rise, it actually looked down into the front of the building where Porter was holed up.

The large, paved section of the short city block was almost completely devoid of any vehicles, having been cleared earlier by the authorities. In fact, the only cars up here were a few police cruisers parked at strategic points and a single, official-looking sedan.

Behind us on the next block was an enormous electrical sub-station that serviced a large portion of the city. Flanking the building on the left was another portion of the substation, and on the right was an open lot that butted against Biddle Street. A second vacant warehouse sat behind the one before us with aging railroad tracks in between.

Upon initial inspection, there didn't really seem to be any place for Porter to go where he wouldn't be spotted immediately—even if he was able to get past the local perimeter. I found a small amount of solace in that fact considering that I had left Felicity essentially alone.

I was just pulling the headset off and handing it back to the pilot when my door swung open. The roar of the helicopter's engine, which had leapt in volume the moment my ears were uncovered, now vaulted up the scale even farther. I turned quickly, somewhat startled.

"MISTER GANT?!" A voice managed to make its way to me from the parka-wearing young woman who was holding the door wide.

I nodded at her, fiddled about with the release in my lap until the belt came free, then pulled myself out of the seat and through the opening. Ben was already climbing out of the back and levering the door shut when I set foot on the pavement.

I turned back and gave the pilot a quick nod as I shut the front door and felt it latch. The three of us then hunched over beneath the rotor wash and scurried away toward the dark sedan several yards to the south.

I heard the repetitious thump growing behind me as the collective once again tilted the rotating blades and applied lift to the aircraft. The whine of the engine rose, and the helicopter hovered upward.

"I'm Agent Kavanaugh with the hostage negotiation team," the young woman told us as we came to the rear of the four-door vehicle, carefully modulating her voice against the sound of the aircraft. She quickly popped the lid on the trunk and after reaching in, withdrew a Kevlar flak vest. "Before we go down to the street, Mister Gant, you need to put this on."

"What for?" I asked. My voice was starting to go hoarse from all the yelling. "Eldon Porter doesn't use a gun."

"Standard operating procedure, sir," she returned.

"I don't need it."

She started to respond then paused as the helicopter rose past us and nosed off into the night sky, taking with it the brunt of the noise. As it faded into the background, she dropped her volume several notches and spoke. "Mister Gant, let me explain this briefly. Number one: you are a civilian, and from this moment on, you are my responsibility. Number two: the simple fact is we have no way to know for certain what he has with him in the way of weapons. Number three: as long as you are on the scene, you go by our rules. And, finally, number four: we don't have time for this. So put the damn vest on now!"

"Fine." I gave my reluctant agreement and started shrugging off my coat. "Give it to me."

I had been subject to wearing one of these before, and I'd hated every minute of it. Granted, it had been right at the end of a muggy Saint Louis summer. The temperature had been hovering around ninety even though it was the middle of the night. And, on top of that, I'd been plagued with an aggravating itch that the vest had rendered unreachable for the duration.

Still, even discounting all of those factors, body armor had been one of the most uncomfortable things I'd ever worn.

I slipped into the vest and in the process realized just exactly how sore I was. My body creaked like an old, wooden sailing ship, and I suspected I had bruises forming on top of bruises. I grimaced and forced my torso into the armor then wrestled with the Velcro straps. I wriggled about inside the somewhat bulky protective garment as I smoothed them down. Agent Kavanaugh inspected the closures, taking a moment to rip several of them open and pull them tighter.

"I was thinking I might like to breathe," I declared with a sarcastic bite as she tightened the last one.

"I was thinking I might like you to walk away alive," she retorted without looking up. "You're no good to us dead."

"Thanks for the compassion," I scoffed.

She didn't miss a beat with her own acerbic reply. "You're welcome."

Ben handed me my coat, and I struggled to pull it back on over the vest.

Agent Kavanaugh was already climbing into the driver's seat of the sedan when she called to us. "Come on!"

We followed suit; Ben took the front passenger seat while I jumped into the back. I was still pulling my door shut when Kavanaugh spun the tires against the slushy pavement and expertly whipped the vehicle around in a tight half-donut.

I rocked inward and felt the door partially latch then sat up and looked forward. I happened to catch a quick glimpse of Ben's injured right hand as he twisted to look back at me. He was holding it balled up in a tight fist and cradled against his chest. Even in the dark, I could tell it was covered in blood, and when I looked up at his face, I saw immediately that he was mutely coping with severe pain.

"You really need to have that hand checked out, Ben," I told him. "It doesn't look very good."

"What? You a doctor all of a sudden?" he retorted.

"Ben…"

"Don't worry about it. I'll get it taken care of when this is over."

We rocked to the side as Agent Kavanaugh whipped the vehicle out of the lot at a sharp right angle, sped forward, and then made another ninety degree turn to the right. She accelerated down the hill, only to quickly apply the brakes, fishtail the sedan through another right hand turn, and bring it skidding to a halt diagonal to the curb.

"Well, that was fun," Ben quipped as he turned back to the front and reached across with his left hand to open his door.

Our no-nonsense escort already had my door open and was hustling me from the back of the vehicle. Once I was out, she led me toward a small clutch of very serious-looking individuals.

A trim man, looking to be in his late forties or early fifties, was at the center of the activity. He was wearing a headset that appeared to be connected to a large, gadget-laden, black box. Upon close inspection, the container looked to me like a deep suitcase. The hinged clamshell of the case was wide open, displaying a patch panel and compact recording equipment, as well as an array of switches and dials.

He fixed his gaze on me and gave a questioning raise of his eyebrow. He must have received a response from Agent Kavanaugh as he immediately executed a satisfied nod of his head and continued talking.

"Yes, Eldon," he said into the headset microphone. "He's here. I'm looking right at him. Can't you see him from the window?"

He grimaced for a moment, and I wondered what Eldon was saying to him. His response that followed a few seconds later gave me a clue.

"No, Eldon, I'm not trying to trick you into giving away your position. I just want to make sure you know I'm telling you the truth. Yes… Yes, I know. Yes, that is him. Okay, fine. Now, according to my watch, we came in well under your deadline."

He continued staring at me with that as his only acknowledgment of my presence. Around us, members of the team appeared to be taking notes while others seemed to be in the process of arranging them on a large board.

"All right, Eldon," he said. "I can let you talk to him for a minute, but I'm going to need something from you... Hey, Eldon, I kept my end of the bargain. You wanted Mister Gant here, and I made good on my promise. He's on site. This is all give and take, Eldon."

I studied the man as he worked, wishing I could apply the same detachment that I was witnessing in him. At the same time, I wondered if that detachment was merely a stoic front and that perhaps he internalized these things even more than I did.

"Okay then. I want you to put Miss Sullivan on the line, so I know she is okay. Simple, right?" He paused for a moment. "Give and take, Eldon, give and take. Right now it's your turn to give... Okay... That's good... Thank you."

He paused again, and I waited.

"Miss Sullivan?" the man suddenly said with a questioning note in his voice. "This is Special Agent Scott McCoy with the FBI. Have you been harmed in any way? Miss Sullivan? Miss Sullivan?"

Agent McCoy's eyes hardened, and the lines in his face grew deeper as he frowned. In that instant, he actually seemed human as opposed to just the detached automaton I'd been watching for several moments.

"That wasn't much of a conversation now was it, Eldon?" he said into the microphone. "Okay... Calm down, he's right here... Yes, I'm going to put him on the line. Hold on."

McCoy twisted back a half turn to the box and pulled out a handset. When he turned back to me, he held it down to his side and fixed his stare with mine. "All right, this is how we need to play this, Mister Gant..."

I shot him a concerned glance, looking first at the handset by his side then at his headset. He noticed it immediately. He turned the handheld phone up so I could see it. "We're fine, there's a talk button on this, and right now my headset is muted."

I nodded, feeling a little chagrined at having questioned him.

"Now, I'm going to put you on the line with Porter," he continued. "We will be listening in. The only thing I want you to do is calm him down. Once you've done that, we take over again. It may sound crass, sir, but you just became a carrot for us to dangle in front of him."

"That doesn't bother me," I returned. "But you probably aren't going to like how I calm him down."

He shook his head at me. "Mister Gant," he said. "We heard your conversations with him earlier so we get the picture. Truth is I don't particularly care what you have to do as long as you don't make him any promises. I just want that hostage out of there alive."

"Believe me, the feeling is mutual," I replied.

He held the handset out to me. "Press the button to talk, and let it go if you want to say something to us without him hearing. Remember, NO promises. I'll handle the negotiating. Understood?"

"Yeah," I affirmed. "You negotiator. Me carrot. No promises."

I stepped forward and took the device out of his hand then drew in a cleansing breath. I let it out slowly from my mouth in a thin cloud of steam and then felt myself join with a solid ground. I placed the handset to my ear and squeezed the talk button.

"Listen up you sonofabitch," I said with more than just a hint of sincere anger. "You are really starting to get on my nerves."

CHAPTER 34:

I turned to face the building as I spoke. It didn't exactly tower over us, but at five stories, it definitely required a rearward tilt of the head to see the top. Large windows were spaced at regular intervals across the brick face, vertically rectangular with a slight arch at the top of each. Unfortunately for us, every one of them was securely boarded over with aging plywood.

I had to lean from side to side as I inspected the scene before me because for some reason, Agent Kavanaugh had placed herself between the structure and me. I was at once reassured and at the same time annoyed by what I considered to be an inexplicably overprotective gesture.

"You tell them not to even think about coming in here, or she's dead" came Eldon's frantic response from the earpiece. "I know every move they make. Do you hear me?"

"I think we all do." I gave a terse response.

He didn't even acknowledge my comment, moving straight into a demand instead. "Where have you been?"

"On my way here," I responded. "Why? Are you getting lonely?"

"Shut up, Gant," he spat. "Just shut up!"

"Fine," I answered. "I really didn't want to talk to you anyway."

I loosened my grip on the handset, keeping it to my ear, but allowing the talk button to release, effectively muting my side of the conversation.

"Gant!" his screaming voice issued from the earpiece. "Don't you hang up on me, Gant!"

I took a moment to gaze up and down the street. The semicircle of squad cars I'd seen on the television earlier had now been rearranged into a strategic perimeter. I immediately spotted police officers from at least two departments, not counting the highway patrol. That isn't even to mention the FBI agents that were clustered around me.

Paramedics were already on the scene, preparing for the worst or maybe even the best. Who could say? I guess it just depended upon which side of the fence you were standing on. At any rate, I noticed that at the moment, one of them was closely inspecting Ben's injured hand.

"GANT!" Eldon screamed again.

I continued holding the handset but simply listened. My fingers would tend to twitch as he spoke, and an angry retort was caught somewhere in the middle of my vocal chords. I consciously forced myself to remain quiet and several times found myself willing my fingers to loosen before they could connect with the switch.

Several steps to my right I saw a small group of plainclothes officers. I assumed them to be detectives attached to the Major Case Squad; primarily because at the center of the huddle was Lieutenant Albright giving instructions with animated thrusts of her hands. They were close enough for me to hear her talking but too far away for anything to be intelligible. As I stared at the clutch of officers, Albright's gaze met mine. She paused and frowned severely, fixing me with the proverbial look that could kill. After a pair of seconds, she looked away and continued her briefing.

"Gant!" Porter's voice came again. "I know you're there! Gant!"

I kept waiting. I was banking on the fact that his attention would focus directly on me and that he would forget about Star. As long as he was ignoring her, he wasn't hurting her. At least, that was my simplistic theory.

I could feel the tension rapidly increasing around me. Some of it was mine, but the majority was coming from the lead hostage negotiator and his team. They couldn't say that they hadn't been warned. For all intents and purposes, they knew what I was going to do once I got on the phone—even if my current ploy was somewhat off my previously traveled path. Still, I had to give them credit for their level of patience. Even with the mounting pressure, no one jumped the gun, and they let me continue playing it out my way.

I'm sure they were all speculating on whether or not I knew what I was doing, and if I had to guess, I would bet that someone was standing by to pull the plug on me at any moment. What I wasn't about to tell them though, was that I was dwelling on that very same issue myself. I was making this up as I went along, and my imagination was getting very weary, very fast.

"Goddammit, Gant! I'll kill her! I will!"

I looked up at the building once again. I didn't know if he was watching me at the moment, but based on the earlier exchange between him and Agent McCoy, I gathered he was able to see me if he wanted to. For me, the façade was a visual connection, so I continued to scan the boarded-over windows in search of his face.

I slowly depressed the talk button and then began speaking. "Goddammit? Did I hear you right? My, my, my, Eldon. Taking your Lord's name in vain?"

"Don't push me, Gant!" he shot back.

"Isn't there a commandment about that or something, Eldon? You know what? I think there is. Seems to me it goes: Thou shalt not take the name of the LORD thy God in vain."

"Don't you dare pass judgment on ME, Gant."

"Why not?" I asked with mock surprise. "Turn about fair play, Eldon."

"Goddammit, Gant! I said…"

"Again, Eldon?" I cut him off. "What happened? Don't tell me that somehow the devil got behind you."

"I told you I'll kill her!"

"Yeah, you keep saying that," I spat. "So what's stopping you?"

"I will, Gant! I'll do it!"

"You talk a good game, but I don't think so, Eldon. Not this time, and let me tell you why." I continued with my explanation, ignoring his insistent commentary. "You need Millicent. You need Millicent to get to me. That's what this is all about, isn't it, Eldon?"

I waited for him to reply and heard only labored breathing at the other end, so I pressed forward.

"See," I told him. "What you really want is to kill me, not her. We both know that. Hell, everyone here knows that. You've made no secret of it. But there's something else we both know: if you kill Millicent, about two seconds later a team of heavily armed SWAT guys is going to screw up your little world.

"If that happens, Eldon, it's all over. There's no way you'll ever get to me. How do you think your God is going to feel about that?"

"My God is a compassionate God," he snarled.

"No, Eldon," I countered. "I've read your book. I know what it says. Your God is a vengeful God."

"Thou shalt not suffer a Witch to live, Gant," he finally replied. "And she's a Witch. She must be punished for her sins."

"Are you still stuck on that?" I admonished. "You know, when I read that particular passage, there was a lot more to it than that. Are you using some kind of abridged edition?"

"Vengeance is mine," he returned.

"Saith the Lord, Eldon," I came back immediately. "Let's get the quote right if you are going to use it. Or, is it maybe that you're trying to tell me that YOU are the Lord? If you are, then I think we are talking about a major sin here. Hubris, idolatry, the whole nine yards."

A quiet lull followed my observation, and I listened closely to the sounds coming from the handset. I wasn't entirely sure what I was hearing at first. As the noise began, it sounded like sobbing, but after a moment, it inched up in volume and started taking on the properties of a throaty chuckle.

"Glad you find this all so entertaining, Eldon," I chided.

"You're good, Gant." Porter finally eked out the words through the insane laugh. "I'll give you that, you're really good. But I'm not fooled. Maybe a man without true faith would have fallen for your lies but not me."

"Well, Eldon," I answered in a pseudo-friendly tone. "You know how it is. Satan has an agenda, and he expects me to keep it."

"Don't mock me, Gant."

"Who says I'm mocking you, Eldon? You're the one who keeps telling me that I'm doing Satan's bidding."

"You know what I mean."

"Do I?"

"Stop trying to mess with my mind, Gant." He hardened his voice. "It won't work. You know my path is clear, and nothing you say can shake my belief."

"Fine," I replied. "You're right, let's just quit screwing around."

"Yes, let's."

The conversation had moved through a series of levels since it had begun. In my mind, I seemed to have accomplished the task given me by Agent McCoy, but he had yet to assume control of the phone. I decided I would just keep going until someone took the device away from me.

I wasn't really interested in chitchatting with Porter, to be honest. There were several things I wanted to say, but they didn't fall under the heading of pleasant conversation. I mentally scrolled through the list but realized quickly that the majority of them might very well undo what I had just accomplished.

I wasn't sure what my next comment should be. I didn't quite know how fragile the calm was that I had reached with Porter. I suppose what finally came out of my mouth was as much a surprise to me as it was to anyone else. What's more, the calm with which I made the comment was actually startling.

"Come on out and get me, Eldon, I'm waiting right here."

"With a small army," he spat.

"Hey, you invited them when you kidnapped Millicent," I chided. "Don't lay that one at my feet."

"I'm not coming out," he replied.

"Okay, then what do you suggest we do about this?"

There was a heavy pause before his voice issued from the earpiece. "You come in here."

"You see, now, Eldon, I'd love to do that," I offered. "Really I would, but I don't think the gang down here is going to allow it."

"It's heresy for them to protect you that way."

"Protect me?" I responded with feigned surprise. "They aren't protecting me. They're protecting you. You see, Eldon, everyone down here knows that I have every intention of killing you."

His next words came as an even hiss. "You come in, and I send the Witch out."

As I'd been expecting, someone took the phone away. Not physically from my hand, but in a sense, the method was just as unceremonious. This time there was no warning click as there had been when I was back at the apartment. No rush of static. No beep. No nothing. The handset simply retreated into the all too familiar thickness of electronic death as the line was instantly severed by the HNT.

"Eldon, Mister Gant isn't here to negotiate with you," I heard Agent McCoy begin. "Now, I gave you something you wanted. It's time for you to give something in return…"

I turned back to face the team and held the now-useless phone out in front of me. Agent Kavanaugh appeared by my side and took the device from my hand then settled it carefully into the large gadget box. When she had said I was her responsibility, she had apparently been serious.

"Don't trust me?" I quipped, keeping my voice low.

"It's not a trust issue, Mister Gant," she returned.

I answered with a shake of my head, "Could've fooled me."

She took me by the arm and began guiding me away from the group. "You've been very helpful, Mister Gant, and you did very well on the line. Especially using the hostage's first name repeatedly."

"Yeah, I read about that somewhere," I replied. "But it won't work with him. He doesn't care about her identity."

"That remains to be seen," she returned. "As well as you did, however, I would question the wisdom of that last ploy."

"You mean when I told him I was going to kill him?"

"Yes sir," she acknowledged.

I glanced over at her as we walked, and I spoke with absolute sincerity, "Who says it was a ploy?"

"I know this is an unpleasant situation for you to be in, but we need to ask you for some more help," Agent Kavanaugh told me.

We were sitting in the back of a large panel van, the inside of which looked like a compact conference room, communications center, and armory all rolled into one. I was holding a thermos cup that was half-filled with coffee. I had accepted it when it was offered but after a couple of sips, came to the conclusion that I didn't really want it. Not that it was bad or anything, I was just far too wired to even think about drinking it.

As it was, the only reason I was still holding the container was that I didn't seem to be able to find a place to put it down. Any space that appeared like it would fit the cup was already supporting something else far more important looking and in the case of the electronics, far more expensive.

"Forgive me for asking then," I replied, fighting to keep the shortness from my voice, "but if you need my help, shouldn't I be out there instead of in here?"

The entire day, right up to a very few moments ago, seemed to have been built around an ever-increasing urgency. Now, suddenly that imperative had slammed face first into an invisible wall. That barrier had presented itself in the form of the standard operating procedures for hostage negotiation.

"There's no rush," she told me. "This is standard procedure. It takes several hours at least before Stockholm Syndrome starts taking hold."

"I already told you this wacko doesn't care about her identity," I remarked. "You aren't going to get any Stockholm Syndrome. He doesn't play by your pat psychological profile."

"We know what we are doing, Mister Gant."

"I'm sure you do under most circumstances, but you're wrong this time."

"How do you know that?"

"Long story. You wouldn't believe me if I told you."

She looked back at me and frowned then absently drummed the end of a ballpoint pen on the notepad she was holding.

"Be that as it may, you're safer in here," she finally replied.

"From what, Agent Kavanaugh?" I asked as I motioned in what I thought was the general direction of the warehouse. "He's hiding out in the building. What's he going to do to me?"

She pointed toward the opposite corner of the van. "The building is that way."

"Sorry," I snapped. "It's been a really freaking long day."

"I understand that." She nodded sympathetically. "But as I told you earlier, we don't know for sure what Porter has in there with him, and now that the urgency of the moment has passed, we want you to stay out of sight."

"Unless you expect him to throw loose bricks at me, I doubt you have anything to worry about."

"Mister Gant," she said. "Apparently, I am not making myself clear. While we do not know this for a fact, we do have every reason to believe that Porter is armed."

"You mean with a gun?" I shook my head and asked the question with an overabundance of incredulity in my voice. "No way. That's not his style."

"Style or not, Mister Gant," she contended. "The second victim this morning was shot once in the back of the head. That tells us he has a gun."

It took a moment for what she had said to register. When it did, I'm sure the look of confusion on my face had to be textbook.

"Whoa, whoa, whoa." I waved my free hand at her. "Back up for a second. What second victim? What are you talking about?"

"At the scene on Locust where Mister Harper was found, a second body was discovered. The victim was male, approximately mid-sixties and apparently homeless. The current theory is that he entered the warehouse in search of shelter and stumbled upon Porter in the act of... Well, you know."

"How do you know it was Porter who killed him?"

"Fingerprints on the body," she returned matter-of-factly. "Porter apparently had Mister Harper's blood on his hands already."

The image of Randy's corpse imprinted itself on my retinas, dancing in the air before me like a three-dimensional movie. I stopped for a moment and fought back a wave of nausea.

I shook my head again when the feeling passed. "No way. This doesn't add up. Porter doesn't use a gun, and besides he kills Witches not homeless people."

"What about Mister Kasprzykowski?" she asked, stumbling over the name. "He wasn't a Witch."

"Okay, I'll give you that," I replied. "But even then, he killed him with a blow to the back of the head with a hammer."

"Yes, and he killed this homeless man with a gunshot to the *back of the head*. I'm certain you know that Porter has a criminal history, Mister Gant," she continued. "Several of his earlier crimes involved handguns."

I closed my eyes and started rubbing my forehead. My perpetual headache was working its way around the inside of my skull. The pain was thick and just the other side of normal. As usual, I couldn't put my finger on the cause other than to say that it was coming from a source beyond the physical realm.

"No. No way," I said. "Porter doesn't have a gun."

"Mister Gant." Agent Kavanaugh took on a concerned tone. "I really don't understand why you are having such a problem with this."

"*Twilight Zone*," I muttered.

"Excuse me?"

"*Twilight Zone*," I said a bit more clearly as I re-opened my eyes and looked up at her.

She shook her head as a mask of obfuscation passed over her features. "I don't understand."

"Ask the big Indian outside," I told her. "He'll explain it to you."

CHAPTER 35:

"What did he say to you during the first conversation this morning?" Agent Kavanaugh asked.

We had been sequestered in the back of the panel van for something close to half an hour by now. She had all but dismissed my objection to the idea that Eldon Porter was using any type of firearm, as well as my suggestion that she talk to Ben for an explanation as to how I could be so certain. Of course, I don't suppose that his answer would have been any more convincing than mine.

"Which part?" I asked, still trying to temper my impatience at the "hurry up and wait" overtone of the current situation.

The order of the moment was taking the form of an in-depth interview of yours truly. The questions that comprised the Q & A ranged from the expected to the seemingly non sequitur. She had already made several queries that appeared to come from far left and well over the horizon, leading me at times to simply stare back at her with a dumbstruck gaze.

She gave me a quick shake of her head. "Any details you can remember. Any at all."

"Let's see," I sighed heavily. "He quoted a few Bible verses to me, then informed me that he intended to rape my wife. Is that what you want to know?"

The abruptness in my voice was unmistakable. Any attempt at disguising my anxiety was effectively rendered null and void by my rapidly hardening attitude.

Kavanaugh stared back at me for a moment, wagging the ballpoint pen back and forth between her thumb and forefinger as she drummed it on the legal pad in her lap. The rhythm of the nervous tick wasn't helping my headache in the least. If anything, it was simply reminding me that it was there. I was just about to reach out and snatch the pen from between her fingers when she stopped.

"Mister Gant," she began. "I know this is hard, and trust me, I realize this doesn't seem important to you, but each detail gives us something more to work with."

"Forgive me," I told her. "But some of your questions really haven't made much sense to me."

"On the surface, to most people, they don't," she agreed. "But we aren't in a normal situation here. Specific details are important to the overall profile of both the individual and the situation."

"Maybe I'm dense, but I don't see how some of the things you've asked can relate to all of this."

"Believe me, Mister Gant, you would be amazed by what seemingly insignificant details can sometimes mean the difference between peaceful resolution and tragedy."

"Maybe so, but ten minutes ago you asked me what color coat he was wearing earlier today. I mean, come on…"

"Do you play chess, Mister Gant?"

"Yes," I answered. "And will you please call me Rowan? I've been getting 'Mistered' and 'Sir'ed' to death today."

"All right, Rowan," she continued. "As a chess player, you are certainly familiar with the concept of a stalemate, correct?"

"Of course."

"Well, that's exactly what a hostage scenario is. A stalemate. A big, hairy, no-win situation. The thing is, the hostage-taker doesn't know this. We do, but he doesn't. His mental state usually places him in one of two frames of mind. Either he believes he has the upper hand and will be able to force his demands on us, or he is in such a state of desperation that he believes he cannot win.

"The second state is the worst because that is usually when he will start killing hostages in an attempt to regain perceived control of the situation. Our job is to make an end run around the stalemate by convincing him that we are as concerned for his well being as we are for the hostage or hostages."

"I understand that," I said. "But the color of his coat?"

"Sometimes, even when you think it is going well, something that appears wholly unrelated can make everything go sour." Kavanaugh sighed. "Let me give you an example. I worked a hostage negotiation three years ago in Nashville, Tennessee. It was a bank robbery gone bad. The gunman had five hostages, but things had stayed fairly calm. We were in the ninth hour, and everything was going by the book. It really looked like we were going to be able to bring on a positive resolution with no casualties, not even the gunman.

"As a good faith move for the release of one of the hostages, we gave in to a request for soda. A specific brand of root beer actually." She paused for a moment. There was a distant look in her eyes that bespoke of repressed sadness and maybe even a modicum of self-blame. She looked down at the notepad in her lap then back to me. "Two minutes after we sent it in, the gunman went berserk, and without warning he killed the hostage he had told us he would release. He shot her point blank in the back of the head as he shoved her out the door.

"Her name was Becky, and she was a twenty-three-year-old teller-trainee with a husband and a one-year-old daughter." She paused again as if taking a moment to force the memory from her mind, and then asked, "Do you know why he killed her?"

I simply shook my head.

Her expression moved in the direction of controlled anger for a pair of seconds and then blanked to a professional, matter-of-fact countenance as she looked me in the eyes. "Because the soda was in a can instead of a bottle. We had missed a detail."

I couldn't think of anything to say that I was sure hadn't already been said. I let out a heavy breath and closed my eyes. I had been able to feel the burst of anguish that came from Agent Kavanaugh as she relayed the incident. To be honest, when she had first started, I wasn't entirely sure the story was going to be anything more than a textbook example. That thought proved itself to be wrong within the first few sentences.

Still, had it not been for the empathic connection now presenting itself, I'm sure I would have believed she had fabricated the whole thing simply to benefit her explanation. I think maybe Ben's jaded attitude had done more than just begun to wear off on me. It had become an integral part of my personal makeup.

"So…" She stopped short. I watched as she consciously took a deep breath herself, and then she began again. "So, I know that some of my questions might seem off the wall to you, Rowan, but there is a reason for them. Everything matters even if you don't think it does."

"I'm sorry," I muttered.

She shook her head. "Don't be. I didn't tell you that story to make you sorry. I want you to understand. As long as you do, that's all that counts."

"I think I do."

"Good. Now can you give me any details from that call?"

I nodded. "I can try."

I searched my memory for a moment, trying to remember specifics of a conversation that seemed to have taken place ages ago but in reality was no more than twelve hours old. My thoughts were muddy from lack of sleep and an overabundance of sensory input. I swam through the murk and seized on the snippets I found floating about the dark mental waters.

"His biblical references were all Satan specific," I finally recalled aloud. "Ecclesiastes three, three. Second Corinthians, Book of Revelation. I'm pretty sure they were all from the King James Version."

Kavanaugh scribbled a note on the legal pad. "Why does that stick out in your mind?"

"Because he follows the covenants and procedures of the *Malleus Maleficarum*," I told her and then added a short explanation. "It's a Witch-hunting text that was written by a pair of inquisitors posing as theologians in the year fourteen eighty-four. The King James version of the Holy Bible wasn't published until over one hundred years later in sixteen eleven."

"What do you think is the significance of that?" she pressed.

"It's probably just a part of his mental state," I offered. "It may be nothing. Truth is, the King James version of the Bible is the most commonly available, but what is so peculiar to me is that he has gone to a great deal of trouble to research things. From the *Malleus Maleficarum*, to various practices of the Inquisition, and even the pomp and ceremony of the executions. When I had my run-in with him last year, he was wearing the clerical collar of a Catholic priest. So in a way, I would have halfway expected him to use the version of the Bible connected with that period of history. All of it is the Christian faith, yes, but the translations aren't exactly the same.

"However," I said, "The prison ministry that is most likely responsible for sending him down this path is Evangelical, Old Testament, fire and brimstone. His indoctrination would have come from the KJV, so the discrepancy might be moot."

"You never know. So your perception is that he is confused?" Kavanaugh asked as she scribbled.

"Absolutely," I agreed. "Or at the very least, mislead."

"What about his threat to rape your wife?"

"That was yet another thing that tied in to his research," I stated flatly. "And he even told me as much. The fact is that it wasn't uncommon for inquisitors to rape the accused as a form of torture. But the real reason he made the threat was to piss me off. What started out for him last year as a re-establishment of the fifteenth century Inquisition has now become focused on a personal vendetta."

"Because you shot him?"

"That's part of it, probably," I acknowledged. "But I have a feeling that I was on his list long before that. When he makes references to me being the spawn of Satan, it's not just a metaphor. I think he honestly believes, that by killing me, he is effectively beheading the monster. Eliminating the source of WitchCraft."

"Why do you think he became so focused on you?"

"Just lucky I guess," I quipped and then made a dismissive gesture of apology. "I'm sorry. Seriously, if I had to guess, it was probably because at the time he started his crusade I was in the public eye. There was a newspaper article running about me because I was teaching an ongoing alternative religion and tolerance seminar for the city police department."

Kavanaugh nodded thoughtfully and underlined a couple of specific passages in her notes. "Is there anything else you can remember from that conversation?"

I took a sip of the coffee from the thermos cup and realized it had cooled considerably. Still, it wet my throat and that was primarily what I was after.

"His manner of speech, maybe," I replied.

"How so?"

"This morning he was much more formal. He seemed calm, and his selection of wording was less conversational and more like it was staged. That's pretty much how he was that night on the bridge as well. Deliberate and rehearsed."

"That's not uncommon when dealing with a psychosis," she returned, making a quick note. "The insane will often slip between conversational and non-conversational English. It's an indicator of the individual's current state of stability."

"Yeah." I nodded in agreement. "But this whacko is a wildcard. It's when he sounds rational that I really get worried."

"That's how most of them are," Agent Kavanaugh replied with a curt nod as she proceeded to circle a few more spots within her page of notes. "I want to go ahead and get this out to the team so they can get it up on the board for the negotiator," she told me as she stood up, still perusing the handwritten words. "I shouldn't be gone for very long. There's an agent right outside…"

"…To make sure I stay inside," I completed her sentence.

"I was going to say, in case you need anything," she replied flatly.

"Yeah, okay," I said, unable to keep all of the sarcasm out of my tone.

"But since you brought it up…" She purposely allowed the comment to go uncompleted.

"I'll be good," I replied. "But could you do me a favor?"

"What's that?"

"Ben Storm," I said. "The detective I was with. Could you let him know where I am? He tends to worry like a mother hen."

"He already knows," she told me. "But I'll say something to him."

"Thanks. I appreciate it."

"No problem."

CHAPTER 36:

A gent Kavanaugh had only been gone for a minute or so, and I was finally starting to come down from the most recent in the daylong series of adrenalin dumps my body had been experiencing.

I looked behind myself, first over my left shoulder; and then over my right, just to make sure I wasn't about to touch something that I shouldn't; then I leaned back against the wall of the van. This was no easy task considering the bulk of the flak vest I was trussed up in. If I hadn't thought Kavanaugh would throw a fit, I would have taken it off before she returned.

The metal bench I was seated on wasn't exactly comfortable, but it beat standing. I gave a quick glance down its length and postulated that I just might be able to stretch out on it if I positioned myself correctly. After a healthy measure of seconds spent considering the idea, I decided I had better not.

It seemed ironic to me that I had just been sitting here discussing the mental state of Eldon Porter with an FBI agent because in reality, right now my own psyche was as fragile as spun glass. I was rafting on emotional whitewater, and my oar was lodged under a boulder two hundred yards behind me.

On the one hand, I was relieved that Porter was holed up in the building because at least now we knew where he was. On the flip side, I feared for the safety of his hostage, not to mention the overwhelming guilt I felt because that hostage was Star.

Then there was everything in between. I was jittery, disgusted, sad, excited, angry, and virtually any other emotion you could think of, all at once. I was struggling with the sudden shifts from one to the next as I would run through the full range, only to find myself repeating it all over again in the very next moment.

The one thing that remained constant was the fact that I was just flat out exhausted.

I tilted my head back and tried to relax. I knew Agent Kavanaugh would probably be back any moment, and as soon as she was, the questions would start all over again. Her story had impressed upon me the importance of this interview, but I was still dealing with my overwhelming impatience.

What my irrational brain wanted me to do was rush into the building and bring about an end to Eldon Porter once and for all. What my logical brain wanted for me was to go to sleep. The few hours I'd managed to abscond with earlier had held me over for a while, but they were nothing more than a stopgap. I needed to be unconscious for a while—a long while—but I was afraid that wouldn't be happening anytime soon.

Drained as I was, I knew I wouldn't be able to fall asleep even if I tried. The headache that had started me on this odyssey was still in place and stronger than ever. It was going to be a while yet before I got my reprieve.

I found myself denying the diametrically opposed ideas being tossed about by the hemispheres of my brain and concentrating instead on the events of the past twenty-odd hours in search of answers to yet unasked questions. I was methodically trying to remember minute details of the day, unimportant and utterly mundane but details nonetheless. However, each time I would happen upon a gem to grasp, my overtaxed brain would release the previous tidbit and send it floating away into dark obscurity. The whole exercise quickly turned into a game of "keep away," where I was the odd man out, desperately chasing after things that I remembered and then promptly forgot again.

I allowed myself to slouch lower then shoved my hands into my coat pockets for lack of anyplace else to put them. My right knuckles immediately thumped against something hard. I pondered the sensation absently for a moment and then wrapped my fingers around whatever it was and pulled it out. I'm not sure what my clouded brain was expecting, but it was only my cell phone. I vaguely recalled someone giving me my charred coat at the hospital, which must have been when I recovered the device. I guessed that Felicity must have transferred it to this jacket when we arrived home.

The sight of the phone in my hand renewed a little hope. It reminded me that I wasn't as cut off from the outside as I had been feeling. I punched the power button and waited as the lights behind the dialing keys winked on, then the display flashed my number across the screen. I automatically thumbed out the pattern of Felicity's cell number that my hand had memorized then hit send and put the phone to my ear.

I listened as the ring tone sounded at the other end a trio of times before ending abruptly in the middle of the fourth. The half-buzz was followed by a tired but familiar Celtic-patterned voice.

"Aye, Rowan?" Felicity asked.

"Yeah, honey, it's me," I replied. "Where are you?"

"We're at the hospital. University down on Kingshighway."

"Good hospital," I murmured. "So how are you doing?"

"I'm fine," she said. "What about you then?"

"Tired and achy," I admitted. "But still in one piece."

"Aye, you'd best stay that way."

"I don't think I have much choice," I told her. "The FBI has me sitting in the back of a panel van trussed up in a bulletproof vest with an agent right outside the door."

"Good for them," she answered. "Remind me to send a thank you card."

I ignored her jibe. "How's Constance?"

"Aye, it looks like she'll be fine. The doctor didn't want to tell me anything at first, but I convinced him I was her sister."

"And he fell for that?" I asked. "You two don't look anything alike."

"Aye, and what's your point then? We're twin sisters from different parents."

"Yeah, sure," I half chuckled. "I can see that."

"Anyway," she continued. "She has a broken nose, a concussion, two broken ribs, and a fractured wrist. Most of it came from the airbag they think."

"Guess it could've been worse if there wasn't an airbag."

"Aye."

"So what about you?" I asked. "Did the doctor check you over?"

"Aye, I'm fine, bumps and bruises, nothing more. I'm mostly worried about you and Ben."

"I'm good," I told her. "Ben's hand is really messed up though. Last time I saw him there was a paramedic looking at it for him. I suspect he'll need a trip to the hospital before it's all over. Have you called Allison?"

"Aye. She was frantic at first, but you know how she is. She's a nurse. She's used to this kind of thing, especially out of Ben."

"Yeah, I know."

"So what IS going on there?" my wife asked, her voice turning serious as she left the chitchat behind. "I've been watching the television, but they aren't saying much."

"Well, they got me here in time to appease Porter," I replied. "For the moment anyway. Right now, I'm sitting in the back of a van, like I said, and they keep interviewing me."

"What for?"

"Looking for angles to use while negotiating with him."

"Aye, do they actually believe they can negotiate with that monster, then?"

"Yeah, they do."

"What about you?" she asked after a pause. "Do you think they can?"

"No," I almost whispered. "No, I don't."

We both fell silent, neither of us willing to press forward with the conversation but neither willing to say goodbye either. The digitally reproduced sounds of each other's breathing issuing from the phones became a tenuous connection between us—distant and artificial, but better than nothing.

My fearful thoughts combined with the hollowness in the pit of my stomach, and I became the first to break the lull. "You know he's going to kill her no matter what, don't you?"

"Row... Don't say that," Felicity appealed softly.

"He will," I continued. "I can feel it."

"Don't you go and do something stupid, now," she said. "Okay?"

I didn't reply.

Her voice came at me again, "Rowan? Answer me."

"Yeah," I finally said. "Nothing stupid."

"*Caorthann...*" Her voice was ringed by sadness and filled with resignation as she whispered the Gaelic pet name.

"Really, sweetheart," I assured her. "Back of van, FBI, cops everywhere. I don't think there's anything I CAN do other than sit here."

"Aye, but I know you."

"They have a chapel there?" I asked, trying to divert her attention.

"I'm sure they do, why?"

"Maybe you should go light a candle for Star," I offered.

Her reply told me that my gambit didn't work as planned. "Aye, I think you mean I should go light a candle for you."

There was no suitable reply that wouldn't either confirm her fears or force me to lie to her. Remaining silent would just do the same. I said the only thing I could, "Maybe for both of us then."

"Aye," she whispered.

I knew that unchecked, we would continue to sit there clinging to the cellular thread that now linked us together in the physical world. As much as I wanted to give in to that comfort, I made the decision that I knew she wouldn't.

"I've got to go, honey," I said. "They're going to want to start asking me some more questions in just a minute."

"I love you, Rowan."

I replied softly, "Yeah. I love you too."

I pulled the cell phone away from my ear then allowed my hand to slide down across my chest and fall into my lap. Without looking, I depressed the end button and disconnected the line. Closing my eyes, I left my head tilted back and began wondering about the wisdom of having made the call.

I wanted to be certain that she was okay, and I wanted to get an update on Constance but that information had come at a price. I wasn't foolish enough to think that Felicity believed for a minute that I would be standing idly by at this scene. Not with Star's life resting in the hands of Eldon Porter. I was convinced she hadn't even believed that when she made the decision to stay behind with Agent Mandalay. But she had come to terms with it.

My phone call may have served to do nothing more than open a wound. It very simply could have been an inadvertent reminder of the dangerous uncertainty that I faced—and my melancholy, a possible harbinger that Ben's promise to her could well be broken. Dwelling on the fact officially made me feel worse than I had before I dialed the number.

I breathed in a deep lungful of the chilly air then tilted my head back forward and glanced over at the door on the rear of the van. It had been several minutes since Agent Kavanaugh had left to hand over the information to the rest of the HNT. Considering that I hadn't given over anything of much relevance, at least in my eyes, I was beginning to worry. Something was taking far too long.

With the momentary diversion from my migraine gone by the wayside, the pain had returned full force, hammering away even harder than before. As I sat there, I felt a creepy wave of gooseflesh climb up my back until it reached the base of my neck. I shivered with a chill as the sensation traveled back down my spine then spread out through my body. I fell into an eerie state of semi-catatonic nothingness that made me feel sick to my stomach.

I jumped with a start and caught an outbound breath in my throat as my cell phone began pealing out the *William Tell Overture* in dull electronic tones. When my muscles tensed, the various bruises I had acquired reported in sharply then settled back into dull aches with unwavering loyalty to the task. I forced my body to relax and rolled my head as I allowed myself to continue exhaling.

"Oh yeah, you're real stable, aren't you?" I chastised myself aloud.

I turned the face of the phone up and inspected the screen, fully expecting to see the words "Felicity Cell" in a blocky, liquid crystal font. Instead, I was greeted with the words "New Number" and a string of unfamiliar digits.

I stared at the display for a moment as the refrain began bleeping out again and then punched the center button and brought the device upward.

"Rowan Gant," I said.

"It is about time you turned on your phone, Gant." Eldon Porter's voice issued from the speaker. "I have been trying to reach you for almost an hour now."

"So sue me, asshole," I replied.

"I don't think so," he replied. "I would rather just kill you."

"Same here," I shot back. "So shouldn't you be talking to the hostage negotiator?"

"Agent McCoy bores me," he remarked. "All give and take, I did for you, now you do for me. It is really very obvious that he does not see the point behind all of this."

Each sentence chilled me even more than the frigid weather outside. His voice had returned to the flat, rehearsed tenor I had discussed with Agent Kavanaugh earlier. His sentences were overtly devoid of contractions and spoken with an air of self-anointed superiority. There was a purposeful calm about him—a frightening preparedness that struck me like a cold blade directly into my heart.

"And that point is?" I asked.

"I think you are well aware of that, Gant," he replied.

"Yeah, just checking," I quipped.

I knew from his tone there were literally no words from me that would keep him at bay. Not now. Not anymore. We were moving forward to the next phase.

I was wondering why the HNT hadn't severed the connection by now. It took a few seconds for me to remember that this was the first time he had ever contacted me on my own cell, so it was a line they wouldn't be monitoring.

Still, they knew about the two different cell phones he was using, so they should be on top of it, unless... A random idea flitted in from the left side of my brain to give me pause. If he had two cell phones, why couldn't he have three? If he did, then chances were the HNT had no idea this call was even taking place.

"Well, whether he sees your point or not, he's the only one who can negotiate with you," I said. "So maybe I should just go get him."

"I would not do that if I were you, Gant," he answered coldly. "My negotiations with them are finished. This is between the two of us and no one else."

My heart thumped in my throat, and I felt my adrenal gland begin pumping again. The waiting game had reached its end whether the FBI liked it or not, and it was all about to be over before they could turn to the next page in the playbook.

I was wrong. This wasn't moving into the next phase. It was jumping directly to the end game.

I forced myself upward and barely missed clanging the back of my head on an equipment rack as I stumbled. I twisted to the side and started moving toward the back of the van. Agent Kavanaugh had said there would be someone right outside. My mind began racing, searching for a way to get that agent's attention without tipping off Porter.

I realized I had to keep him talking, so I said the first thing that popped into my head. "So what did you call me for, Eldon?"

"I have a question for you, Gant," he said.

"What's that, Eldon?"

What I got back in reply was nothing short of a lit match pressed firmly against my already short fuse.

"How loud do you think I will be able to make your wife scream?"

CHAPTER 37:

I felt my face grow hot as repressed anger was released directly into my veins alongside the rushing adrenalin. My free hand balled into a solid fist, and at the same time, I heard the tight squeak of my skin against hard plastic as my other hand involuntarily attempted to crush the cell phone.

"You're dead, Eldon," I growled through clenched teeth. "Understand me? You are dead."

"How bad do you want to kill me?" He spoke the question with the same nonchalance as someone asking for the correct time.

I snarled my retort, "I think I made that clear enough."

He began his reply in an imperious voice. "Do you think you can get to me…"

"Not with cops everywhere," I spat. "And you can bet that's the only thing keeping you alive right now, you bastard."

"I was not finished, Gant."

"Ask me if I care."

"You do."

"I doubt it."

"Now," he began again. "What I was going to say is this: Do you think you can get to me before Miss Sullivan's sentence has been duly and properly executed?"

His words struck me with as much force as a punch square to the jaw.

"You said this was between you and me!" I barked.

"Second floor, Gant. How fast are you?" he asked, then without waiting for an answer he pronounced, "Thou shalt not suffer a Witch to live."

"Porter!" I shouted.

Stealth was no longer an issue. I bolted for the back of the van, and in my haste, my hand missed the latch on the door as I threw myself against it. The sound of my shoulder thudding against the metal struck first and was followed immediately by the physical jolt vibrating through my frame.

Desperation-induced clumsiness was doing everything in its power to impede my progress as I fumbled with the lever. I felt my hand connect and pushed heavily downward on the latch then leaned into the door once again.

Sound was buzzing in the earpiece of the phone the whole time. Porter's self-righteous voice continued rattling against my eardrum with sickening clarity. "Wherefore, since you, Millicent Renee Sullivan, are fallen into the damned heresies of Witches…"

"He's doing it!" I was screaming even as the door was beginning to open. "He's getting ready to…"

The rest of the words caught in my throat as an icy blast of wind hit me in the face. The door was swinging wide in surrender to my attack, and my momentum kept me moving forward. My stomach leapt then fell with an odd, tickling sensation as a split second of weightlessness struck. It was only then I realized I had launched myself into nothingness. I felt myself pitching forward and began to flail my arms in an attempt to regain my balance, but it was too late. My exit was anything but graceful as I completely missed the step and stumbled down to the wet pavement.

I'm still not entirely certain which event in the quartet came first: me hitting the asphalt, the intense flash of light, the wildly screeching siren, or the deafening explosion. In retrospect, it didn't really matter; they were all so close together that for all intents and purposes, they were one and the same.

The cell phone popped out of my hand and skittered a few feet away on the street as I rolled. Chaos was the only word I could use to describe the scene before me as everyone's attention was directed away from the building. On the tiered parking lot above us, a squad car was warbling out every emergency tone in its arsenal of noises. Every source of illumination on the vehicle, from light bar to headlights, was flashing. The windshield was a shattered maze, and the driver's side windows were completely missing. Smoke was rolling upward from the openings, and an orange glow was filling the passenger cabin.

I had absolutely no idea what had happened. My mind was paging through scenarios, attempting to wedge the few available pieces of the puzzle into place, but every picture I imagined seemed far from likely.

I scrambled across the slush for the cell phone and placed the wet device against my ear as soon as I clamped my hand on it. Though I had to strain to hear him over the background insanity, Porter's voice was still bleeding from the earpiece with ominous portent, "...Have refused the medicine of your salvation, we have summoned..."

"NO!" I screamed.

I dragged myself up to my feet and wheeled around, looking for the federal agent who was supposed to be posted outside the van but found no one. All attention was still focused on the bedlam surrounding the patrol car. I wheeled around, looking for anyone I could but again found not a soul anywhere nearby. Everyone seemed to be converging on the raucous patrol car.

"...away and seduced by a wicked spirit..." Porter continued.

I had heard these very words from him before, and I knew them well. The recitation was an official proclamation of Star's guilt and final sentence. He would be following immediately with her execution. Even with the pomp and circumstance of the pronouncement, there would be no time to wait. He had already begun; she was going to be dead in less than a minute.

The dark, prophetic sensation that had been plaguing me was now a set of icy fingers clawing at my throat. I felt myself moving forward with deliberate intent. The doorway of the building seemed an almost unattainable objective in the distance, but it loomed clear in my sight, beckoning me.

By the time I took my fifth step, I was at a dead run.

"MISTER GANT!" I heard Agent Kavanaugh's voice in the distance behind me, but I didn't stop.

Figures I had not previously noticed were now coming out of the shadows as I barreled through the SWAT perimeter. These men had been the only ones not completely diverted from their mission by the insanity on the parking lot above. Still, they were staged at a distance from the entrance and focused on impending entry into the building. Whether by pure luck, the situation, or fate alone, I was yards ahead before I began to hear their shouts.

"GODDDAMIT, ROWAN!" I picked out Ben's voice bellowing from within the jumble of others that were ordering me to stop.

My cell phone flew from my hand as my arms pumped in unison with my legs. I was starting to wheeze as cold air rushed in and out of my lungs. I wasn't in the best of shape to begin with, but the bulk of the flak vest and my coat weren't helping either.

My knees were complaining, and a sharp chill was biting into my leg where my pants had soaked up wetness from the slush on the street. I ignored the pains that were vying for attention throughout my body and pushed myself forward. I could hear the clamor of footsteps behind me and felt a momentary wave of relief. I couldn't stop to tell anyone what was happening, but if they followed me in, that would be good enough.

I launched myself over the low curb and on my first stride was across the narrow sidewalk. With far more agility than I had displayed exiting the van, I hit the low stairs and propelled myself past two of the three and directly onto the landing. I threw a forearm up in front of my face and allowed the inertia I had built up to coil into my body as I hit the door.

The barrier was already unlatched, and the force with which I struck caused it to fling wide, impact an interior wall, then bounce back. I thrust my arm out to the side and caught the door before it could hammer back into my face then drove inward through the darkness.

I was already several steps into the building before I began to slow. I could hear a gathering commotion through the door behind me, but thus far I was the only one who had entered. Part of me wanted to wait for the SWAT team to catch up, but I knew that there was no time.

My labored breaths were grating in my ears and sending cold stabs through my chest. My heart was thumping out of control, and I could feel my right leg beginning to cramp. I winced at the pain and stumbled as I wandered through the dark interior.

Some small amount of light was streaming in from the door to my rear, but "small amount" was the operative phrase. It did little to illuminate the interior much beyond the first few feet. Porter had said second floor, but I had no idea how this building was laid out. Not to mention that it had been abandoned for Goddess knows how long.

Piles of unidentifiable debris announced themselves solely by feel as I thumped against and tripped over them. The one thing I could say for certain was that several of them were very hard.

My eyes were finally beginning to adjust to the darkness but not quickly enough for the given situation. I had no idea where the stairs were in this structure, and I still couldn't see enough to find them. My throat began to constrict, and my chest felt tight as a wave of panic washed over me. I could hear the blood begin to rush in my ears and fear commenced stabbing me in the back with repeated thrusts of gelid anxiety.

"...Therefore, following in the footsteps of the blessed Apostle Paul..." Porter's voice came to me as a distant echo.

I swallowed hard against the constriction in my throat and pushed forward, staggering through the darkness with my hands waving blindly in front of me. It took one half dozen steps and something hard biting into my shin before I careened into a cold wall.

The cramp in my leg blossomed, twisting the muscle down the back of my calf into a secure knot. Fiery agony shot through the appendage as my knee automatically bent in an attempt to hide from the onslaught.

I caught my breath and grunted as I fought to ignore the pain. I pushed myself away from the wall but left one hand against it for support as I limped along.

"PORTER! YOU SONOFABITCH!" I screamed.

My words glanced from the walls of the empty building, fading away on the heels of a sharp echo. An almost solemn silence followed the last audible reproduction of my voice, then after a measured beat, his voice began again.

"Millicent Renee Sullivan. By this our definitive sentence we drive you from the ecclesiastical court, and abandon you to…"

I had no idea exactly how long I had been in the building at this point. I assumed, however, based on his cadence and the words spoken, that it had only been a matter of seconds. My eyes had adjusted enough that I could now make out murky shapes but not much more. I twisted in place, looking frantically for a direction to go.

"…Secular court, that having you in its power now moderates its sentence of death against you…"

The echo of Porter's voice bounced around the building, repeating itself into silence. I tried to follow the sound and found myself spinning in a confused circle, knowing only that it was coming from above.

I knew I couldn't waste any more time. The sentence had been pronounced, and there was very little ceremony left before he carried out the execution. I whipped my head around and made a snap decision, picking a direction to try, in hopes that it would lead to what I sought. I took a quick look down and to the side, scanning for obstacles before pushing completely away from the wall.

Light flashed behind me, and I heard scrambling footsteps as the SWAT team entered. A momentary swath of white luminance cut across the wall then along the floor in front of me before swinging in the opposite direction. I assume it had come from one of their flashlights, but the source was moot. While it had been dimmed by distance, it was still enough to give me what I needed.

Pure luck, magick, divine guidance of The Ancients. I had no idea what was responsible. All I knew was that had I not been looking in the exact spot at the exact instant the light passed over, I would have missed the stairwell through the opening just ahead of me.

CHAPTER 38:

"**H**E'S ON THE SECOND FLOOR!" I screamed aloud to the SWAT team as I leapt forward, aiming myself at the opening.

I couldn't be sure if they heard me or even saw me. I didn't think about it until later, but my sudden movement could very easily have gotten me shot. Whoever, or whatever, was watching over me was apparently still on the job.

I ran my shoulder into the wall and groped for anything I could use to steady myself. My fingers fell against something hard and ice cold. When I tightened my hand, I recognized what I was gripping to be a solid metal handrail.

I turned my face up and saw a faint yellow glow, telling me there was some form of light ahead.

The cramp that was seizing the muscle in my right leg was still impeding my motion to the best of its ability as it caused me to list to the side. I threw my left arm out and began pulling myself hand over hand as I struggled up the littered stairwell.

"...And having before us the Holy Gospels that our judgment may proceed as from the countenance of God..." Porter's ominous voice was becoming louder with every step I took.

"...By this sentence we cast you away as an impenitent heretic and sorceress."

"PORTER!" I screamed again as I strained to make my way up the stairs.

I caught my right foot on the edge of a crumbling step and slipped to the side. I quickly grabbed the handrail and corrected for the misstep before tumbling back down.

"In accordance with the thirty second question we do hereby deliver you unto the power of our most Holy God. As you, Millicent Renee Sullivan, are damned in body and soul, your sentence on this day is death."

I was only a few steps from the top when I heard a metallic squeak pierce the night. It came as a slow, repetitious noise, fading then sharply breaking through once again. I was certain I could hear a whimpering sob behind it.

"The sentence, to be executed immediately and without appeal in the manner of hanging."

The high-pitched squeal made a violent increase in cadence, sounding like metal spinning quickly against metal, all while in desperate need of lubrication. There was a creaking noise in its wake, and I heard a choking gurgle.

The muscle in my leg was beginning to untie, and I pushed hard, taking the last two steps at once. I arced myself out through the doorway at the top and out onto the creaking wooden floor.

The light of countless candles stationed about the large room created glowing pockets in the darkness that spread illumination in toward center. Porter was standing near the center of the space, staring directly at me. Next to him, swinging two feet above the floor was Star, partially nude and streaked with blood. The noose was tightening around her neck, and even at this distance, I could see her kicking and bucking her body against the constriction.

Porter's solemn voice hit my ears with absolute clarity. "May the Lord Jesus Christ have mercy upon her soul."

Whatever it was that I screamed, it was completely unintelligible, even to me. The sound was that of a madman—a banshee's wail that froze blood solid even as it ran through veins. It was a cry that could only emanate from something not of this world.

I ran head on at him, striding harder than I believed myself capable and ignoring any pain or complaint my body elected to issue. My hot breath continued to expel in the tortured scream right up to the point where I slammed into him full force.

He had braced himself for the impact, but my momentum was more than he could bear. He folded over at the waist as I drove into him, and we both crashed to the floor in a tangle. I was at the top of the pile, and I pushed myself up with my left arm then brought my right over in a wide arc toward his face. He threw his own arm up and tried rolling to the side, which brought my fist slamming hard against the back of his shoulder. I pulled my hand back and drove it home once again as he moved, glancing downward along his back.

I pushed back and dragged myself up to my knees as he scrambled away from me. Rage was telling me to dive on him and continue punching. I was just about to give in to the anger when as I leaned back to launch myself, something thudded against the back of my head. I wheeled about in search of the unknown attacker, swinging my left arm out in a stiff arc.

Instead, I saw a pair of legs dangling in front of my face and heard the gurgling whimper of the young woman hanging above me. I got to my feet and looked up, frantically following the noose from around her neck up through the aged block and tackle, then back down to where it was tied off on a supporting column.

I rushed across to the column and began working my fingers into the knot. The nylon rope was twined about a large steel spike that had been driven deeply into the age-hardened wood. It was solid and had obviously been placed there long ago. I fought to loosen the tight braid, but her weight pulling back against it was making the task all put impossible.

Panic began to seize me once again, competing with the rage for control of my conscious self. I hooked my arm over the taut angle of the rope and pulled down, lifting her a pair of inches farther from the floor but gaining some slack on the knot. I hated doing it, but it was the only way I could think of to get the leverage I needed. Just as I began working the tangle loose, hot pain bit into my back, and I was forced hard against the upright beam.

Air expelled from my lungs, and my hands flailed away from the task. I felt the rope snap taut once again, and it flung my arm up like a catapult. A heavy fist, or so I thought, connected with my side. The punch was concentrated on a pinpoint and sent a lance of pain through my ribcage. I sucked in a quick breath as I was jerked backward, and I leaned into it, spinning myself in an arc with my right arm flailing upward and out ahead of me.

I connected with something both soft enough to qualify as flesh and hard enough to qualify as a skull. I stumbled through the spin and fell downward while holding my side. I landed on the plank floor with a heavy thud. My coat was seriously impeding my ability to move with any agility whatsoever as was the flak vest. I found myself wishing that I had gone ahead and removed them when I had the opportunity.

I looked up to see that my blow had rocked Porter backwards, but unfortunately, he was none the worse for wear and was now bearing down on me. The reason behind the extreme concentration of the strike to my ribs became immediately apparent when I saw the dim light flicker from the blade in his hand.

I tried to kick away as he literally fell on top of me, but I was too late. My mind flashed on the SWAT team downstairs, and I wondered why the hell they weren't up here yet. Porter's body pinned my legs, and for the first time, I saw his left hand gathered into a misshapen claw as he thudded it against me like a club. I jerked my head back just in time to see the knife arcing through the air above me, clutched tightly in his right hand.

I threw my left arm up to block and felt his connect. I was too late to halt the stab or even deflect it, but I did manage to slow it somewhat. Still, it kept coming, and I closed my eyes. Dull pain erupted through my chest as the large blade came down straight where my heart was thumping wildly. I felt a tingle through my flesh somewhere just to the left of my sternum, and I winced. I wondered for a brief second if this was how it felt to be stabbed because I had expected it to be far more acute.

I exhaled and opened my eyes slowly to see that the knife was still clutched in his hand with the shiny blade lying horizontally across my chest. I sucked in a quick breath and immediately balled up my fist.

I slammed my right hand hard against the side of Porter's face as I fought to kick away from him. I felt my own pain as my knuckles glance downward, grating across his teeth and ripping a gash in them. He howled as I quickly seized his left wrist and twisted the appendage as hard as I could.

He rolled away, and I scrambled to my feet. Behind me I could hear footsteps as the SWAT team made their way up the stairwell. Only a few more seconds, I mutely told myself. A few more seconds, and this will all be over. I started again toward the rope holding Star aloft and heard Porter's near breathless voice wheezing as it came toward me.

"As you, Rowan Linden Gant, are damned in body and soul, your sentence on this day is death." He inhaled with an audible heave.

I spun back toward him and steeled myself. He was standing a few steps away with the knife raised over his head. Standing as tall as Ben, he towered over me, but I held fast, still reaching behind me for the rope.

"The sentence..." he sputtered, then coughed. "The sentence to be executed immediately and without appeal..."

He launched himself at me and brought the knife downward. I tried to sidestep him but still caught the brunt of his force against me. I let out an agonized scream as the blade ripped through my coat sleeve and bit into my upper arm. I screamed again as he wrenched it back out and made a second attempt at aiming the weapon.

Out of reflex, I stretched my hand up and grasped his forearm, locking my elbow so that he couldn't thrust the knife downward. We struggled in a violent twist as we pushed against one another.

Shouts from the SWAT entry team sounded from across the room as a flurry of footsteps vibrated through the wooden planks that made up the floor.

We stumbled backward in a clench, and as we began falling, I heard the sound of something wet splattering nearby. Somewhere in the back of my mind, my olfactory sense absently registered the pungent odor of urine and bowel.

I crashed downward with Porter on top of me and immediately heard a loud creak followed by a sharp crack. A fraction of a second after the disturbing noise bit into my ears, the section of floor we occupied gave way and opened up on the room below.

The sensation of weightlessness I had experienced earlier when I vaulted from the back of the van was now magnified tenfold. We seemed to float in place for a brief moment, and then we plummeted downward in a tangle of arms and legs.

When we hit bottom, we were engulfed in a cloud of dirt and dust that had collected over the years. We had started rolling to the side as we fell, so the detritus that was once the floor above now rained down on and around us. There was enough trash covering the floor to cushion a portion of our fall, but as we hit I felt my left forearm snap. The sharp pain shot up into my shoulder, and I let out a yelp. I think I would have passed out had it not been for the adrenalin coursing through my veins.

Porter had rolled almost completely under me before we hit, and he had taken the brunt of the impact. He was definitely injured, but he was still alive.

He was still struggling to regain his breath as I pushed myself up onto my knees with my one good arm. I groped through the debris with my good hand and felt the handle of the knife. My fingers closed around it automatically as the rage once again took control.

I felt myself raising the knife as a swath of light fell across us. I heard a commanding voice call out, "Police! Drop the weapon!"

I hesitated for a moment, a dim pinpoint of logic winking at me from behind the curtain of rage that shrouded my mind.

"DROP THE WEAPON!"

The light of rationality faded to black, and I felt my hand begin downward.

I only remember three things after that: a bright flash, a loud explosion, and the feeling that my chest had just caved in.

CHAPTER 39:

The first thing I did was cough.

The second thing I did was groan.

The third thing I did was open my eyes.

When my vision started to clear, I could see that there was a white ceiling above me—but not too far above. At least that is how it looked. My depth perception seemed to be a bit off for some odd reason.

There was something resembling artificial light filtering in to aid my sight, which was a far cry better than darkness. Why darkness stuck out in my mind I didn't know, but I didn't need to give it much thought to decide that I preferred the light.

There was a lot of noise too. Things like distant voices and staticky radios. I picked out the rumble of a motor and even a few electronic sounding beeps. There were countless other things, both identifiable and not, but I very quickly grew tired of trying to associate names with them.

Everything in my head was a jumbled blur. I had no idea where I was or why. There wasn't an inch of my body that wasn't killing me, but at the moment the real pain seemed to be centered on my chest. Just the very sensation told me that I had been hit by something, but I couldn't begin to say what. I knew what it felt like, and that was a freight train; but since I appeared to still be in one piece, I decided that might be an exaggeration on my part.

I lay there for a moment trying to remember. There seemed to be something important stuck in the back of my head, and it was fighting a desperate struggle to be released from its holding cell. It felt like an imperative, something urgent, but I couldn't connect with it and that just brought on a feeling of frustration.

"Hurts like a motherfucker, don't it, paleface?" Ben's words worked their way into my ears over the multitude of ambient sounds.

I rolled my head in the direction of his voice and blinked, then I blinked again. When I was still unable to focus, it dawned on me that I wasn't wearing my glasses. Somewhere in the dark ball of memories that was bouncing around inside my head, I seemed to recall having lost them. But at the same time, I remembered having another pair. The attempt at reasoning just made me hurt even more, so I gave up and centered on his blurry face.

"What?" I croaked.

He started to repeat himself. "I said, hurts like a motherfu…"

"Yeah," I eked out the gravelly word to cut him off. "I got that." I cleared my throat and coughed again before continuing. "What hit me?"

"Piece of lead," he said. He held up his hand, thumb and forefinger spread slightly apart, then added, "About so big, actually. But it was movin' pretty fast."

"Porter shot me?" I asked.

"No, not Porter."

"YOU shot me?!" I half yelped then immediately regretted it.

"Hell no," he returned. "SWAT did it. If I'd shot you I probably woulda aimed for your goddamned hard head."

"They shot me?" I muttered.

"Hey, look at it this way, white man," he offered. "You just joined an elite club. That friggin' vest you were wearin' saved your ass."

"But they shot me," I said again, confusion permeating my voice. "Why?"

"Row, what the hell? You got amnesia or somethin'? They didn't have much choice. You were gettin' ready to stab Porter to death with a big ass butcher knife. Don'tcha remember?"

His words triggered the mechanism that released the lock on the cell door, opening it wide to allow the urgent memories of the evening to flood back in. Everything rushed to the front of my brain and then vied for my undivided attention. One item stood out from all the others, and I seized on it immediately.

"Star?" I asked. "How's Star? Is she okay?"

My friend stayed conspicuously silent and simply looked away.

My brain was adjusting to the blurry picture being fed to it by my uncorrected vision, and I watched as he brought his left hand up to smooth back his hair then massage his neck.

"Let's talk about that later," he said.

"Tell me she's okay, Ben," I insisted.

He hung his head down and continued to work his fingers against a muscle in his neck. His only audible answer was a heavy sigh.

The stark memory of the wet sound just before Porter and I crashed through the floor returned to echo in my ears. The phantom odor of urine and feces sharply tingled my nose, and I instantly realized I had been standing next to Star when she had died.

I wanted to cry, but my body refused. It had nothing left to give. Not now, anyway.

"They should have let me kill the sonofabitch," I muttered.

"I'm sorry, Row," he returned quietly.

"At least tell me they shot him too," I said, my voice a mixture of pleading and demanding.

"No," he shook his head as he uttered the word. "He's already been transported to the hospital."

"Critical?"

"No. He's worse off than you," he replied, "but not critical. He'll make it."

"Too fucking bad," I said.

"He's off the street, Row," he offered. "It's over."

"Yeah. Tell that to Randy and Star."

"Row..." he let his voice trail off.

"What happens now?" I asked.

"Whaddaya mean," he replied with a shrug. "We're sittin' here in the back of an ambulance. They'll be takin' you to the hospital in just a few."

"So that's where we are," I said.

"Man, what did they dope you up with?"

"The way I hurt? Nothing."

"The way you sound? Something," he replied.

"So which one?"

"Which one what?"

"Which hospital?"

"Oh, yeah. I already asked 'em to transport you to University." He picked up on where he thought my mind was going. "Felicity will be waitin' for ya'."

"Where did they take Porter?" I asked.

"Not there, so don't worry."

"Where then?"

He shook his head. "No way, Row."

"So maybe I'm just curious," I returned.

"Uh-huh, yeah, sure," he grunted. "I know better. You ever hear the term 'malice aforethought'? How about 'premeditation'?"

I stewed in silence for a moment.

"You know, this is gettin' to be a pattern with you," he announced. "This is the second person you've tried to kill in less than a month."

I knew that the other person he was referring to was the deranged rapist who had kidnapped Felicity on Christmas Eve. I had come very close to pulling the trigger on the gun I'd had aimed at him that night. Fact is I did pull the trigger; I just managed to point it somewhere else first.

"Can you blame me?" I asked.

"Hell no." He shook his head as he answered. "But like I told ya' last go around, you need to keep that to yourself 'cause not everyone is as open-minded as me."

"Yeah, right," I grunted and then came back around to the original question. "So, hospital, then what?"

"Home I guess," he returned.

"Just home?" I questioned. "So I'm not under arrest or anything?"

"Shit, Row," he exclaimed as he began massaging his neck again. "Not as it stands now, but I can't really tell ya' what's gonna happen at this point. This whole scene is a clusterfuck."

"How so?"

"Did you happen to catch that big boom just before you went runnin' across the street like the *wild man of Borneo*?" he asked.

"Uh-huh. What was that all about?"

"Flash-bang grenade," he told me. "Special ordinance, used by SWAT entry teams for the element of surprise. Seems that one went off in the front seat of a highway patrol Interceptor."

"How did that happen?"

He shook his head again. "You're askin' the wrong Injun, Kemosabe. Nobody knows. Hell, nobody even knows what it was doing there to begin with. Right now the SWAT commander is crawlin' all over the guy who was in charge of the van because accordin' to the inventory, that's apparently where it came from. The hubcap chasers are pointin' fingers at City and SWAT. City is pointin' fingers back at 'em since it went off in their car. The Feebs are pointin' fingers at EVERYONE and claimin' that Federal shit don't stink. And to top it all off, since Albright's site commander, she runnin' around spoutin' crap about chargin' everybody with everything."

I groaned. "Including me I'll bet."

"Yeah," he confessed. "She's taken your name in vain a few times, but I wouldn't worry too much about it."

"So what about her?" I asked. "Is she so above reproach?"

"You mean tonight?" He scrunched his face.

"Now, earlier, any of it," I replied.

"Well, she's site commander so the buck stops with her," he offered. "But she can bury the whole fuckin' thing and lay it on someone else, which is what she'll do, guaranteed."

"What about earlier?"

"We'll see," he returned. "I'm talkin' to IAD in the morning."

"You think they'll listen?"

"Dunno," he confessed. "All I can do is try. It might take you pressing charges to get anything done."

A paramedic climbed into the back of the ambulance with us and pulled the door shut then quickly checked my restraints.

"We're getting ready to roll," he said. "How are you feeling, Mister Gant?"

"How do I look?" I asked.

He grinned back. "Okay, sir, we'll have you at the hospital in just a few minutes."

"Feel free to take the scenic route," I quipped.

"Ignore 'im," Ben told the paramedic. "He ain't exactly natural."

I rolled my gaze back to my friend. "So what we were talking about…"

"Yeah?"

"If that's what it takes, let me know, and I'll do it."

"Okay."

I turned my face back to the ceiling and tried to relax as we began moving. Settling in, I noticed an extra set of pains coming from my left forearm. I slowly cocked my head at an angle and saw the edge of an inflatable splint encasing the appendage. Then I remembered the snapping sound of the bone and felt slightly queasy.

Flashes of memory whirled around inside my skull, always seeming to come back around to Star hanging from the end of the rope. I wondered, if I hadn't hesitated, would it have been different? If I'd just been there a few seconds sooner, could I have stopped it all from happening? Or at least gotten her down before she choked to death?

As random thoughts tend to do, something that Agent Kavanaugh had said flitted past, and I latched onto it in an attempt to divert my mind. I mulled the comment over for a moment then twisted my head back to face my friend.

"Did Porter have a gun?"

"The scene hasn't been cleared yet," he returned. "But they haven't found one yet, no. Why?"

"Something Agent Kavanaugh said."

"About the bum from this morning." He gave me a knowing nod as he made the statement. "Yeah, I heard. Even if they don't find one, that doesn't mean anything, Row. He coulda ditched it. Probably did in fact."

"But he didn't have one." I tossed his original answer back to him.

"Not that we've found." He cocked his head and looked at me. "Is there somethin' I should know?"

"No," I said in a dismissive tone. "Not really. Just do me a favor. If you see Kavanaugh, explain *Twilight Zone* to her and let her know I was right."

"Jeez, Row." He shook his head. "You and your hocus-pocus."

"Yeah, me and my hocus-pocus," I muttered.

The ambulance rocked as it bounced over what was probably a curb then listed slightly as it hooked into a turn. Ben reached out to steady himself, and I saw his right hand was tightly wrapped in gauze once again.

"So how is your hand, Tonto?" I asked.

"Hurts like a motherfucker."

CHAPTER 40:

"An overwhelming sense of apathy and withdrawal is not that uncommon, Rowan." Helen Storm's friendly but analytical voice filtered into my ear from the telephone. "It does not mean that you are unsympathetic."

The clock on the coffeemaker read 6:58 a.m. I had fully expected to connect with the answering service when I dialed the number to her office. I knew it was early, but I had gotten tired of waiting for business hours to roll around. I had to admit that I felt an almost cathartic sense of relief when she actually answered instead of them.

"But if I had been there ten seconds sooner, Helen..." I submitted.

"It probably would not have made a bit of difference," she told me. "Rowan, understand that you are human. There is only so much that you can do. Millicent's loss is a horrible tragedy for you to contend with—both of you. However, you cannot and should not obsess over something of which you had no control."

It had been a little less than thirty-six hours since my life had run headlong into the floor of the abandoned building at the corner of Ashley and Second Street. At least, that is how I was feeling.

Felicity and I had talked, and she had certainly helped me, but I wondered if I had done her any good. We both had a lot to work through, on many levels. Our relationship had never been more solid, but emotionally we were both chewing our fingernails. We had agreed that we shouldn't try riding it out alone, especially not after everything that had happened.

"Her parents called me last night," I murmured.

"How did that go?" she asked.

"It wasn't pleasant," I returned with a sigh. "As far as they are concerned, their daughter would still be alive if she had never met me."

"Rowan, you must understand that they are grieving a terrible loss, just as you and Felicity are. Anger is a stage of grief. They will reach a point where they will realize that you are not at fault."

"I don't know, Helen," I replied. "That should have been me not her."

"You know full well what Eldon Porter's intent was all along, Rowan. What you are experiencing is normal, but still, you cannot torture yourself for an act that someone else committed."

"Survivor guilt," I returned softly.

"Precisely," Helen acknowledged. "Now, when can the two of you be here?"

"I don't know," I answered. "Ben is supposed to show up any minute to help us move things back over to the house. Felicity has already gone to pick up the dogs, and we're supposed to pick up the cats this afternoon."

I gingerly cradled the phone between my shoulder and ear, wincing as it found a bruise to rest on. Using my right hand, I tugged the carafe out of its niche on the coffeemaker and topped off my cup. There were still a few inches of brew left in the Pyrex globe, but they probably wouldn't last long considering how fast I was going through it.

The much-worshipped java machine was the last thing left to pack, really. We hadn't brought that much with us when we'd been sequestered here to hide from a madman. Our suitcases were already packed, and a half-dozen medium-sized boxes stuffed with various personal comfort items now rested on the small, dining room table. The last box was sitting on the kitchen counter patiently waiting for the coffeemaker to occupy a space within.

After I crammed the carafe back onto the hotplate, I picked up a spoon and jammed the handle beneath the cast on my left arm and dug gently at an insistent itch.

"What about this evening then?" Helen asked.

"We don't want to impose on you, Helen," I told her.

"You won't be," she returned with an almost cheerful nonchalance. "I will come over to your house, and we will order out pizza."

"But, Helen…" I began to object.

"No buts, Rowan. The two of you need to deal with this. Trust me, I am a doctor. I know these things."

I couldn't help but allow just a hint of a smile to pass across my lips. "Okay then. If you insist."

"I do," she replied. "If it will make you feel any better, you can buy."

The smile grew larger, and I even chuckled lightly. "Deal."

Her voice took on a mischievous tone, "Do you like anchovies?"

"I love 'em, Felicity not so much," I replied.

She chuckled. "So you will have to buy two pizzas then."

"I think we can do that," I replied. "And Helen, we really appreciate this."

"I know you do," she assured me. "How does seven sound?"

"Seven is perfect."

"Seven it is. I will see you both then."

"Okay, bye."

"Bye."

There was a forceful rap on the door just as I dropped the handset into the cradle. I took a quick sip of my coffee then set the cup back on the counter before exiting the kitchenette, hooking around the table then moving through the small living room.

I undid the deadbolt then unlatched the door and pulled it open. As expected, Ben was standing on the other side, a familiar flat box resting in his hand like a platter.

He looked me over then said, "You look like shit."

"Yeah, nice to see you too," I replied as I stepped aside and allowed him to come in. "There's some coffee left if you want it."

"Got a cup?"

"Look in one of the boxes on the table." I waved as I shut the door. "There should be some travel mugs in there."

He had set the box of donuts on the counter, so I flipped it open and dug out one that looked as though it might have jelly or something injected into it.

"They were outta glazed, can ya' believe it?" Ben asked rhetorically as he drained the coffeepot into a large plastic mug bearing the logo of a particular film Felicity often used.

"Just stick it in the sink," I told him as he started to stick the carafe back on the burner. "I need to rinse it out before I pack it."

He nodded as he twisted then set the pot down in the sink. Turning back, he snapped the lid onto the mug with his good hand.

I swallowed a bite of the donut as I held up my cast-encased arm then said, "Looks like we have one good pair between us."

"Yeah, well at least you broke your left," he returned. "I shoot with my right you know, so now I have to fly a desk for at least six weeks."

"I thought that was all you did anyway," I jibed.

"Yeah. Funny." He rolled his eyes. "So where's Firehair?"

"Picking up the dogs."

"At seven in the morning?" he asked. "Did she miss 'em that much?"

I nodded. "Yeah, we both did I guess. But the real reason is that Joe and Terri both work Saturdays, and she wanted to pick them up before they left. It just works out easier that way."

I finished off the jelly-filled pastry in a series of quick bites as I moved in past him. Stopping at the sink, I twisted on the faucet and then began rinsing out the carafe.

"That's cool." He shrugged, turning to face me, and then he took a sip of coffee. "Not like you have that much to move anyway."

"True story," I agreed.

"By the way," he said suddenly, thrusting the coffee mug at me like a pointer. "Talked to Deck. He said for you to get your sorry ass up to the hospital and visit him."

"Carl Deckert said that?" I chided.

"Okay, so he didn't say *that* exactly, but I know he'd appreciate the visit."

"Yeah, we will. How is he doing?"

"Good." Ben nodded. "He's good. They had to do a triple bypass, but he's feeling good. Looks like he'll be taking an early retirement."

"How is he feeling about that?" I asked.

Ben shifted to the side as I reached around him and began disassembling the coffeemaker—emptying the grounds into the trash and rinsing the various parts.

"I don't think it's settled in yet, but he seems okay with it. Said something about opening up a PI shop or doing some consulting."

"He'd be good at that," I offered as I shook the excess water from the filter basket then began reassembling the device for easier transport. "How about Constance? Any word from her?"

"Yeah, she's gettin' out today. She'll be on desk duty for a while, but that's what she normally does anyway."

I finished stuffing the coffeemaker into the box on the counter, affecting the task one-handed, then hooked my arm around the cardboard container and moved it in with the others on the table.

"So, Ben," I started as I turned back to face him. "Something has been nagging at me."

"Whassat?"

"When we met Carl over at that house, he showed me the Witch jar," I outlined.

"Yeah. That was friggin' disgusting," he replied as he screwed up his face for a moment.

"Whatever." I dismissed the comment. "But there was something else. I was supposed to see some drawings or something that Porter had made?"

"Yeah. Pretty simple stuff really. I'm not sure what you were s'posed to get off 'em to be honest."

"So what were they?" I pressed.

"Bunch of stars. Kinda like the one you wear," he replied and then started in on his coffee again.

"Pentacles?" I asked with a note of disbelief. "Pentacles? Pentagrams? Are you sure?"

"Well, they weren't exactly like yours," he told me, shaking his head and shrugging. "They had eight points, and yours only has five, right?"

"Right," I nodded as I spoke. "But his had eight?"

He rolled his eyes up and looked like he was searching his memory. "Yeah, eight."

"Protection Hex," I muttered.

"Come again?"

"That would be a symbol of protection," I explained. "Something commonly referred to as a Hex Sign. Used most often by the Pennsylvania Dutch and other persons of Germanic descent. They were painted or placed over the doors of barns to protect against bewitching and evil magick among other things."

"Kinda fits with the jar full of piss then, doesn't it?" he returned.

"That's my point," I told him. "The page from *Hexen un Hexenmeister*, a Witch jar, a Hex Sign…"

"Yeah, what?" he looked at me expectantly.

"There just seems to be a lot of ties to Germanic folklore," I answered as I mulled the information over. "Something just feels hinky about it."

"You mean like hinky ha-ha or hinky hocus-pocus?" he asked.

I bypassed his question. "Did they ever figure out what was up with that flash-boom thing?"

"Flash-bang," he corrected. "Not yet. There's still a lot of finger pointin' goin on. It could be a while before they figure it out. So what about this hinky thing?"

"Why did that go off at that exact instant, Ben?" I asked.

"Who the fuck knows?" he shrugged. "That's what they are investigating." He cocked his head to the side and gave me a serious look. "Are you thinkin' it was on purpose?"

"To create a diversion so I would go in there," I answered.

"That would mean a dirty cop, Row, and I know you're thinkin' Albright."

"Did you know that Albright is actually the Americanized version of the German surname Albrecht?" I asked.

"Row." He shook his head slowly. "I see where you're goin', and believe me, I think she's a loon myself but helping a serial killer? That's some serious shit to accuse someone of, white man."

"I know, Ben." I gave my head a quick shake. "But it adds up."

"For you, yeah," he told me. "But I dunno what IAD would say."

"Have you talked to them yet? About the other stuff, I mean?"

"Yeah, they're lookin' into it," he replied then took another quaff of his java. "Good thing I've got a friend in there, otherwise it might have been just another cluster."

"Are you going to tell them about what I just told you?"

"Lemme think on that, Row." He shot me a wincing look. "Like I said, that's some deep shit to pile on."

"I know, but it feels right," I replied.

"You're sure it's not just because you hate each other?" he asked.

"I'm sure."

"Well..." He paused for a moment. "Like I said, lemme think on it and see where everything goes."

"Okay," I replied. I'd spent enough time arguing my point over the past few days. I didn't have the energy to press it. At least not right now. "So we should get loaded up. Felicity is just going straight to the house."

He pushed away from the counter and headed for the boxes on the table. "Lead on, Kemosabe."

"Missed a spot." Ben pointed at the floor as he made the comment to Felicity.

She was just making the last of her third pass through the house with a bundle of straw that was bound tightly to a gnarled, old tree branch. The broom normally hung on the wall in our kitchen, positioned over the back door, but right now it was clasped in her hands as she moved fluidly throughout the entire house.

"Shhhh, Ben," I admonished as I shuffled past him.

I was following behind my wife with a large bunch of white sage that had been tied into a smudge bundle. The end was a glowing red coal, and a healthy cloud of pungent smoke was billowing up as I waved the sage about.

Ben coughed slightly then continued to watch us from his seat at the breakfast nook in our kitchen without further comment.

Felicity ended at the back of the house with a strenuous flourish of the broom out the open door.

As she shook it, she held her free hand up, three fingers pointing toward the sky, then began to speak. "Lord and Lady, hear my plea, keep us safe from things unseen. Protect these walls from evil deeds, but allow good spirits to plant their seeds. This cleansing now I do complete, ye things unwelcome must retreat."

As she finished the recitation, she scribed a pentacle in the air with her fingers then pressed them against her lips and thrust her hand outward as if throwing a kiss. She stepped aside, and I tucked the burning sage between the fingers of my cast-encased hand. With my good appendage now free, I reached into my pocket and withdrew some salt, which I immediately sprinkled across the threshold.

Ben was staring at us with a bemused look when we reentered the kitchen. I had tamped out the sage bundle and left it on a plate in the atrium to cool, so I went over to the sink and brushed the excess salt off my hand.

"So what was that all about?" my friend asked.

"Cleansing," Felicity told him. "This place felt very weird when I came in."

"You've been gone for almost three weeks. Whaddaya expect? It always feels weird to come home after bein' away."

"Not this weird," I told him. "Something strange was here."

"Yeah, about ten different coppers that I know of." He nodded. "And several of them are pretty strange."

"My point exactly," Felicity explained. "They brought something in with them."

"Do you know if Albright was ever here?" I asked.

"Yeah, probably," he replied. "Yeah, I think she was. Why?"

"That would explain a lot of the negativity," I replied.

"Yes, it would," Felicity agreed.

"What was that? A 'yes'?" Ben jibed and then affected a bad Irish accent. "What happened to 'Aye me good laddie boy and then and such.'"

Felicity just looked back at him as he sat there grinning. "I got some sleep, Ben. And, I don't say 'laddie boy,' so give me a break."

The phone rang, and I looked up with what had to be a startled expression on my face. I don't know why, other than the fact that almost every time I had answered a phone in the past few days it had been unpleasant.

"You want me to get that?" Ben asked, leaning toward the device.

"No," I shook my head as I started across the room. "No, I'll get it."

I had covered the few steps by the third ring. The caller ID read all zeros with the word "UNAVAILABLE" below them. I frowned and picked up the receiver. "Hello?"

There was no answer at the other end. "Hello?" I said again.

I was certain that I heard the heavy breathing of someone on the line issuing from the earpiece as the hairs instantly rose on the back of my neck. A stab of pain bit into my shoulder and my scalp tightened as the dull thud of a headache began to tap out its rhythm on my grey matter.

There was something that sounded like a heavy sigh then the line clicked and went dead.

Five Months Later

EPILOGUE:

The television set tossed light out into the room as the picture flickered and changed. The logo of the news station sat prominently in the corner, proudly displaying the network affiliation along with the current time.

It was 7:32 in the morning.

The picture suddenly switched to a shifting, bright background overlaid with an artistic shot of a hovering helicopter, complete with the slow motion blur of its rotors blending into the gradient of colors. The words BREAKING NEWS slashed in bold letters across the screen, and a fanfare of syncopated beats underscored the image.

The screen switched again to a fresh-faced, young reporter holding a logo-adorned microphone. Behind him was a lush scene; leafy trees and dense vegetation disappeared into the unfocused depth of field. It was immediately obvious that he was in a rural or wooded area somewhere.

As he held one hand to his ear, presumably listening in for a cue, he began to speak.

"Thank you Chloe and Russ, I'm on the scene at Rafferty Park overlooking the Missouri River where last evening a jogger made a gruesome discovery. Mike Rickman was coming down this path when he stumbled upon what appeared to be a badly decomposed human arm.

"Authorities were called to the scene and after a thorough search have confirmed finding more remains in a shallow grave well off the path.

"While there has been no confirmation as yet, there has been speculation that the body may be that of Tamara Linwood, the grade school teacher who disappeared from the parking lot of Westview Shopping Mall back in January of..."

The man watching this particular television set this morning might have had an interest in the story had he been able to hear or see it. Unfortunately, he was sprawled on the hardwood floor, face down in a puddle of coffee where his cup had shattered.

He convulsed and postured as the sudden seizure ravaged his body, forcing him to bite his tongue and writhe as if holding the bare end of a live extension cord.

Photograph Copyright © 2004, K. J. Epps

ABOUT THE AUTHOR

M. R. Sellars has been called the "Dennis Miller of Paganism" for his quick wit and humorously deadpan observations of life within the Pagan community and beyond. However, his humor is only one facet of his personality, as evidenced by the dark thrillers he pens.

While being fast-paced, intensely entertaining reads, his books are also filled with real-life pagan dynamics and even a dash of magick! All of the current *Rowan Gant* novels have spent several consecutive weeks on numerous bookstore bestseller lists. *The Law of Three*, book #4 in the saga, received the *St. Louis Riverfront Times People's Choice award* soon after its debut.

An honorary elder of *Mystic Moon*, a teaching coven based in Kansas City, and an honorary member of *Dragon Clan Circle* in Indiana, Sellars is for the most part a solitary practitioner of an eclectic mix of Pagan paths, and has been since the late seventies. He currently resides in the Midwest with his wife, daughter, and a host of rescued felines. His schedule never seems to slow down and when not writing, researching a project, or taking time to spend with his family, he can be found on the road performing workshops and book signings nationwide.

At the time of this writing, Sellars is working on several projects, as well as traveling on promotional tour.

For more information about M. R. Sellars and his work, visit him on the World Wide Web at www.mrsellars.com.